They were men.
And Hitler had
for hati

THE
HOMESTEAD
GRAYS

WALKER: who downed a flaming string of Nazi planes and reaped Europe's sensual pleasures. **FREMONT:** a West Point career man who would die for his dream. **SKINNER:** an Olympian in Berlin in '36 who had a score to settle with "the master race." **ARCHIBALD:** who feared his sexual secret would explode and destroy them all.

"Dramatic . . . draws you in slowly but surely until you're reading a mile a minute."
The Christian Science Monitor

"Wylie's the best black novelist to emerge since James Baldwin. . . . His breathless air battles have seldom been bettered."
Dallas Times Herald

"First-rate. . . . There are passages that remind this reader of James Jones in THE THIN RED LINE with their brutality, soul-searching truth, and vitality."
Best Sellers

THE HOMESTEAD GRAYS

James Wylie

AVON
PUBLISHERS OF BARD, CAMELOT AND DISCUS BOOKS

AVON BOOKS
a division of
The Hearst Corporation
959 Eighth Avenue
New York, New York 10019

Copyright © 1977 by James Wylie
Published by arrangement with G. P. Putnam's Sons.
Library of Congress Catalog Card Number: 77-3641
ISBN: 0-380-38604-6

First Avon Printing, September, 1978

AVON TRADEMARK REG. U.S. PAT. OFF. AND IN
OTHER COUNTRIES, MARCA REGISTRADA,
HECHO EN U.S.A.

Printed in the U.S.A.

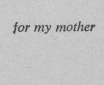

for my mother

Fate often allowed its victims time to prove themselves.

KOMMODORE JOHANNES STEINHOFF
Sicily, 1943

In pictures, the snapshots hurriedly made, a little faded, a little dog-eared with the thirteen years, they swagger a little. Lean, hard, in their brass-and-leather harness, posed standing beside or leaning upon the esoteric shapes of wire and wood and canvas in which they flew without parachutes, they too have an esoteric look; a look not exactly human, like that of some dim and threatful apotheosis of the race seen for an instant in the glare of a thunderclap and then forever gone.

WILLIAM FAULKNER

PART ONE

ONE

It was nearly sunset. High above the broad valley gigantic shafts of mellowing sunlight slanted down majestically to the earth. Far away, miles away, endless green fields of spring wheat swelled heavily, emulating the motions of the sea. A coldish wind, which had arisen deep in central Africa and cooled on its flight to the Mediterranean, swooped off the mountain tops still glistening vaguely where the snow had not melted. The pilots, most of them, said little as they walked along the flight line out to the place where the photographer had set up his tripod. Taking the official squadron portrait the day before they were going up to meet the Luftwaffe for the first time made them edgy. Those who were proud or elated kept it to themselves and hoped to get copies of the picture soon.

Nervously, bumping each other awkwardly in a rush of subdued excitement, they lined up four abreast, by flights. On the grass off to one side, the ground crewmen, in soiled khaki fatigues, lounged around the chuckwagon, eating their lunch of pea soup, boiled eggs, and sandwiches. They found the pilots an interesting group: glory-seeking, headstrong, quick to take up unusual challenges, smart-talking, and a little oblivious to things, a little too anxious to hold their heads higher than a black man was supposed to.

No one had missed the picture-taking. Walker was there, standing boldly and a bit ludicrously in his sheepskin thigh boots which he claimed had belonged to a British scout pilot in World War One. He was a short thick man and seemed to wallow in the deep boots. Today his large and poignant eyes were at peace. The ragged, curly mustache covering half his upper lip did not look funny. The veil of clever boyishness which usually dominated his round dark countenance ("Baby face me") was gone. He stared into the camera with an artlessness so restrained that Donny Beaumont and Carl Jennings, who flew tailass in his flight, leaned forward to see his face. Only Jennings noticed that Appaloosa, Walker's plump blackand-white spotted cat, peered out from his arms with the same helpless quietude.

The pilots of the 74th Squadron, United States Army Air Force, Medjez-el-Bab, Tunisia, moved in closer. Then someone laughed out loud. It was a bitter and frightened laugh. It had to be Skinner.

"Forgive me," he said quietly to the men nearest him. "It just came out."

They nodded and pulled at their tunics and flight suits and leather jackets. Suddenly Skinner felt a surge of hysterical merriment coming over him. He fought it down violently, holding himself in a pose both stiff and tenacious, a pose he always took when being photographed.

He had been through this kind of thing so many times before. He had dozens of hopeful and faded group pictures back home: old pictures of him as an All-Oklahoma halfback with the high-school football team, snapshots from his days as a trackman at Howard, tiny candid camera-glimpses of him at the Olympic Village in Berlin seven years ago when he had failed to win a medal. And pictures from Spain, lots of photographs from Spain, showing him in Barcelona cafés and on troop trains, surrounded by naïve anarchists and romantic farm boys; there were also blurred images of his taut, handsome figure striding through the trenches and fighting in the Sierra under the assumed name of Lieutenant Douglas, fighting until the terrible end. Two weeks later he had been photographed in Paris, in a hotel bedroom, this time by a French woman who said she loved him.

The camera clicked for the third time. Lieutenant Colonel Jonathan Fremont, the squadron leader, got up and waved at the man behind it.

"That's all, Dick. I think we look pretty good," he said warmly.

"Whatever you say, Jonathan," the man replied. He was not an official photographer, but Captain Richard Beasley, the squadron flight surgeon, a big bushy-haired man of forty-seven who wore a full beard against regulations.

Folding up his tripod, he moved up to Fremont slowly, watching the men drift away or form small groups and light cigarettes.

"Better let 'em mess around for a while," he said affably. "I don't want too many dropping in after dinner for sleeping pills."

Fremont murmured in agreement and gazed out across the valley. The beginning of a mauve twilight was setting in. The white cottages among the fir trees on the other side of the field stood out delicately. His sharp eyes inspected the eighteen brand-new P-51 Mustang fighters sitting in their dispersal areas, noses lifted elegantly to the blue African sky. The crews had done a good job with the tan-and-green spotted camouflage. The planes looked incredibly malevolent. Fremont couldn't take his eyes off them.

Beasley, his tripod under one hefty arm, eyed Fremont. He had never seen his old friend and childhood buddy so withdrawn, so expectant.

"How about some gin rummy and a drink before dinner?" he asked. "It's quiet in the infirmary."

Fremont looked at him, angry with himself for having brought anyone out here who knew him this well.

"All right, Dick," he replied.

"Kissin' cousins!" Walker said, kicking at the grass as he watched them go. "They can kiss my motherfuckin' ass, both of 'em," he muttered, reaching into his pocket for a pack of Camels.

"I didn't know they were related," Carlson Jennings said casually as he flicked open his lighter.

Walker leaned his head toward the younger man, the tail-ass turkey in his flight, and took a puff. His eyes were filled with disgust. Appaloosa clawed at the soft suede of his flying boots.

"Listen, Sonny Boy," Walker said sharply after a long

hostile moment, "when we go up tomorrow, you stick with me like I was your mammy's left tit."

Jennings sighed, dropped his own cigarette and ground it out. He'd never really gotten accustomed to smoking, anyway.

Half an hour later Horace Walker, an overloaded dinner tray in hand, passed a window in the combat mess and slowly came to a halt. Crouched low in an old vineyard planted right up to the kitchen door was an officer of the U.S. Army Air Corps. Walker saw the bars on his collar stand out in the fading light. A truck started up in back. It emerged from around the side of the mess. The huddled figure tensed like a sprinter in the blocks and then broke clumsily from the dense brown webbing of the vineyard to overtake the rumbling truck in three long bounding strides.

Walker turned back to the roughly paneled room and put his tray down on a table where Skinner, Jennings, and another pilot named Blackie Chenier were sitting. Rufus, a huge Saint Bernard and the squadron mascot, waddled by.

"I just saw Archibald out there taking off for town," Walker said. "We ain't been here but a week and already this nigger has found some pussy."

"Little Arab boys aren't exactly pussy," Skinner remarked. Seated at the end of the table, he was smoking a pipe between sips of the rough local brandy and reading a newspaper. Appaloosa sat in his lap, narrow-eyed with contentment.

"Yes, but does Archie know that?" Walker asked slyly.

Everyone laughed a little. Flight Leader Travis Archibald was a notorious closet homosexual. It was said he had once attacked a patient in a hospital where he was working as a porter.

"I'm shocked," Walker announced. "I really am. I can't have this sort of behavior, consorting with children and such, goin' on in my squadron."

There was not much they could say to this. Chenier cleared his throat. Jennings stared into his bread pudding. Walker made sense. Logically, he should have been their leader, but somehow command had been conceded to Fremont from the outset. Walker blamed the Army ("They give it to the West Point man every time"), the politicians, and even his own men, although he knew this was unfair. Tonight he did not press his claim.

"Why so glum?" he asked Jennings.

"Oh, I don't know," Jennings replied, his voice riding the edge of irritation. He didn't want to talk to Walker. Walker was too mercurial. One day he would tear his room apart, and the next day he was all right again. Jennings found him maddening. No matter how hard he tried, he could never understand Walker.

"Don't worry, the Germans are worried about you too," Walker said in Jennings' ear. "They know they can't handle you."

"We'll never see any Germans," Jennings snapped. "The Army doesn't want us to fight. We're kidding ourselves. They're going to leave us in this valley until the end of the war."

"Boy could be right," Chenier added.

"Hell, no. Not with these new airplanes," Walker said. "They mean for us to fight. I know they do."

"They were going to send us to Liberia," Jennings said, almost to himself. "Or have you forgotten?"

Walker slammed his fork down and turned away from Jennings. He addressed Skinner with elaborate courtesy. "What are Germans like to fight against, Perc? You saw them in Spain. How did you all do against them?"

Skinner lifted his small, handsome head. He looked exotic and wistful.

"We lost," he said absently, then returned to his paper.

After the evening meal, Jennings, Skinner, and a contingent of other pilots trooped over to the Operations hut where, hands in pockets, they examined the alert list for tomorrow's mission. The names of all the regulars were there, arranged neatly by flights. The men in front stared at the list for a long while and then moved away to allow the others who'd come up to get closer to the bulletin board. Somebody said he wanted a drink, but before long, word spread that the base club was locked tight. There was a lot of grumbling and cursing. The men went back to their rooms unhappy, yet too skittish to be bored.

The sun was about gone now, melting down over the Atlas Mountains to the west. In the officers' quarters, lights

went on. The checker games and the card games that
would end in irritable exhaustion at 0300, a mere two
hours or so before breakfast and the briefing, all these
ritual games had begun. There was little conversation.
They had all seen enough war movies to know when not to
talk, when to do nothing but smoke and play at being
calm, play it out to the very end. Still, if Fremont had
come in and asked if everything was all right, he would
have received a dozen different babbling answers.

The big floor-model Stromberg Carlson radio in Chenier's room boomed out:

As a bullet seeks its target, shining rails in every
part of our great country are aimed at Grand Central
Station, heart of the nation's greatest city. Drawn by
the magnetic force, the fantastic metropolis, day and
night great trains rush toward the Hudson River,
sweep down its eastern bank for one hundred forty
miles, flash briefly past the long, red row of tenement
houses south of One hundred twenty-fifth Street, dive
with a roar into the two-and-a-half mile tunnel which
burrows beneath the glitter and swank of Park Avenue, and then . . . Grand Central Station . . . crossroads of a million private lives. . .

A loud click sounded in the room. The announcer's
voice disappeared.

"This is too damn much noise. I'm turning this shit
off," Walker said as he wheeled to leave.

Chenier watched him with an icy stare. He was cleaning
his .45, and he slammed the magazine in angrily and
tossed the heavy pistol onto the bed with the same motion.

"Why you want to turn my story off?" he said in a hurt
tone of voice. "Why you want to fuck with me?" he yelled
as Walker ambled away. "You ain't the only one in here
afraid."

Up and down the corridor, doors closed discreetly.
Appaloosa was tossed out of one room with a yowl as
her master approached. In the dimness Walker scooped
up his cat and patted her head.

"Fuck these people," he said affectionately to the cat.
"What do they know about us anyway? When have they
ever heard the tunes of glory? Never. Never, that's when."

Appaloosa nuzzled his bare chest, and Walker went into his room.

Fremont picked up the field telephone in his caravan on the first ring.

"Three Messerschmitt 109s closing the field boundary, sir," the night Operations Room clerk informed him calmly.

He hung up and went outside without bothering to switch off the lights. This was not an attack. He guessed that much.

He saw the Messerschmitts a long way off. His sharp eyes picked them up a little before the other pilots who had gathered around him did. Their engines sounded too loud and a little ragged. They were coming in very low, three abreast, their bright yellow spinners growing larger and larger in the dull afterlight. The small band of men around Fremont stood its ground against the growing noise, against the dust raised by the three barely visible aircraft streaking on with deadly, bestial sleekness. They were only yards away now. Everyone saw their exhaust stubs emitting a vivid fierce blue fire. Overhead they came in an eloquent rush, hanging close to the ground before finally nosing into a long, beautiful climb which revealed their delicate blue undersides marred only by the squared black-and-white wing crosses. The Messerschmitts turned high in the sky with the thoughtless grace of seagulls. The outside man was going to top RPMs to keep up this illusion of easy perfection.

They didn't fire.

"They're probably out of ammunition," Fremont said to the men closest to him. "If they keep this up, soon their tanks will be dry."

"They're coming in for another run, Colonel," an excited voice behind him announced.

The run was very slow this time. The Messerschmitts had throttled back and they almost glided over the field, daring anyone to lift a gun against them.

"These are bad people," Chenier said, laughing uneasily. "Crazy or very bad one."

Fremont smiled to himself. He was tempted to wave at the Germans, to acknowledge their superb display of bravado as the aircraft floated just beyond the reach of the amazed pilots. At the end of the runway all three planes went to full power and rocketed up and out of the valley as quickly as they had appeared.

"We've got to try that sometime," one of the men put in. "That's my kind of sophistication."

"See you in the morning, gentlemen," Fremont said.

It was only when the pilots had bade him goodnight and moved on that he realized that not everyone had left the barracks.

Fremont set out across the field. It was a cool night, star-splashed and quiet. The young spring grass felt very spongy and alive under his heavy shoes. The presence of the Messerschmitts had alarmed him, alerted him to something terrifying in his adversary: an evil glamour, a harsh-tempered cleverness, a confidence he hadn't seen in his own men. Of course, the flyover had been foolish, he knew that. The base was beyond the range of any known German fighter. After a long, dark flight across the sea, those Messerschmitts would be lucky to crash-land on the southern beaches of Sicily. What they had done was merely psychological retaliation, probably for the nightly raids of the British Wellington bombers on their bases. But they had come around for a second pass, come around with near-empty engines and slipping fuel gauges, and Fremont could not forget that.

The base was large for a squadron, nearly fifty acres, and Fremont decided not to go too far. He circled back through the dispersal area, wondering why Beasley hadn't come out and stood by his side. The ground crewmen called out to him and saluted pridefully, then returned to their work. There was a mechanic for every plane in the squadron because no white man would ever think of letting these men here touch his airplane. They couldn't do the job, the Army said. Never. Engines were complicated; *they* were rudimentary. Besides, who wanted to depend on a black man, thank a black man?

"Evenin', General," a figure in khaki fatigues said to him as he passed the hangar. Fremont forced a thin smile, for this kind of informality always irritated him. He looked closer. The man was Dummy Jones, Walker's mechanic, a tough, frenetic little man who was sitting in the cockpit of a P-51.

"Jones, I don't want you men taxiing these planes out to the line. I want them towed," he warned. They weren't going to listen, Fremont understood that. In a couple of nights they'd be riding around the field with only the landing lights to guide them. But he wanted no accidents tonight.

He stood looking at the P-51 for a long moment. The Mustang was a beautiful airplane, faster, more devilishly sleek, heavily armed, and more powerful than any other combat plane man had conceived right up through this chilly North African night in the year 1943. Fremont strode up to the craft and touched it lightly. It was hard to see his hand against the tan and green smudged Mediterranean camouflage.

He returned to his caravan. He poured some scotch into a heavy glass and added a splash of the local bottled spring water. This theater of operations was strange and perplexing to him: idyllic mountain valleys farmed by picturesque Europeans, yet not fifty kilometers away, the scorching desert, a continent in itself, that seemed irrelevant now. To the north began the Mediterranean, blue and wide and deep. Air-sea rescue was next to impossible, he'd been advised. Sighting conditions were bizarre, tactical circumstances unpredictable; the clouds and sky lulled you to sleep. It was a lovely place to die.

He wished there were some Germans around. He longed for a final spasmodic battle with .88s lighting up the night and tank formations appearing from nowhere. The absence of Germans from the land made everything unreal. But the Germans would not be returning. El Alamein had happened. The shock of Stalingrad last winter was still fresh enough. The Afrika Korps had dissolved into the dust storms, the blinding sun, the snake- and lizard-infested scrub. Its remnants had fled from the desert they loathed, leaving behind the infernal heat and tormenting flies, leaving everything to the British, who seemed to like it.

Fremont sipped his drink. According to Intelligence, the Luftwaffe pilots huddled at their temporary airfields on Sicily were exhausted. Their fighter *Gruppen* were smashed or in disarray. The pilots were bitter, for Hitler had forgotten about their heroism in the desert and ordered them to remain in the disintegrating pocket around Tunis and fight to the last man. ("Europe is being defended at Tunis," he bellowed.) The evacuation went forward only when it was already too late. The German flak gunners fought demoniacally, insanely, and enabled the heavy Siebel ferries to escape with men and unreplaceable supplies. Meanwhile, the fighters, the Messerschmitts and Focke-Wulfs of Fliegerkorps Tunis, returned from Sicily in brave relays. Two and three times a day they set down on the tiny strip under continuous artillery fire and took out their faithful ground crewmen, jamming men in their underwear behind the pilot's seat, streaking through the Allied ground fire and out over the misty, treacherous sea.

Fremont's confident brown eyes roved about with just the faintest trace of satisfaction. His caravan was sumptuous, with rich polished wood and shiny brass fittings for the twin desks folded against the wall. Electric lights in carefully detailed glass shades burned overhead. The sleeping quarters in the rear were slightly elevated and partitioned off by a heavy dark-red curtain. This luxury had belonged to an Italian general killed a year ago in the desert. A British colonel had appropriated it in Egypt, had it pulled across Libya, and sold it to him for a hundred and fifty dollars when his outfit was being transferred to Tebessa in Algeria. A few days before, when Omar Bradley had stopped by to see the new black squadron ("Jonathan, Ike wishes you good luck"), he'd been more than vaguely surprised to find its commander living in such splendor.

"You'll never be a general now," someone had said jokingly as Bradley's car left, and Fremont had smiled because people had been saying that for more years than he could remember. Beasley had said it years ago in Los Angeles when they were the only black students at their high school. At MIT, where he went for a year to study aeronautical engineering, they just laughed indulgently at his military aspirations and told him to stick around and be a great engineer. On reaching West Point, he encountered a withering, vicious hatred. He had no friends, none. Once, a red-haired prostitute, dead drunk, was found in his room; fortunately, he was in New York that weekend. He garnered many more demerits than he earned, took several slaps in the face, and graduated third in his class, the top student in engineering and one of the few black men in the last fifty years.

The Army never had the vaguest idea what to do with

him. They sent him to Negro colleges to teach military science to youngsters who would not believe he'd gone to West Point. Then he was shipped to the Royal Military Academy, Sandhurst, in a two-year exchange program. He learned to fly in England, grew a thick mustache, and developed an interest in opera and poetry. He perfected his French and took on the appearance of a star, an elegant liaison officer. He was widely known now and hated, although promotions came easily. His father left $75,000 to be divided between him and his sister, who was the only black obstetrician in the western half of the United States.

The squadron was Fremont's gift to his father's memory. The older Fremont had tried to enlist in the Air Service during World War One and had been virtually laughed at. ("We do not contemplate the creation of any colored aero squadrons at this time.") For years afterward he had pleaded and failed, lobbied and failed, to get black men into the Army's air-training schools. He was an idealist soured by the reality of black people's keeping house and sweeping up.

Fremont took out a sheet of writing paper and began a long letter to his wife and sons in Los Angeles. Tomorrow, after the mission, he expected to be very tired.

TWO

FIRST LIGHT CREPT into the valley, mingling with the darkness until a soft, pinkish aura was everywhere and the distant white cottages stood out, mute and solemn. At the dispersal area the ground crews moved around briskly. From where he lay shivering in a thicket of dense bushes, Archibald watched them standing by the mobile generators as the Mustangs' electrical systems were tested one last time and then charged. He could see the long heavy belts of .50 ammo being fitted into the wing panels. Hardly anyone talked. Once in a while a field telephone rang and someone picked it up out of the grass.

Archibald began to crawl. His long body slithered over the ground and in no time he had worked his way a couple of hundred yards. Archibald was a durable, dark-skinned, rather ugly man with small, remorselessly sharp eyes. His nose was broad and flattish, and his upper lip, which looked swollen, curled back, leaving only a small space between his nose and mouth. Behind his back a few of the pilots called him the Ubangi, but they respected him. He was a kind and considerate man. He never made advances and he was generous with money and whatever else he had; yet he was not really liked.

Abruptly, he came to a halt near the Operations hut and listened tensely. One of the clerks came out, went a few steps, and stopped to check some papers on a clipboard. Archibald moved away, drifting well beyond the hut. He began to pant in sudden fright. He got up, walk-

14

ing gingerly on the tips of his toes. The officers' quarters came into view and he began to run. He had to get inside before the Ops clerk came to wake him. He fell, got up instantly, and stumbled on, knifing through the bushes and trees right up to the back entrance of the big Quonset hut. In moments he was inside his room, stripping bare. The Ops clerk was knocking at each door as Archibald sauntered down the hall to the shower room, whistling very softly.

"Briefing at 0600 hours, sir," the clerk announced when Skinner appeared before him. Skinner was fully dressed, and the clerk's eyes lingered enviously on the white flying suit the handsome little man wore with such casual style.

In the nearby rooms Skinner heard other pilots moving about. He went to his footlocker, opened it carefully, and removed a long-barreled Colt .45, replacing it with his regulation automatic. He read the blurred old inscription: "Amos Skinner, Oklahoma Territory, 1884." Then he began to load his grandfather's pistol, which had kept him alive several times during the civil war in Spain.

He had about him this morning his usual noble bearing. He was dark, with some Cherokee blood, and did not really look like a black man. White people found him fascinating. Women thought him exotic. Skinner was proud and confident, yet he kept to himself a lot.

Carlson Jennings stood before a mirror and brushed his hair. He wore a tan army shirt, tie, leather flying jacket, and long white scarf. He looked ridiculous, but since he was the quietest and most well-mannered of The Homestead Grays, no one would call it to his attention, except perhaps Walker. His rakishly dressed roommate, Donny Beaumont, sat rigidly on the edge of his bed, smoking a cigarette in an ivory holder and sneaking glances at him. He assumed Donny was annoyed because he had been kept up half the night talking about Von Richthofen and manhood and the exploits of pioneer aviators. Jennings was a smart youth, both energetic and cerebral. He held two degrees in physics from New York University and flew next to Beaumont in B Flight; yet it did not occur to him that Donny, like everyone else, had little faith in his flying skill and felt sure that this first encounter with German pilots would be his last.

Striding anxiously through his own room, Walker

thought, *No way I'll be taken alive. No days like that. Either I'll drown, or if I come down on land, we shoot that shit out and decide right there. That's the way a real man is supposed to die, anyway. Nobody's goin' to drag my ass in a truck or put me in a fuckin' zoo. Not that I should be thinkin' this way, anyhow.*

He was heavily armed as usual, sporting two .45 automatics, extra ammunition, a bone-handled, razor-sharp hunting knife in one boot ("When I go, *beaucoup* Germans go with me"), and his personal survival kit whose contents he refused to divulge. He had planned to carry grenades, but Fremont had heard about it and ordered him not to. People laughed when he described his fear of capture by the Germans ("Black as I am, there's no tellin' what they'd do with me").

"Sir, the briefing will begin at 0600," the Operations clerk announced as Fremont came to the door of his caravan.

Fremont nodded. "Thank you, Corporal," he replied, saluting the slim young man standing at the foot of the wooden steps leading up to his quarters.

The clerk lingered for a moment. Like everyone else at Medjez-el-Bab, he knew that today's mission was the first by an all-black squadron in the United States Army Air Force, but he made no reference to the fact.

"Would you like your breakfast brought to you out here, Colonel?" he asked.

"No thanks, Corporal," Fremont said. "I'll eat with the men."

"Better hurry, sir," the clerk added. "Most of them have already gone over to the mess."

Fremont closed the door and put on his leather flying jacket and overseas cap. He was six feet one, standing half an inch over Archibald, almost too tall for a pilot. More than any other quality, he conveyed strength, distinction mixed with strength, and a suggestion of naïveté. His eyes betrayed little except harshness and an unwillingness to compromise. The thick mustache he wore looked like an ornament from an earlier time. He felt irritated and untested.

He'd been up for hours and had gone through his daily regimen of exactly twenty-two minutes of brutal calisthenics, followed by a shower under the rusty old oil drum set up in the back. He saw Archibald as he circumnavigated the base, but decided to take no action, not now, anyway. Fremont checked his .45 automatic and slid it into a shoulder holster. He tied his white silk scarf loosely and foppishly. Then, smoothing down his curly hair in the back with one hand, he left the caravan.

When he arrived at the mess, the pilots were sitting at tables by flights, eating rapidly and talking in loud voices about the Messerschmitts which had come over last night. He sat down with Butters, Johnson, and Ben Majors, the men who would be flying with him, and had a big American-style breakfast of eggs, Spam, buns, and black coffee. No one looked at his watch. But when Fremont got up, the men began to saunter out behind him, hands in their pockets.

A few minutes before 0600 everyone was seated on the rough benches in the Briefing hut, either staring down at the dirt floor, sneaking glances at Fremont because he probably knew what the mission was, or peering at the covered map on the stage for some clue of what was to come. The Operations Room group strode in on the hour and briskly moved right up front.

The Operations Officer, Lieutenant Duane Osborn, stepped forward, arms behind his back.

"At ease, men," he said in a quiet, peremptory voice.

Osborn was short and about to be fat because he sat at his desk fourteen hours a day trying to get missions for a squadron nobody wanted to see in the air. He smoked too many cigars, always anticipated trouble, got out of bed in the middle of the night to make decisions, and ignored men with half his intellect who called him a nigger on the telephone.

"You men are new to the Mediterranean Theater and things are a whole lot different here, so let's look at the background picture before we discuss specifics," Osborn said crisply. "First of all, Germany's out of Africa, half out of Russia, and in deep trouble everywhere. The German pilots on Sicily are exhausted. North Africa has broken their spirit, at least temporarily, and bombers are fanning out from this coast every day, hitting them at their bases, keeping them in the hole. Earlier this week we leveled their Focke-Wulf assembly station at Bari on the Italian mainland."

There was some whistling and good-natured clapping and genuinely astonished murmuring, but Osborn pressed on as if no reaction at all had come from the young men sitting in front of him.

"The British fleet has begun to show itself off the east coast of Sicily. Sicily is the prize out here. It's the way home. Don't forget that, because Sicily is what we are building toward."

At this point Norvel Donaldson, the tail-ass pilot in Archibald's flight, got up and left the Briefing hut. He held his stomach like a man in sudden, overwhelming agony. Fremont eyed him with fierce distaste. Donaldson had to know that a pilot could go on sick call only before the mission for the day was announced, never afterwards.

"Your mission for today will take you to the island of Pantelleria," Osborn said, unveiling his one-to-twenty-scale operations map. "It is one of several islands we would like to secure and make into forward bases. Ultimately we won't be able to do much from North Africa. Sicily is just a bit too far away, so for tactical purposes we need these islands. This morning a squadron of B-17 Fortresses will bomb the only airfield on Pantelleria, here at Marghana, where the Germans still have a few Messerschmitts and some spare parts they badly want. You will rendezvous with this formation as they come off the target and escort them to the Tunisian coast."

The pilots' sense of relief was palpable. With the main day-bomber attacks tying down the German fighter defense on Sicily, this would be an easy mission. Osborn gave the rendezvous coordinates, magnetic course out and back, and the radio-telephone call sign and channels.

"One more thing," he added, with a warning finger raised. "There is very little air-sea rescue in this theater. That is why I haven't given you a frequency. If you go down, get out of your airplane fast and stay in the dinghy. We'll try to find you. That's a promise."

Next, the meteorologist moved to the center of the small stage. Hardly anyone remembered his real name because for months he'd been called Nature Boy, a nickname forced on him by Walker. Nature Boy wrote poetry, some said. He was also a butterfly collector and during his free hours he could be found photographing, sketching, and cataloguing the profusion of wildflowers on the near mountainsides. He took the business of weather very seriously and checked with the bases in the area several times a day. He was shy and learned. He was well-liked.

"Good morning," he said, clearing his throat a bit. "Nothing but good news this morning. The ground mist out there is lifting and should be almost gone by the time you take off. You'll find some light stratocumulus at three thousand feet, about two-tenths cover. Above it ceiling and visibility are unlimited. There will be some rough air in the form of a strong crosswind meeting you at eight thousand feet neat the Tunisian coast. These winds can be mean. Try to ride above them."

Here Nature Boy stopped abruptly, for he had quickly run through his brief report. He looked out at the pilots seated in the garish light of the Briefing hut. Slowly his eyes moved over them. They were so naïve, so engrossed and so rapturously naïve, he scarcely believed he knew any of them.

"Good luck," he said, nodding to the show of raffish clothing, silk scarves and daggers and custom-made flying suits.

The Intelligence Officer, Lieutenant Todd, moved up. He was a vain, strutting fool who carried a .45 around with him at all times. His job was to study the theater of operations, collect information from pilots, assess it, and offer advice in planning missions. But ever since word had gotten out that he'd been barred from a Situation Conference in Algiers, no one had taken him seriously.

"Gentlemen," he began pompously, "I'm going to need your help. I want you to bring back all the data you can on Pantelleria. This is vital because we don't know exactly what the Germans intend to do with it. Try and see all you can and note any unusual structures, installations, and so forth."

"Okay, Cap," someone shouted, as if to dismiss him from the stage.

Todd smiled indulgently and leaned on his .45 in a slightly exaggerated posture. "One thing I ask you, men. Bring those bombers home. I have reports that the Luftwaffe has been instructed to go all out against the Fortresses. They'll do anything to knock out those ten-man crews. These are desperate people, so keep a sharp lookout. Any questions?"

Walker bounced up. "Will the German radar on Sicily have a fix on us?" he asked.

"Good question, Lieutenant," Todd replied slowly. He pulled at his upper lip pensively. He knew that the Germans had a big new radar disc and monitoring section on Mount Erice in western Sicily which covered all of North Africa, but he simply said, "You'll be picked up on their screens. Sure. But undoubtedly you'll be too far away for them to do anything more than take notice of you. The primary task is still to get those ships home."

"Yes, sir," Walker answered sardonically.

"Any other questions?" Todd asked, rising on the balls of his feet. "None? Okay, that's it."

He hopped off the stage and was replaced by Fremont. "Synchronize watches at 0614," he said. "Start engines at 0630. Takeoff is at 0632. Watch your radio discipline. I want no chatter. All right, you flight leaders, see me up here for a minute."

Absolutely no one moved. They remained, stunned and mulish, on the benches.

"We all heard the Colonel," Walker said in a voice soft and vicious, "so let's get up and move ass on outta here."

Parachutes and escape kits were handed out in the equipment room at the rear of the Operations hut. A covered truck pulled up around front and sat waiting stolidly, its exhaust pipe giving off a slow, rasping sound. The pilots jumped aboard and slid down on the benches. It was cold in the truck. Someone banged a fist on the cab. As the truck began to move, Jennings burst excitedly from the Operations hut, calling desperately, then breaking into a ponderous, stumbling, high-stepping gait, with two enormous bundles in his arms.

"Pull over. Make him pull over," he shouted to the amused faces crowded under the canvas covering. His parachute sailed into the back of the truck, and he began to run faster. He got quite close now and heaved up a big package. Taut, straining hands reached for him and jerked him right up off the road. He dropped, panting, onto the cold floor. Somebody put a cigarette in his mouth. Beaumont struck a match. A couple of guys patted him on the back. Jennings looked around and saw one of the reserve pilots, Orlando Jones, sitting in the gloom.

"Where the hell is Donaldson?" he asked no one in particular.

"Bellyache," was the derisive answer. "Right before the mission assignment."

A grave stillness prevailed. Beaumont held Appaloosa on his lap. Rufus, the squadron mascot, bounded out of nowhere and came lumbering futilely after the truck, barking and baying. At the dispersal area everyone jumped out quickly. The camouflage nets were off the planes. It was 0620. The men moved away in groups of four, parachutes flopping low on their backs as the flight leaders tensely went over last-second details.

Dawn had taken over the valley when Fremont reached his P-51. His boots wet from the morning grass, he climbed deliberately up on the wing walk and released the canopy button. He had cranked the canopy all the way back before it slowly came to him that none of the other pilots had entered their airplanes. They were waiting, he realized, to grant him the honor of being the first in his cockpit. Fremont dropped into the narrow seat, fastened his safety belt and shoulder harness, then waved at the others irritably. He covered his preflight check rapidly, but with great care. When he glanced around again, the mechanics were scurrying everywhere, shouting, and gesturing. The whole thing was so bizarre and grotesquely touching it made him angry. For a moment he despised those inane little black men in grimy fatigues running about, doing everything too snappily, a shade too crisply. They reminded him of the day Mrs. Roosevelt and Lord Halifax, the British Foreign Secretary, had come to watch the squadron practice formation flying at Tuskegee. He had never forgiven them for being so amazed, so condescendingly dumbfounded by what they had seen.

A handful of photographers from stateside magazines and the Signal Corps moved up to the periphery of the dispersal area. Then a car pulled up, and men set down two newsreel cameras on spindly tripods. Fremont eyed them with contempt.

Dummy Jones stood on the wing walk chatting with Walker while he pulled at his harness straps to make sure they were tight. Walker found this annoying.

"She topped up?" he asked, feeling idiotic.

"Couldn't get another drop in her. You could go to China in this airplane," Dummy said, staring into his face.

Walker nodded. "Thanks for puttin' in this extra shit," he said quietly, without looking at the other man. He was nervous. He wanted Dummy to get the hell off his plane.

"Oh, that's nothin'. Spitfire boys had rearview mirrors and look what they did."

Walker didn't answer. He glanced at his clock. A hand grabbed his shoulder poignantly. "So long, buddy."

Then, from the ground: "Don't bend up that auxiliary headset. I can't get you another one."

Walker waved, forced a hard little smile, and closed the canopy roughly.

0626. Interior check repeat. Skinner's elegant hands flitted about the cockpit, releasing levers, priming switches. Control lock on stick released. Clock set and ticking. Fuel shutoff lever on. Parking brakes set. Ignition off. Oxygen-gauge pressure at 400 psi. Test flow perfect. Gun-heater switch off. All thirty-five items covered. Skinner leaned back and sighed deeply.

0627. Activity on the field had slowed. The mechanics stood almost at attention beside the auxiliary starter-generators near each plane. The sun broke through, and Skinner could see the portly shape of Doctor Beasley, one foot on the running board of his ambulance. Some big fire extinguishers lay half obscured in the grass. Skinner waited, pulling gently at his helmet strap.

Jennings was the only pilot not in his plane. Scattered on the ground lay his leather jacket, scarf, pistol, and parachute. He squirmed violently, endlessly, in an attempt to get into the electrically heated flying suit he had brought all the way from the States. Perspiration ran down his face and into his eyes. He gasped. The heavy coils in the suit cut into his back and for a few seconds he was completely immobile.

From around the side of his aircraft came a furious, beleaguered figure, his mechanic. The man fell upon him with diabolical purpose, tearing the suit from his body.

"Leave it alone," he cried wrathfully. "Leave the son of a bitch alone! You got to turn that engine over on time."

He slipped the parachute over Jennings' shoulders and pushed him into the plane. Then he tossed up the jacket, pistol, and scarf as Jennings tried to go through his preflight. Jennings gazed at the bank of big round instruments in front of him. He peered at their esoteric markings, and it all meant nothing to him. The mechanic appeared on the wing, hurriedly tightening his straps. A leather flying helmet was placed on his head as he sat motionless. The mechanic glanced at his immobile face and deadened hands.

"She's checked out," he said snidely. "She's ready. Start her at the signal and I'll goose her up from outside. Good luck, boy."

The canopy slid over Jennings. He saw Walker bare-headed, wearing a light headset and sunglasses. On the Mediterranean a man in a dinghy could last forty-eight hours, he'd read somewhere; then he would become very badly burned and die of thirst and sunstroke. The throttle in his airplane was racked open one inch so he'd be able to take off. Jennings shook his head in confusion.

The red second hand on his clock swept around. A loud rustle came through the headset, followed by a strong voice: "It is 0630. Switches on."

Jennings checked to see if his propellor was clear, as he'd been told to do each and every day of flight school. One shaky hand groped for the ignition switch. The Mustang started with a roar so ferocious it jarred him. A haze of light blue exhaust smoke trailed over the wings. Jennings feared a runaway engine until he heard the harsh crescendo of other planes around him. A low whine emanated from his instrument panel. The pressure gauges began rising slowly. It all looked normal. He calculated the oil pressure would reach 50 psi within thirty seconds of engine start and knew he would not have to restart. A sharp bang on the fuselage signalled the moment when his mechanic disconnected the external power source. Automatically, he moved the battery switch to ON.

His head was beginning to clear. His hands moved easily, free of any cramping sensation. Confidently he placed the supercharger at HIGH and warmed up the engine at 1300 RPM. He glanced out over the dispersal area. The sun was very strong now. Mechanics were dashing around, unplugging batteries, pulling chocks away from the wheels. As the engine revolutions built steadily up, Jennings went through his regulator and manifold-pressure checks. Fremont's plane began to taxi. The ground crewmen sprang forward, hanging on to the wingtips, helping the aircraft to pivot on the still-wet grass. Jennings realized his plane was moving and looked down casually to see his hand firm on the throttle.

The planes, low, rakish, and fiercely powerful, lined up on the runway in a cloud of dust. Beaumont's wingtip nearly touched his; ahead, only the top of Fremont's canopy was visible. He wiggled his surface controls for free movement. He noticed all the mechanics were standing in the grass not far off, the wind pulling at the long bills of their fatigue caps. Some of them were crying. Other men came running from the hangar area. A red flare shot up and Fremont's plane swooped down the runway, lifting off perfectly. His wingman, Butters, tore after him, then Pedro Johnson and Majors. B flight began to roll. Jennings released his brakes and eased the throttle forward. The heavy plane charged ahead, rattling slightly, rocking leftward until he gave it some right rudder. He heard it roar away in eagerness. Objects on the ground fell by with compelling swiftness. The aircraft suddenly felt lighter, smoother. He saw no runway beyond the gray, translucent arc of his propellor. The landing-gear warning lights blinked out and there was a muffled click under his feet. He watched the coolant and oil temperatures, then pulled back gently on the short stick between his legs and felt the long climb-out begin.

Now the valley spread all around him. It was not as green as it looked from the ground. At the base of the foothills, the wheat fields dropped back and a colossal landscape of wildflowers took over: they cascaded madly and luxuriantly among big boulders in incandescent shades of canary, vermillion, and sky blue. Beyond the boulders, in duller patches of green, flocks of goats browsed right up to the snow line. Jennings smiled as one of the Arab shepherd boys waved forlornly at his plane.

"Attention. This is Broadsword squadron." It was Fremont, reminding them of the call sign. "Check airspeed. Form up on me immediately. We have a rendezvous to make."

Jennings searched the sky before him. Fremont's flight was already flying in perfect finger four: leader out front, wingmen staggered to port and starboard, Ben Majors, the tail-ass turkey, hanging in.

The squadron moved into battle formation, two flights

ahead, two behind. This was the easiest formation to fly on a straight course, and it offered excellent cross fire. Below, the green mountainous Tunisian landscape drifted slowly by. Fremont's flight moved on swiftly and purposefully as an arrow, but everywhere else the Mustangs rose and fell unevenly. Jennings could sense apprehension all around him. None of the pilots wanted a time lag between his movements and the others, yet no one could keep his ship steady. They were struggling to fly station and this was unusual. Their big propellor discs flickered in the sunlight. Jennings saw Beaumont's helmeted head clearly, goggles up, oxygen mask dangling to one side. On the radio Skinner and Archibald were reprimanding their flights for sloppy flying. A click came through his headset.

"Broadsword Two-four. Get your ass in here. You're flying all over the goddamn sky," Walker snapped.

It took a minute for Jennings to realize he was the fourth man in the second flight and that, like every pilot, he had to be constantly aware of his code designation.

"Roger," he said quickly.

But Walker had switched off, so he pulled in closer to Beaumont, who looked concerned. Jennings fixed his eyes on the altimeter and turn-bank indicator for a while. It was a perfect day, just as Nature Boy had forecast. They swam in a limitless blue sky, the soft morning sun bouncing gently off their canopies. Jennings began to daydream. In flight school they'd been told that the beginning fighter pilot had to learn to stay alive without being unduly cautious. At this juncture that didn't sound too difficult. And in spite of his meager skills, Jennings was not worried, for it had also been stressed that the successful pilot did not belong to any recognizable type.

"Leaving Tunisian coast at four-eight," Fremont broke in, to advise them they were over water now and had departed Tunisia at forty-eight minutes after the hour. Sixteen minutes since takeoff.

Almost immediately they began to bounce in the sustained turbulence.

"Broadsword squadron, fly to eight thousand feet."

They climbed with surprising ease and leveled off.

"That's the way, Broadsword Two," Walker called.

Far down, the Mediterranean, bluer and more elusive than anything Jennings had ever seen, drifted toward a

horizon blurred by the eternal haze between sky and sea.
It looked like infinity, the point where the earth simply
dissolved into ether. But at the same time they gained on
it. The instruments read normal, yet the Mustangs hung in
a state of weightlessness, not seeming to move. Jennings
lived within a narrow vista encompassing the high vault
of the sky, the distant sea, a warming sun. And suddenly
he was afraid. Nervous voices, terse phrases, shot through
the radio as each man sought to stay in contact, sought to
break the terrible isolation.

Fremont called. "All Broadsword aircraft. Climb to ten
thousand feet and go to oxygen."

When they had gained altitude, the radio chatter began
to increase. Fremont glanced over and noticed Butters
wiping perspiration from his brow with one arm. "Broadsword squadron, clear this channel! Cut out the jabbering.
That's an order," he barked into the microphone, surprised
at the savagery in his voice.

Everyone lapsed into the solitude of his own thoughts
and fears. Fremont knew radio discipline was tough to
learn, even for veteran pilots who flew together in small
groups all the time. Invariably one man talked, and then
all the others did. The result was always confusion, disintegrating patterns of attack, panic, death. The leader had
to be heard at all times. There was no other way.

Moving his head in a slow, rotating motion, Fremont
searched the sky around the clock. This was the fighter
pilot's best defense against surprise. ("Look everywhere,"
they had said in training. "Then look again for the man
you didn't see. He'll be the one to get you.") Fremont
hoped the others hadn't forgotten. He almost reminded
them, but they were on course to the rendezvous and things
were quiet. Besides, Ops had told him the Germans on
Mount Erice monitored every voice transmission in the
Med area and translated simultaneously. With a new squadron beginning to bounce all over the place again, he was
not anxious to see any Messerschmitts today.

The tension and isolation were nearly over now. At their
flying speed, Pantelleria was less than twelve miles away.
Fremont double-checked his compass, then broke radio silence.

"Broadsword aircraft, test guns," he said calmly.

Short bursts of machine gun fire erupted all around him and died instantly in the rarefied air.

"Check gunsights," he added quickly, remembering now that these checks should have been performed earlier in the mission.

They approached the rendezvous point, flying east into the sun. The outline of Pantelleria slid out of the hazy sea ahead and sort of wandered toward them, minute by minute. They closed the rendezvous point right on time, to the second. Butters smiled over at Fremont and raised a clenched fist. Everyone watched the heavy, elongated B-17s, which hadn't been visible moments before, drift in a wide circle and assemble as they came off the target. Their white condensation trails were short and neat, like skid marks in the sky. On the ground at what had been the German airfield at Marghana, ugly plumes of deep black smoke spread out over the terraced and rocky landscape. Fremont called in.

"Greentree formation leader. Broadsword is here to pave the way home."

No answer came. Puzzled, Fremont repeated his message. Long seconds passed. A voice, reluctant and bored, broke through the light static.

"Well, thank you kindly, Broadsword."

Butters stared across, his eyes wide with anger, but Fremont didn't see him. He was listening to the open channel.

"Goddamn nigger upstarts," the copilot said bitterly.

"What did they do, send those damn niggers?" another voice snapped.

"Can't you see, dumbbell? They're right there, plain as crows on a clothesline."

The whole bomber formation was on the radio now, irate, vicious, and resentful.

"Who the fuck are they in American planes? That's all I want to know. Who the fuck let this happen?"

"I don't know, Johnny. Once you get to Africa, I guess they just take over."

"Man, I thank my lucky stars the krauts don't know about this."

"Look at 'em. They can't fly. Look at 'em, bunched up tighter than a donkey's asshole."

The Mustang pilots glanced at each other, astonished

and bewildered, ashamed, then furious. Walker tore off his oxygen mask and screamed obscenities through the canopy. Fremont was afraid of a collision.

"Keep station! Keep station, Broadsword!" he shouted.

But Walker would not listen. He nosed in too close to the lead Fortress, pounding his canopy. The starboard waist gunner, his pink face betraying amusement, yelled back as he leaned casually on his machine gun in the big side window. Walker's canopy slammed back. He was screaming. The port waist gunner left his post to come over and enjoy the fun. Suddenly the starboard gunner stood up, spit on his hands and leveled his machine gun directly at Walker. Fremont desperately ordered Walker back into the formation. Crazed laughter and taunts came through the radio as the other crews heard what was going on. The Fortress squadron leader chuckled softly. Archibald pulled his flight of Mustangs up, moving above and a little behind the bombers. A few of the top turrets with single machine guns followed them menacingly. The giggling and chatter vanished. Hard breathing came through the headsets. It was quiet and very sunny.

Fremont noticed the sun coming directly into his eyes again. They had flown in a circle and were facing east. He called the bomber leader once more, intent on conveying the responsibility of command to him. He felt weak and absurd.

"Greentree formation. This is Broadsword. We are taking up escort position."

"With four planes over my tail, man? Son of a bitch, you can kiss my ass."

Fremont looked at the lead ship, *Cotton-Eyed Joe,* not knowing what to do. He searched again. Dozens of black flecks seemed to hover against the sun. For a moment he was too shaken to make a sound. Then his voice returned, with incredible composure.

"Messerschmitts at twelve o'clock."

From their great altitude the gaggle of enemy fighters rocketed down on them. They were in fact Focke-Wulfs, dark green, thick, and lethal. They split into pairs, swooping in every direction. The Fortress gunners fired, their .50 caliber guns sparking from all over the big airplanes. It made no difference. The Germans swarmed in. A P-51 disintegrated in the pop-pop-pop of a 20 millimeter cannon, its flaming remnants dropping through the fireball and down to the glassy sea. One of the bombers, *Lonesome Polecat,* rolled over, engines boiling with fire, and plummeted in a tight spiral while its wings gracefully fell away as if they were supposed to. Fremont saw no parachutes.

His radio rasped loudly. An urgent voice cried out. "Attention. Broadsword leader. Look behind you. Behind you!"

A Focke-Wulf, the white spiral on its prop spinner grinding hypnotically, lined him up. He broke sharply left in a seizure of cold, instant fear, calling for Butters, who had vanished. Planes were all over the sky, floating like buzzards. The German was closing on him, and Fremont saw with alarm how casually the other pilot imitated his every move. He jammed the throttle forward. The horizon dropped. His Mustang streaked down and down, twisting a little, diving for life. A loud bang came from his port wing. The German had holed him. He was still there and obviously enjoying the way Fremont had chosen to open the fight. Snatches of radio transmission leapt out of the headset ("Shoot. Shoot. Shoot the fucker! There's one under you. Get him. We're burning. I can't see anything in here. Help!"); another bomber was going down somewhere. It was all rapid and indistinct. He could hardly breathe, barely see. At 500 feet he leveled out and his body went cold for a moment. Instinctively he wavered and snaked over the water, following a violent course of evasion. The German remained smoothly on his tail, flying as calmly as if he were following a guide wire. Fremont called for help. No reply. A burst of cannon fire ripped over his canopy. He could see the big Focke-Wulf's cowling drawing closer. Desperately, he went to half power, skidding out in a wide circle, forcing the German to fire at maximum deflection. Then he quickly dropped 200 feet. The shells were not even close. He shot the throttle into full power, breaking from the sea like a sailfish, climbing for the sun, for the advantage of altitude, rising through the ragged battle. The Focke-Wulf, its pilot shaking off surprise, came up after him. Minutes went by as they rode up at a sharp angle, the horizon falling behind. But Fremont broke out on top first, at 25,000 feet.

He banked right, racking his plane around, turning into the attack as he had always been told to. The Focke-

Wulf broke leftward, beginning a turn on its own. Fremont zoomed after it, and they began to turn together over the silent, beautiful sky. He rattled out a long burst, hitting nothing. They flew tightly, like two cadets practicing formations. Once or twice the Focke-Wulf opened a perfect angle of deflection between them, waggling his wings. Fremont was awed, chilled. Here was the classic sporting gesture he'd never expected to see. He was being given a chance to kill another man because that man respected his skill, admired his fortitude. He waggled his own wings in response, believing for a second that he had gone mad. A single puff of smoke came from the Focke-Wulf's exhaust. He was throttling back, getting ready to claim his kill as the other plane lunged past. Fremont stiffened, sank into confusion, drifted back to shocking alertness. He pulled the nose of his Mustang up slightly and slipped to the right with his left wing down. He was directly behind the German. The Focke-Wulf filled up his sight. He held the stick absolutely still, steadying himself. Streams of .50 caliber machine-gun bullets laced out from his wings, ripping into the enemy aircraft even as it began to smoke heavily. The canopy was thrown back. A German, short and blond, emerged, stepping onto the wing root with a curious, weary smile. He was not aware that his parachute was on fire. It opened briefly and then ignited, flickering away like a candle dropped down a well.

Skinner watched the Focke-Wulfs in perplexity, following their paths and routes as they knifed through the confusion all around him, flying in pairs, picking out sure targets, never remaining long in level flight, invariably destroying the airplane they were after. Two of them sailed down again, this time in front of one of the bombers. They attacked, flying head-on. Blinding flashes came from their cannons, and the big forward dome, the greenhouse, disintegrated. One man, a navigator or bombardier, pitched into space amid a torrent of splintered glass. Tracers sought out the bouncing wings. The Germans took their time, cutting loose with long bursts. Soon, both starboard engines were absorbed in flames. The Fortress shuddered, then began to fall away as another Focke-Wulf streaked underneath and shot the ball turret to pieces.

"Let's get them, Three-one," Hollyfield called from his wing. He sounded anxious and incriminating.

The Focke-Wulfs spotted them, wheeled and came on.

"Stay with me, Three-two," Skinner warned. "Stay with me no matter what, or they get us both."

"Roger."

Again, the Focke-Wulfs attacked head-on and abreast. Skinner watched them grow larger and larger. He kept his nose level. The Germans fired, but only at Hollyfield. His Mustang jumped under the salvo of cannon fire. Part of his right aileron was blown off, the wing badly holed. As he labored to right his plane, the German pair dipped into a shallow dive and prepared to turn on both of them. Skinner banked around to face the onslaught.

"Dive, Three-two. Dive. Pick me up later."

Hollyfield plunged into a diving turn, and his pursuer overshot him. Skinner fired at the other Focke-Wulf, hoping to beat it off before it got close and bore in with its powerful 20 millimeter cannons. The German rolled over and dived, his blue-bellied craft blending into the haze and water. Skinner went down after him, lost him, and then picked out the black crosses on his underside. He was nearly 2,000 feet below. Skinner fell swiftly, ignoring the sky and the sea, looking only at the German. His airspeed rose tremendously and the Mustang roared. The Focke-Wulf began a split S, which was almost always followed by a dive. Skinner followed him into the top of the S, switching on his illuminated sight, but suddenly the German fooled him and shot upwards and right by him in a steep full-power climb. He pulled up, tracking the Focke-Wulf, rocketing imperceptibly closer, urged on by wariness and confidence. Then, in one cavalier motion, the other plane looped into a Cuban eight. Skinner reached the top of the figure eight and panicked for an instant when he realized that any other craft in the sky could blow him to pieces. He tumbled out of the maneuver, rolling over twice. When he searched for the Focke-Wulf, it was gone.

"You should have had him," Walker broke in on the radio. "He's mine now."

Above, Skinner saw a Mustang flash by. Walker climbed with the Focke-Wulf, masterfully breaking left and right in its slipstream, as if he did it every day. At 30,000 feet, they leveled off. Walker tried a badly angled deflection shot from slightly above and missed. The Focke-Wulf whipped around, its pilot apparently sensing there was an amateur on his tail. A hail of tracers raked the Mustang, and in seconds the German plane had slipped off Walker's right wing, flipped over gracefully, and gone into a split S. It vanished before Walker could move his stick. His canopy and starboard wing were full of bullet holes, but the control surfaces held firm.

Walker sat shivering for a while, describing aimless circles in the sky. He pushed the regulator to one hundred percent oxygen and felt a little better. Still he was afraid, stunned by how quickly he had lost the initiative and been thrown on the defensive, fighting not to die, praying for help that was not there. Suddenly he was angry. He began cursing wildly and banging his fist on the top of the stick. He didn't see the Focke-Wulf which had glided elegantly down behind him until his plane was nearly in cannon range. They had told him always to face the man on his tail and he did, but this time the big radial engine was just about on top of him. He refused to dive, and looked down with some satisfaction as the enemy plane streaked under him so close he could see its peeling paint and the blistered areas around the exhaust stubs. Abruptly the Focke-Wulf darted away, making for a lone Mustang which was idling along, not even bothering to take evasive action. The gas tank was hit. Flames billowed out on all sides. Walker saw the pilot throw himself clear without crawling out on the wing. He dropped like a stone before his parachute finally jerked him upright. It was all quick, vivid, and terrifying.

Walker cut back on his power and ranged in wide circles around the descending pilot to keep him from being strafed. He could not be sure who the man was but suspected it might be Jennings. Walker followed him down, staying fairly close until he hit the water and cast aside his parachute with some difficulty. Pathetically, he bobbed on the endless sea. Walker was enthralled. He was so absorbed by the wretchedness of the small dark figure there in the water that he actually thought at first that the big boat coming out of a nearby cove was an air-sea rescue launch. The boat moved over the water powerfully, sending out a rough, wide wake. It passed within fifty yards of the downed pilot. Black smoke wafted up from its engine. The deck was protected by light flak and machine guns.

"Diesel ferry making for the open sea," someone informed him on the headset. "Can you handle him, Two-one?"

Walker snapped off his radio without answering and eased into a gliding turn. He spied the German Navy flag now, but could not understand why they didn't fire on him. The white stucco houses of Marghana drifted by on his left. People had come to the edge of the water to watch something. Leveling out, he saw it too. A Flying Fortress, two of its engines feathered, droned along barely a hundred feet above the water reflected on its undersides. The top turret was blown away. Walker could see the port waist gunner hanging dead in his harness. The survivors worked frantically, flinging everything possible out of the plane, even ammunition and guns. The ship had to be lightened; it was the only way to try and make a run for land. The first burst of flak from the ferry killed everyone standing in the doorway. Another salvo tore the plane in half and it exploded seconds later, simply metamorphosing into a rising sheet of bright orange fire, like a dirigible igniting. The Germans continued firing. Fifty-caliber machine-gun bullets whipped up a froth of wavelets, but there was nobody in the water. The men in the ship were all gone.

The ferry changed course for Pantelleria in a wide arrogant arc, its flak guns pointed skyward. Walker flew low in a circle outside their range. He prayed they would not see the fighter pilot in the water, but they did. Instantly a pair of Mustangs dived on the ferry, but it threw up a tremendous curtain of flak and they had to pull up. The ferry crept closer to the Mae West floating on the calm deep blue sea. The pilot tried to submerge himself, but his life jacket held him up. He attempted to swim away. The Germans came alongside and snatched him from the sea, tossing him brutally on the wide flat deck of the pontooned boat. Walker's heart tightened. He girdled the ferry as closely as he dared and dipped one wing in encouragement. Shame and pathos overwhelmed him. He climbed out.

The weaving and buzzing of airplanes had slackened somewhat. Walker could make out a bomber here and there, Mustangs grouped around it. He searched the sky. Ahead and below, not a thousand feet away, was a Focke-

Wulf, its pilot looking for strays, for one more target, one more victory toward his Knight's Cross. Stealthily, Walker dropped down a hundred feet at a time, gazing at the altimeter as it fell back. He was too wearied and saddened for anger. His senses were vague, unalert, peculiarly numb. The Focke-Wulf skidded left as Walker followed it through his illuminated sight dispassionately, as if he were a scientist at his microscope. He led the plane beautifully and fired a long burst from each wing which converged a few hundred yards on, just as the Focke-Wulf passed through it. Walker watched the pilot jump and yank and twist in his shoulder harness under the pulverizing bullets. The plane tumbled away, hopelessly out of control. He did not bother to follow its downward path.

Jennings was at 40,000 feet, just 1,800 feet, a few ticks on his altimeter, from his airplane's ceiling, the point at which it would no longer climb but would hang stubbornly in the clouds until its fuel was gone. He did not search the sky. Focke-Wulfs couldn't fly at this altitude, and so at least he was safe. Blood dropped from his nose into the oxygen mask, hitting the rubber with a dull, pattering sound. He had trouble breathing, trouble understanding why he was still alive. The Germans had had him on the deck twice, slicing the air around him with tracers. Yet his plane had not ignited; somehow he had shaken them off, dodging madly over the sea, angling out and away from them as if he had known what he was doing. Twice more, Focke-Wulfs had ridden his tail, only to have him turn and come at them in a suicidal rush. He had gotten close enough to see the faces of the pilots, suddenly agonized and frozen before they had dived him. Walker had saved him once, Hollyfield once.

Jennings blacked out for an instant in a dive and actually skimmed the water as someone screamed into the headset for him to pull out. Everything else was fragmented into hideous images, grotesque voices: bomber crewmen petrified in the doorway, unable to jump as their huge plane plunged for the sea; flaming Mustangs, beautiful in their death roll; someone in the water, dark and indistinguishable against the bright orange of his life jacket. Then there was his one aggressive moment of the whole battle, a quick pass out of the sun, aiming for the black Luftwaffe cross outlined in white, flying in on it until it seemed to touch his nose. Squeezing the gun switch. An empty click. The guns jammed.

Total silence swept through the heavens. Fremont heard nothing but the drone of his engine. He looked around as Butters took up station off his port wing. They examined each other quizzically. Their fuel running low, the Focke-Wulfs had vanished, disappearing all at once, probably at a prearranged signal. Only friendly planes remained.

"Broadsword squadron. Assemble by flights. Assemble by flights."

Slowly the planes began to cluster in around him.

"Request permission for damage check, leader," Walker said.

"Hurry it up," Fremont said irritably. "They may be back."

A Mustang came so near to Walker that they almost touched wingtips. Walker tested his controls for free movement, then the inspecting aircraft glided around him searching for external damage.

"You're holed pretty good and there's a big cannon bull's-eye right at the base of your air scoop. You'll live."

Fremont switched channels. The leader of the bomber squadron was there.

"Broadsword leader, I can only raise twelve of my ships. We've got a lot of men hurt bad. Suggest we make for Bizerte and emergency landing."

"Acknowledged," Fremont said icily. The man had not paid him the courtesy of inquiring about his own casualties.

They set out over the sea, moving toward the faraway blue haze which indicated the horizon. No one talked. Everyone was aware of the missing aircraft, of the man floundering helplessly in the water. Flying two flights on each side of the damaged bombers, they slowly lost a bit of altitude and watched their clocks, waiting to see land. Most of the waist gunners on the Fortress were not at their stations. Most of the glass turrets stood cracked and shattered, their machine guns askew. Fremont could hear the bombers asking for landing clearance. He spied a ship, a destroyer, cutting through the glassy water.

Soon the coast of Africa appeared. Low, fleecy clouds cast shadows on the massive greenish landscape. The leader of the bomber formation broke into Fremont's fleeting sense of relief.

"We're about home, Broadsword," he said in a mildly apologetic voice. "Don't feel bad about what happened. You all boys tried. They just had the whole thing sniffed out," he went on plaintively. "They took away the initiative. Some days it's like that. Well, so long now."

"So long, Greentree," Fremont answered. He didn't like this countrified fluency with the ways of disaster. He knew his own squadron would take all the blame when the bomber pilot wrote out his mission report.

The bombers dropped down to 3,000 feet and banked left toward a distant runway slotted into the rich brown-and-green plateau. Someone began laughing raucously and whistling into the headset. Admonitions and curses failed to silence him. He whistled so shrilly that helmets had to be removed. The chortling and giggling continued, twisting into a cunning and whimsical frenzy of humming and bizarre noises.

"Who is that man?" Fremont demanded.

"Four-four," Archibald answered. "My tail man. A replacement. Jones, sir."

"Is he injured?"

"No, sir."

At that moment the delirious laughter stopped. A Mustang shot by overhead, roaring away at full throttle. Whooping cries of exultation blasted through the radio.

"Request permission to divert runaway aircraft home."

"Negative, Four-one," Fremont replied, watching the graceful Mustang grow smaller in the high sky.

"I can bring him back, sir. Jones listens to me," Archibald insisted.

"Preserve flight integrity," was the cold reply.

"He's firewalling, sir. He'll be out of gas soon. Give him a chance. He didn't know he was going up today."

"No matter what happens, don't go to your reserve tank, Archie. I don't want to lose my flight leaders."

"Yes, sir. I understand."

Archibald zoomed past the squadron, but Jones had all but disappeared. It looked hopeless.

THREE

Two INJURED MEN landed first, their Mustangs wobbling and bouncing almost out of control as they touched down. Hollyfield went in next. His overheated engine smoked heavily, and he glided the last thousand feet. Fremont could see he was on the verge of a stall just before his wheels reached the runway. The go-round light was flashed again as he prepared to come in; another pilot with engine trouble dropped down to earth. When Fremont taxied in, his mechanic came running up and signalled to him where to park. He cleared the engine with a burst of the throttle and switched off. The silence was oppressive. Slowly Fremont realized he was dazed. The mechanic opened the canopy and helped him out of his harness quickly, not saying a word. On the ground his legs went weak, making it hard for him to shake out the stiffness. He noticed his clothes were sodden with perspiration. Looking around unsteadily, Fremont saw one of the fliers being assisted into the back of an ambulance.

Osborn's jeep ran over the grass and pulled up right alongside. Without bothering to take the cigar out of his mouth, he saluted as Fremont got in beside him. He drove rather slowly. Osborn was a mediocre pilot, and the confusion of actual combat always disturbed him.

"We monitored the whole mission carefully," he said after a while. "Those jughead crackers cost you three minutes. It's all down on paper. They've got no case."

"They've always got a case," Fremont said wearily.

37

"Here's the breakdown," Osborn continued. "Ike Fox from C flight and Spain Kelly, Archie's wingman, are both gone. Ben Majors ditched over the sea."

Fremont turned to him in anxious surprise because Majors was in his own flight. But Osborn didn't take his eyes off the road.

"His radio went out before he could get off a Mayday. Air-sea got him. He'll be back here in an hour."

"What about Jones?" Fremont asked briskly.

"Jones ran out of gas somewhere inland, in the desert. He crash-landed, but his ship is still flyable, only he can't take off in the sand. He's walking around. Archie ordered him to stay with the ship. Soon as I can get a fix on him, we'll have a tractor out there."

Fremont watched the little fat man next to him puff on his cigar. As always, he was relaxed and nimble-minded. For a moment Fremont wondered what on earth Osborn would do after the war.

"We lost a man in the sea," Fremont announced.

Osborn pulled at his cap very tensely. "Ollie St. Clair, sir. A promising young boy, too. We can't do a goddamn thing for him. Not a thing, sir. I pray to God the Luftwaffe sends him to a POW camp before the SS moves in. It's entirely possible the SS will not find out about him for some time. But eventually news of who he is and what he is will get out. There's no way to stop that. Soldiers always talk."

"Notify headquarters formally of his capture. Then telegraph the Red Cross in Geneva, using my name and rank. Tell them he's the first black boy the Germans have gotten. Have them make inquiries. I want this thing public. It's the best hope."

"I'll do that, sir," Osborn answered flatly.

They drew up in front of the caravan. Fremont spoke rapidly, his voice full of subtle agitation. "Clear out the belongings of Kelly, Fox, and St. Clair pronto. Send me their personal effects along with St. Clair's file. And the minute Jones sets foot back on this field, I want to see him."

Osborn smiled a bit. "Tomorrow's mission assignment ought to be coming through in a couple of hours," he said smartly.

"Just let the pilots know after dinner that they'll be

flying in the morning," Fremont replied. He wanted Osborn to go now, but the Operations Officer looked up at him from the jeep, one heavy arm curled around the top of the wheel.

"Sir, I hate to say this," he began quickly, as if he'd already reasoned the whole thing out, "but I think we can expect an inquiry into today's action. The bomber boys at Headquarters just won't stand for the loss of four planes on a routine mission. They'll blame you all the way back to Washington."

"This wasn't a routine mission," Fremont replied evenly. "We were jumped by more than fifty enemy planes, Lieutenant."

"I know that, Colonel," Osborn said, "yet you might not have been if Walker hadn't broken air discipline and challenged one of the Fortresses. That broke our back today."

In the middle of the afternoon a clerk brought the intelligence reports to Fremont's caravan. He glanced through them quickly, knowing from the start that they would make the pilots look foolish and contradictory. He felt the whole intelligence procedure, with its absurdly detailed questions ("Are these the F-Ws with the new fast-firing cannons? Spirals on their spinners or not? Make up your mind"), was unfair to his men now, when they were so unaccustomed to the speed and intensity of the air war. Besides, he did not like Lieutenant Todd, the Intelligence man. Todd was a little too stagey, too meticulous. He had a gift for pretension.

Fremont pulled out a big map of North Africa, Sicily, and the Mediterranean, spreading it over his spare desk. He savored the map. ("You'd make a top staff officer," a professor at the Point had told him once, after all the other cadets had left the classroom.) Sicily was not going to be an easy campaign. The Luftwaffe was skilled at regrouping and was at its most dangerous when things were desperate. Hitler had made his pronouncement ("Not one German soldier must leave this island"), then brought in reinforcements from the Reich. Sicily was mountainous, rough to fly, especially at the lesser altitudes where the hot air caused severe downdrafts. Every mission was certain to be brutal. Fremont expected withering ground fire from camouflaged batteries, a tactical art at which the

Germans excelled. The RAF was losing a dozen planes a week in France and the Netherlands that way. And, of course, there would be the inevitable improvisations: collapsible buildings, phony airfields, a new rocket, something. Yet he relished the whole thing because the Germans were mad and romantic; they were still sporting enough to play with death in the midst of chaos, like the man he had killed this morning. In the end, perhaps sadly, they would lose. Their army was low on fuel and some of its best divisions could not be kept on an island that must eventually be surrounded and overrun. Germany was destined to vanish from Sicily, leaving only artifacts, as the Greeks, Carthaginians, and Romans had done.

The telephone buzzed softly. "Sir, Lieutenant Jones is back on the base. He's on his way to your quarters."

Jones came in, saluted, and took a seat in the campaign chair alongside the desk. The men faced each other. Jones had a reputation as a gambler and a fighter. He was supposed to be dangerous in a quiet, backcountry way, but this afternoon he appeared self-absorbed, dirty, and slack. Fremont sighed heavily.

"What happened up there today to make you break air discipline and leave the formation, Lieutenant?"

"I lost my head, sir. Something happened. I felt pressure all over my head. I no longer knew where I was or what I was saying."

"I see," Fremont said. "Well, you're through here. Your presence in the formation would only hurt morale. I'm sending you back to Tuskegee to work with some of the younger pilots coming along. Get packed, Lieutenant. You leave for Algiers tonight. Ops will have your traveling orders."

"Tuskegee," Jones said vaguely. "Tuskegee all over again. Well, I kinda figured that."

"I'm sure you did."

Jones got up. He pursed his lips. "You got it all figured out, right, Colonel?" he asked, staring at the shelf where Fremont's leather-bound editions of Caesar, Napoleon, Thucydides, and Rommel stood elegantly.

"Come to the point, Jones."

A cunning pair of eyes met his before flicking away.

"You should never have let those white boys talk to us that way," he said angrily. "You should have left them.

Left them or fired warning shots to make them shape up. They went to *their* guns mighty quick, I noticed. Everybody feels the same way. They all think you were wrong. Dead wrong. Spain Kelly and Foxie were good buddies to me and as far as I can see, they died for nothing."

"They might have died anyway," Fremont replied impatiently. "No one knows what will happen in an action."

"We were over enemy territory. You shouldn't have just sat there and taken all that shit."

"I understand what you're saying, Lieutenant," was the calm answer, "but I want to caution you. We do not fire warning shots at Air Corps personnel no matter what happens. That's what they want us to do, you damn fool."

Jones smirked. Fremont was obviously disturbed and this pleased him.

"Headquarters was on the phone half an hour after I landed," Fremont said. "They suggested we might need a psychologist up here to interview these men. This outfit is being carefully watched. We can be shipped back to the States anytime, and I'm not going to have that."

"I don't care what you say!" Jones shouted defiantly. "You're wrong. These pilots want to be treated as men or they'll start killing. I know that for a fact."

Fremont was ready to hit him in the mouth. But he could see that Jones was right in a sense and, at the same time, stupidly destructive. He loathed people who did not think things out clearly. He ignored Jones for a couple of minutes and then asked coolly, deprecatingly, "Why are you in this war? Why did you bother to come out here, Lieutenant?"

Jones was confused for a moment. But he regained his composure triumphantly. "I came out here for my salvation as a man," he replied with bitter directness. "I thought you understood that much, Colonel."

As evening descended on the field, a mood of insidious depression took Fremont. Jones had made him see what a disaster the operation had been, how close it had come to catastrophe. He felt terribly lonely and wondered if command of the squadron would not eventually be pulled from his grasp. He told himself an official inquiry into the mission was really the thing to fear most. Squadron leaders were easily replaced, and Fremont knew he'd made a lot of enemies over the years. Dozens of senior officers all over this theater, some of them former classmates, would relish news of his dismissal. With four B-17s lost in a single day, he had no right to feel secure.

A loud knock sounded at his door. One of the Operations Room boys stood in the waning sunlight.

"Sorry to bother you, sir, but the strangest message just came through on the teletype. Someone at Headquarters sent it," the clerk added, handing the yellow paper up to Fremont:

> COLONEL: BIRD OF ILL WILL IN YOUR NEST.
> THIS TO ALERT YOU.
>
> PARTY LINE

"Who else has seen this?"

"No one, sir. I came straight here."

"What's your name, Corporal?"

"Reeves, sir."

"Reeves, you are not to mention this communication to anyone. Ever. That is a direct order."

"Yes, sir."

"In the future bring all similarly worded messages directly to me."

The clerk saluted obediently. Fremont folded the paper and put it into his breast pocket thoughtfully, as if to indicate he knew what it meant. But the corporal was not fooled.

FOUR

A THIN WHITISH MIST clung to the ground outside as the pilots came into the Briefing hut. Walker surprised everyone by suddenly throwing an arm around Norvel Donaldson's neck ("I going to yoke you like a mule so you won't run away no more. . . .") and playfully holding him down until he sprawled on the floor. A harsh, insulting laughter filled the hut as Donaldson scrambled to his feet, but Jennings did not think it was funny. He felt sorry for Donaldson because he drank heavily and should not be flying an airplane in combat. Like the other men, Jennings was tired. He hadn't slept much. Yesterday's air battle had unreeled through his mind all night, vividly, then elusively. He hadn't been able to remember what he'd done or failed to do. Incidents, bare fragments of the battle, had stood out in his memory as he had strained to see some coherence in all of it. Finally he had come to believe he grasped the whole operation, even though it had happened quickly. Even though it had gone by so fast, all the thinking, emotion, and action compressed into those seventeen or so minutes had left him staggered.

"Good morning, gentlemen," Osborn said crisply. "I have good news. Today we go to Sicily."

Some of the fliers murmured; some smiled a bit. They appeared relaxed and had already begun to take on the arrogant and cynical look of the fighter pilot. This was good. It would make them more effective, make them take more chances. Osborn went to the map.

43

"Southwestern Sicily is the operational area we've been assigned to. This is a rough area, let's make no mistake about it," he said. "The terrain is rugged, and General Galland, the leader of the German fighter arm, has four *Gruppen* here, as against two on the other side of the island. What we are to do is hit communications, tear them up. Knock out military trains. Keep those people short of heavy trucks. Hit staff cars hard. You never know, it might be Rommel or Galland. Watch the trees by the roadside. The Germans like to park there by day and move at night. Another thing, try not to hit civilians if at all possible. Many of these civilians leave their villages during the day in donkey carts. They're all over the goddamn place, but we've got to try to spare them. We may be in Sicily ourselves this summer."

Jennings stood up, cap in hand. "Sir, is there any word on Ollie St. Clair?"

"No, Lieutenant," Osborn replied, staring right past him. "We have no word as yet on St. Clair. We are making attempts to find out what the Germans have done with him. It is hoped that he is still in the hands of the Luftwaffe and that with Red Cross help he can be gotten into a camp for Air Force prisoners."

"Thank you, sir," Jennings said.

The men looked at each other with a sort of shrewd glumness. It was clear now the best St. Clair could hope for was solitary until the end of the war. The white boys would probably not want him in their camp.

"Today P-38 Lightnings will be operating in an area just east of you, so look out for them," Osborn continued. "The Germans don't like Lightnings. They shot the first three P-38 squadrons out of the air until cover tactics were devised. Now the Lightnings have turned mean. They hit everything viciously and rip up the roads in southern Sicily so they won't have to lug a lot of ammo home. They're good boys to have on your flank."

"If you say so," somebody said laughingly. Osborn showed the hint of a tough smile, then withdrew it.

"Gentlemen, there is one thing I'm going to caution you about every time you come in here," he said, pointing a stubby finger. "Keep track of your fuel. Don't go to full power unless it's necessary. Sicily is a long way from home and you're flying over water. Please be careful in this regard. Repeat. Be careful."

Nature Boy appeared and told them what was already apparent: it would be a beautiful clear day, a perfect flying day.

When Lieutenant Todd stepped up, a host of derisive stares met him. Some of the pilots crossed their arms and pretended not to listen. Todd ignored this coolness and hostility. He knew the men were furious about his reluctance to confirm Walker's kill, but he didn't care. He didn't know a melee had almost broken out in the Debriefing Room yesterday.

"Frankly, the reports I got from your first mission were pathetic," he opened brusquely. "Today, I hope you can do better. I want info on troop movements, truck convoys, et cetera. If you see something suspicious on the ground, do me a favor and check it out. I would also like some facts on enemy aircraft. We've heard the Germans have beefed up the armor on the 109s and FWs. If you shoot for weak spots on these planes and nothing happens, don't take it as a personal failure; forget about it. This is a technical war. These things have significance. That's all."

"You can say that shit again," a snarling voice replied. A current of bitter, mirthful laughter circulated among the fliers.

Fremont got on the stage. "A warning. Any man who breaks air discipline for any reason is on his way back to the States tonight. Keep off the radio unless you've got something important to say. The Germans can monitor us and they have translators. Okay. Start engines at 0645. Takeoff is at 0648. You flight leaders see me up here. Dismissed."

"We had a time getting some of these planes back into shape last night, sir," Fremont's mechanic said as he tightened the harness straps.

Fremont nodded. He'd meant to come out and check on damage with the line chief, "Big Chief" Harris, but there had been little time.

"You all must have run into some real veterans yesterday. Understand you got a kill, sir," he continued in a voice full of admiration.

"Yes, I did," Fremont answered modestly. He turned a bit in the seat to get a better glimpse of the mechanic.

"It's only right. We wouldn't be out here fighin' if it wasn't for you. That's the way the men feel."

"What's your name, Private?" Fremont asked.

"They call me Friday, sir," the man replied as he stepped off the wing walk and began his final exterior inspection.

Archibald came tearing up on his motorcycle and parked it in the grass. Jennings watched him from his aircraft. He didn't notice his mechanic appear from under the plane, wiping oil from his hands with a heavy cloth.

"You jammed your trim tabs," the man said accusingly. "And they shot part of your rudder away. Did you know that?"

"I thought she was in pretty decent shape," Jennings said cheerfully.

"Decent shape, my ass. You popped God knows how many rivets. What were you tryin' to do, sir, break the sound barrier?"

"I'm sorry if I'm making a whole lot of trouble for you, Sergeant, but it can't be helped," Jennings said.

"Well, I appreciate you doin' your best to spare me this way, Lieutenant," the mechanic answered, "but a couple more days like yesterday and this airplane, tough as she is, has got to go in the shop for major repairs. That is if you don't fold back the wings first."

Angrily Jennings closed the canopy. It was almost time for takeoff.

Showing the precision of carrier pilots, the Mustangs streaked away at five-second intervals. They assembled into battle formation beautifully, as if the squadron had flown daily since the beginning of the war. At 8,000 feet Fremont took them east through the astonishingly limpid sky. As they passed the ruins of Carthage, the men hand signalled one another to look down. Then they skirted Cape Bon and moved out over the sea. The rear flights bobbed a little in the slipstream of the plane up front, but everyone seemed to hold station easily. Fremont really wanted another kill today.

No one broke radio silence. The solitude of the Mediterranean set in and stayed with them until Fremont saw the faraway white sands of a beach coming up out of the vapor which cloaked the blue horizon.

"Victor squadron. We are closing the coast of Sicily. Keep a sharp eye out for fighters and don't leave the formation unless I give the order. Maintain radio silence."

The high dazzling sky, the legendary Sicilian sky they had heard about, opened above them. Circling the town of Castelvetrano, the squadron dropped to 5,000 feet over the melancholy white houses stacked up in tiers around a neat idyllic little harbor. Fremont ordered a cutback in RPMs. They glided swiftly over the land, over the eternal olive groves and vineyards, above the tall pines and elegant cypresses, along the dusty roads. They saw no people. It was all so strange, this combination of warmth and bleakness, so different from the green hills of North Africa. Slicing toward the coast again, they made for Chinisia. The ghostly, predatory shadows of their planes fled across the picturesque houses. Along the road between Chinisia and Marsala to the north, an old man leading a donkey cart waved at them. At Marsala they bore due east on the second leg of a triangular course intended to bring them out at Castelvetrano. Nowhere could evidence of German soldiers be found. The penetrating heat of Sicily steamed up at them from the yellowish primeval barren earth. One hour had elapsed in the air, an eternity on the island below. Twangy indistinct voices, the P-38 pilots operating east of them, wafted through the static and ether into their headsets. A flat plain dotted with low scrub spread in front of them. Walker was the first man to see the train.

"I've got a fix on it," Fremont answered coolly to Walker's excited call.

The train was moving slowly, laboring along the narrow tracks at a right angle to the nose of Fremont's Mustang.

"Why don't we attack, leader?" Walker asked impatiently.

"Maintain radio silence," Fremont warned.

They continued on their course, passing a few miles south of Castelvetrano and heading out over the empty sea. Here they wheeled about in a big circle knowing it would be difficult to spot them even with binoculars; the train did not pick up speed. Unfolding his map on one knee, Fremont spoke calmly to Butters.

"This must be the Castelvetrano-Agrigento line, Roy."

"Yes, sir. It seems to wind all over this coast."

"How many fighter bases have the Germans got between these two towns?"

"One on the map, sir, although there is a base just north of Castelvetrano, and they probably have some planes camouflaged at a forward position somewhere."

If the radar on Mount Erice picked them up, there could be trouble. Off Fremont's starboard wingtip the train crawled across the sparse landscape, its old engine idly sending up balls of cottony white smoke.

"Go down and have a look, Roy."

"Right, sir."

"Victor Three-one and Four-one. Take your flights and climb to seventeen thousand feet. I'm depending on you to keep us from getting surprised."

The flight leaders acknowledged the order crisply. Eight Mustangs pulled out of the formation and lifted upwards, climbing toward the sun. Butters sailed over the plain below at 500 feet. As his shadow reemerged on the other side of the train he called in, rasping out his information.

"Four coaches, One-one. Four open boxcars covered with tarpaulin. A caboose. Civilians on train. No Germans in sight."

"We're going in, Roy. Come around and follow the run."

Fremont alerted his men. He heard Walker whoop with joy. He edged the stick forward and the Mustang gained speed immediately. Johnson came up near his wing. They cut a long, swooping path through the air. Beneath them the ground blurred. The sensation was intoxicating. Directly ahead of them the train meandered along when suddenly Fremont saw German helmets at the windows and men running inside the coaches. Machine-gun fire streamed up at them. Tarpaulin flew in all directions and a light flak gun was cranked up furiously by its crew. German soldiers were everywhere, firing from the windows, setting up their guns between the coaches. He passed over too quickly to do anything, but Walker's flight fired away and men tumbled from the train, rolling into the scrub. They climbed to 2,000 feet and swept around for a second pass. The defensive fire was thick. A light flak gun sat in each of the boxcars and the train was moving faster now. Most of it was passing between two hills as Fremont came in again. His cannon fire missed badly, churning up the earth.

A machine gun on the rear platform of the caboose flicked up at him. He heard the sharp ping of a hit on his fuselage. This time he climbed higher to get the sun squarely at his back and wait until the train cut across open country again. Butters was beside him, shaking his head in annoyance.

"Victor aircraft," Fremont said intensely. "When they hit that flat we'll lead them a little and go for the engine. Use your cannon and get in close."

The train fled across the straightway, throttle open. Fremont kept the engine in his sight, watching its size increase. He saw a man stoking wildly. Two kneeling soldiers fired from the coal pile with murderous determination. The cockpit smelled of cordite as the cannon popped off its rounds. He pulled up to the left in a steep bank with the other Mustangs in tow. Steam poured over the engine, but its pace barely slackened.

"It's armor-plated! A goddamn armor-plated engine," someone cried in excitement verging on despair.

"Bore in for the center of the train," Fremont ordered.

Once more they swept down, cannons blazing. Half of one coach flew into splinters. People were lying in the aisles, bloody and askew, as Walker's flight pounded the train until, abruptly, it came apart, the first of the rearward cars lurching off the tracks and onto the sandy ground.

"You handle that, Two-one. We're going after the rest," Fremont said as his flight broke to the east and climbed into position.

"Look alive there, tail ass," Walker snapped at Jennings, who had been slow coming around. "We go in two abreast this time. Bluey and me will work 'em over with the cannons. You and Beaumont use the .50s. Strafe hell out of anything movin'."

Beaumont came alongside and together they watched the first element go down. Their accuracy was astounding. The boxcars shuddered and then exploded in a brilliant rolling ball of fire which carried fifty feet into the air and gave off waves of heat that distorted the scenery for miles. The Mustangs got clear just in time. Shock waves still buffeted the atmosphere as Jennings and Beaumont headed in, firing long bursts. Dead soldiers and their equipment were flung all over. Jennings could hear the skeletons of the boxcars burning violently.

"Six men," Beaumont cried as they passed the wreckage. "Six men ran from the caboose before the explosion. Some of them had briefcases."

"You sure, Donny?" Walker cut in.

"Yes," Beaumont said. "I have them in sight. They're moving south toward a farmhouse."

"I see the bastards. Okay. We'll take 'em first. You and tail ass mop up."

Like a true predator, Walker flashed down and circled in behind the fleeing Germans. The two men with briefcases were fat and could barely run. On hearing the planes, they all spread out. Fifty caliber bullets the size of a man's index finger stitched the earth around them in straight lines. Four Germans fell, but the man holding the document cases stumbled on.

"Pick a man and stay with him," Walker yelled as the second element took up the chase. The officer Jennings was after veered all over the scrub. He wore shining boots and had a yellow stripe going down the side of his pants. As Jennings drew near, one gloved hand shot into the air as if to ward off the airplane. A short burst from the fifties spun him around crazily. He died without letting go of the briefcase.

"Good shooting," Walker cried, his voice full of satisfaction. "All my boys shoot good."

Jennings smiled broadly and saluted Beaumont.

What was left of the train had eluded Fremont by gaining entrance to an area of twisting, hilly terrain where no clear shots were possible. Tantalizing puffs of smoke rose from between the hills as the tracks followed a strange roundabout route. Butters reconnoitered ahead and reported a short straightaway leading into a tunnel where the train would be safe and unreachable.

"We'll only have time for one more pass, leader," he warned. "If they stop in these hills, we may have to give it up. Estimate in four minutes fuel will become critical factor."

"All right, Victor One aircraft," Fremont said. "You all heard Roy. This is probably it for today. We'll come in four abreast. Stay low. Hit the locomotive. Aim for the wheels and drive shafts."

Fremont's men began their run a mile away at 200 feet

just as the locomotive emerged onto the straightaway. It was all going to be one pass. Onward they came, hurtling toward the engine and four ragged reddish-brown coaches. Machine gunners on the tender picked them up. Spurts of light lashed away at them. Hits were scored, but the planes came on, roaring, throwing up clouds of dust. Then Majors, the outside man, was hit hard. He screamed into the headset. His plane rocked, and fire was concentrated on it. One wing scraped the ground. He lost control and the Mustang cartwheeled on its wingtips, flinging debris everywhere. Flames streamed out of it, all over it, and it bounded on heavily toward the train, struck the tracks and came to rest, a shapeless, hideous conflagration against the mouth of the tunnel where the engine plowed into it at top speed and blew up instantaneously. A man covered with flames broke into the open. He dashed over the scrub beating at his clothes, as people and soldiers leapt from the fiery coaches and fled in all directions.

Fremont's flight turned to starboard and gazed over the holocaust in disbelief. After two circuits the order was given. "Victor squadron, assemble at ten thousand," Fremont intoned sadly. "It's time to go home."

FIVE

THE NEXT DAY, Walker arrived at the Operations hut with the second truckload. After landing, he took his time, talking with Dummy about new spark plugs and an oil pump for the engine, drinking a Coke. The Debriefing Room was still crowded when he got there. Pilots in their sweaty flight gear sat around writing reports and chatting about the truck-convoy attack, using their hands to indicate the motions and attitudes of airplanes. Osborn patiently questioned some of the men, Todd the rest. Walker found a seat next to Hollyfield and filled out his forms, not unaware that people were watching him. Presently he ambled up to Todd's desk and turned a chair around in front of it.

"Well, Lieutenant," Todd said, looking over the papers. "I see you've enjoyed some more success."

"I think so," Walker came back politely. Fremont's kill was already in the books, but Todd so far had ignored his claim of a Focke-Wulf on the first mission and Walker was seething.

"What aircraft type was this you got today?" Todd asked, staring at him.

"It was an artillery spotter plane. A Storch," Walker said.

"A Storch in that area? That's unusual. What was the angle of deflection?"

"About thirty degrees," Walker answered coolly. "It folded up like a model airplane."

Todd flashed an amused smile, as if to say he did not believe a German-made aircraft would just fall apart.

"Any witnesses?"

"I saw it," someone shouted. It was Ross Greenlee, Walker's wingman, the pilot everyone called Bluey. He stood boldly, hands on hips, with his leather jacket open. Todd noticed that all of them were looking at him in anger and resentment. The only sound in the room was the swish of a big black electric fan overhead.

Walker had been waiting for this moment. He struck. "What about my claim the other day? The Focke-Wulf."

"Well, that's pending," Todd replied sharply.

"Pending on what?" Walker said with narrowed, venomous eyes. "On what, you bastard?"

Todd leaned forward stiffly.

"Look. Right now it's a probable. That may be all you get."

Walker's hand dropped, touching the hunting knife in his boot.

"What the fuck are you talkin' about, man?" he cried in something like anguish. "I gets nothin'? I get a handful of shit, is that it? Is that the payoff?" he yelled.

"I didn't want to go into this with you until a decision was made. But you've forced the issue, so I guess you've got to know, Walker. The film in your gun camera came out blank."

A wave of ugly, embittered grumbling broke out in the room.

"This doesn't mean you won't get your kill. Under regulations all I need is a witness not in your flight who saw the airplane crash or the pilot bail out. I've been asking around."

"You're a liar!" Walker screamed. "I would have heard about you askin'. I would have heard!"

"Did he ask any of you all?" Walker shouted.

Most of the men shook their heads or turned away in embarrassment. They waited. The situation was nearly out of control.

Walker peered at Todd.

"I'm going to do away with you motherfucker. I'm going to kill you!" he exclaimed. Tears of panic and frustration filled his eyes. He tore the knife from his boot and held it over his head with both hands. Todd stared at the sharp glinting blade. His face was strangely composed. He made no move to run. Everyone waited in horror for the brutal

sucking noise as the knife plunged into Todd's chest. But
as it came slicing down, a hand caught Walker's wrist and
twisted it savagely. The knife fell away. Osborn slammed
a shoulder into Walker and he went sprawling to the floor,
groaning in surprise.

Some of the pilots laughed, but relief showed on all
their faces.

"You men get the hell out of this room," Osborn said,
waving an arm. "Clear it out!"

As the men left, Walker searched the floor for his knife.
Todd remained behind his desk. When no one was looking,
he snapped his holster down.

"Get your ass over here, Lieutenant," Osborn yelled at
Walker. "Get over here on the double when I talk to you."

Walker came sullenly.

"Lieutenant, you are to check in with the flight surgeon
and get something to settle you down," Osborn told him in
a cold, deliberate way. "If you don't, if you sneak back to
quarters, I'll have you grounded. Maybe for the duration
of this war. And give me that goddamn knife," he said,
snatching it away.

Walker looked hurt. His childlike face fixed on Osborn.

"You let being a first lieutenant go all to your head," he
cried. "You paint me as an outrageous person when I'm
not. I merely seek justice!"

"Get out of here," Osborn said.

Todd watched Walker go. He touched a sleeve to his
forehead. "I'm sure glad you were here, sir," he said in a
strained, quavering voice. "That crazy bastard might have
killed me."

Osborn murmured something. He turned over Walker's
knife in his hand and studied himself in the large shiny
blade.

"Who did you ask for confirmation on that FW?" he
said, glancing at Todd now.

Todd sat down behind his desk. He appeared slightly
stricken.

"I want names," he heard Osborn say. "I want a full
report on the failure of that gun camera. Tonight."

No operation was assigned for the following morning,
and immediately Fremont suspected trouble. It was after
midnight when a teletype message came in from Party

Line at Twelfth Air Force Headquarters warning of a full base inspection at 0800.

A brigadier general and his party of five arrived on the hour.

"Good morning to you, Colonel Fremont," the brigadier said coolly. "I'm General Barker."

Fremont saluted as slowly as he dared. Barker was tall and slim for a man in his forties, but he seemed ordinary, devoid of either presence or good looks. His blue eyes were tinged with outrage. His small prim mouth was tightly shut. He had the annoying habit of wrinkling his forehead. The war had pushed too many men like Barker to the top. In a brief exchange of glances they despised each other.

"This is my executive officer, Captain Paul Love," Barker went on, nodding to a younger man with clean, even features who, surprisingly, stepped forward and shook Fremont's hand after saluting.

"I've heard about you, Colonel," he said politely, although his eyes contained a suggestion of something deeper and more serious.

Fremont acknowledged him brusquely.

"This little inspection isn't aimed at you or your men," Barker said with a snide touch of grandness. "We hit every base in this theater. Keeps people sharp. But some need it more than others, if you know what I mean."

Barker's men fanned out all over the field, barging into huts, tramping around the dispersals, sneaking into the kitchen ("What the hell do you people eat anyway?"), searching everywhere for infractions. None was found. The pilots, dressed and shaved, sat in the mess hall talking quietly, reading, writing letters home, obviously on standby. Everything seemed to run efficiently. The infirmary was spotless and devoid of malingerers. All of this left the inspecting officers with nothing to report. Their instructions from Barker had been to order a stand-down if adequate reasons could be found. Now they looked foolish and it enraged them. Osborn overheard Barker tell his men to get back to the car immediately to avoid the humiliation of being invited to lunch.

Shortly after sundown the day they went back on operations, Walker took his corncob pipe and set out for a walk. As the reigning squadron ace with three kills in the air and one on the ground, he was not interested in the big discussion at the base club about the disappearance of German fighters on Sicily. There was no point to it, and besides, he did not believe Germany was anywhere near finished. What he wanted tonight was a woman, but according to reports all the ladies of the village were being closely watched. He considered going back to his room and getting stoned on cognac like Donaldson, yet that seemed too dreary for such a gorgeous night.

He disappeared into the blackness beyond the fringe of huts, smoking his pipe and speculating about the passengers in the Junkers transport he got that day. *Must have been Galland and some of them other generals,* he thought. *Galland and his staff boys, that's who it had to be flyin' low like that almost in the goddamn trees. They must have been sneakin' out to one of their secret airfields for a conference. Well, that's all broke up now. They'll have to walk over half of Sicily to get a hot meal tonight.*

When the door of the Operations hut opened, Walker stopped. He saw Todd clearly in the light bursting over the damp ground. Carefully he puffed at his pipe, observing everything. Todd wore his sidearm as usual and held a portfolio tightly in one hand. He looked very important from this distance. He'd slipped into the night, when Walker heard a jeep starting up. Out of idle curiosity he strode in the direction of the only road leading from the field. He picked up a bicycle along the way but didn't mount it. Todd's jeep passed twenty yards from him, and as it did, a spark of mean suspicion urged Walker to follow Todd, to keep Todd in his sight no matter what happened.

Todd gained the road swiftly. The olive trees and vegetable gardens kept by the French settlers spread out on both sides of him. He passed small, verdant fields filled with plump sheep and cattle. He was obviously unfamiliar with the road, for he drove cautiously, slowing at every turn. Halfway to the village, he swerved onto a path skirting a large wheat field burned by the Germans and headed into the foothills. In his excitement Walker pedaled hard to keep up. Twice he was nearly thrown from his bicycle by big stones impossible to see by the light of the quarter moon. The jeep vanished occasionally in the swirl of its own dust, then reappeared, small and fleeting against the darkness. Walker got off the bicycle and trotted with it across country, enveloped now in a nameless premonition he found both absurd and dreadful, ludicrous and appalling. *It's not a woman up here this far from everything. It can't be,* he told himself. Pretty soon he noticed something bulky and ominous in Todd's headlights. Leaning the bicycle against a tree, he scuttled up the path and silently crept in closer. Todd was parked behind a Dodge staff car belonging to the U.S. Army. Brigadier General Barker and his executive officer got out wearing khaki trenchcoats.

The younger man stood off to one side as Todd came up. His back was to a meadow lush with wildflowers. Here Walker lay down, motionless as a corpse.

"What are you bringing me here, Lieutenant?" Barker said brusquely, snatching the portfolio.

"Copies of mission reports and the evaluations of personnel you asked for, General."

Barker walked into the jeep headlights, flipping through some papers in a folder.

"This doesn't really look very good," he said sharply. "It looks like a lot of shit."

Todd sighed loudly and kicked at the pebbles under his shoe.

"I don't think this is the way to get on in the Army, Lieutenant," Barker continued in a loud bullying voice. "I want personal stuff, Todd. Who drinks. Who takes pills. Who fucks the white women in town. See what I mean, son?"

"I'll try," Todd said without much conviction. "But I'm in a hole with some people in town. I've got to have some more money tonight."

"What kind of dummy are you, playin' cards with Arabs?" Barker asked.

"Give him something," he snapped to the executive officer, who produced an envelope from his pocket.

"Lot of important people in Washington put their money into that envelope for you, boy," Barker warned him. "They want something back. I want you to come to me with something I can use to send these niggers back to Alabama where they belong. Don't you let me down, Todd."

"Yes, sir."

"As long as you understand. Now get your ass on back before they miss that jeep."

Todd stuck the envelope in his tunic and saluted the brigadier. Walker watched him move away.

"Trouble with Todd, sir?" the young captain asked as Barker came up to the car.

"Just once I want to see a nigger who earns his keep," Barker answered.

Todd's headlights turned around down on the lower path and struck for Medjez-el-Bab, much faster now. The captain got in on the driver's side and Barker's car pulled off in a trail of dust which settled on Walker as he lay smothered in the beautiful flowers. He remained there for a long while, finally turning on his back to study the stars overhead.

That's why I didn't get that first kill, he thought. *I wasn't supposed to get that much credit. Well, Horace, you've seen it all now. For the hundredth time. Seen how they use us and twist us. We don't really have a chance no matter what it is we try to get into. All we are here is a bunch of boys who want to fly and help the country win. But no, they won't let us do it. Afraid we might get a little glory, and that would be too much glory for us. Goddamn it to hell! Something led me up here tonight, made me come up here, and I don't know what it is. I wish I'd stayed in bed and never seen this shit. But it's too late. I did see it. I saw the light and there has never been a man who could run away from the light of truth without knowin' what he had to do. It don't work like that. I know now what I gotta do. It's all clear to me, just as clear as them stars. I can't run from the light once I've seen it. No, can't do it.*

Toward the end of the week Carlson Jennings wandered into the base club one evening and found Skinner sitting at a table. Skinner motioned to him in that friendly, restrained manner he had and Jennings walked over.

"Have a hamburger with me, Carl," Skinner said.

Jennings sat down. Together they surveyed the club, which had taken three weeks of part-time labor by the whole outfit to build. It was a small and intimate place styled to resemble a lounge club back home, with deeply

curved and padded banquettes, indirect lighting, red ta-
blecloths, a bandstand for musicians, and a long bar
stocked with good liquor bought out of the squadron fund.
Drinks were cheap, and the juke box, crammed with El-
lington, Coleman Hawkins, and Billie Holiday, did not
require coins. Both officers and enlisted men ate and
drank here.

"Wish we had some women around this place," Jennings
said as Skinner returned with their hamburgers and beer.
"Bluey was talking about bringing in some Arab women
from Bizerte, but nothing came of it."

"Don't worry about women," Skinner said with a smile.
"They'll turn up. They always do."

"People say the women in Mcdjcz-cl-Bab are curious
about us," Jennings went on. "I sure wish they'd show it."

"You've got to help them along," Skinner advised him.
"Let them know where to meet you in the valley after
dark. You'll get what you want."

"Hope so," Jennings answered, biting into his hamburger. "Hope I don't get robbed out there in the dark."

Skinner laughed. Neither man spoke again until they
had finished eating.

"Have you heard anything about Ollie St. Clair?" Jennings asked.

"We aren't going to hear anything more about Ollie,"
Skinner said quietly. "They've sent his belongings stateside. You must have been told."

"Maybe I was," Jennings said. "But Ollie was here
not long ago helping us build this goddamn place, and
now everybody chokes on his name. What are we here
for, to forget each other?"

"That may be part of it," Skinner answered softly, and
put a sympathetic hand on his shoulder.

Skinner had never forgotten that final briefing at Tuskegee before they went north. A highly placed Intelligence
Officer from Washington spoke. He told them not to be
captured under any circumstances because the Nazis considered black people members of a degenerate race. A
captured pilot would be very lucky if he was shot. Most
likely, he would be taken to a special hospital outside
Berlin where advanced racial experiments were performed.
("President Roosevelt is aware of this possibility. He is
deeply alarmed.") At this hospital, surgeons transplanted,

implanted, and grafted vital organs. Inmates found themselves exposed to dangerous rays and virulent diseases. The officer went on to explain that the provisions of the Geneva Convention were never meant to apply to black men. On finishing, he asked the pilots to vote on whether they would go into combat with L tablets to kill themselves before they could be captured. Walker shouted him down in a voice quavering with rage and shock. The officer was told to get the hell out of the room and never come back.

"Why on earth are we flying, Percy?" Jennings asked after a while. "I wake up at night sometimes and wonder what brought me here. I feel like I've lost my way."

Skinner shrugged and sipped his beer. "The psychologist back in the States said he found a large element of suicide in the boys. He said none of us could stand ourselves and we were looking for a situation which doomed us."

"Fascists will always say that about people they want to see dead," Jennings retorted.

A relaxed, wistful smile came to Skinner's delicate face. "In Spain there was a lot of talk about the death wish. All of it came from the other side, though. The peasants wanted to live more than anyone. They wanted to live so badly it tore at your heart some days just to watch them."

"Are we like them?" Jennings asked.

"What do you think?" Skinner said.

The club began to fill up as ground crewmen and clerks and fliers came in from the dice and poker games which had just broken up. Skinner disregarded the increasing hubbub and laughter to concentrate on the music coming through a speaker near their table. He loved jazz and kept a large record collection in his room, where he could lose himself in its dreamy intimacies. He heard the second of the shots outside, then the third and fourth, followed by a few more, all evenly spaced as if the men shooting had faced off and were firing deliberately. Finally the last shot snapped into the night air, flat and ominous. Someone screamed. Somebody was cursing. As he and Jennings slipped through the side door, Skinner heard a gun click empty. Terrible screams rent the night. Men ran outside. A figure in uniform was on the ground, wriggling in awful pain. It was Todd. He was sprawled grotesquely in the grass, clutching his smoking .45 in one hand. His lower shirt was heavy with blood. He shivered, pulling at the wound in his stomach. Other people appeared.

"Must have been about cards or something," an indifferent voice said. Jennings was appalled.

"Who did this to you?" Skinner asked the tortured figure. "We have to know."

Todd stared dumbly at him, still holding the pistol. His eyes were weak and nearly crossed.

"He was drunk," Todd whispered fiercely before passing out.

Late the next afternoon Fremont slowly paced back and forth in his caravan, alternately sitting for long, anxious moments on his bed. Todd had been on the operating table last night for three full hours. They had had to dig deep for the bullets. He had lost buckets of blood. He was still in trouble, lying heavily sedated under an oxygen tent. Osborn had been assigned to conduct an immediate investigation and get the facts within twenty-four hours. Ten minutes before, his phone call had come. He was on his way over, and it seemed a little too soon.

"Sir?"

It was Osborn, calling him through the open door. He came in and sat down. He put his cap on his knee and removed a small black notebook from his breast pocket.

"What have you got?" Fremont asked.

"Nothing," Osborn replied, going through the pages of small script in front of him. "Statements of people who were with Walker last night when the shooting happened. Enough alibis to wallpaper every john on this base."

Both men looked at each other. Fremont nodded his head. He had been afraid of this.

"Todd spoke Walker's name under the anesthesia," he said to Osborn. "He pleaded with Walker not to shoot him again."

Osborn remained silent.

"Ops, what is your opinion of Horace Walker?"

"Damn good pilot."

Fremont stirred impatiently in his chair. He pulled a manila folder out. "Todd beat Walker out of an FW

kill and Walker came at him with a knife for it. How
do you interpret this?"

"Colonel, may I say respectfully that I don't deal in
interpretations. What we have here is a mass of circum-
stantial evidence, and nothing more. The Army hates this
kind of case, sir. They'll call it nigger violence and throw
it back in our faces."

Silence took over the room. They got up and moved
to the door. Fremont clapped Osborn lightly on the shoulder and they parted.

Fremont remained in the infirmary until long after midnight. It was quiet. The only sound was the humming of
the auxiliary generator. The infirmary was actually a small
hospital thoroughly set up so that wounded officers would
not have to be transferred to regional hospitals where
their appearance in the wards alongside white officers
might cause a social and morale problem. Fremont distinguished Beasley's heavy footsteps slowly coming down
the hall. The big man in surgical green filled the doorway.
Smudges of blood covered the front of his gown.

"Todd's out of danger," he said, taking off the gown
wearily, "although he'll need at least a couple of more
transfusions."

"Any possibility of a relapse?"

"There is always the possibility of a relapse when a
man is shot three times in the stomach with .45 caliber
bullets," Beasley answered. "Fix me a drink, Jonathan."

Fremont poured out some scotch.

"Without these facilities Todd would have died," Beasley said. "He was on his way when they brought him in
here."

"This is a terrible thing, Jonathan. If Todd had died,
we'd have an investigating committee in here, followed by
criminal proceedings. We'd be disgraced."

"I'm aware of that, Dick."

"Then what the hell are you going to do, Colonel?"

"What do you want me to do?"

"Get rid of Walker. Ship him out of here. He made
a mess of another man last night. Todd's going to have
problems for the rest of his life."

"Dick, it would look mighty strange for one of us to

suddenly show up in the States without explanation. Walker would be showered with questions."

"What questions?"

Beasley pulled at his drink. He was beginning to discern something much bigger in all of this, and it worried him.

"Jonathan, was that a way of telling me Walker had his reasons, maybe good reasons?"

Fremont said nothing. He stared rather vacantly at his old friend. He was thinking about that first warning from Party Line. He had been thinking about it all day.

"Are you in trouble?" Beasley asked.

"We're all in trouble."

"What can I do?"

"Keep Todd alive. I can't tell you any more now."

SIX

WELL BEFORE THE TRUCK rolled into the dispersal area the ground crewmen had removed all chocks from the airplanes' wheels and laid out a rough network of boards to help them taxi over the soggy ground. For the third day in a row it had rained, and a steaming mist came off the grass into the slightly humid air. The mission was definitely on. Every mechanic stood by his Mustang, shivering in coveralls that were soaked through and clammy with cold. Fremont addressed the pilots clustered around him.

"We'll form up very low today, at nine hundred feet, and go into tight formation before we hit that undercast. Trim your airplanes at a climbing speed of one hundred seventy miles per hour. Do not exceed a thirty-degree angle of bank if we have to turn. While we are in the undercast, every man must keep station perfectly. The pilot who leaves his station will probably be killed and bring down other men with him, so exercise extreme caution. Takeoff is at 0700. Observe ten-second intervals. Good luck."

The men trotted through the chilly dampness to their planes. This morning's mission would be arduous and taxing. They were going to the island of Sardinia, a full two hundred miles west of Sicily. Sardinia was a forbidding place, nearly as large as Sicily itself, but far more isolated, primitive, and exotic. Banditry and revenge murders were commonplace. And Osborn said Luftwaffe pilots had been killed merely for their boots and medals. No one wanted to crash-land there.

In the last week or so, Sardinia had been watched scrupulously, hour by hour, as if it were a dormant volcano whose crust was beginning to heave. Supposedly the only planes there belonged to a depleted reserve *Staffel* badly in need of spare parts and gasoline. But recently, brand-new machines had appeared out of the hazy skies to intercept and destroy larger and larger numbers of British bombers, Mitchells and Marauders, making day raids on Sicily. Desperate battles lasting for a hundred miles were erupting even when the bombers flew at very low altitudes. The intruders had to be coming from Sardinia. So far, unarmed photographic recon planes had been unable to locate their bases. Now the job was given to Fremont, and it was to be done promptly.

Fremont's Mustang streaked down the runway, sending up a fine spray, and took off right on time. As the rest of the squadron assembled, Fremont was worried. None of the planes had been run up carefully or checked as thoroughly as he liked. They had a lot of ground to cover today, and the time had simply not been there. The four flights packed in closely. They swooped up into the undercast and climbed. Visibility did not exist, just instruments and nerves, composure and silence. Fremont could not see Butters at all. He only knew that if Butters moved abruptly, if Butters grew careless and banked beyond the thirty-degree mark on his turn-bank indicator, a collision would be inevitable. But no one used the radio; no one lost that surge of fine concentration needed to get them through.

At 6,700 feet they broke out into the midst of a gorgeous day. The squadron held in near-perfect formation and headed due north. They could expect to be intercepted within half an hour. The Luftwaffe Aircraft Report Center at Trapani was probably plotting their course at this very moment. Big breaks in the clouds opened. Below, the sea appeared greenish and wind-driven. Everyone was vigilant. They were on a new course, a totally unknown course. Fremont wondered if his squadron hadn't been pulled from western Sicily because it was getting too many opportunities for kills and promotions and glory. That was the kind of reward he expected from the Army after fourteen tough missions. Since Todd had been hurt, a pattern of subtle harassment had set in: unreturned calls and messages, delays in getting operational assignments and spare parts. But he couldn't think about those things now, up here. He checked the sky carefully and scanned his instrument panel. The ship was in perfect trim.

They rose through the thin, patchy cirrocumulus to 22,000 feet and flew at 350 miles per hour. A mood of eerie quietude had taken hold. The sun shone with a strange diffused quality, neither strong nor weak. The headset crackled loudly. Jennings came on, his boyish voice straining to sound calm and controlled.

"Six strange-looking enemy aircraft below us," he said. "Directly below. Estimate their altitude at nineteen thousand feet."

Fremont broke in at once.

"We can't see them, Two-four. They're bunched underneath us. Describe and give bearing."

"Bearing our course," Jennings said excitedly.

His Mustang dropped 500 feet, but he didn't notice. He peered down at the German planes with uncertainty. The planes appeared very fast and were driven by two wing-mounted engines whose long cowlings bulged grotesquely forward, well beyond the nose of the craft. Atop the slender fuselage sat a peculiar-looking greenhouse which slanted ahead and straight down at an angle. The two-man crew in the greenhouse searched the sea below. Jennings relayed this information to Fremont, who asked if there were any other distinguishing features.

"Yes, sir, there are two machine guns mounted in barbettes on each side of the fuselage aft of the canopy. Probably remote-controlled. That is the only visible armament. White spirals on spinners. Camouflage is new. Very dark brown underneath and on sides, lighter earth color on top. Sardinian camouflage, sir."

"Well done, Two-four."

Just then, the tight formation of six planes materialized below the leading edge of Fremont's starboard wing. He saw their white crosses clearly. They possessed the bulk of small bombers, but moved with deadly assurance and speed.

"Attention, Jupiter squadron," Fremont said. "Have

spotted pack of six Messerschmitt 410 bomber-destroyers. Full armament unknown. Will duplicate their course."

The Germans continued their watch over the sea, staring down through tremendous rifts in the clouds, patiently scrutinizing the grayish-green water for something their radar section told them was down there, moving blindly toward them. Fremont speculated on what would happen if they glanced up and saw fifteen Mustangs prepared to dive.

"Turn onto course three-zero-zero," he said very quietly into his microphone.

The squadron dodged from cloud to cloud, flying skillfully enough to keep its massed shadow off the long airy canopies of the Messerschmitts. The men gestured actively and kept in touch with hand signals.

"Steer to two-nine-zero."

Slowly the bomber-destroyers began to lose altitude. They had a certain primitive, brutal grace despite their nose-heavy design. The pilots' oxygen masks dropped away from their faces and they strained to examine the empty sea more closely. The Mustangs kept their distance, flickering through the clouds in a slight bank to port, sights on, gun switches on.

"I see a flock of B-17s down there. Way down, flying below five hundred feet!" Jennings yelled into the headset.

The whole squadron made them out now, detailed and tiny as model airplanes, as they raced along in tight formation thousands of feet below, barely visible despite their tan-and-green North African camouflage. Fremont waited to see how the Messerschmitts would deploy. Ops had mentioned that the Luftwaffe considered dropping bombs directly on the Fortresses or suspending bombs from planes above for them to crash into. Cautiously he led the squadron closer. The low-level stratocumulus was thicker than he had anticipated. The Messerschmitts disappeared for moments at a time. Then the bombers vanished.

Down the Mustangs glided. Fremont knew something was wrong. He sensed an important maneuver of some kind had already taken place. When they broke out of the clouds and haze at 3,000 feet, only four Messerschmitts were around. Suddenly the bombers came into sight again, flying wingtip to wingtip, terribly low, almost at wave-top level. The Germans swept in, four abreast, and went at them head-on. The Fortresses moved at top speed, closing the distance rapidly. Abruptly it happened. The second and third Messerschmitts, the middle men, fired tremendous cannons concealed in their forward bomb bays. The planes lurched sideways under the powerful recoil. Two of the bombers out front were simply blown to pieces, instantly reduced to clouds of fiery orange light on the water. Then all four Messerschmitts opened fire simultaneously. Cannon flashes lit up the sea as if a naval engagement were taking place. Fortresses dropped into the water, dying like quail. From behind the formation, brilliant streaks of white light ripped into the big planes. The other Messerschmitts attacked at the rear with 21 centimeter rockets. Bombers veered away, burning brightly as men dove from them, swimming for their lives. Fremont attacked.

He gave no command; he simply attacked, throwing himself at the 410s in front. He bore in close, heedless of the fuselage guns nipping at him. The planes were bigger than he expected. His cannon tore at one, shredding the armored glass canopy, killing both crewmen in seconds. He pulled up hard, gritting his teeth against the G forces, fearful of catching an air scoop full of water.

Mustangs buzzed everywhere after the fleeing Germans. Skinner stormed in head-on, where his adversary resembled a praying mantis, with its strange canopy bulging on each side like a pair of eyes. He was almost obliterated by an enormous 50 millimeter cannon shell that whistled violently as it sailed overhead. All of his machine-gun and cannon fire slammed into the heavy plane. Nothing seemed to happen, but as he streaked over the German, smoke began to stream from one of the big cowlings. He whipped around tightly, aware now that no one else was going for the plane. It was his. Again he cut loose with everything. And the Messerschmitt began to climb. He overshot it, surprised and angry with himself. The black swastika painted on the tail zoomed upwards. Skinner went to full throttle, burning up his precious reserve of combat fuel. For a cumbersome plane the 410 climbed exceptionally well, and he had trouble gaining altitude for another pass. But nothing could outclimb a Mustang. When the bomber-destroyer finally leveled off at 12,000 feet, Skinner dipped into a shallow dive and concentrated his fire on the pilot and copilot, who never saw him. They flung their arms about in agony before slumping dead. At last the Messerschmitt spiraled away, yet it was not burning or really crippled. Skinner watched it head for the sea like a drone and he realized this airplane frightened him. It frightened all of them.

Orange-and-yellow dinghies crowded with men dotted the sea around huge oil slicks where eight of the bombers had plunged into 700 fathoms of water. The survivors waved and cheered the Mustangs regrouping just above their heads. The four remaining bomber-destroyers had slipped away, taking cover in the haze and clouds. The Fortresses bunched together and continued on, skimming the waves as they ran for Algeria. Fremont radioed the position of the downed crews to Bizerte, although he knew the bombers had already done so. He waggled his wings in farewell to the men on the water and pulled his squadron far up into the sky, topping out at 20,000 feet, where they swung onto a course for Sardinia.

Time passed. A man cleared his throat. Hesitantly Butters spoke to Fremont. He was angry and disappointed.

"Squadron leader, damage reports not good. Fuel situation is critical. Imperative we return to base at once."

Fremont checked his gauges. Rage mingled with frustration ate at him. He could hear Butters breathing.

"All right. Roger, One-two."

They regrouped and swung onto a compass heading for Bizerte. Most of them were exhausted and had trouble monitoring their instruments. Walker had to snap at his men several times before they would hold a loose formation.

In a series of delicate and subtle shadings the sky darkened and grew ominously full. Whereas moments before, the vast deserted sea had glittered idly, now it appeared flat, gray, and sullen. Crosswinds sprang up, bucking the airplanes harshly. Many of the engines sounded unsteady and rough. Fremont did not mention the storm, although its presence was evident. Calmly he ran through a list of preparation checks.

"Mixture control to normal. Pilot-heater switch on. Check gyro instruments for correct settings. Lock those shoulder harnesses good. If you're getting too much static, turn off the radio. Maintain original heading. Under no circumstances are you to make any turns."

A hard rain slanted down viciously through rents in the clouds, pelting the canopies unrelentingly. The temperature dropped. Men shivered in their cockpits, unable to see anything, tense with concentration on their instruments. Enormous lightning flashes cascaded to the sea west of them. Airspeed indicators fell off and rose again in the face of the violent, gusty headwinds strong enough to bring on the beginning of a stall. Out front, Fremont fought determinedly to hold a fairly straight course for Africa. For the first time he was truly apprehensive. Ice gathered on the carburetors in several planes, causing an extreme roughness that could only be eliminated by clearing the engine and using fuel desperately needed to get home. Hollyfield and Archibald twirled away in huge calamitous downdrafts and came back to the formation slowly, uneasily. Somewhere ahead, the coast of Africa spread out waiting to receive them. But the rain did not slacken. Then Bluey broke in to say he had just seen an air-sea rescue launch bobbing in the water, and they were now over the continent.

Contact flying was impossible. Within the canopies heavily beaded with rain and clouded by heat condensation, no landscape existed. It was very dark. A few men had their cockpit lights on full-bright, even though this was prohibited during the day. Winds swerving off the mountains blew them east and then west of their course. Fuel was pitifully low. The menacing growl of thunder and vivid lancing shafts of lightning seemed almost predictable and tedious now. Upon entering the valley, they cut altitude to 1,500 feet. Every jeep and truck on the base lined the runway with their lights on.

Jennings looked down wryly and turned back to his instruments. His manifold pressure and RPMs continued to drop off. The engine spat and coughed badly, and he could no longer tell himself the trouble was spark-plug fouling. His engine had been wrecked by overspeeding in his dive and would fail at any moment. Fearfully he notified Walker, who replied, "Get on the base-frequency channel, boy. What the hell can I do up here?"

Jennings' tingling hands pushed clumsily on the channel-selector button. He identified himself.

"This is Ops, Jennings," Osborn said pleasantly. "What's wrong?"

"I pulled maximum Gs coming out of a dive. My engine's shutting down."

"Move the mixture control to RICH. Trim off that nose a little. Is she coming back?"

"No, sir," Jennings said quietly.

"You'll have to bring it in dead stick, Carl," Osborn said.

Jennings could hear him calling the squadron on another channel to put them into a go-round pattern. He watched his propellor blades start windmilling.

"Are you carrying any hot ammo?"

"About two hundred fifty rounds."

"Get rid of it."

He squeezed the gun switch. Short bursts of harsh orange fire spurted from the leading edges of his wings.

"I want you to make it fast and clean, Carl. The boys are flying on their own sweat."

"Roger."

"Check hydraulic pressure."

"Pressure normal."

"Okay. Get your landing gear down and flaps up."

Jennings worked the landing gear and flap handles on his right side awkwardly. Thick rivulets of water streamed off the canopy.

"Fuel shutoff lever off."

"Right."

"Can you see the runway?"

"I make out something between the trucks."

"Head for it. Into the wind. Try to keep one hundred seventy-five miles per hour at the start of your glide. That will give you maximum distance."

Jennings held the stick firm in his gloved hand. He turned off switches rapidly and closed the throttle. The airplane sank. He was both wary and alarmed because without power there is no real sensation of landing. He couldn't see ground. He maintained maximum glide, stopping the flap lever at thirty degrees, saving the last twenty degrees of flap to overcome possible mistakes in judgment. Gravity tugged at the seat of his pants. For a long time nothing happened: he just glided, nose down, one hand on the stick, one on the flap lever. Below, the

truck headlights got bigger. He listened to the wind screech
and moan through his cockpit. Blue dots running parallel
along the earth, the runway lights, opened up on each
side. He noticed shadowy figures clinging to the cabs of
the trucks in line.

"Battery disconnect switch off. You're on your own,
now," Osborn said as the radio went out.

Jennings stared at an imaginary line between the blue
lights and applied back pressure slowly and subtly. He
was moving very fast. The Mustang hurtled by the first
of the trucks, wheels groping for the slick runway. The
plane settled gently, but streaked on and on. Jennings
strained and cursed in his harness, jamming the brakes
hard. They took hold, let go, then squealed harshly. The
fire truck and ambulance flashed by on his right. At the
end of a long, wild, wobbly skid the plane bolted from
the asphalt and slammed to a stop, heaving up and down
on the shock absorbers in the landing gear. There were
still a few trucks in front of it. Ground crewmen appeared
from the blackness like elves, climbing anxiously onto
both wings. Someone opened the canopy. Quick hands
cut him out of his harness. He was yanked away from the
aircraft and pulled over the wet grass as the fire truck
lumbered up. Everywhere men shouted. Almost at once
Mustangs dropped out of the dark sky, one right after the
other, and roared down the runway, their tan-and-green
North African camouflage glistening brilliantly in the
headlights.

SEVEN

THE NEXT MORNING they slowly departed from the Briefing hut, heads down and collars up to keep the water from trickling down their necks. Through the humid mist they could just make out their planes tied fast in the lashing rain. Walker held his coat over his head and smoked a cigarette. He bumped into people without apologizing.

In the mess hall a big fire was going. The men had coffee and cocoa. They were still disappointed over not reaching Sardinia, but no one talked about it. They settled in at tables to read, play chess or cards, and write letters. Jennings, Donaldson, Archibald, and Walker found themselves together discussing the Messerschmitt bomber-destroyer and the awful way it simply annihilated other airplanes.

"They say American boys are pouring into Bizerte and Tunis by the shipload. They'll be going after Sicily any day now," Archibald said, changing the subject.

"Sounds like you believe anything Osborn tells you," Walker answered. "Sicily ain't it, Archie. It's a diversion, man, a mere diversion. That main thrust will probably go right through Sardinia and Corsica into southern France. Why fuck with a long campaign in Italy?"

"Well, Italy *is* one of the Axis powers," Archibald said in his prim, curt way. "Not that it matters a goddamn, because we are not going to see Europe, anyway. We were only meant to take part in this little sideshow. Nobody wants to see us get in on anything big."

"Why are you always so full of shit, Archie?" Walker asked. "And what's happened to you dudes?" he inquired of the other pilots. "In Flight School you became men. You were daredevils with your mustaches and silk scarves and pretty uniforms. Fighter pilots, man, motherfuckers all. I anointed you with nicknames. Now I find you steppin' around real careful, just like chickens in the yard tryin' to stay out of their own shit."

Faint smiles and pleasant laughter met this outburst. But Donaldson cleared his throat and interrupted. "Archie's probably right," he said uneasily.

"Who the fuck gave you a speaking part?" Walker said, with roving and amused eyes. "You must have lost your bottle somewhere, talkin' out of turn like this.

"There's no way they'll let us go to Europe, surrounded by white troops. There'll be riots," Donaldson blurted out. "Everyone knows it. Look at our record. Pushed out of those training fields in the North to avoid race riots. At Tuskegee the white boys were always saying they'd come down the road and get us, fuck us up good. Everywhere we go, somebody objects, somebody is ready and waiting to block us. It just adds up, that's all."

"We'll see Europe yet," Walker said with a conviction that took hold among the tired men. "We'll even see Paris. I *feel* we will see it."

"Wouldn't you like to see Paris, Norvel?" he asked.

"Maybe," Donaldson replied sheepishly. "Maybe someday, Walker."

Walker took out a Camel and lit it. The room had lapsed into near silence. Outside the clouded windows, rain sluiced down off the roof. Walker peered over Jennings' shoulder as he wrote a letter.

"That's a whole lot of words you got there," he said respectfully. "Who you writin' to, Sonny Boy, your momma? Or is it some little pair of tits who thinks she's as good as your momma?"

"It's my mother," Jennings said.

"That's good. I like to see a boy who respects his mother. God knows I wish I could write to my poor ma."

"Is she back home?"

"No, man. She's gone. She took the ferry to the other side in thirty-six, that summer. I sure miss her."

"You were out of college then, weren't you?" Jennings asked.

"Yeah, I was out. I had a degree to teach. I was even certified, but there was no jobs. They even closed the grade school in my hometown."

"Did you ever come to New York? A lot of people went into teaching there. My mother taught first grade."

"I tried to get to New York, boy," Walker said. "I really did want to see that big old city, but I never made it. Chicago curtailed me. So did Detroit and Cleveland. You got to remember this was the Depression."

Jennings nodded. He had never seen Walker as open or talkative.

"In the Depression I did nothin'. I niggered around from one end of the country to the other. I was a real nigger, believe me. I was always at somebody's back door, beggin' for scraps of food. I would steal chickens at any opportunity, snatch people's clothes right off the line, take the baby's milk from your front porch. I tried to end my life once by jumpin' in a river with rocks in my pockets, but some hoboes saw me and pulled me out. Why, my own family wouldn't have anything to do with me. They said I'd gone crazy. And I had."

"But you recovered," Jennings said. "You're here."

"I ain't recovered," Walker replied in a voice full of sadness. "I just outlasted my destiny. Like every goddamn fool, I hopped the freight train for California. Carried suitcases and pails of water for people in those trailer camps and auto courts. Not our people, of course. One night I was real hungry, so I let a bunch of white boys talk me into goin' to a diner with them to eat. I couldn't get served. Some of the men inside dragged me out and tried to blackjack me to death. They beat me until they was tired and they left me for dead. Didn't see right for a month. Where there was one hobo, I'd see two. Once after I was fired out of a dishwashing job in Oklahoma City, I read about this group in a newspaper my sandwich was wrapped in. ('Here's your severance pay, you crazy black bastard,' they said to me.) It sounded like a good idea, flyin'. You had money comin', food comin'. I found a freight train and came on down."

"Are you glad you did?"

"In a way, Sonny, but don't crowd me. This group has

a long fuckin' way to go," Walker replied. "This Hun
we're fightin' is a natural warrior. He's an advanced man,
a technical man tough to equal. And our people have got
to make their mark in this war. We got to, or we won't
get nothin' when it's over. Nothin'!"

It was after midnight. Todd was the only patient in the
infirmary. He gently opened the drawer of his nightstand
and removed his toilet case. He pulled out a thick roll
and began counting. Nothing had been disturbed. He
still had 40 fifty-dollar bills, 300 English pounds, and as-
sorted French and Swiss franc notes. He was still all
right. But without a gun he felt helpless. Not that anyone
knew he had this much money.

He sighed and picked up a magazine. He remained weak
and a vague aching sensation twanged beneath the bright
pink surgical scar on his belly. He had no idea when he
might be released. Every time he mentioned it, Beasley
was evasive.

Most of his life things had been quite different. In Fort
Wayne, Indiana, where his father was a moderately successful realtor in the black district, he was branded early
as a show-off because he liked to excel. Soon his quickness
of mind and precociousness soured into hostility and an
obnoxious swagger. It was the only way he could protect
himself against other people's standards, and he grew to
like it too much. At seventeen he got a white girl pregnant. After the abortion he was rushed away to Fisk
University in Nashville ("Become something," his father
warned. "Become a man or don't come back"), where he
arrived driving a white Buick convertible.

In spite of good grades he was seldom around school.
Many of his best friends were older people, poker players
and numbers people off campus, people who appreciated
his style. He loved money and gambling and carried a gun
even then. As the war drew closer, he took Civilian Pilot
Training courses, never believing he would actually fly.
Instinct and cunning told him to try for Army Intelligence
so that when Germany lost the war he could get in on
the spoils. For six months after graduation he trained in
Washington, the only black face in any classroom he entered. When Fremont began forming his squadron, the
Army transferred him to Tuskegee to be its Intelligence

Officer. It wasn't long before Barker, then a full colonel at the new Pentagon Building, contacted him with an interesting offer. He was asked to make off-the-record intelligence assessments of the squadron's combat performance. The pay would come out of general research funds and it would be very good. He accepted, knowing somehow this was why they had let him into intelligence work in the first place.

Now he was in real trouble. He was sick, friendless, and isolated. Outside, life rambled on. The Mediterranean war was unfolding toward its climax. Engines were tested day and night, heavily loaded trucks moved past, men called to each other, but it was all terribly remote from him. He wished he had not been as cool and forbidding. He wished he'd made at least one friend, someone who might come in and play cards and talk a few hours. But there was no one. Caution had urged him to exist on his wits; comrades asked questions, especially in the Army, and his life could not bear the weight of too many questions.

To his surprise, Captain Love, Barker's executive officer, had been on the base at least once that he knew of and hadn't tried to contact him. He wondered what Barker was thinking. Barker was ruthless and very careful and probably had given him away. Todd was anxious all the time, now, and was beginning to depend on sleeping pills to get any rest. He had considered writing to his father for advice, but had no idea how to begin the letter, how to describe what had happened, because it was all so casual and subtle. *Go to Fremont,* something told him. *Lay it all out in front of Fremont,* right now.

He let the magazine slip out of his hands and off the bed. The light switch clicked softly. Despite the total darkness it was difficult to sleep. At 3:00 A.M. the corpsman would give him a mild pain-killing shot that would help him to relax, so he dozed fitfully.

Out of nowhere came a sharp, metallic sound. The big flame of a cigarette lighter roared up and burned dangerously close to his nose.

"Motherfucker," a deep rasping voice said. It was Walker. The barrel of his .45 entered the circle of light, and Todd gasped. He trembled as the gun came right up to his temple and rested there coldly and heavily.

"As soon as you can travel," Walker whispered hoarsely, "make it your business to do so. If not, I'm going to kill you. I'm not going to expose you or tell what I know. I'm just goin' to kill you outright like the low-down nigger you are. Keep that in mind."

The lighter went out. Todd felt the pistol withdraw from his head. He wanted to cry, but he fainted.

Nearly a week passed before the rain ended, giving way to the gentle heat of early summer. Slowly the valley dried out. The men spent more time out of doors now, playing basketball or volleyball or just sunning themselves in armchairs appropriated from all over the base. Fremont had fresh flowers brought to his caravan every morning.

It was midday, but Skinner remained in his room. He understood German and was listening as a voice wafted out of his table radio and described the fall of Pantelleria in heroic terms of sacrifice and valor. Skinner grimaced and lit a cigarette. Pantelleria, pounded into an unrecognizable wasteland of rubble and shattered dwellings after two weeks of bombardment, had surrendered without a shot being fired as an invading force of British troops came ashore in their landing craft.

Lately he'd been pondering the invasion of Sicily, which everyone knew was coming soon, perhaps in a few days, certainly within weeks. Osborn had already announced an important briefing on Sicily for tomorrow, and this aroused a subtle fear in Skinner. Although he concealed it smoothly, Skinner was horribly disappointed in his performance as a fighter pilot, shocked that enemy planes did not fall out of the sky when he pressed his gun switch. He felt tense and outside of things. It was true that he owned one kill, only three less than Walker, but that kill had come against the Messerschmitt bomber-destroyer which he hadn't smashed or even flamed. A familiar sense of futility swept over him.

He was twenty-eight now, and since he'd left Oklahoma ten years before, much of his life had turned down unexpected pathways. He had first come east in 1933 to Howard University in Washington, where his aim was to become a doctor like his father. In high school he was an all-state halfback and one of the best prospects in the

Southwest, but no school in the area dared offer him a scholarship. Scouts from the Big Ten and California came to see him play every game of his senior year. His father urged him to apply to Harvard and Yale. Yet deliberately he chose Howard, a black school, in order to assert his independence and hide a certain inchoate bitterness welling up in him. He did quite well at Howard, never failing to make the Dean's List. The professors said his amiable and gentle assurance was money in the bank for a doctor.

He joined the track team, practicing daily until he excelled in the sprints and shorter relays. In time he began winning at meets and heard his name mentioned as a possible world-class runner. By the middle of his junior year Skinner married, mostly out of loneliness and confusion. His bride was the beautiful and energetic daughter of a professor he liked. Two months later she was pregnant. He felt trapped and escaped from their small dreary apartment to run during the evenings. When a coach offered to send him to the Olympic trials in Chicago, he accepted immediately. Only once after that did he see his wife and daughter again.

At Chicago he was brilliant enough to make the team. People began to whisper that he had a chance to beat Owens and Metcalfe in the Games set for Berlin during the first two weeks in August. He reveled in the gay life aboard ship, practicing starts on the deck with Owens and then going to parties that lasted half the night. He was more free and adventurous than ever before in his life. In the last days before sailing, invitations had come from groups hoping to establish rival games to what was certain to be a Nazi spectacle. He was asked to take part in the Workers' Olympics in Antwerp, The Peoples' Olympics in Barcelona, and The World Labor Athletic Carnival on Randall's Island in New York City. But Skinner never truly considered any of them. He was young and desperately wanted a real Olympic medal, preferably a gold one. The team disembarked at Bremerhaven and moved by train to Berlin, marching four abreast into the beautifully landscaped Olympic Village. Skinner still had the suit he wore that day, folded neatly at the bottom of his footlocker.

He was placed in a double room with one of the high jumpers who later won a bronze medal with the best effort of his life. Most of his time during those first days was spent at the stadium. In the grayness of rainy weather that would last throughout the Games, the immense sloping oval of the stadium seemed to close about him. He felt like a gladiator existing under the menace of terrible retribution. On opening day, an Aryan youth appeared and put his torch to the brazier framed by blackening clouds. *"Deutschland über Alles"* was sung fervently, with a mass ecstasy that bewitched him. Huge banners swayed to and fro among the crowd. The Olympic bell was rung. Outside the stadium, *Hitler Jugend* holding torches lit a path to the outskirts of the village. The profound righteousness in all of it intimidated Skinner.

The next morning he was eliminated. It happened quickly, without any real anguish, as seventy thousand people, avid and intense, sat holding their umbrellas in a light rain. When his heat in the 100 meters was called, he went to the starting blocks. A fraction over ten seconds later he finished fifth and jogged halfway around the track in quiet disappointment. That afternoon Jesse Owens won the second of his heats in the 100 and his first in the 200. Abruptly the Games focused on him. For the rest of that week Skinner lounged on the infield in his sweat clothes and watched Owens become immortal, race by race. His clean, surging power never slackened. He possessed a mythic grace, a titanic vision of himself, that drove the Germans wild. He became their champion because he ran for immortality, that, and nothing else. Each of his pure swift questing challenges for a gold medal brought people to their feet in a rising of infernal and unstoppable rapture. "O-wens. O-wens. O-wens," they chanted insanely. Skinner nearly expected to hear the *"Horst Wessel Lied"* after Owens' fourth and last gold medal. He was terribly proud of Jesse, especially after his victories forced Hitler to flee from his box to avoid the traditional handshake ceremony.

Then, in all the tumult and singing, all the rhythmic chanting and the national anthems, he came together with Helene. She was German and a member of the women's track team, blonde, fresh, vigorously ravishing. They fell in love almost immediately. She was enthralled by his dreamy embittered outlook and compelling handsomeness, all this contained under a silken mahogany skin. He adored her beauty, her strength, and her fierce intelligence more

than anything he could remember. It made no difference
that she was already engaged. ("I am a terrible athlete,"
she said in her lovely amused way. "I pushed myself very
hard to get on this team because my fiancé is an SS man
and National Socialism will not allow us to mate unless I
win a Reich Sports Medal. Of course, now I shall have
to forego that medal.") When his roommate was told
about Helene, he moved out in half an hour. A couple of
the sprinters begged him to stop seeing the girl. Skinner
listened to their reasonable arguments, their reasonable
fears ("You'll be found dead, Percy, and none of us will
ever know what happened"), and then went his own way.
Ever since childhood he had feared white people would
spoil his life and vanquish him, perhaps without truly
meaning to. Now that fear was subsidiary. He no longer
cared.

They enjoyed Berlin immensely during the Games. Its
polish and wicked sophistication made Washington look
like the cow town it was. The nightclubs and cabarets,
where they often saw middle-aged Olympic officials with
two or three stunning young girls each, put on acts Skinner found astonishingly erotic and cynical. Invariably the
most striking women in the room took note of his penetrating good looks. ("You see, darling," Helene whispered
happily, "they are staring at you. They want what I have,
but I don't want what they have and it incenses them.")
And he was inwardly pleased. Still, beyond the revelry
there was a grimness about Berlin. Soldiers, mainly young
officers, were everywhere. An inordinate number of people seemed to be part of paramilitary organizations. Too
many people had caps, badges, crosses, varicolored uniforms, insignia, and armbands. They all had a place, a
position in the national destiny that was too energetic and
serious to remain dormant for long. Skinner did not want
to fight Germans.

After a display of mass gymnastics by German sporting
clubs, the Games ended with dozens of powerful searchlights forming a cupola over the stadium as the Olympic
bell tolled for the last time. Things changed. During the
festivities, people had been tolerant and curious about
them. Now, they met angry, incriminating looks on the
street. Helene dropped out of the university and rented
an apartment in a working-class district where her fiancé

could not find them. Weeks passed. They went out only
at night. They grew closer and were desperately in love.
A neighbor told them a Gestapo man had inspected the
mailboxes that morning. Next day he was back, asking
questions. Helene phoned her father for money. He informed her the Reich had filed an official complaint with
the American ambassador. He pleaded with her to come
home, but obstinately she refused. ("Then you must leave
Germany," he warned. "Tonight if possible. You are en-
dangering all of us. Go to Paris and end this bohemian
affair in the proper surroundings.") Early that evening he
met them on a back street. He brought a Mercedes coupe
and 1,000 marks plus some American dollars. ("If you
drive all night, you can reach Strasbourg by morning. Don't
stop unless it's necessary. Our friend has no papers," he
said, shaking Skinner's hand coldly.) Arrogantly, they
stayed on the autobahns and crossed half of Germany before the middle of the night. An hour before dawn they
were in Mannheim, just miles from the French border.
Helene began to speed. The kilometers fell behind. Then
cars appeared, blocking the road. They cut across a field.
Shots were fired and the tires went out. They kissed hungrily and wildly in the strange silence. ("Run straight
ahead, Percy. The French border can't be very far," Helene told him. "Run. I will get to Paris in a few days by
way of Switzerland.") With tears in his eyes he loped
across the field and into the woods, stopping for a moment to watch the cars pull up alongside the Mercedes.
Helene waved defiantly. Men in long leather overcoats
stared in his direction.

In Paris he learned that Jesse Owens, exhausted by his
climb to glamour and fame, had been badly beaten by
Metcalfe at a meet in Cologne. Owens rebelled violently
when a tour of Scandinavia was planned without his con-
sent and left for home. Almost penniless, Skinner remained in Paris for three weeks. Helene never came. They
never saw each other again. He returned to Washington a
haggard, spent, and romantic figure. On campus many
laughed at him ("White girl broke Percy's heart!"). Following a long, hysterical confrontation ("You shamed me
and your child. Shamed us to death. You're crazy. Crazy!")
his wife divorced him in Mexico. His father was sympathetic, even a bit envious, he suspected, but it made no dif-

ference. He staggered through that last year of college, thinking of Helene every day, every night. On graduation day he sailed for Spain to fight with the Republicans. The thought of existing as a black man in the United States frightened him to death.

EIGHT

FREMONT SAT OUTSIDE his caravan in the warm afternoon sun and read a letter from his wife in Los Angeles. Her words were calm and controlled. Everything was fine. Mark and Tony were enjoying school. They sent their love and hopes for his safety. For a moment he wished he'd married a more flamboyant or excitable woman; but then, she would probably be in the process of divorcing him right now. Marva would be there waiting if he ever got back to America, for that was her way. She was well-educated and dependable, yet he didn't know if he really loved her. More than anything, she was the kind of woman he felt he ought to be married to—a dull, superior woman who would produce intelligent children. Suddenly Fremont was overwhelmingly glad the war separated them.

He thought about Jan, the blond Dutch schoolteacher in the village. She was a beautiful woman, but he had known many beautiful women since he had started spending a lot of time away from home. There had been a nurse in Washington at Freedmen's Hospital and an English professor at Tuskegee. Fremont knew there would always be other women, and somehow he blamed Marva for it.

He was anxious to fight again, but he anticipated no operational assignments for the time being. Osborn had told him all squadrons still on the North African mainland were being held back. Where would the invasion hit, Fremont wondered.

After the evening meal he shaved, put on a class A uniform and brushed his hair with the silver-backed brush his father had given him when he graduated from the Point. He got into his jeep and removed a slip of teletype paper from his breast pocket. The man who called himself Party Line had urgently asked to meet him at a house in Medjez-el-Bab, and intuition told Fremont to be wary. He considered not going at all, but an angry curiosity impelled him to meet this person, probably an obscure communications clerk, who had assumed such great interest in his squadron. The jeep moved slowly over the field. Osborn's heavy-legged stride came through the dusk.

"You look sharp, sir. Anticipating a good time?" he said pleasantly.

"I'll let you know, Ops," Fremont answered.

He drove quickly across the floor of the gigantic valley and into the village. The European quarter with its beautiful stone cottages was serene. He saw clean pink faces around the dinner table at one window. People on the street acknowledged him in their ambiguous, restrained fashion. In the Arab district things were quite different. Here narrow alleyways wiggled by on every side. Men in caftans drank small cups of black coffee outside their cafés and ignored him. Within rooms shielded by beaded curtains, whole families squatted around dim oil lamps eating. He gave the address to a small boy who trotted in front of the jeep, directing him onwards. They stopped before a massive door in a high white wall. Fremont knocked. A veiled woman led him through a series of darkened rooms and up a back staircase to a door which he opened. Captain Paul Love rose from behind a table and saluted him.

Fremont was careful not to betray the extent of his surprise. He returned the salute elegantly and scrutinized Captain Love, who appeared taller and more polished this time. The trace of ingenuousness he remembered from their only other meeting was no longer apparent. Fremont saw now that it had been a highly calculated gesture.

"Good to see you again, Colonel," Love said. "I apologize for all the melodrama, but it was time for us to meet alone. I suppose you've discovered the weak link in your outfit is Lieutenant Todd."

Fremont nodded and sat down. "What do you want, Captain?" he asked quietly.

"I'm here to apprise you, Colonel Fremont, that the

conservative elements in this Army are mustering a strong effort to have all Negro troops brought back to the United States. Your group may be returned to Tuskegee Army Base any time."

"We knew that when we came out here," Fremont snapped.

"I understand," Love said.

"Who do you speak for?" Fremont inquired.

"I can't say too much now, Colonel," Love replied carefully. "But I speak for the right people, the progressive people in the Army who are supporting what you've accomplished."

"I see," Fremont said dryly.

"There are influential people at home who are watching everything we do out here very carefully," Love went on. "They have access to the White House. In their opinion, many of the Army's present commanders are weak, inefficient, and hopelessly bigoted. These men must be weeded out now, before any invasion of Europe can be attempted. The Army has to be made strong and viable for the assault on Germany and for whatever comes after the war. This is paramount. We don't really know who our allies will be when this thing is over, so we must gather internal strength. It is not a question of racial discrimination or morality. It is really a military question. We will need men of your military caliber, Colonel Fremont."

To Fremont, it all seemed too precise and theoretical. He wanted to tell this earnest young adjutant that bigots would always exist and mediocre men always found a way to sully the plans and hopes of people greater than themselves.

"By the way," he said casually, "Lieutenant Todd was shot by someone in the squadron a couple of weeks ago. He almost died."

Captain Love's eyes appeared to waver slightly. He drew his face together in an expression of distaste.

"Who did the shooting?" he asked seriously.

"We don't know," Fremont explained. "Todd gambled. It may have been a personal grudge."

"Why didn't you make contact, Colonel?"

"I didn't know who you were, sir," he answered snidely.

Love shot a cold glance in his direction, and Fremont smiled just a bit. He was sure Captain Love feared that

Barker knew all about the Todd shooting, knew all about his friends in Washington, and had already made his countermoves. He was never more glad to be a mere fighter pilot. He got up and excused himself.

Outside, over the low roofs of the town a starry sky held sway. Fremont ruminated over what Love had said as he climbed into his jeep and headed out into the countryside. (He didn't notice General Barker's staff car parked in a narrow street near the house.) Idealists like Love rarely won, because their sincerity and quiet passion were not enough when confronted with evil. He knew something about evil.

In 1917 and again in '18 some of his father's well-meaning friends urged him to enlist in the Air Service of the Signal Corps as a pilot. He was turned down and angrily went to Washington, where he waited on a bench all day to see an Air Service official who might hear his case. At 5:00 P.M. a secretary told him the man had gone home for the day. Soon after, the war ended, leaving him silently embittered. He went into teaching and pleaded with his students to consider science and aeronautics as a career because technology was certain to be the next important breakthrough for mankind. For nearly twenty years he put forth his ideas in speeches and on the editorial pages of black newspapers. Crusading in his tweed suits, bow ties, and ranting voice, he was dismissed as a fool and a dreamer.

Yet by late 1938, as Germany grew more bellicose, his ideas gained some favor. He rallied his friends in Congress and a few curious philanthropists. In early 1939 they got an amendment attached to a defense bill directing the Secretary of War to lend equipment for aviation training to a group of black colleges. The program was called Civilian Pilot Training. The elder Fremont was overjoyed. He attended inaugural ceremonies everywhere and made rousing speeches. One spring night that year he died in his sleep.

The first CPT graduates encountered trouble immediately. Their applications for advanced flight training were filed and forgotten. They were turned away from the gates of every military field in the country. Young Major Fremont stepped forward and protested. Slowly and in secret, a compromise was reached, settling on him. A year after

his first disappointment and respectful letter to a friend
in Congress, an order came down from the Air Corps.
He was to form an all-Negro pursuit squadron at Tuskegee
Institute in Alabama. That was all. No instructions were
given. Everything was up to him.

In October of 1942 the Tuskegee base finally opened,
and 354 men arrived, many of them from CPT courses.
They sat in the hot sun along the road. Fremont met each
man at the main gate and shook hands as they moved past.
Right away, he warned them that only twenty places
existed in the squadron being formed, and he could only
take the best available pilots. A few more might be kept
as instructors or be considered for administrative jobs in
later squadrons. Those who completed training and got
their wings could not expect to live long. The odds for
combat pilots were only one in three. The program was
considered experimental. No one believed black men could
fly and that was a big part of the challenge. Anyone who
still wanted to try was welcome aboard. They were thanked
for coming and wished good luck.

Walker was the first man to solo. He alighted on the
runway beautifully and then took off again, buzzing the
field upside down. Quite soon he became a leader, bestow-
ing nicknames, listening to problems, and picking his fa-
vorites, a sort of informal squadron from among the men
still left. Somehow he nourished the irrational hope of
being named squadron leader, but no one thought he had
a chance and he was hurt. ("I'm from your side of the
tracks and y'all won't put in a good word for me," he
said accusingly.) He and Fremont almost never spoke.
Their meetings were charged with cool resentment and
wariness. Fremont's ideas, like handing out shotguns so
the cadets could learn how to lead a target and gain a
feel for deflection shooting, bored Walker to death. He
advanced swiftly on his own and was the only pilot to
master aerobatics.

After a while just fifty cadets remained in the program,
and the atmosphere at Tuskegee changed. A sort of regimental swagger came over the men. The first pipes, mustaches, silk scarves, sheepskin boots, and corduroy jackets
appeared. People strutted a bit more and were no longer
afraid to describe dogfight tactics with hand gestures. They
drank scotch in the barracks at night and feigned a calm

and elegant cynicism. All of it was overdone, but the men felt these days were very precious to them. They became as romantic as schoolboys and treated anyone who washed out of the program respectfully, almost as if he had died in combat. Every man sensed it was a triumph to get this far. They truly valued themselves, perhaps for the first time.

It wasn't long before the Army started paying more attention to them. Generals made it a point to visit them when they were in the area. Usually they departed with puzzled skepticism. ("They fly well. I'll give them that much. But they're showmen. I sure as hell wouldn't want them around when a fight started.") A trickle of important dignitaries materialized: Secretary of War Stimson, then Mrs. Roosevelt and Lord Halifax, the British Foreign Secretary, leaning against their Packard limousine and holding binoculars as the cadets practiced formations. Magazines sent their best men, and Fremont was photographed for the cover of *Collier's*, sitting in the cockpit of a Mustang, gazing into the empty blue sky. *Collier's* never used the picture.

At other bases in Alabama, Mississippi, and Florida, new squadrons moved on to the war fronts. Fremont's men grew impatient. They'd absorbed as much as they could without experiencing actual combat and began to suspect the Army might not let them go overseas. Calmly though, Fremont chose the twenty men who would travel with him, die with him. Their names were posted on a bulletin board in the mess hall. A week later, they received their wings at a graduation ceremony held in a placid meadow. Pridefully he pinned the silver wings over each man's left breast pocket as flashbulbs exploded and the guests clapped emotionally. To everyone's surprise, they entrained for New York thirty-six hours later. The scene at the railway station was a medley of jubilant shouts, wails, and hopeful smiles. Somehow, when the train had gone, the platform and tracks were littered with flower petals.

The trip from Tuskegee to Pennsylvania Station in New York lasted three days. The train pulled its way across the primal landscape of the Deep South, past fields and shacks where ragged black people came out and waved forlornly. ("They know. They know it's us.") All of that first day and most of the second, men sat gazing from the windows, perhaps realizing how deprived they had been, how easily cast aside by history into this elegiac and haunted backwater.

"I feel like Lenin crossing Germany in his sealed train," Walker muttered to himself, staring out at the sunset. "The countryside is rolling past a little fuzzy. I work at my desk over important papers. A whole people is depending on me."

Jennings smiled and continued with the newspaper he was rereading. Walker turned to him abruptly.

"I'm scared, Sonny," he said quietly. "I ain't never been nowhere before. I don't know how to act, what to say. This is hard. If I'd known it was goin' to put this kind of burden on me, I'd stayed pickin' in trash cans."

In New York there was time for just one wild night in Harlem before they assembled at Bush Terminal in Brooklyn. From inside the gate, Jennings watched Fremont say good-bye to his wife, a tall plain woman in an elegant cloth coat. They kissed sedately and she put the boys in a black Lincoln convertible and kissed him again, this time more passionately. In the terminal yard thousands of servicemen milled around looking for their loading areas and dodging the fast little narrow-gauge trolleys. Jennings showed his orders, then strolled by the dainty picket fence and MP guardhouse at the entrance to his pier. Beyond, it was dark and rather cool. A very high pitched roof soared above him. Crates mounted up on every side. Those workmen who noticed him studied the lieutenant's bars on his shoulders uncomprehendingly. Some shouted insults ("Impersonating an officer in wartime. These niggers never learn"), or tried to spit on him. He saw some of the other fliers about a hundred yards ahead, but made no attempt to overtake them. Instead he walked briskly, arrogantly, ignoring the dead weight of his heavy bag. At the gangplank, standing in an enormous shaft of sunlight, he hesitated, then left the soil of his country behind.

They sailed three hours later in a filthy, vermin-infested ship packed to the engine room with a brigade of black laborers. Immediately, a general rowdiness broke loose. By the second night, all the ship's rules were being flaunted. Men smoked on deck at night, left lighted portholes open, and made noises that carried for miles. Other captains in the convoy protested, but little could be done because the ship's officers remained secluded in their quarters and ignored what was happening. Uneasiness reigned. No one in the squadron knew exactly where they were going, although they believed it would be Liberia, or Dakar in Senegal. Sometime during the following night, their ship separated from the convoy. At sunrise they discovered themselves alone except for a single destroyer escort. The weather got warmer. Donny Beaumont and Walker began watching for German submarines. Two muggy days passed. Suddenly Gibraltar was sighted in the strong yellowish late-afternoon sun. Men rushed on deck, cheering and shouting as the rock swelled up massive and brownish in the incredibly blue water, beckoning them on to North Africa where German armies had so recently been smashed and routed.

Fremont listened to his jeep's engine running smoothly in the evening silence. He heard crickets. As he pulled up beside his caravan he marveled at the freshness and naïveté of that moment. It all seemed so very long ago.

A week later Todd was out of the infirmary, walking with the aid of an aluminum cane. Beasley said he would need for at least two months. The frenetic activity he'd been hearing from his sick bed had all but ceased now. He guessed the beginning of the Sicilian ground campaign was very near, but no one said anything to him about it. Osborn had been friendly and solicitous when it came to his health, yet seemed to avoid discussions that might be construed as official Army business. In the Operations Room they were glad to see him, glad and at the same time unquestionably distant. Todd was upset and offended. As he set off on his afternoon stroll in the ripe early summer heat, a mood of quavering bitterness took him. Fremont was cutting him out, treating him as if he were dead, the way all the other pilots did. On top of this, Barker had sent him a letter ("It's been a long time since you wrote to your pappy. He's worried. This is no way to treat the man who brought you into the world"), and he was terrified of replying. He considered a confrontation, a complete break with Barker, but that looked dangerous. Suddenly he wanted a drink, the feel of smooth playing cards in his hand, the sympathetic attention of a woman bought for the evening. He started back towards the field and found an empty jeep near the dispersal area. He'd already turned it around when a familiar figure hailed him. It was Fremont.

"Good afternoon, Lieutenant," he said amicably. "Mind if I hitch a ride with you?"

"No, sir," Todd replied, smiling tentatively. "Which way you headed?"

"Off you can take her out into the valley. I like going out there. All that serenity makes you think."

"I understand, sir."

Rapidly the base fell behind. A virginal and total silence prevailed. For thousands of yards in each direction rich grasslands spread to the far mountains, which looked menacing and impenetrable in the golden haze. The jeep squeaked a little as it ran onwards.

"How are you feeling, Todd?" Fremont asked, gazing at the inscrutable landscape.

"Pretty well, Colonel. Sometimes I'm unsteady in the mornings, but I'm coming back."

"Glad to hear it," Fremont said. "What happened was a real shock to the men. Now that you're coming around, maybe we can get some answers from you."

Todd drove a bit faster. He was sweating. He had been afraid of this, afraid Fremont would come after him this way.

"I don't remember much of that night, sir. I'd been drinking," he replied, watching his passenger from the corner of one eye.

"Who shot you, Lieutenant?" Fremont inquired casually, hands resting in his lap.

"I don't know, sir. Honestly," Todd answered in a strained voice. He was driving too fast now. The grass to either side blurred when he looked at it.

"Did he know what we both know about you?" Fremont continued, looking at Todd fiercely, bursting with an intensity so abrupt it appeared diabolical.

"What the hell are you talking about?" Todd said, glancing at him wildly.

"Did he know you were a Judas, a traitor?"

Todd's feet punched at the brakes. The jeep skidded to the right and stopped in a long violent semicircle.

"I'm no Judas!" Todd cried, his voice full of strange

pathetic dread. "Why did you call me that? Why did you have to say 'Judas'?"

Fremont stared at him dispassionately. He unbuttoned his breast pocket and took out the yellow slip of paper bearing the first message from Party Line. Todd read it twice, then once more, his mouth forming the words. When he faced Fremont, his eyes were large and glassy and tear-filled.

"You always knew," he said tremulously.

"Not always," Fremont answered quickly. "I only knew someone would let us down. I'm very sorry it's you, Todd."

"Why did you send Walker to kill me? You didn't have to do that."

"I didn't send Walker."

"You did!" Todd shrieked. "You know you did. Why lie about it now?"

Fremont made no reply. He eyed Todd with anguished contempt.

"No. Wait a minute," Todd smirked bitterly. "You wouldn't. You're too high and mighty for that, too fine a person. But they'll get you anyway, you smug son of a bitch. You want to prove you're better than they are, and they'll kill you for that, Colonel. In the end they'll rip your guts out like wild dogs," he said, handing back the piece of paper. "Because that's what they are, wild dogs."

Fremont remained calm, but inwardly he was enraged and uncertain. A strange light in Todd's eyes cast doubt upon him. Life seemed monstrous. He felt frail and taut. In some way he was depending on Captain Love, that much was clear to him. He sighed wearily, lowering his head in confused resignation. Beside him Todd wept.

NINE

It was 0530. Darkness had not yet lifted from the valley and a quarter moon still sliced the sky brilliantly. In the Briefing hut it was cold. The men watched intently as Osborn came onto the stage flanked by two Operations Room clerks, both armed and looking unduly grave in their close-cropped army haircuts. The clerks stood at ease. Someone locked the back door.

"Gentlemen," Osborn said, "the Allied invasion of Sicily began this morning at 0245. Seven divisions, British and American, preceded by two divisions of airborne troops, are going ashore along a hundred-mile front on the south-eastern quadrant of the island. We have reports that British glider troops and our own airborne men are widely scattered. So far the beachheads are holding."

"This is more like it," a voice called out.

Osborn went to his maps. He appeared tired and large circles of perspiration showed under his arms and at the center of his back. Lately he'd been unable to stop gaining weight and the top of his pants was folded over his belt. A lot of the fliers now called him Sarge, but never to his face.

"The strategic objective of this campaign," he began, "is the city of Messina here in the northeastern corner of Sicily opposite the toe of Italy. If Messina is captured early, the German and Italian forces on the island will be trapped. We will then have the alternative of striking

94

at Italy itself or attempting an invasion of France through Sardinia and Corsica."

"That's what I said," Walker cried to no one in particular. "Hit up through those islands."

"This thinking," Osborn said, "is predicated on a lightning campaign. Any prolonged resistance will change things considerably, so let's not dwell on it. Here is the general strategic situation facing us this morning. The Italian army has four infantry divisions on the island plus a variety of coastal units bringing the total to eight divisions, two hundred thousand men in all. The coastal battalions, which have prime responsibility for repelling our forces, are in reality a negligible factor. They are composed of old men who are badly commanded. Supplies are short. Their guns are antiquated, useless against modern ships and tanks. In addition, Commando Supremo, the Italian General Staff, has these battalions hopelessly strung out, sometimes twenty-five miles apart. Harassment from the Italian navy is not expected. Their fleet is immobilized at La Spezia in northern Italy for lack of fuel. The weakness of Axis naval and air forces has placed most of the burden for Sicily's defense on ground troops."

"How many Germans, sir?" a man in the back asked.

"Thirty thousand crack troops," Osborn snarled. "To the west the Fifteenth Panzer Grenadier Division has been split into three task forces. The Hermann Göring Division is operating as two combat teams oriented to the south and east. In between them are the Italians. Right now we have the advantage of being on the coast where the roads are good and we can move out. Once we turn inland, things are going to be different. We could be fighting in those mountains forever. Only around Catania here in the northeast below Messina is there a plateau of any size. We have to punch through this line of enemy forces which is contracting around the landing areas and make our way to the Catanian plain. That's what this thing is all about."

"Are German reinforcements expected?"

"I don't know, Jennings. Let's get down to the goddamn specifics. Your mission today will be to form part of an air umbrella over the First Division beachhead at Gela on the south shore. Gela is not far from your operational area. The terrain will be familiar. Now, truthfully, I don't know what the Luftwaffe will do today. They are hurting.

Four days ago B-17s got one hundred of their reserve fighters on the ground at Gerbini, so they could be out of it entirely, but you never know. A note of warning. There are beachheads to the north and east of you. We want to minimize accidents and collisions. Stay over Gela. Protect those ships. Please do not roam because concentration of strength is vital here. This is the most important thrust of the war so far. Any questions? All right, get going, and needless to say, good luck."

At the dispersal, Fremont's men huddled around him in the darkish light. He could not see their faces. The muted orange color of their Mae Wests stood out weirdly as he reminded them of the magnetic course out and back, air-sea rescue frequency, and call sign for the day, the kind of information pilots forget quickly after a long layoff. Then they sprinted to their planes in the cool morning air.

Jennings was glad to be in his cockpit again. The familiar smell of perspiration, stale cordite, and hot rubber reassured him. The squadron took off in the first fine rosy flush of dawn, exhaust stubs blazing. Moments later they were over the sea, whose bluish-green surface was streaked by swaths of pink sunlight. Nothing moved in the water or in the sky. The Mustangs held perfect formation.

Fremont eyed the quarter moon waning in the heavens, that moon by which thousands of paratroopers had plummeted from their planes onto Sicily, that moon whose meager light had hidden an armada sneaking up on her shores. His Mustang was in immaculate condition. The extra wing cannons, armor plating, and bomb-rack fittings caused not one millimeter of imbalance. She ran more smoothly than a new touring car, and Fremont was pleased. There was always a healthy exhilaration in flying, in leading your own squadron.

Pantelleria squeezed over the horizon and drifted toward them. Pantelleria was where they'd been blooded, where St. Clair was captured and then forgotten. The island appeared smaller than five by eight miles, standing as it did like a sort of crown on a pedestal of sheer and dreadful cliffs. Never again would Messerschmitts emerge from underground hangars hewn out of those cliffs.

The air was vibrantly clear. As they approached Sicily, the morning sun turned the sea orange with its soft grandeur. Ships of the enormous task forces which had put American troops ashore on four beachheads were bobbing in the westerly gale. Gela lay straight ahead in the middle of the American sector. Many miles east, the British under Montgomery were executing a five-pronged attack. Fremont made out their ships far off. Below them stretched the outer line of cruisers, troopships, destroyers, and battleships ushering the invading armies. LCMs jammed with helmeted men raced ten abreast for the shore, cresting the large swells, spilling men onto the wide, sandy beach. Behind them came the DUKWs, the amphibious trucks which just drove up on the land to be unloaded. LCTs holding five forty-ton tanks apiece rendezvoused at their release points. Men on the beach assembled and moved up tentatively as the battleships cut loose with their terrifying broadsides, heaving up the earth well ahead.

The squadron went inland, finding the countryside placid and empty as always. Soldiers and tanks were nowhere to be seen here. They turned back over the beachhead, holding at 30,000 feet. Light spotter aircraft zipped over the level plain near Gela, Piano Lupo, searching for targets the eager battleships could smash. Way below, a covey of Thunderbolts and Lightnings beat off a few stray Messerschmitts. The air was thick with radio transmissions, voices tense and droll and unmistakably American. Some of the men were disgusted and disappointed now. There was nothing for them to do but fly in wide circles at 30,000 feet and protect their altitude. It was boring work.

They swept high over the beachhead like a flock of pigeons. Initially the two ships materializing in ghostly fashion on the blue water went unnoticed. Neither the Germans nor the hapless Italian navy dared enter the Mediterranean, everyone knew that, and so the ships plowed onwards toward the LCT rendezvous points. They might have gotten much closer, but quite abruptly the following ship, a camouflaged destroyer, turned about and ran. Fremont now saw they were both German ships. The size of the invasion fleet obviously had frightened the destroyer. Her companion, a sleek light cruiser, changed course and boldly made for the troopships where men were still descending into the clustered LCMs.

Fremont pressed his microphone button. "Ajax squadron. Attack intruder ship. Attack. Attack!"

Instantly all sixteen Mustangs slanted down out of the
sky, engines screaming, and headed for the cruiser. At
10,000 feet light flak opened up, clouding the air with
black smudges. The cruiser held her course. Jennings noticed a battleship slipping from the line. They flattened
out and came in low, just above the whitecaps, peppering
the hull with cannon fire, raking the deck with bursts of
.50s. The six-inch turreted guns raised up and fired sighting shots. Fremont racked them around tightly. He came
in again, cutting through the web of tracer shells all
around, firing all three cannons at once. The Mustang
lurched hard. Sailors on the deck fell to their knees or
were flipped backward. Both turrets amidships wheeled to
face this crazed onslaught. Rapidly the ship executed a
half-turn to port, and Archibald's flight missed it entirely.

"Spread out in a line by flights," Fremont ordered.

Walker's flight jutted in front of the others. He was
surprised at the length of the boat, at the exactness of
its details. It looked like an expensive toy, low and swift
in the water. He poured a stream of cannon fire into a
porthole near the water line, then pulled up and struck at
the wheelhouse with all his guns. Glass splintered in the
sunlight; bullets tore into his airplane, pinging loudly.
I'm going to upend this motherfucker, he thought, drawing
back harshly on the stick. Somewhere behind, a fireball
erupted in the sky.

"Chenier," a flat voice said. And that was all.

At 20,000 feet they banked for another run. Smoke
drifted up from the cruiser, and she had completed a full
circle. The battleship, slightly out of range, blazed away
at her, its enormous eleven-inch guns belching fire. Smaller
ships, a handful of destroyers, made for her hungrily. Fremont took them down. The sleek whitish-gray hull grew
larger. All turrets and antiaircraft guns fired. Two hundred shells a second flicked through the air. Some of the
men yelled in exhilaration over the din. "Hold your fire
until we're on top of them!" Dead men were flung about
on the decks, yet those still moving went on without panic,
and Walker was infuriated. Before anyone else he squeezed
his gun switch. Then they all fired, cursing and yelling.

On the climb-out another plane was hit. Jennings saw
a fiery turret extended to full elevation and then watched
one of the Mustangs simply stop climbing and shudder in

the air before dropping away. The pilot's chute opened almost immediately, dazzling as a white carnation on the surface of a pond. Someone was on the radio to air-sea. They were many miles from the beachhead now, nearly isolated from everything. The fleeing cruiser, boiling with thick black smoke, snaked over the placid water for the horizon. Jennings followed its path sadly. In less than half an hour bombers from Algeria would send it hissing and steaming to the depths of the sea.

That evening most of the pilots retired to their rooms early, and by 0100 all but one or two lights had winked out. The men were very tired. They had flown an afternoon strike over the beachhead and in five hours would be briefed for takeoff at sunrise. Sitting in the warm stillness of his caravan, Fremont reflected on how silent the mess had been tonight. It was always subdued when a man was missing, and no one felt quite relaxed until Osborn came in and said Jack Hobdy, the downed pilot, was on his way back to Tunis aboard an empty troopship. Hobdy was the fourth man in Archibald's flight to be shot down, killed, or captured, and the men didn't like it. Archie was unlucky, they said. He wasn't masculine enough to be a flight leader. Something had to be seriously wrong for him to lose that many pilots.

Fremont snapped on the radio, searching through the static for an English-speaking voice. The British were still broadcasting. An announcer said most of the American paratroopers and British glidermen who'd been spread over a wide area had coalesced toward the middle of the morning. They had roved about in small bands cutting communications and ambushing reconnaissance parties. A few key pillboxes and bridges had fallen to them.

By late afternoon a major counterattack was mustered. The Hermann Göring Division, led by heavy tanks, moved against the Americans at Gela. Messerschmitts sank two ships standing offshore. Simultaneously the Livorno Division attacked the town of Licata just north of Gela. Furious defensive fire and naval guns completely decimated this division. Survivors were observed staggering around, driven delirious by the shock of concentrated shelling. Near Gela, German tanks withdrew when spotter planes laid them bare to the battleships moving in.

It all sounded fairly good. A division had been driven from the field and this was always encouraging. But it had happened in the wrong place, on the approaches to western Sicily where there was nothing to be gained. The British, racing up the east coast for Messina, would get all the glory. American strength and staying power weren't being respected. Patton's genius was being used to guard Montgomery's asshole. That was the deal.

And then, of course, there was always Todd to worry about. He'd fucked up again. An argument with the Arabs over a card game had flashed suddenly into a gunfight. Dozens of shots were exchanged. A French civilian, a middle-aged woman, took two bullets in the thigh and Twelfth Air Force Headquarters was notified. So far they'd said nothing. Todd was confined to quarters, but there was no way he could be kept on the base. Fremont decided to write to a friend in the Pentagon, asking if any black MPs were available for overseas duty. He went to bed.

The next few days were vivid, fragmented, and eternally long. The squadron seemed always to be in the air, always firing and diving and recovering. Again the Germans thrust at Gela, coming within 2,000 yards of the shoreline where their tanks raked the supply dumps before an inferno of falling shells drove them back for good. Forty tanks were smashed. Then the American 45th Division broke through and captured 125 planes at a forward airfield near Comiso. British forces snatched Syracuse and moved on. Many of the Italians, especially older men, simply gave up after the Livorno Division was ripped apart in a couple of hours. Still, Patton was gravely concerned. He ordered airborne reinforcements for the Gela beachhead. The operation disintegrated when frightened American gunners fired on their own planes. Twenty-three were lost and a lot of the paratroopers drowned. Those who jumped found themselves spread over the whole sector. Nothing stopped.

Near the end of the week Fremont returned to his caravan late in the afternoon and found Walker sitting on the steps in the long, pleasant shadows. His ragged mustache and small snub nose lent a boyish quality to that dark rotund face. His cap sat on the back of his head and a cigarette jutted from one corner of his mouth. Appaloosa was with him, pulling at his sheepskin flying boots. She was heavily pregnant and Walker spoke to her in low, scolding tones.

"Look at you. How am I goin' to carry you to Italy with all them babies in your belly, you damn fool."

He looked up casually.

"Afternoon, Colonel."

"Hello, Horace," Fremont said.

Walker stood up, but his head barely reached Fremont's chin. Fremont ushered him inside.

"Mighty nice in here, Colonel," Walker said, glancing around at the paneled walls and leather-bound books.

"Thanks, Horace. May I get you a scotch?"

Walker nodded. "You're a gentleman."

Glasses in hand, they eyed each other carefully. They hadn't held a real conversation since the squadron left Tuskegee and both men were a little tense. Walker looked ridiculous in his high boots.

"Sir, I came here to talk about that gunfight in town the other night. You know what happened. Lieutenant Todd was run out of a card game by some Arabs. He got mad and cut loose with a pistol. Like to killed everything in sight. Now people in the village are hot with us. They claim we're just a bunch of niggers, and the men are unhappy. Their friends don't speak anymore and they feel the whole thing is unfair to them, downright unfair."

"Few things in this world are fair, Horace," Fremont said. He didn't want to talk about Todd.

"That's right, Colonel," Walker said. "And that's what bothers me. I see Todd walking around here free and easy. I say he shouldn't be part of this outfit."

"You say nothing!" Fremont retorted savagely. He slammed down his drink. "This is an administrative matter."

"This is a squadron matter," Walker said in a loud voice. "One night I followed that motherfucker up into the hills. He met with that general who was here one time on an inspection. They talked about ways to fuck us up and send us back to the States looking stupid and incompetent. You call that an administrative matter. Huh? Is that all you call it?"

"I know about that," Fremont said quickly. "I've known about Todd ever since we got out here."

"And you did nothing?" Walker cried.

"I used my discretion as a commander," Fremont snapped. He felt threatened.

"You did nothing!"

"And what did *you* do, Lieutenant?" Fremont asked.

They stared at each other silently.

"I acted!" Walker hissed out the words in a low voice.

"You made an attempt," was the scornful answer.

"You got Barker after your ass now," Walker came back. "His kind don't play with niggers. Your nice white friends can't help you now."

"Don't go too far, soldier."

"I know they've helped you, all those progressives in their bow ties. They treat you like a West Point man, but that doesn't mean shit to me, Fremont. To me they look like those Germans in Berlin who want to sew another leg on me. It's that white face. It's been there over my shoulder every day of my life, tellin' me to move on. Tellin' me I was never shit."

He lowered his head, then abruptly raised it to Fremont again, eyes filled with pain and a frightful poignancy.

"These people don't need you, Colonel. They'll make you a general someday, but it won't mean anything, man. Nothin'. A black general gettin' on the back door of a trolley car? You'd be the funniest thing next to Donald Duck, yes you would. This here is something among black men. Back home we'd settle it that way, like men do, and finish off that son bitch."

Fremont shook his head wearily.

"I ain't had no home for a long time, not truly," Walker went on. "It's been so long I can't hardly remember it. Being out here with these boys means a whole lot to me. I feel like a human being out here, and I'm not going to be stripped of that. Never again. You hear what I say?"

"Horace," Fremont said quietly after a long while, "what you suggest is not possible."

There was no response. Walker stared into the empty whiskey glass before him.

On Sicily the campaign developed quickly. Oberkommando der Wehrmacht brought in two tough divisions, the 1st Parachute from France and the 29th Panzer from Calabria in Italy. Still, the Germans pulled back in a delaying action. Fremont saw their only hope was to

shorten the front and try to hold a fortified line. The
Italians would be of little help. The Italian military was
very near the end. While Montgomery plodded toward
Messina, Patton broke out brilliantly in western Sicily
where the terrain was suited to his armored columns. He
ransacked town after town, herding thousands of listless
Italian soldiers into captivity. Trapani, base of the Luftwaffe Aircraft Report Center, fell, so did Marsala, and
then Palermo. Suddenly in the east, Montgomery was
blocked at the entrance to the Catanian plain. The Luftwaffe began to drift away. Some of the men in the squadron thought the capture of 125 planes at Comiso had
robbed them of an opponent. But others felt the German
lust for air combat was gone; so many aces had been
killed, so much ground lost, it was tragic and lugubrious,
something the Germans looked for in life. Walker remained outside the arena of these discussions. He brooded
a great deal and quarreled with Dummy Jones, his mechanic, nearly every day. Fremont knew Todd did this to
him, yet he was afraid to ship Todd back to the States.
Once Todd was out of sight, there was no telling how he
might be used against them.

The dazzling Sicilian sky opened over their canopies as
the squadron flew inland on a routine ground-support mission. Mount Enna was easily visible, and so was Etna off
in the distance behind the German lines. Sicily had changed
for them, though, and each man felt it. It was no longer
the elegiac island of their lonely fighter sweeps. Its ghastly
beauty, which they considered their own province, was now
despoiled by men and machines. Villagers stood mutely
by while giant tanks squeezed through their narrow streets.
Below, an American column snaked its way along a road
obscured by dust. Half-tracks camouflaged with branches,
6 x 6 trucks, jeeps, and Sherman tanks ground forward
against the enervating heat. The soldiers down there
looked very slow.

Donny Beaumont glanced at Jennings' Mustang holding station perfectly near his starboard wing. For a long
time he'd worried about Jennings, but now he seemed
resourceful enough to survive. They flew in silence, and
out of nowhere it started. Machine-gun bullets just streamed
into the cockpit, their heavy impact pinning Beaumont
where he sat, dazed. They seemed never to stop coming.

Blood gushed from his nose and mouth. He couldn't speak or yell. Spattered blood covered the instruments. "Donny! Donny! Donny!" Jennings screamed into the headset. A feeling of euphoria took Beaumont. He smelled fire and smiled. The silhouette of a Focke-Wulf passed over him as he floated down.

Planes whirled and dueled everywhere in the sky, guns sparking evilly. Tracers meandered in all directions like paper streamers thrown into the air. The radio chatter was excited but disciplined. ("Don't turn with the son of a bitch. Break right. Right! I'm coming up to help you.") The FW that got Beaumont pulled up and away, racing for the protection of the sun. Walker streaked up after it with Jennings tight on one wing. Jennings screamed curses and fired long bursts that had no chance.

"Get the fuck off my wing, boy. Get away from me," Walker said coolly as he watched the brown-dappled German craft climb like a rocket.

Jennings fired another burst, almost hitting Walker, then banked to starboard and plunged downward. Walker turned off his radio and eyed his adversary in the total silence surrounding them now. *Nothing outclimbs a Mustang,* he told himself. *All I got to do is stay with him, hang on with him like he was a big old fish and we was on a line together. He's got to dive soon. He can't outmaneuver me up here against this engine I'm sittin' behind. Look at him try and get me mad. He's trying to make me shoot and miss so I'll get madder and lose him in the dive. This is Horace Walker out of Texas, boy.*

At the exact same instant both planes rolled over and dropped earthwards, engines whining. Walker was close enough for a shot, but he did not fire. He merely studied the twisting turning aerobatics of his adversary, the backward dive, the split S, all of it. Never once did the distance between them change, and now the German had to be desperate, had to be calling madly for help. The horizon fell away. Walker gripped the stick tightly. Everything on the ground seemed to bulge up toward him. The FW flattened out, darting over the countryside, barely visible in its brown-mottled camouflage. Still Walker was there. At last, he fired a long deflection shot just as his quarry slipped into a wide, dipping circle. He used only his machine guns.

Smoke billowed from the cowling. The FW swung around and tried to climb. Cannon fire would have finished it off, but Walker made no move. He saw the pilot struggle in the heat and smoke of his crippled plane. He was going too fast for a crash landing and couldn't possibly bail out at this altitude. For some moments he wavered, glancing fearfully over his shoulder. The aircraft erupted into flame and finally hurtled into the hills where it exploded with a childish bang. When Walker rejoined the squadron, the Germans had fled. On the road, trucks started up and soldiers began marching again.

That evening, the squadron held a memorial service for Donny Beaumont, with Jennings, Osborn, and Fremont delivering eulogies. Todd was there, standing among the fliers, looking thin and deranged. But Walker did not come. ("I did what I could by the boy. What the fuck can I say now? He's gone, that's all.") Fremont presided and used the occasion to remind his men they had voted down a squadron chaplain, and it might just be a mistake. No one paid any attention. They left the brief service still confounded by Beaumont's death, stunned by its exquisite suddenness. Everyone liked Donny. He was an original Homestead Gray, an element leader, a good pilot who always encouraged the replacements when their confidence faltered. Jennings could not hold back the tears. He dreaded going back to the room they shared, quailed at the prospect of seeing the Operations people take away Donny's belongings. Skinner made his room available for the night, and Jennings mumbled something about appreciating it. Skinner seemed to be flying poorly. Today he'd gotten credit for an FW slowed down by ground fire from half-tracks on the road. The pilot parachuted safely and made for his own lines. The whole episode was tainted by luck, and fliers never really trusted luck. It gave out too quickly.

Some days later startling news came through. Mussolini had been deposed and was under arrest. The aged king of Italy, Victor Emmanuel, was now Commander of the Armed Forces. He had appointed an elderly field marshal to be Mussolini's successor. The Fascist party was dissolved, but constant radio messages warned the people not to expect immediate peace. Around the field, hardly anyone bothered to talk about Mussolini's dismissal. It seemed a trivial matter while Germany still held most of Europe and was successfully fighting off the bomber campaign designed to level her cities. Besides, there was an important mission early in the morning.

Suddenly it was August. The Allied armies had clawed over Sicily for more than three weeks and at last only the extreme northeast corner of the island remained a battleground. Here the Germans fought brilliantly to preserve their escape routes, beating back attempts to encircle them, cutting up the small amphibious landings in their rear, holding mountain passes to the last rifleman. The Catanian plain was lost to them. The fortified line at the base of Mount Etna had shrunk and disappeared. Each day the squadron noticed more dead men on the roads. Pack horses struggled across the virtually impassable terrain. Howitzers fired on German positions continually until the guns became so hot their camouflage nets burst into flame. Naval guns from battleships out of Palermo joined in and B-17s droning up from captured airfields in the southern half of the island were very active. But it was the fighters who went in close and killed the soldiers holding those tiny impregnable hilltop towns, Triona, Cesaro, Randazzo, San Fratello, haunting names no one had ever heard of before. The Squadron hurled itself against these towns every day, morning and afternoon, grappling with the exhausted Germans struggling to hold the high ground. At night the Germans slipped away, demolishing bridges, feverishly sowing minefields and booby traps in their wake. Hospital tents with red crosses on top sprouted over the landscape. Destroyed tanks and heavy vehicles lay all around. And yet the nearly spent Allied troops dragged themselves through the immense heat of the Sicilian summer, lurching toward Messina. From the air they looked pitiful. Fremont's men saw how badly they lacked the gallantry and flair of the enemy, but no one mentioned it.

As they drew closer to Messina more and more flak guns dotted the countryside. Around the port itself five hundred guns pointed to the sky, the heaviest concentration anywhere in the world at that moment, heavier even than the inner defenses of London. Flak ships plied back and forth along the strait, waiting for their prey.

Secretly, the German evacuation began. Naval barges,

Siebel ferries, troop carriers, and motorboats streamed along half a dozen ferry routes every night. Meanwhile, all sorts of ominous news burst from the radio. German divisions, moved in from France, now practically occupied northern Italy. Somewhere in North Africa, representatives of King Victor Emmanuel were said to be negotiating a surrender with the Allies. Night and day the evacuation was pressed forward. The war momentarily slipped beyond Fremont's men. Forty thousand Germans, a tenth of them wounded, escaped Sicily with 10,000 vehicles. The Italians, running their own ferries, miraculously took out 75,000 men. When Patton arrived in Messina barely a half hour before Monty, he found nothing but dynamited piers and wrecked warehouses, gloomy and desolate in the hot sun.

Late morning had come. In his empty caravan Fremont stared past the drawn red curtains into his sleeping quarters, perhaps for the last time. He continued packing his books and personal things for the transfer to Catania in eastern Sicily where, forty-eight hours before, the squadron had been ordered to move. Outside, he heard the men moving about, calling, and sometimes laughing, but never with the absolute freedom and innocence of other days. He ran one hand gently over the richly polished wood of his desk. What had happened on Sicily bothered him. The thirty-eight days of brutal fighting seemed terribly inconclusive. Strong arguments for a German success could be drawn from it, for Sicily really led nowhere. Ahead stretched the gnarled wasteland of southern Italy. It looked like a long war. And yes, he also regretted leaving North Africa now that the time had come. Tunisia possessed an easy charm he'd been blind to. He'd noticed it in the French couple who agreed to store his caravan in their garage in the European section of Medjez-el-Bab.

He stepped outside. There was a tableau of activity everywhere he looked. Several of the pilots bickered stridently with the Berber merchant who came to repurchase their bicycles at a cheap price. Someone, it looked like Butters, smashed his bicycle with a hammer to prove to the Arab a fair exchange had to be made. Walker wheeled up in a jeep and let Appaloosa out. She had recently given birth to kittens, which Walker had distributed to the French and Arab children in the village.

"Saw a whole bunch of Italians in town," Walker said to the pilots hemmed in around the merchant. "Had some fine looking gals with 'em too. One of the kids told me they left out of their homes in Medjez and went up into the hills when the Germans passed through. They been campin' up there all this time. Sure wish I'd known. People need a helpin' hand at times like that."

The valley was unusually placid and pastoral today, shrouded in a soft, highly diffused light which cast faint shadows. Out on the main runway a twin engine C-47 Dakota turned around and began to taxi. Osborn, his Operations people, and their equipment were leaving, accompanied by the mess crew and some of the mechanics. Fremont walked over to where Beasley stood watching the battered overloaded transport struggle to take off.

"Sorry we couldn't squeeze you in on this run, Dick, but they only gave us one plane and he's limited to a couple of trips," he said amicably.

"Oh that's all right, Jonathan," Beasley answered with a smile. They chatted about the war, about how badly it was going for Hitler and what his rages and desperation must be like. Beasley expected Mussolini to be resurrected soon, but they both knew it would make no difference.

"Jonathan," Beasley said, glancing over at the pilots, "as a doctor I don't like the look of your men today, not at all. They're drained, more than they know. This is perfectly natural, a bad letdown now that the campaign is over. But accidents happen on days like today."

"I'm forewarned. Anything else, Dick?" Fremont asked.

"Yes," the big man replied carefully. "I've been watching Todd, and he's in trouble. He's showing signs of paranoia, Jonathan. He just shouldn't be here. I've got a friend on the psychiatric ward at Walter Reed. How about letting me get Todd out of here on a medical transfer? The man needs help."

Fremont sighed. Todd was nowhere to be seen. He'd gone out on the first flight without authorization.

"I'll give your request real consideration, Dick," Fremont answered.

"You're a decent man, Jonathan," Beasley said with a sincerity that irritated Fremont. "By the way, I'm bringing over a load of vermouth and English gin. After you're settled tonight, come by my tent."

At the dispersal area the men stood around smoking cigarettes and talking casually. A sullenness and reluctance clung to their voices and gestures. It was clear they detested the idea of going to Sicily, hated the thought of living in all that heat among half-starved and suspicious peasants. Briskly Fremont called them together.

"The squadron will be split. We'll take off fifteen minutes apart in groups of eight. Lieutenant Skinner will lead the second group. Stay on course and be sure to hold formation. I won't tolerate sloppy flying today and I mean it. All right, T.O. is at 1320 hours. Let's get out of here on time."

Quickly he strode to his plane without looking back at the men. His mechanic had left some flare cartridges in the grass and he put them into pockets on the calves of his flying suit. Rather deliberately, he folded his map over to show the route and studied it for a minute. He noticed many of the pilots inspecting their planes or consulting with mechanics and, taking this as a sign of readiness, climbed into his Mustang. Friday appeared on the wing walk and tightened his harness.

In the shade under one wing of his plane, Walker knelt and delicately tied a blindfold around Appaloosa's head as Dummy stood guard.

"If you knew how high you was goin', it like to drive you crazy," he said to the confused animal.

All engines started on time. The eight Mustangs roared up into the sky. Jennings gazed down at the white cottages, at the lilac-tinted almond trees and the firs along the road. He saw the village nestled in on itself, the wheat fields, the stunning flowers, and the mountaintops, now scorched by the summer sun where once they had been green with wet spring foliage. Then, in a moment, it was gone. North Africa was behind them.

They moved out over the Mediterranean. Peace reigned. No ships marred the dazzling surface of the water. No radio traffic came through the headset. Being jumped seemed out of the question, but instinctively everyone searched the skies. Fremont, hardly aware of his powerful droning engine or the craft behind him, thought about Beasley's suggestion concerning Todd. It was a tempting idea, sending Todd to Walter Reed, almost too simple and tantalizing to be good. He wondered if Beasley knew Todd had worked to betray the squadron. It was possible. Coming out of anesthesia, wounded men often told all the secrets of their lives to whoever was near.

Capo Passero, the southernmost tip of Sicily, lay ahead. Fremont ordered a change of course and they stayed out over the water. Siracusa and Lentini, prominent east coast towns, drifted by off the port wing. All the men noticed the bright flat ribbon of the east coast road, which had been traveled by the British not many days ago. Mount Etna, a powerful and mysterious pyramid of rock, rose up into view. Fremont cut altitude and they circled inland lazily, preparing to come in at Catania. As he ended his final approach, Fremont saw that the runway was heavily cratered. On touching down, he had to swerve wildly to keep from ground-looping his plane. The others alighted very cautiously and slowed their machines at once as he taxied on, surveying the horrible landscape all around. Their new base had been completely wrecked by heavy bombers. The hangars and administrative buildings were pulverized to ruins played over by the drooping tendrils of melted steel girders. What had been the control tower was a heap of rubble. Fremont cleared his engine and switched off in disbelief. He opened the canopy. The hot sticky windless air burned his lungs. Smashed German planes, fighters and bombers, lay randomly on the auxiliary runway.

"Signore Generale! Signore Generale!" some of the Sicilian workmen filling craters called to him respectfully as he descended from the cockpit.

A man was running toward him headlong. He recognized Osborn tramping through the waves of heat shimmering thickly up from the ground. His crumpled tropical uniform was badly stained and his face contorted by distress as he reached the plane.

"Colonel Fremont," he cried in a winded voice. "Sir. This just came in," he said, handing over a teletype message.

Fremont's hands trembled. His voice was faint, incredulous.

"I've got to return to Washington at once," he said to Osborn. "The War Department has called me to an inquiry. And, by the way, I'm taking Todd with me."

PART TWO

TEN

THAT EVENING Fremont and Todd left Catania by truck and throughout the warm night rumbled along the zigzag roads traversing Sicily. At first light they came into Trapani at the western end of the island. Trapani was small, lovely, and very hot, a typical Sicilian town distinguished only by the pyramidal staunchness of Mount Erice, where the big Luftwaffe radar disc had been located. In the middle of the morning a cargo plane ferried them to Algiers. Before sunset they took off in a C-47 for the long exhausting trip to Washington. None of the half dozen passengers sitting in narrow seats along the walls bothered to introduce themselves. Fremont and Todd, who slept all the way to Casablanca, were isolated at one end of the plane. Todd seemed oblivious to the harsh cold at 15,000 feet. He curled up on the metal flooring comfortably, as if a warm fire were burning a few feet away. This despite the fact that last night he had awakened in the truck, his eyes blank and catatonic as he screamed at Fremont, "You sneakin' son of a bitch. You sent Walker to kill me. Admit it. Admit it!" and then gone back to sleep as if nothing had happened.

A mood of foreboding took Fremont. The everlasting drone of engines pulled him farther away from Sicily and his squadron. He picked at the bread, cheese, and tomatoes in the basket given him by the workers at the field and wondered if he would ever see Sicily again. He felt lost in the sky somewhere between the brown earth below and

the high equatorial sun. A copy of *Adler in Süden,* the Luftwaffe newspaper for men serving in the southern theater,
rested on his lap, and out of boredom he attempted
to read it. His German was weak, but what came through
appalled him. German fliers were being congratulated for
their heroic defense of objectives they'd abandoned without
a fight. It was all lies and propaganda. He flung the paper
away in disgust.

At 1350 hours of the second day they reached Dakar
in Senegal. The heat was staggering and almost immediately they got back into the plane only to find it filled
with strangers: French generals, civil servants in pin-striped
double-breasteds, tall lean black men wearing fezzes who
seemed uninterested in their presence. Engine trouble de-
layed them for three hours as the plane baked on the runway. The stench inside was suffocating, but no one left
his seat. Dinner time had come and gone before they got
underway again, and perhaps hunger made everyone nervous, for the volume of conversation suddenly expanded.
Fremont watched the French generals carefully. When
they spoke, everything was succinct and clear. They were
the right sort of people, rational and humane, the kind of
men to be found at the top of any officer corps. Fremont
wondered if men like them, thoughtful men, might soon
come forward in Germany to seek a political solution to
the war. And if they did, decency would make it impossible for the Allies not to hear their arguments. They
would, after all, represent reason. If Hitler were dead, the
war might end through negotiation, no matter what anyone
said now. But one never knew; fair hair and blue eyes were
a language in themselves.

The two nations of Guinea, Portuguese and French, slid
by underneath them. Ahead, off the starboard wingtip, lay
the immensity of the South Atlantic where German surface
raiders had run wild two years before. Fremont wished
Osborn were making this trip. Good old Osborn. He was
obviously stunned when the link between Todd and Barker
was explained to him, yet he never asked why he hadn't
been told before. He pledged loyalty and support instantly,
and this made it easier for Fremont to get away fast. Skinner was made acting squadron leader, although some of
the men objected. His own choice intrigued Fremont. He
liked Skinner. The man was from a background like his

and would appreciate Osborn's steadiness. ("If things don't go well, get rid of him," he confided to Osborn.) Still, he was not a true squadron leader, not at all. Once again Walker had been wronged. Walker had stayed away when most of the others shook his hand and wished him good luck before the truck moved off into the Sicilian night.

A white tropical moon shone through the transport's windows as they touched down at Monrovia, Liberia. A stumpy black man in an Air Corps flying suit used signal flags to direct the plane onto a taxiway. In the run-down terminal Fremont pushed his way through the babble of races and languages and angry customs officials. The Frenchmen disappeared quickly. Fremont and Todd slept on benches in the terminal that night. All of the following day they crossed the Atlantic as the C-47 bobbed in strange upper air currents and lunged toward the bulge of Brazil at Recife, where they remained long enough to refuel and head northwards to Belém, not far from the mouth of the Amazon. Both men were exhausted by now. The engines started to run quite roughly and they barely made it to Georgetown in British Guiana. There, ground crewmen went to work anxiously. In the next thirty-six hours Port of Spain, Trinidad, a long arc of minuscule islands, and finally Puerto Rico all fell behind. They came down on American soil at Pensacola Naval Air Station in Florida.

The plane emptied and they found themselves alone in the steamy silence. A tall, trim figure emerged from the cockpit.

"Last stop, gents," the copilot said jauntily. Something in his bearing was both innocent and snide. Fremont hated the type.

"Sorry, but you'll have to hop another bird. We were lucky to get this far. They come down on us awful hard if we crash in the States with passengers aboard. You men are officers, anybody'll take you on."

Fremont saw it was futile to argue. They got off the plane and wandered around in the heat for an hour before finding another transport headed north. Over South Carolina they ran into a violent storm coming from out at sea and were forced to land at Charleston. Fremont wasn't sure Todd could make it to the railroad station. He perspired heavily and seemed on the brink of incoherence much of the time. Luckily a black soldier driving a truck picked them up on the highway.

After washing in the colored bathroom, which reeked of old urine, Todd returned strangely refreshed. They stood at the end of the platform together with the other black passengers and crowded into the antiquated and fetid Jim Crow coaches when the train arrived. Stops were made in practically every hamlet. Soon, it was impossible to move in the aisles. Fremont gave his seat to a woman who put three tiny children in her lap. He thought of the train they'd torn apart in Sicily and was heartsick. Todd simply stared at the bedraggled faces above him and never got up. They pulled into Union Station in Washington forty-five minutes late. A tide of black people carrying cardboard suitcases and cloth bundles streamed up the long train shed and out into the dark rainy night. Fremont approached the long line of yellow cabs hoping someone would have the courtesy to take an officer where he wanted to go.

"You don't ride here, Billy," the first driver in line said. "Colored cab stand two blocks back," he snarled, jerking his thumb.

"I'm going to kill somebody now that I'm home," Todd muttered as the slashing rain ran down his face. "I'm going to kill until they blow my head off. See if I don't."

"Aren't we going to the officers' barracks?" he asked bitterly after Fremont had given an address to the driver of a dilapidated Chevrolet taxi. "Or don't we have reservations?"

"Shut up, Todd," Fremont answered coldly.

They sped through the wet streets, past blacked-out public buildings. The cab took them to a large Victorian house in the middle of the black district. It was a boarding house run by a Miss Olivia Smalls. Beasley had mentioned it many times ("Taking a girl to Miss Olivia's is like going down a mine shaft, Jonathan. The Gestapo couldn't find you"), and for now there was no better place. He and Todd were shown to a double room in the back. Fremont drifted into a deep, exhausted slumber and was not aware that Todd got up twice during the night.

The next morning, alone in a taxicab on the way to the Pentagon, Fremont was nearly overwhelmed by a spell of dizziness. He peered from the backseat with quavering uncertainty, for he was badly disoriented. They had crossed seven time zones since leaving Catania, and Washington seemed as remote as a city on the Ganges delta. Its slow, countrified pace had quickened. Some of the metropolitan seriousness of New York was in the air, but only in a good-natured middle-western way. Soldiers moved out about everywhere, especially officers, who ruled the sidewalks and seemed to have commandeered the best hotels.

As public buildings, dazzling white in the late summer sun, passed by, Fremont's thoughts shifted to Todd, who was a terrible burden to carry on his back. It was mainly because of Todd that he was here in Washington now, battling once more for the right to exist as an American fighting man when he had hoped that struggle was far behind him. Anxiety over the War Department inquiry crept upon him. He didn't really know what to expect, and for this reason he decided to keep Todd close to him just a while longer. It was plain luck he hadn't shipped Todd out before. No matter what happened now, luck would play an important part, and Fremont strained to discern how it could work in his favor. Firstly, Barker must not be allowed to snatch Todd away. Only Todd could incriminate Barker if things came to a crisis. Todd had told him all about their involvement and how it went way back to the beginning of the program. He feared Barker, that much was clear, but he dismissed Captain Love. He thought Love was merely ambitious and this comforted Fremont a bit. He had never really felt free to contact Love when the recall order came through. Now, his caution looked very sensible and fortunate. Still, something nagged at him. Todd was dreary and detached, probably at the onset of some mental disorder. In his present state he would make a poor witness before a committee of austere generals. Perhaps Beasley's friend at Walter Reed might agree to hide him for a while. But no, he was safer at Miss Olivia's where the presence of a black soldier would go unquestioned.

To gain entrance to Room 1050, D ring, Fremont had to ring a buzzer in the hallway. He stepped into a paneled room with leather sofas, and a rug on the floor. A major, several full colonels, and even a few generals sat around reading newspapers and waiting. Wary, unfriendly eyes sought him out, examined his immaculate uniform, then slid away. A corporal took his name and disappeared. Several men were called into another room before his turn came. Then he found himself in a bare office, sitting across from a rather distant and correct first lieutenant.

"Lieutenant Colonel Fremont, the War Department plans to conduct a formal hearing into the conduct of your squadron," the man said.

"I understand."

"The hearing will come in about a week. The Department will advise you of the time and date in a few days. Please leave an address and telephone number where you can be reached."

Fremont wrote this out on a slip of paper and gave it to the pale, controlled young man on the other side of the table.

"Is this an officers' residence?" the lieutenant asked with a faint, disapproving smile. "I'm not familiar with this part of town."

"It's where I'm staying, Lieutenant," Fremont said sharply.

"Very well, sir."

The long gently winding corridors beyond the high-security area were crowded. Fremont walked along briskly. Aside from orderlies, he was the only black man in sight. He recognized an occasional face from the Point, yet no one greeted him. He felt terribly lonely. Snatches of conversation, much of it denigrating the campaign on Sicily, floated around him. So far as he could tell, everyone seemed absorbed in Europe, absorbed in the bombing offensive against Germany, which was going badly, and in the prospective invasion, surely the last chance for many to make their reputations. He didn't notice the middle-aged man in a soiled white suit and panama hat who came out of the press room as he passed. The man scuttled behind him. Finally he came alongside and cleared his throat loudly.

"Colonel Fremont, sir?" he asked tentatively.

Fremont remembered the face vaguely. His pace slowed.

"Detwiler, sir. *Memphis Evening News*. I followed your men all through their training. Fine American boys."

"Hello, Detwiler."

"May I have a few lines from you, Colonel? How is the

war going in the Mediterranean? Do your men like fighting Germans?"

"You don't want to know that," Fremont said.

Detwiler stared at the floor. A crooked smile touched his thin lips.

"No, sir, I don't want to know that," he replied with sudden frankness. "I want to know a lot more. Maybe I shouldn't be tellin' you this, but Major Shaw and Lieutenant Colonel Stowe, the only other commanders of black boys, are also in town, all the way from the Pacific front. Do we have a divine coincidence here? Are you fellas gettin' together socially, or could this be Army business?"

"I'm not at liberty to divulge any of that. See the others."

"Can't," Detwiler said, grimacing up at him. "They've become very, very busy."

"I'll bet they have."

"So you're takin' the same line?" Detwiler inquired in a slow, mean way. "Well then, let me ask you one more thing."

"Make it the last."

"Is it true that your squadron, your own hand-picked boys, have been graded out as the worst in the Air Force? Is there any truth in that statement, Colonel?"

The two men stared at each other tightly. Detwiler was amused, trashy, insolent, and very sure of himself. A faint aroma of bourbon came off him. Fremont wanted to knock him down, yet he maintained his composure.

"Why, you're just the great stone face this mornin', aren't you, Colonel, sir?" Detwiler said. He wheeled around and was gone.

Fremont reached the Communications Center. *Better advise Osborn I've arrived in Washington,* he thought. He wrote out a brief cable. Again, he had the feeling someone was watching him. This was getting to be too much. He was an officer and wanted the courtesy of his rank. He turned around angrily. The man before him was black, tall, rather husky, and wore a second lieutenant's bars on his shoulders.

"I'm very sorry," Fremont stammered.

The man said nothing. He saluted briskly, forcing Fremont to look at his face. It was Orlando Jones, the pilot who had broken formation after the first mission and crashed in the desert.

"Hello, sir," he said softly.

"Hello, Lieutenant."

"Jones, sir."

Fremont remembered him quite clearly now. Jones had come to his caravan surly and frightened. They had argued and nearly fought. But his assignment was Tuskegee, not the Pentagon.

"I don't recall sending you to Washington, Jones," Fremont said in a not unfriendly way.

"I was washed up at Tuskegee, Colonel," Jones admitted. "They found me psychologically unfit to fly, but we both knew that already, didn't we, sir?"

"I'm afraid so," Fremont said.

"The Army posted me here. Usually I work the night shift. It's a big job for a black fellow, at least that's what they told me."

Fremont smiled a bit.

"I'll take your cable, sir."

"Thanks, Jones."

"Another thing, Colonel. I want to apologize for the way I acted overseas. That wasn't really me."

Fremont nodded thoughtfully and the men parted.

It was beautiful outside and Fremont headed for the bridge to town, knowing there would be no black taxi drivers on this side of the river. Behind him an Army staff car with Captain Paul Love at the wheel gained ground and shot past. General Barker turned around in his seat and examined the tall, brown-skinned man.

"There's my nigger," he said quietly, biting off the end of a long cigar.

Two evenings later Miss Olivia's niece, a scrawny and sullen girl of sixteen who worked in the house as a chambermaid, knocked on Fremont's door.

"There's a soldier downstairs to see you," she said crossly. "He's white. He claim to know you."

Fremont looked over at Todd, who was asleep in the next bed. Then he put on his shoes and went downstairs. As he passed the dining room door, the boarders around the table examined him with curiosity.

In the parlor, midst the dark turn-of-the-century furniture was Captain Love. This time Fremont was not at all surprised. He'd been expecting Love, although thousands of miles lay between this house and their last meeting place. Immediately he decided not to mention Todd was in Washington.

"Colonel Fremont, sir, it's good to see you again," Love said, stepping forward to shake his hand.

"I didn't expect to see you in Washington," Fremont replied. "You get around, Captain."

"Sir, I'm sorry I've been so secretive," Love answered. "Now that we're home, I'm free to tell you that I have been acting in my capacity as an aide to the Army Chief of Staff."

"Very impressive, Captain," said Fremont, raising an eyebrow.

"Thank you, sir," Love replied with a trace of that innocent smile Fremont remembered from their first encounter. "Colonel Fremont, what we both fear has happened. The hearing you have been summoned to is being called by some of the most conservative elements in the department and the Army. General Barker is merely one of their representatives, and far from the worst, I assure you. These men are very unhappy with the fact that Negro soldiers have gone abroad and distinguished themselves. They feel the black man's place is at home and intend to make this official policy. Their plan is simple—redeploy all black fighting men within the continental United States where they can be formed into a defense brigade."

Fremont turned away, but Love continued momentarily. "I know it's terribly disappointing, but there is a way out of this. And I would like you to consider it."

"What is it?" Fremont asked.

"Just this. Agree here and now to accept the withdrawal of your squadron from Sicily for temporary duty in the United States. In a few months, when things are quiet, your men will be returned to the front. They'll be needed, sir. Pilots are in short supply. We all know Italy is going to be tough, awfully tough."

"You're talking like a goddamn fool," Fremont said. "We'd never get back into the war. Our morale would be shot to pieces. I won't do it!"

"It's an intelligent compromise, sir," Love said.

"It's bullshit!" Fremont shouted. "Bullshit!"

Love sat down on the edge of a stuffed chair. He rubbed his hands together.

"I've found out some things about the hearing you ought to know," he said in a dry voice. "It will be a closed hearing and all testimony is to be placed under top-security classification. Senators and congressmen, chiefly men from the South who are connected with the armed services, will be on hand. They know all about you and your father. This kind of thing can turn into an execution very easily, Colonel. I've seen it happen before. These men resent intruders in their world."

"And I resent them!" Fremont yelled.

"I know that. I understand. But let me caution you, Colonel. Don't bring a civilian lawyer. It can only hurt your case. My advice is to show no rancor. Play the good soldier, if not for yourself, then in all decency for your men."

"Don't you dare ever tell me how to conduct myself, you son of a bitch."

"Colonel, where do you imagine you are going with all this fury?" Love asked patiently. "In the name of reason, please accept the compromise you have been offered. It is politics, yes. But very necessary politics at this moment. You must trust me, sir."

"I cannot," Fremont answered coldly. "You represented yourself to me as an emissary from the right people, the enlightened people in this army. Now what you are perpetuating is yet another wrong, another injustice. If black men don't fight in this war, they can expect nothing when it is over. Therefore I must fight what you propose, fight it and reject it."

"But why?" Love exclaimed, getting to his feet. "Why? If you're worried about honors and acclaim for the black man, I am prepared to guarantee you your first star within a year. You will be the first of your race to attain the rank of general. You can have that in writing. Isn't the fact that you'll be a general proof of my intent?"

"I'd be the only general leading a squadron," he said with a smile. "I'd be ridiculous, to myself and everyone else. Don't ask me to become a fool."

"I am very sorry, Colonel," Love said. "I thought a man in your position, a distinguished man, would understand and accept these things more readily. I'm afraid you will be destroyed now. Good night to you, sir."

"Good night, Captain."

About twenty minutes later, while Fremont still seethed with frustration and near panic, he was called down to the pay telephone in the hallway.

"Operator callin' you back. They claim it's long distance," one of the boarders said, handing him the receiver.

His wife's faded and scratchy voice far away in California came through to him. They chatted tensely and affectionately for a moment.

"I called because there's trouble here," he said at last. "We may be brought back to the States. I'm going to fight it."

She was calm, telling him he was doing the right thing, undoubtedly what his men would want.

"Jonathan, I want to come to Washington. You need someone by your side."

"I'd prefer you didn't," he said stiffly. "Please, Marva. Things may get rough here. I may be cashiered. Stay with Mark and Tony."

"Of course," she replied in that cutting, civilized way she had. "I'll be the dutiful mother as always. But I want to ask you something, Jonathan. Have you got a woman there?"

"What the hell are you talking about, Marva?" he shouted in the phone.

"Is that affirmative?" she said in a fluttering voice. "I only want to know. That's all, just to know."

When he looked at the receiver it was back on the hook. He hadn't even spoken to the boys.

"Stupid bitch!" he hissed, slamming the side of his fist into the wall.

As he got to the foot of the stairs, Miss Olivia appeared. Instantly he realized she had been eavesdropping. She sashayed up to him, a short, plump brown woman who supposedly had been one of the great beauties in Washington twenty-five years ago.

"Colonel, may I have a word with you?" she said cutely. "You'll have to excuse me, my memory isn't like it was. Who did you say sent you all to me again?"

"Doctor Richard Beasley," he replied, straining to be polite.

"Oh, yes," she said, averting her eyes in a gesture both coy and shrewd. "Then you know Doctor Beasley?"

"Yes, ma'am, I do. I serve with him."

"In the Homestead Grays, them people that fly airplanes?"

He nodded.

"All right, Colonel," she said touching him on the arm with a reassuring pat. "Just checkin'. Whole lot of funny people come to a roomin' house, you know."

Soon after, he left the house and made his way through the neighborhood of neat middle-class dwellings to a main thoroughfare, where he looked for a cab. Todd was still asleep and would probably remain in the room until he awakened much later to take up his strange nocturnal life. Cabs came by, slowed, then saw his face and sped away. He walked about a mile. Police cars looked him over. Finally a black taxi driver on his way home agreed to take him to the Pentagon for a five-dollar bill.

He considered what lay before him at this hearing and felt tempted to call his father's old friends in town, the good liberal congressmen and columnists who would surely help. Yet he could not. This was one battle he wanted to fight alone, without aid of philanthropy. He preferred it that way. Besides, there was no reason to believe an outcry would save him. Love was probably right about that.

"They gone over into Italy," the driver said, breaking into his thoughts. "Did you hear about it?"

"Turn on the radio, please."

A small yellow light appeared on the dashboard and Fremont heard a voice say, "This is the Mutual Network with a repeat of an earlier bulletin. Tonight the Allies are back on the continent of Europe. General Bernard Montgomery's British Eighth Army has come ashore at Reggio on the Italian mainland across from the port of Messina. Initial resistance is light. We will keep you informed throughout the night."

The driver turned to a station playing big-band music. Fremont drifted back into his reverie. Marva had acted very stupidly on the phone, talking like that. In all the years of their marriage she had rarely shown jealousy before, but now he sensed a strong resentment directed toward him. An undertone of dissatisfaction and unrest had been discernible in her last few letters. It was probably the strain of the war, the fear of his vanishing, never to return. Fighter pilots never lasted. His death would leave her to struggle with the boys by herself. All this had to be getting to her. Perhaps it was just worry and nothing more. What would she be like after the war, he wondered. Would they both have changed too much, lost too much? Or was their marriage disintegrating now? Anything was possible. Marva was an attractive woman in her plain, cultivated way. There might be another man, a genteel, tennis-playing doctor, a nice professor, a rational calm man who would know how to ingratiate himself. He decided to call his sister in Los Angeles and make tentative inquiries. Then he realized he really didn't care.

Jones spotted him the minute he walked into the Communications Center. He had a cable from Osborn. An impressive unit citation for the attack on the German cruiser at Gela had come through. Momentarily Fremont was cheered. Osborn had anticipated trouble and moved to buoy his spirits. He appreciated it.

"Any reply, sir?" Jones asked, pencil and pad in hand.

"Yes. Tell him everything is in jeopardy. Tell him we may be recalled."

Jones wrote it down rather slowly. When he looked up, Fremont was gone.

He walked back into Washington. He realized that the war had changed him, given him more assurance. He didn't care if he never got that first star. He only wanted to be a warrior, that and nothing more. Justifying himself to mediocre men, explaining his conduct to bureaucrats and alcoholic senators bound by rigid policies and ancestral hatreds, these things were farthest from his mind. He'd found it amusing when Love talked about cleansing the army of its incompetents. Tonight, he wondered if Love was amused by his plight, if the man was that uncharitable.

Next morning he awoke in a mood of foreboding and depression. He had breakfast downstairs with Todd, who seemed peculiarly bright and fresh.

"Remember, Lieutenant, at the hearing you will testify fully to the nature of your association with General Barker," Fremont said to him.

"Okay, Colonel. Whatever you say," Todd answered blithely.

Fremont reasoned that since the hearing was closed to the press, Todd was his only means of discrediting the charges against him. He lapsed into gloom and thought again of the faraway Mediterranean, the limpid sky, the warm sun, and the not uncomfortable feeling of constant danger. He thought of the men, Skinner, Jennings, Hollyfield, and all the rest, even Walker. Throughout the day he was tense and also very annoyed with Todd, who appeared to think or care about nothing as he played endless games of solitaire. Fremont could not wait for the hearing now. He was tired of sitting around this dreary rooming house, tired of Todd's vacuous manner, his trivial habits. For long stretches of time he feared he didn't even exist. He began to feel he was nothing more than a creation of his father's friends and the newspapers. Todd had said his enemies would rip him apart like wild dogs, and he believed it. But when? When?

He left the house before six o'clock, unable to face the bland conviviality of Miss Olivia's boarders around the dinner table. At the Pentagon, Jones had another cable. The squadron was in good spirits and behind him all the way. He strolled outside, both gladdened and deeply anguished. It began to rain lightly.

When he returned to the house, Miss Olivia's slim and sulky niece met him in the downstairs hall.

"Miss Olivia want to see you," she explained sourly, pointing to a door in the back that Fremont had never seen open.

He knocked and entered a small, pleasant sitting room. Miss Olivia was in a rocker, knitting. Oscar, her boyfriend, an out-of-work jazz musician, sat on a sofa in his yellow vest, reading a newspaper. The sweet smell of bourbon hung in the air.

Miss Olivia rose at once and threw her knitting into the chair. Fremont saw that she was livid.

"Now you listen here, Colonel, or whatever the ·fuck you are," she cried in her brassy, cutting voice. "I don't like a lot of crazy shit goin' on in my house."

Her strong, malevolent gaze stunned Fremont.

"I'm talking about this," she said, opening one meaty

fist to reveal several broken ampoules in the center of her brown hand. They gave off the odor of a harsh chemical.

"Morphine!" Oscar said.

"I found one in the bathroom the other day," she said, pointing a finger savagely. "That's why I spoke to you. Now I'm tellin' you straight. *I* don't play this shit," she yelled, flinging the ampoules to the carpet. "I hate dope in my house!"

She trembled with fury, hands on hips.

"Olivia, please," Oscar said. "I told you. Maybe the boy was hurt fightin' for the country and took to the habit that way. Don't be so quick to condemn a man."

"You shut up, you fat-ass fool," she said without taking her eyes off Fremont. "I put a roof over your head, Oscar, and don't forget it."

"You, mister," she snapped at Fremont. "You get that nigger dope fiend out of here tonight. Better still, do it right this minute or I'll have the MPs all over you both."

Fremont turned to go, his bearing slow and uncertain.

"Goddamn trash," Miss Olivia called after him. "He's got a hell of a nerve comin' in here and callin' himself a colonel. We ain't got no colonels in the Army. He's an orderly somewhere or a deserter one."

Raucous laughter exploded in the room.

When Fremont reached the staircase, he went wild. He tore up the steps and smashed into the room, which seemed hideously overlighted. Todd got up from his card game on the bed. He looked sickly. His thin smile aimed itself in Fremont's direction. Fremont's fist drove into his face, again and again and again into his bloodied, expressionless face.

"Why? Why? Why?" he heard his frenzied voice screaming.

Suddenly people crowded in the doorway. He seized Todd by the throat.

"Why have you done this to me?" he screamed in confusion. "I don't understand."

Todd sank to his knees. Two figures cut through the spectators and rushed at Fremont, tearing his hands from Todd's throat.

"Oscar! Oscar, call the MPs," Miss Olivia said. "They gone crazy up here."

Someone tripped Fremont and he fell very hard.

"I'm all right," he shouted as Oscar pounced on him. "I'm all right. All right," he said, hanging his head.

He lay there for a while suspended between grief and delirium. Miss Olivia knelt beside him, speaking in an emotional whisper.

"Get out of my house," she pleaded. "Leave before I do something real bad. I see you got troubles. Take them away from me."

Neither he nor Todd spoke as they staggered along the street carrying their bags and jackets. It began to rain much harder. Todd fell twice. He was barely able to stand at all. Walker was right, Fremont thought. He should have killed Todd before he could do any real damage. Now it was too late, far too late. They went on through the rain, dazed and silent. After nearly an hour they arrived at the YMCA, drenched and exhausted. As they came up to the desk, the clerk on duty sneered.

"What do you all want in here?"

"We want a room!" Fremont yelled, pounding on the desk.

"It's a bad night. There aren't any empty rooms," the clerk said as he examined their soaked uniforms. "But since you boys are both officers and gentlemen, I believe we can let you have a cot on the third floor."

A creaky old elevator led them off in the midst of a hideous scene Fremont had forgotten to expect. Hordes of black soldiers slept everywhere, in the rooms, on cots in the hallway, but mostly twisted and heaped on the floor. He stepped gently over the fallen soldiers, whose khaki uniforms seemed encrusted on their slumbering bodies. A bent old man appeared with two folded cots. Fremont cried out in rage and knocked them away viciously. The old man shrugged. He pointed to a corner. Moments later they were both heavily asleep, indistinguishable from the men around them.

In the middle of the night someone awakened Fremont. His eyes opened with effort and he was struck by the oppressiveness of stale air all around. Snores and grunts punctuated the darkness. A hand rocked him again, this time more gently. A match was struck. He recognized Oscar's yellow vest and gleaming pomaded hair parted in the middle.

"This came after you went," he said, handing Fremont a telegram. "Army man brought it, so I thought it was important. Figured you'd come here."

"Thank you," Fremont said in a hoarse voice.

"It's my duty," Oscar replied cryptically. "By the way, don't take what Olivia said too hard. She don't mean half of it."

"I understand," Fremont mumbled.

"Well, good-bye now, soldier," Oscar said. He groped for Fremont's hand in the dark and shook it firmly. "I know who you are. You just keep doing that good job. Just keep on, hear?"

Early in the morning Fremont and Todd left the Y. The streets of Washington were practically empty and had that broad quality of provincialism and grandeur Fremont remembered from before the war. An occasional staff car or jeep whizzed by. A trolley appeared out of a side street. The front half was empty, but the rear section teemed with black people, domestics and laborers and children who waved enthusiastically at them. Fremont said nothing to Todd about the War Department hearing scheduled to begin that morning at 9:00 A.M. Yet he sensed Todd knew. Perhaps he had not been asleep when Oscar came with the telegram.

They went into a drugstore for breakfast. The counter was deserted and they sat down. A big blonde woman in an apron sped towards them.

"You all will have to sit down at the end of the counter," she said in a chiding tone of voice. "You know you're not supposed to be up here."

Todd stiffened. His eyes roved about crazily in his badly swollen face. Calmly, Fremont directed him down the counter.

Todd was showing disturbing signs of wear. The last remnant of his cockiness had faded. It seemed impossible that he'd once strutted upon the stage in the Briefing hut, talking down to men far braver than himself. Dark smudges of fatigue had surfaced under his eyes. He'd lost weight and his uniform hung baggily on him without any crispness or definition. He was both dreamy and intense, like a man in the grasp of undeciphered forces. Fremont guessed his dose of morphine was wearing off, but he couldn't be sure.

"Lieutenant, are you still willing to confront General Barker?" Fremont asked him.

"I am," Todd said in an odd tone.

"You understand where the advantage lies in this situation?" Fremont pressed him.

"I feel I have to do something for you and the men," Todd answered with a strange, quiet passion. "You were right. I am a Judas. I loved money and what it could get me more than I loved life itself. It's disgusting. Filthy, low, and disgusting. I hate what I am, Colonel. You should have beaten me to death last night."

They finished breakfast in silence. After the meal he asked the waitress where they could get a cab.

"There's a big colored cab stand three blocks down and two across, gents. Whole lot of cabs down there this time of day. Can't miss the place."

Fremont left her thirty cents in change, but as they were leaving, Todd whirled and knocked the change all over the floor.

"Now ain't that just like a nigger!" the waitress screamed after them as she squatted daintily to pick up the money.

At the cab stand Fremont watched Todd closely. The prospect of arriving at an official hearing with a morphine addict at his side was at best disquieting. In fact, this entire morning seemed darkly inchoate. He got into the back of the cab and slammed the door.

"Lieutenant, go back to the Y and remain there until my return," he said through the window. "Do not leave the building. That is a direct order."

To his surprise, Todd saluted briskly and strode away.

As he entered the Pentagon, Fremont became aware that his uniform was rumpled. A horror at the way he looked, at the suggestion that he might be slipping, surged over him momentarily. In the busy main lobby he stopped and got a shoeshine, then he found a telephone booth and dialed the Press Room. He didn't really know what he was doing. It was all intuition, that and pure, cold fear. Detwiler, the reporter from Memphis, came on the line and he repeated the carefully phrased words he'd rehearsed in the cab. A big story revolving around him might break in a couple of days. It could be bigger than the news that

General Patton had slapped a shell-shocked soldier in a hospital tent on Sicily. It could make Detwiler a name in Washington.

"Appreciate your call, Colonel. Thanks. I'm glad you see who your real friends in this city are."

For security reasons the hearing room was located deep within the building. Military policemen stood at either side of the padded leather doors. The room faced an inner courtyard where trees had begun to shed their leaves. Fremont noticed a photograph of President Roosevelt on the wall. At a long polished table in front of an American flag sat three uniformed men chatting and smiling at each other in complete relaxation. General Barker was in the center. The man on his left was a staunch-looking four-star general Fremont had never seen before. The other man wore three stars. Barker looked different in this setting. His expressions and gestures were more subtle. He had the air of a successful politician, not an elected official, but a highly placed personage, a well-thought-of insider's man. Just for an instant, Barker's gaze flicked in his direction. Fremont caught a hint of disdain on his face. The scope of things in this room, at this moment in his life, was very large. Here at last he was being brought to book for his arrogance, for breaching the sacred walls of West Point, for being forward and aggressive with white men of less ability. He had exceeded his orders in life. And now, today, his enemies, his father's enemies, had assembled here in body and spirit to regain their advantage. Fremont was glad he had no counsel. Even the best lawyer was irrelevant here.

Soon the four rows of benches behind him started to fill up. Love came in and nodded casually. Many polished-looking young men in expensive suits arrived. They all appeared to be men on the way up at State and Justice and the Treasury, men who wanted to be in on an important kill just to see how it was done.

Moments before 9:00 A.M., a group of senators and congressmen came in and took seats in the spectator's section. Detwiler in his white linen suit was with them. On the hour, everyone quieted down and Barker rose to say, "This hearing is open. Until a recess is declared, no one may leave the room."

Two MPs stood inside the door now. A second lieutenant, who also functioned as the official stenographer, called out, "Lieutenant Colonel Jonathan Fremont, please step forward."

Fremont got up, his footsteps the only sound in the room, and moved to within fifteen paces of the long table. As he saluted, the three generals scrutinized him. Oddly, General Barker's pale blue eyes seemed the most kindly, although the other men did not exactly look harsh. Barker still appeared ordinary, even a bit clerkish. His thick wavy hair was cut high on the sides. His bland, oval face was tinged by an expression of vague outrage. Clumps of small, misshapen teeth showed in his mouth when he said, "Lieutenant Colonel Fremont, this panel has an urgent question for you. Were you aware when your squadron went overseas that it was considered by the Army to be an experimental unit?"

"No, sir, I was not," Fremont answered. "It was my impression that I commanded an operational squadron like any other."

"That's a remarkable admission, Colonel, considering the nature of your men."

The other generals nodded slightly.

"These are men," Barker went on, "from a race we know little about in this country. I suggest that placing highly complex machines, expensive machines, in their hands implicitly constitutes an experiment."

"It certainly does," General Johnson said, putting on a pair of horn-rimmed glasses.

"I have in my possession," Barker said, "a seventy-five-page document of the conduct of your squadron, Colonel." He lifted a bundle of bound papers. "The Army now knows more about your men than it cares to."

Fremont sighed and stood at ease, hands behind his back. It was going to be a hard morning.

"According to the best psychologists in the Army, the racial type to which your men belong is unstable and lacking in both discipline and initiative. Their reflexes are poor. They lack concentration. Any answers to this evidence, Colonel?"

"The Army gave us wings. That must count for something," Fremont said politely.

"This is accounted for by the fact that the Army must answer to civilians," Barker said quickly, motioning to the men on either side of him. "And these civilians in government must respond to political pressures, very often unfair pressures. It is the belief of this panel that your men are inherently unfit to fly in combat. They lack the character and mettle found in white men. I have seen qualities in my six-year-old grandson that are more admirable than any possessed by your men."

Nervous coughing came from the audience. There was no answer to this, Fremont knew, nothing to prevent him from sounding as violent and irrational as Barker wished. He noticed that the four-star general was uneasy in the face of these assertions. He squirmed in his chair. The other general stared straight ahead.

"Go on to another point, General," the senior officer said to Barker.

Time seemed to pass quite slowly. The ceiling fans were turned on. Thick rolls of paper piled up in the stenographer's box. The squadron's training record was being torn apart. They had spent many more months at Tuskegee than was necessary, and this evidence riled the generals. Fremont tried to explain that his men started without officers, started with inadequate facilities, progressed quickly, and then were held back while other squadrons went to war. The three-star man said white Army instructors at Tuskegee had sworn the cadets were lazy and stupid.

"It isn't true, sir," Fremont pleaded.

"I only know what the record says, Colonel Fremont. The record is official. You are emotional."

At noon they broke for lunch. Fremont simply sank down on a bench, weary after standing perfectly still for three hours. The MPs eyed him with a combination of pity and scorn. An hour later he was on his feet again. Barker went at him viciously, as if he'd been told to finish off this disagreeable business. The squadron's combat record was taken apart mission by mission. Barker pressed hard. Pantelleria was brought up ("An example of rank cowardice. The bomber commander called what happened deliberate murder"); the catalogue of charges and distortions grew, all of them official and irrefutable. They had not failed to go in low on attacks, Fremont cried. They were not frightened by flak. Aggressiveness was their trademark and they had the kills to prove it. Yet none of this counted.

Twelfth Air Force Headquarters had recommended they see no more operational time. Their Mustangs should be taken away, the report said, to be replaced by lesser aircraft. Again Fremont tried to defend his men, but the will to justify himself was no longer powerful enough in him. His answers became more contained and lofty. ("We have served to the very best of our abilities and someday the world will know it.") Shortly after 3:00 P.M., they adjourned until the next morning. Fremont glanced at Captain Love on the way out, but the other man turned away. Detwiler and another reporter scurried past quickly.

Somewhere in the black night, a church bell tolled twice. Todd roused himself slowly, grudgingly, as if it were time to go to work. He checked Fremont, who slept on the other cot in the narrow room. Once it had been a porter's closet and a small slop sink was still on the wall, a festering breeding ground for the roaches that slithered everywhere. Todd fished around in his suitcase and took out a pair of socks. He listened again to Fremont's deep snoring, then stepped outside. Wall lights giving off their meager wattage lit the appallingly familiar scene. Soldiers in uniform lay all over the floor, contorted, grotesque, and as tightly packed as worms in a fishing can. Todd picked his way over their squalid mass, stepping on a couple of them. At the end of the corridor he reached a fire exit and crept upstairs to the next floor. Here the halls were bare and smelled of new wax. Men slept quietly in their rooms. He sneaked into a bathroom and locked the door securely.

He was breathing heavily. He pulled up one trouser leg and removed the small syringe taped to his calf. Unknotting the socks, he produced an ampoule of morphine and broke off the glass top. The needle went directly into a large vein in his arm. It felt good. It was always pleasant, too pleasant. He would not have been able to survive the terrible postoperative pain without it. After a while, he had started buying it from the medical corpsman, ampoule by ampoule. Then he stole it, hoarded it, because morphine made him feel better than anything else ever had. Morphine was *so* good. It stopped all kinds of pain, and he felt safe and secure with it running through him. But he needed more all the time. And when the stuff in the sock was gone, there wouldn't be any more.

A flash of anger touched him. The morphine wasn't working fast enough. He broke open another ampoule and hurriedly injected it. He opened another, but it slipped from his trembling hands and smashed into pieces on the floor. He cursed violently and stamped on the pieces. Pick them up, something told him. Get rid of them. He reached for them, yet they seemed so far away, so small. A pleasant fog drifted into his mind. He pushed at the tiny pieces for a long time until they were all in a corner, then giggled in satisfaction.

The next morning in a coffee shop Fremont said to Todd, "Lieutenant, your assignment for today is to be in the main lobby of the Pentagon Building at twelve forty-five. Be there on time. Please don't keep me waiting."

"I won't, sir," Todd answered quietly.

Fremont got on a trolley car and moved to the rear. He had plenty of time this morning and looked forward to a leisurely trip, for the papers were full of exciting and portentous news. Italy had surrendered to the Allies. She was out of the war. The Germans were moving to seize Rome. Rumors said the Italian government would be set up in a provincial city south of the capital. At Taranto, in the heel of Italy, the British First Airborne Division had landed and been helped ashore by Italian troops glad to be out of the fighting. But the big story came out of Salerno, far up the west coast near Naples. Here, during the night, two British divisions and one American division had executed a complex amphibious landing. The Americans had decided to go in without a naval bombardment. German flares had illuminated the men on the beaches. Many had died and panic had ruled the situation until morning. Everything was now in the balance at Salerno. If the Germans brought up reinforcements, three divisions of good men might be floundering and drowning in the beautiful Tyrrhenian sea.

The precariousness of it all annoyed Fremont. He had studied the map of Italy and knew Salerno well. It was well beyond the range of effective fighter cover. Mustangs and Spits using drop-tanks could only stay over the beach for twenty minutes. The four hundred-mile round trip was bound to be exhausting. Not only that, the whole area was ringed by mountains which gave a perfect view of the landing zone. It appeared to be another fiasco, like the parachute drop at Gela and the aborted amphibious attacks behind German lines in northeastern Sicily. There were not nearly enough men at Salerno to attempt a major landing. Fremont wondered why this invasion had been undertaken. He blamed Intelligence. They must have prepared some very favorable estimates. They must have told the High Command that after the surrender the Germans would get out of southern Italy fast and leave some choice territory around including the port of Naples, the good airfields around Foggia, and undoubtedly Rome itself. Instead a mere handhold had been gained at Salerno, and Fremont was angry. He hated to see stupidity in the field. Then a small smile lit his tired face. He was still thinking like a soldier, reacting with the passion of a commander when, after today, his career might be finished. He continued reading the paper.

At the Pentagon everyone, even the clerks, looked grave and worried. People walked more quickly, more purposefully. When he arrived at the hearing room, it was packed. Many of the spectators, especially the civilians, stared at him openly as if he were already a martyr. The panel of three generals entered and took up its place behind the long polished table. An autumn coolness seeped into the room. Fremont watched the four-star general, who betrayed no emotion. *He feels he's doing the right thing,* Fremont thought. *I know how he feels. He probably knows that Captain Love's compromise was rejected and is puzzled. The other man is different. He didn't like my performance yesterday, weak as it was. He thinks the urge to fight back even a little is unfair. I've always been unfair to what they wanted for me. I've always refused to take my medicine. There is no greater sign of disrespect.*

Fremont studied Barker, who had a stack of notes in front of him and was going through the long report on the squadron. His every gesture indicated tenacity and thoroughness. The other generals obviously liked him.

Just before Barker began, Detwiler came into the room with a group of senators. He winked at Fremont and sat down with an air of fastidious self-importance.

"Lieutenant Colonel Fremont," Barker said. "Is it true that your father, Professor Phillip Fremont, was arrested several times as a public nuisance and for creating civil disorder?"

Fremont stood motionless. "I object to this question," he responded coldly.

"That objection is in order, General Barker," the four-star general said smoothly. "The colonel's father is not part of this inquiry."

The spectators stirred.

"Very well," Barker said, "let us go on to the matter of Lieutenant Percy Skinner. Colonel Fremont, were you aware that Lieutenant Skinner embarrassed this nation before the entire world by remaining in Nazi Germany after the last Olympic Games to conduct a sordid love affair with the daughter of a prominent family?"

"I recall reading something about it at the time, yes."

Fremont heard whispered curses. He was being blamed for Skinner's audacity, but he didn't care.

"According to other sources Percy Skinner also fought on the Republican side in the Spanish civil war," Barker continued. "He lived in Spain under the name of Lieutenant Douglas. There is no record of his having returned to America with the Abraham Lincoln Brigade. In fact, he is known to have fought until the end of the war as an independent soldier of fortune. His mistress was a Communist. His closest friends were Communists."

The three-star general took off his reading glasses and slammed them down. Barker stood up, a repressed fury glinting in his eyes.

"This is the kind of man you are asking us to accept as an officer in the Air Force. He is a disgrace to his uniform and his country!"

"What have you to say to this, Colonel Fremont?" the senior general asked.

"Nothing," Fremont answered.

"Nothing?" the general said incredulously. "Colonel, I think you should know we are prepared to terminate the hearing at this point if you wish."

"I do not wish it," was the icy reply.

"Carry on, General Barker."

"Horace Walker," Barker said as he studied an index card. "Horse thief."

Laughter exploded through the hearing room.

"And a vagrant arrested in five states," Barker went on as the spectators roared with amusement.

"Shut up! Shut the fuck up in here," a ragged voice bellowed over the laughter, which died out quickly as people looked about in shock and irritated surprise.

Fremont turned around. He noticed Love standing in the back row and then saw Todd knifing across the room toward the table, his aspect busy, frantic, and deranged. He seemed to have sniffed out the smell of humiliation in the air. His brown eyes were full of mistrust and comic savagery.

"I had to come," he whispered, brushing past Fremont. "I couldn't wait."

He strode right up to the table and stopped in front of Barker, whose face was slack with astonishment and panic. Many of his index cards tumbled to the floor.

"Hello, General," Todd said with a nervous stutter.

Barker didn't answer.

"I said hello!" Todd shouted. "Don't you look at me like I'm just a nigger in the street. I'm an old friend. You were going to do a lot for me, remember?"

Barker tried to get up, but one of the generals had his arm. The senior general grasped the situation immediately.

"What has brought you here, Lieutenant?" he asked in a solicitous way.

"I am here to reaffirm my dignity as a human being," Todd said in a strong but shaky voice.

"That is not really the point of this hearing, Lieutenant."

"Lieutenant Ernest Todd, sir. Intelligence Officer, Seventy-fourth Squadron," was the angry reply.

"I see," the general said thoughtfully. "Am I to understand you are here on behalf of Colonel Fremont?"

"Ask him," Todd cried, pointing a hostile finger at Barker. "Ask that sneaky son of a bitch. He started this whole thing. He had me sent to Tuskegee."

With a barely noticeable flutter of his hand, the four-star general motioned to the stenographer to stop recording testimony. The man folded his arms across his chest.

"Go on," the general said softly.

"I am responsible for what you have been doing to Colonel Fremont," Todd said loudly, his voice enlarged by a terrible sincerity. "I wrote that book you have there," he said, pointing numbly to the official document. "I did it in collaboration with General Barker. I lied. I changed things. I disallowed kills. I did everything I could to fuck things up."

"Get the nigger out of here," a spectator shouted.

The general glanced over sharply and all was silent.

"Barker got to me. He got to me good. He wanted my private assessments. He must have known I gambled all the time and needed money. We always met at night, exchanging papers, arguing. Down at Tuskegee it was under the bridge. In Africa we went up into the hills. I became a night creature, controlled by the night, General. I was a conspirator against my own people for no real reason at all. During the day I couldn't stand myself. I had to get away from myself. I took a little morphine to relax. I started with a little and nobody knew. But that got to be a habit too, like taking money from Barker. I had nowhere to turn," Todd said, dropping his head. "I just slid under."

Fremont watched Todd's anguished reflection in the polished table. He was glad Walker's name hadn't come up.

"Now I'm here to throw myself on your mercy. Punish me. Do to me what you would have done to him," Todd pleaded as he gestured to Fremont.

After a long moment the general cleared his throat.

"Even in a case like yours that is not a simple matter," he said. "I must ask you to put this strange story into a written report and submit it to me for review."

Todd gazed at the general. He seemed trapped in a sort of pure, stupid innocence.

"What am I, a motherfucking fool?" he said, snapping into a peculiar state of alertness.

"Don't use that kind of language in here," the general warned.

"I asked you not to treat me like a nigger. I asked for human consideration," Todd stammered.

"You have been given consideration! You were not called to this hearing."

"I am going to denounce these proceedings," Todd screamed as tears ran down his cheeks. "I am going straight to the President."

Then Todd crumbled. He broke into sobs. Two MPs came up and touched his shoulders gently.

"Put him in a seat," the general ordered.

Fremont watched the MPs lead him away.

"General Barker, continue with your questions."

But Barker could not. His hands shook as he reached for the water pitcher. The three-star general had to pour it for him.

Fremont sat down on a bench in the first row for a moment. Todd had been lodged in a corner seat two rows back. No one came near him. He looked drained, eerie, and quite distant as he sat there smoking a cigarette. Detwiler maneuvered himself into a position between the two men. Todd removed a piece of paper from his wallet and scribbled something on it. Folding it in half, he tapped Detwiler on the shoulder and indicated he was to give the paper to Fremont. Detwiler hesitated, then furtively opened the message. His eyes showed idiotic concern. He glanced back, but Todd wasn't there. He had moved down the row, stepping by people with a ghostly sort of grace, and was on his way out of the room. Detwiler handed the note to Fremont, who sprang to his feet and raced through the padded doors into the corridor.

A middle-aged man came rushing up to him.

"Colored boy just went into the White bathroom," he shouted. "You've got to knock on that door and make him come out."

Fremont punched the man with every ounce of strength in his body. He dropped away, holding his stomach, his speech short-circuited by agony. From behind a bathroom door a shot exploded, reverberating powerfully down the hall. A group of MPs came running as Fremont stood frozen. They flung themselves at the heavy door, first alternately, then together. Fremont threw himself at the door wildly. A large pool of blood began seeping from underneath it, spreading like overflowing water. One of the MPs slipped and fell sprawling into the blood.

"Shit!" he screamed. "Look at me. I got nigger blood all over me."

Spectators from the hearing room flooded into the hall, jamming it so tightly there was no room to run at the door. A flashbulb popped.

"Get that camera," an MP shouted. "This is high-security area. Stop that man. He's from the press."

Detwiler was pinned against a wall.

"There's another one over there."

"You men are in trouble," an MP sergeant yelled, jabbing his club at them. "Do you hear?"

More MPs rushed into the corridor, shutting it off. They outnumbered the civilians and began herding them back toward the hearing room.

"No one is to leave this area. Return to the room, gentlemen. Please, return to the room."

Fremont stood by the unopened door, his shoes covered with blood. He didn't notice Barker until the other man was almost on top of him. Barker's face was composed now. He held a batch of folders and an index card box under one arm.

"Watch out for me, black boy," he said in a low snarling tone. "You step lightly, son of a bitch, because I'm going to chop your pecker off yet."

Then he moved on.

It was the middle of the afternoon. For a while Fremont stopped pacing up and down the length of the big oriental rug in Room 1050 and slumped into one of the leather couches. This was the same room he had reported to on arriving in Washington, but now he was alone in it. Several hours had gone by. The horror of Todd's suicide seemed so pathetic, so absolutely needless. And yet, he'd always expected a tragedy of some kind to be connected with his squadron. It was ordained. But he blamed himself for Todd's death. Somehow he'd let Todd down, failed to see how ensnared he was in his own deceptions. He knew Todd was carrying a .45. He could have taken it away almost anytime, but he hadn't bothered, and he realized now the question of why he hadn't would gnaw at him for the rest of his life.

More than an hour had been consumed in getting Todd's body out of the bathroom. The heavy wooden door proved impossible to batter off its hinges. MPs were forced to break windows and enter through the courtyard. Todd had shot himself in the mouth. His blood-drenched corpse lay directly against the door. His farewell note said, "Goodbye, Colonel. I'm sorry."

The afternoon wore on. The same first lieutenant who had told Fremont about the hearing brought him sandwiches and coffee. His manner remained frosty and reserved. He gave no hint of what might be coming. All around him Fremont sensed the government was operating, tackling the problem of what to do with him now.

In the middle of the evening as Fremont dozed, Captain Love entered the room and sat in a chair across from him. He watched Fremont's bloodshot eyes open slowly and flutter into a sleepy vigilance. "Colonel Fremont," he said slowly.

Fremont cleared his throat and straightened his tie.

"You might have told me Todd was in Washington. We might have gotten to Barker that way, Colonel."

"You could never have touched Barker," Fremont said. He was very tired of white people.

"The Chief of Staff apologizes for not being here, Colonel. He wanted to see you personally, but he's in conference over the Salerno situation."

Fremont nodded his head.

"The Army has decided to sweep this entire episode under the rug," Love continued. "It can do no one any good, and no public mention will ever be made of the hearing or subsequent events. All those present have signed documents to that effect. Detwiler has relinquished rights to whatever stories he planned to write."

"You're very thorough, Captain."

"The Army is thorough, sir," Love said. "It's the best fighting organization man has ever conceived."

"What have you done with Todd's body?" Fremont asked.

"The body is in the morgue at Walter Reed," Love answered. "Lieutenant Todd's parents are on their way to Washington from Fort Wayne to claim it. They have been told he was suffering a mental breakdown and committed suicide. I think his father understands that there is more to it, but he asked for no details."

"Todd was a morphine addict, Captain," Fremont said matter-of-factly.

Love's eyebrows arched upward.

"So that's why you didn't tell me he was around. He must have been very shaky. Well, it's a good thing they only did a partial autopsy."

"Yes, it's a good thing," Fremont said.

Just then a tall, elderly man in a black suit entered. His manner was patrician and almost jaunty. He looked like a banker, and there was a shrewdness about his eyes. Love introduced the secretary of war.

"Colonel Fremont," he said in a rather rough voice. "I find everything which has happened here in the last two days highly regrettable, as you do, I'm sure. But I don't want you to take it to heart. Please. I want you to take it as a part of your squadron's growing pains. Frankly, I'm angry at all this secrecy and head-hunting. A man like you, one of the best we have, ought never to be subjected to it."

"Thank you, Mr. Secretary," Fremont said.

"Oh, don't thank me yet," the secretary answered. "I have a real surprise for you, Colonel. Plans for that new squadron you wanted have been finalized. Yes. They are to begin training next month at Tuskegee Army Base. I'm sure they'll be every bit as good as your own men, every bit."

"We're all sure," Love said.

Fremont examined both their faces, so veiled, so clever and self-satisfied. Here was the price for his eternal silence about this matter. They were handing him his dream, all of his father's dreams. It was impossible to spit it back into their faces. He pretended to grope for adequate words and hated himself for it.

"By the way, Colonel," the secretary went on, "has Captain Love told you that you're on your way back to Sicily? We need men of your caliber over there. This war is far from over."

Fremont nodded.

"Well, good-bye," the secretary said, shaking hands. "Get back to the front safely, young man. The captain will see you to your car."

Outside, in the cool, fresh autumnal darkness, Fremont let out a long desperate sigh. Some yards away at the curb he made out a staff car.

"You handled the secretary well," Love said. "A lesser man couldn't have, you know. I've seen them stumble and fall."

"Let's forget the secretary, Captain."

"Would you like to call anyone, sir? Your wife, perhaps?"

"No, Captain," Fremont said slowly. "I don't believe so. There is one thing I'd like you to do, though."

"Anything, sir."

"You have a young lieutenant named Orlando Jones working here in the Communications Center. I want him shipped out to my squadron. He's going to be our new Intelligence man. We'll train him on the job."

"I'll see that it's done promptly."

They reached the car. The driver, a flashlight in one hand, saluted and opened the door.

"Good-bye, sir," Love said. "Have a smooth trip back."

"Will I be seeing you again?" Fremont asked.

"I'm posted here now, Colonel, so I can't really answer. The weeding-out process I spoke to you about in North Africa is far from completed. We won a round today, sir, not much more."

They shook hands. The car door closed with a muffled slam. Fremont was not surprised to see his traveling bag on the seat beside him. As the car pulled away, a figure in white materialized at the window. It was Detwiler. He gestured frantically, pounding on the window, pleading with Fremont to have the car stopped so they could talk. After a moment he vanished. The car sped through Washington and cut into the country. Soon they reached an airfield and drove right up beside a waiting C-47. Fremont was helped on board. Sitting nervously in the metal seats along the wall were a few high-ranking officers and a couple of well-dressed civilians. They took off from the unlighted field.

It was good to be in an airplane again. The drone of engines calmed him somewhat. Nearly four hours later the C-47 came in at Halifax, Nova Scotia. A pair of British generals in brown uniforms, their long red collar tabs setting off ruddy faces, got on board. They nodded to the Americans and buckled in, smoking their pipes. During the middle of the night they touched down at Goose Bay, Labrador, to refuel. By morning they had crossed the half-frozen Labrador Sea to Greenland, where they ate breakfast in the airport coffee shop. Snow and massive glaciers loomed beyond the high windows. It was all weird and rather soothing. Over the radio came news that the Germans were closing in and the Salerno beachhead might have to be evacuated.

On the long leg across the gray, desolate North Atlantic, Fremont sank into reflection. He already missed Todd, missed his vulnerability, his rages, his sad humanity. He felt ashamed of his conduct with the secretary. He should have forced the secretary to see that a man had to give up his life before a semblance of justice could be done. But it had all happened so quickly and innocuously there was almost nothing to fight against. He was left with nothing, just a sense of his own terrible fraility. Now he was absorbed into the Army more thoroughly than ever before. Never again would he play the role of challenger, because they had given him a lot of what he had asked for. Of course, he still had enemies. Barker, Johnson, and their kind. All of this knowledge made Fremont feel too wise, too knowing. He'd been willing to use Todd, to exploit him in any way, and that would be impossible to forget.

That evening, they closed the coast of Ireland and soon glided into the big grass airfield at Prestwick, Scotland. A car took Fremont to the station in Glasgow, where he caught a train for the overnight trip to Liverpool. Alone in his compartment, he hungered for battle. He read everything in the papers about Salerno. The next few days were spent in a British corvette on its way to the Mediterranean. The officers were delighted to hear he'd been at Sandhurst. In the late evenings they drank rum and stout and discussed the war. Everyone was a little saddened when they finally put in at Messina.

ELEVEN

THE STEAMY PORT was jammed with men, transport ships, and pontoon barges holding bulky engineering equipment. On the busy dockside a sergeant came up to Fremont and handed him a message. The squadron had moved to Matera, a town somewhere in southern Italy. A car waited for him at Reggio, across the Straits. He was directed to a ferry landing. The heavy flat-bottomed boat slipped out over the polished blue water. When it docked, Osborn and Beasley met him at the gangplank, smiling happily.

"Welcome to Italy, sir," Osborn said, taking his bag. "Our transportation is over here."

They were driving a captured German scout car, a *Kübelwagen*, and were very proud of it.

"It'll ruin your back, Jonathan," Beasley said, opening the door for Fremont, "but it's a superb little machine."

Sunset had come. The fiery and moist daytime heat of southern Italy had abated. Fremont, sitting beside Osborn on the front seat of the open car, surveyed the countryside, which glowed with deep, rich browns and oranges and yellows in the afterglow of yet another stunning Mediterranean day. As they sped along the twisting zigzag roads, he knew how glad he was to be back in the war, how truly glad. They saw no one. Most of the towns in this part of Italy, the Calabrian peninsula, were stretched out along the coasts. The interior, hidden from the sea and dotted with small desperate farms and impoverished villages, seemed more lonely and haunted than the far

148

reaches of the Sahara. Beasley studied Fremont. He had lost weight and looked gaunt and irritable. Fatigue bent his strong, erect body a little. His eyes shone too brightly, as if touched by pure, cold, still apprehension. Beasley made a note to give him malaria and typhus booster shots as soon as they reached the base.

"Jonathan, where is Todd?" Beasley asked after a long while.

He told them Todd was dead, that he'd confronted Barker at the hearing and then killed himself in a bathroom. Osborn said nothing and silenced Beasley by glaring in the rearview mirror. It was clear what this trip had taken out of Fremont. Still, they were fighting in Italy and that was what mattered. He produced a cigar, lit it, and tugged at the bill of his cap.

"The Luftwaffe is hurting badly, sir," he said without taking his eyes off the road. "They're short of everything. Göring ordered them to pull things together for a defense of Calabria, but the British overran all the terrain suitable for bases. We haven't done too badly. Skinner was adequate as your replacement, but the men were jittery under him. He had a habit of hesitating when you wouldn't have. Our assignment now is Salerno. The situation has eased and they're moving out now, but for a long while there it was grim. The battleships had to slip in pretty close and Ike was forced to call up heavy bombers from North Africa to plaster anything moving. That kept us on the beaches. We may get another unit citation, Colonel. We were on those Germans like flies trying to get at a piece of watermelon."

A smile touched Fremont's worn face. Osborn knew how to handle him, all right.

"Sir, the men will be really happy to see you," Osborn continued. "They seem to like serving under you. We're in pretty good shape. No injuries. No casualties. Unfortunately, we're short a man. Lieutenant Walker's not with us. He's on a Special Duty assignment. General Johnson at Twelfth Air Force HQ put him on it. Do you know him?"

"He was one of the panel at the hearing," Fremont said with quiet bitterness. "He and Barker tried to get a noose around my neck."

Osborn puffed on his cigar thoughtfully, but his expression did not change. Special Duty operations were top secret and very hazardous and a lot of the pilots who were used never returned to their squadrons.

The *Kübelwagen* rolled along the moonlit road. It was still hot. Occasionally, they passed one of the creaking brightly painted old carts common to the region. An old man holding a brace of goats with rough string tied around one hand called to them.

"Guten abend, meine Herren!"

By the roadside a donkey watched their passage. The scent of pine and eucalyptus was in the air. A velvety purple sky was pierced only by the moon. Fremont swore he could hear the soft rushing sound of the sea, but it was only the wind, just the wind.

Sharp, cramped voices speaking English could be heard now. This was British Eighth Army territory. They had conquered it within a week and Tommies were everywhere. The long thin barrels of their Bofors antiaircraft guns slanted up at the sky. Howitzers and big Sherman tanks rested just off the road.

"We got some rather sad news the other day, Colonel," Osborn said. "I haven't told the men yet because I thought you might want to. Ollie St. Clair passed away in a German prison camp. That's the way the Red Cross in Geneva got it from the German authorities. They say his death was due to natural causes. But they refuse to return the body or say which camp he was in."

Fremont sighed. He'd been expecting St. Clair's death, yet he was still horrified.

"They worked an experiment on that boy," Beasley said furiously. "I know they did, those lousy bastards. But they'll never be forced to admit it, not even when the war is over."

"We can't do anything about it, Doc," Osborn said.

"We can do *something*," Beasley almost shouted to no one in particular. "We can write letters. We can *try*."

"Keep in touch with the Red Cross, Ops," Fremont said wearily. "Badger them for details. Don't let them forget us."

"I'll do my best, Colonel."

"We've got another five miles to Matera," Osborn said. "I picked out the field myself. We're well behind the lines, located in a valley. The town itself is in the mountains.

Many of the people here are living in caves. There's a lot of malaria around, sir, an awful lot. They say wolves sneak into those caves at night and drag away the sick children."

In the distance, Fremont could see lights from the field, and his heart quickened.

Well before daylight Osborn awakened in the darkness of his tent. He lay still for a moment, enjoying the fairly cool night air. His hand reached for the flashlight near his pillow, and he examined his watch by its light. It was 0420. He pulled back the mosquito netting and popped out of bed. The sound of water cascading roughly into a glass reverberated heavily off the canvas walls. Osborn gulped down two salt tablets, then took his pistol, a bath towel, and some soap and left the tent. A breathtaking quiet hung over the field. The only light came from an area where a makeshift hangar had been built. Osborn eased into the ice-cold water lapping against the sides of a cut-down oil drum out back. He shivered uncontrollably but made no sound. Nearby, where he could reach it quickly, his cocked pistol lay on a box next to his towel. Lately, wolves had been seen slipping into the valley around dawn. Someone said they even went after men when driven wild by hunger.

Gradually the sky to the east lightened. Osborn could see the high rock walls of the mountains situated almost around them. Cooking fires were lit near the *sassi*, the cave dwellings below the town of Matera. People were moving around up there. Once or twice during the night he remembered hearing strange chants coming from those caves and wondered what was going on. He decided to ask Jennings later on because Jennings had taken a great interest in the mountain people.

More and more now, the valley became visible. Its eucalyptus trees and oleander bushes, its expanse of sedge dotted with bent and gnarled olive trees, arose from the dark light as if pushed up from the bottom of the sea. The valley was pretty in a way, stark and spectacular in the perpetual sunshine, but for Osborn it lacked the poetry of North Africa. He returned to his tent and dressed slowly. Ten minutes later he was on his way to the

Operations van, which sat near the cottages used as a Briefing hut, social club, and Fremont's personal quarters.

The long, high van looked rather bizarre on its enormous truck tires with awnings coming off both sides and heavy cables running to the generator about twenty yards away. Osborn could hear the generator humming as he got closer and mounted the wooden steps leading into the van. Corporal Reeves, the man on duty, stood up in the narrow interior filled with maps, charts, telephone lines, and file cabinets. He saluted Osborn and handed him a cup of very hot coffee.

"Thanks, Reeves," Osborn said. "How are things?"

"Fine, sir," Reeves answered. "You're right on time as usual."

The bell on the teletype machine rang loudly. A message clacked out on the roll of yellow paper which billowed up in Osborn's hands as he read it. It was pretty much what he expected, and he was pleased. He pictured the way today's operation at Salerno had been assembled. First the big conference at Alexander's underground bunker at Malta or Ike's headquarters in downtown Algiers. Cunningham and Tedder, the overall naval and air commanders, would be there in person or be represented by their staffs. They would decide whether to send bombers on the long run from North Africa, today, and talk about the deployment of tactical fighter strength. Their plan would go to 12th AFHQ, then down to the groups and squadrons nearest the battleground. Now he was reading about it. He was enthralled by it. The scope, organization, energy, and power in this war never ceased to fascinate him. He turned to the corporal.

"Wake the men up, Reeves. Briefing at 0520."

Inside the thatched-roof stone cottage which served as a Briefing hut, it smelled dank. The pale rosy early-morning sky still sparkling with a few last stars was visible through a large hole in the ceiling. There were only two benches, and most of the pilots stood along the walls in full gear, their arms folded across their chests as they waited for Osborn to begin. Quickly, he stepped up on one end of the half-completed stage. The cottage seemed to hold within its battered walls the solemnity of a deserted country chapel, and he liked that.

"We're on search and destroy today," he said to the men. "The Germans are pulling back from the Salerno area much more rapidly than we thought. Keeping contact has been hard. Right now we're moving through ghost towns. We don't really know where the hell Kesselring has moved the bulk of his army, but if they get into the mountains and string out in another defensive line, it could be hell. The terrain favors them, just like northeastern Sicily. A single .88 can cover the whole valley floor and hold up a division. We've got to seek out Kesselring's rearguard people and tear them apart."

He answered all their questions patiently. The German rear guards, mostly crack infantrymen on motorcycles, did their job well. They set up machine-gun nests with sharpshooters above them and retreated smoothly when things got too rough. "Watch for mirror signals in the hills," Osborn told them, "watch for dust plumes from their motorcycles. Never stop searching. Hit anything suspicious. Bore in on them. Bore in."

On the flight line he watched them take off and circle the field, forming up in the clear sunny sky. Fremont, who had been grounded by Beasley for forty-eight hours so he could rest, moved up beside him and looked on silently. He stood straight and was immaculate as always. Osborn's eyes were on the planes, on the men. Takeoff was a poignant moment in the day's routine. Unfailingly it made him feel guilty and treacherous. He wished all planes could return safely and no one ever had to die. But this was impossible and foolish and dangerously sentimental. In the next instant he was angry with himself for thinking this way.

When they left, climbing northeast with deceptive speed, Osborn went to the mess hall for breakfast. He picked rather absently at the unappetizing powdered eggs and sliced fruit on his plate, part of a regimen Beasley had put him on as his waistline began to swell. He would be complaining of fatigue in the middle of the day. Mentally, he followed the path of the Mustangs through the limpid sky, over the high mountains cut by turbulent rivers in deep valleys. He saw the smashed German tanks, the bomb craters, the downed bridges being rebuilt by Army engineers. He saw the Spitfires and Douglas Havocs roaming to the west and for one brief moment wished he too were a fighter pilot. But he'd never had the nerve, the steely recklessness, to fly in combat. Instead he was left with a little envy, a little regret.

He went back to the Operations van and listened in on radio transmissions for a while. The squadron had surprised a large patrol and cut it up. Then, Archibald spotted a pair of .88 guns. They dived on them. No luck. Sherman tanks with infantrymen behind them were moving across a valley toward the guns. Three were on fire. They dived on the guns again. Someone warned about ground fire. No luck again, followed by a lot of angry cursing. Osborn handed Reeves the headset and lit his first cigar of the day. He rolled it in his mouth with roguish pleasure. If they didn't get to Rome soon, he might never lay his hands on another good cigar. He was down to five a day now, and Rome was far away, too far to think about. Once more he took up the headphones. The gun crews were dead. Everyone was excited.

At mid-morning the squadron returned. The ground crews streamed out onto the dusty runway to refuel the Mustangs while the pilots, walking around slowly to get the stiffness out of their legs, ate sandwiches and drank hot coffee. Some of them talked with their mechanics as they ate. Orders were shouted. Men bustled to and fro. Skinner stood beside his plane, chatting with Fremont about all they had seen. Just before takeoff Osborn called them together. He told them heavy artillery pieces and a column of the new Tiger tanks had just been spotted north of the Volturno River.

"Take them out if you can, but be careful. Messerschmitt 410s might be in the area. They've been showing up a lot lately when the chips are down. At Schweinfurt they broke up in the bomber boxes for the first time and scattered planes all over the place, so be on the lookout, especially you men giving top cover. All right, let's clear out of here."

The men jogged back to their planes, parachutes flopping low on their backs.

The valley reverberated with the diminuendo and harsh

crescendo of airplanes taxiing and going to full power. Dust whipped everywhere in vicious swirls. Osborn watched the last plane leave, then strolled back toward the van. His thoughts switched to Walker. He liked Walker maybe best of all the men, liked his brashness and terrific courage under fire. If anyone had better than an even chance of returning from Special Duty operations, it was Walker. But he only had to fail once, fail to blow up a ship or kill an important general on the road, and he might be dead. The strain of these operations was overwhelming, stifling, and a lot of men got sloppy and careless and never came back. Walker wouldn't crack, though, Osborn was sure of that; no, human stupidity, cowardice, and treachery would kill Walker.

Unfortunately the same was not true of everyone. Several of the men now flying might reach the end of their tether soon, without really knowing it. They would continue to go on operations, continue to try for kills that weren't really there, and then come back each day just a little bit more weary and shaken. This was when men crashed and burned on takeoff or were shot out of the sky by some young pilot on his first mission. It always happened that way, and Osborn felt an obligation to spot these men and prevent their disintegration. Skinner was under his scrutiny. Beneath all his composure Skinner never failed to try too hard. For some reason he labored. He never scaled the heights of crazed inner abandon needed to be a top fighter pilot. Walker had guessed he was working on a death wish and was waiting to be mutilated in his cockpit by a rain of shells and bullets. Others felt that Skinner had conceived some kind of feeling of brotherhood with the Germans that kept him from being a killer. He listened to German broadcasts at night when almost everyone else was asleep.

Then there was Jennings. He'd become a stable pilot, but since the death of Donny Beaumont, an uneasy quietude had masked his feelings. He might get over it; he might not. Archibald, who was flying well, could become a problem at any time. Homosexuals had a way of exploding, of being scarred easily and deeply.

Osborn missed the calm regularity of their day patrols out of North Africa. Here in Italy he feared a breakdown in discipline. There was more tension to be dealt with here, more subtle excitement. The front was always relatively near. There were probing and spoiling attacks to think about, even a commando raid or a parachute drop. Also, it was impossible to keep the men out of the nearby towns where they would go hungrily looking for women. Anything could happen, for the men seemed to be more sociable now. Obviously, they thought their presence was more acceptable in Europe than it had been in colonial North Africa where the place of a dark-skinned foreigner was difficult to define in the landscape. Already he had heard it around that Skinner had a woman in Bari, thirty kilometers away. She was said to be quite beautiful and a titled aristocrat, the daughter of a cabinet minister in the exiled Italian government.

That evening after dinner Osborn sat in the Operations van going over the day's debriefing reports. The clarity and precision of these reports (although much was not really accurate) drove him to reflect some more on the life around him. He deplored the fact that life was so untidy, so ragged and fraught with personal involvement and with sensitive people like Todd, Skinner, even Fremont, in his way, too. When he thought about it, most of the men fell into this category. They were too complex for their own good. He was glad to be an essentially simple man and proud to serve in the United States Army, safely removed from his former existence of lower-middle-class struggle. He never really liked striving to be the exceptional black man. Osborn wanted to be normal.

He had been born thirty-four years ago in Philadelphia and had been raised in the same small row house where his father still lived. His mother had died when he was a baby and he grew up under the kindly tutelage of his father, who taught carpentry and drafting in the Philadelphia high schools. Their house was on the edge of a rough Italian district. As a boy, he fought many violent battles in the streets and quickly proved his independence and toughness. After a while the Italians left him alone, but the black boys called him lazy and stupid because he refused to emulate their swaggering bitterness and get into a street gang. Two years in a row he won a *Phila-*

delphia Bulletin circulation contest for newsboys. He was heartbroken when someone stole the trophies from his house and smashed them in the gutter. Still, he matured in his quiet, industrious way, and after high school he moved on to Penn State instead of to the black college in the South his guidance counselor had recommended. Despite his bulk and lack of both height and speed, he made the football team as a second-string tackle. His grades in mechanical engineering kept him on the Dean's List every semester, and he studied business management as a minor.

Upon graduation he descended into oblivion. There were no jobs, especially for a black man. He dug ditches for the state highway department and ran a playground for a while before his father helped him get a job teaching industrial arts in a trade school. He lived at home. Years passed. He put aside the idea of marriage because he was sure his adult life had not yet begun. His girl friends tended to be older women who just wanted to go out and have a good time. When he read about the formation of a black fighter squadron, he was overjoyed. Here was what he'd been scanning the papers for, ever since war broke out in Europe. His blind, dogged intuition had paid off and he felt truly alive and keen to be tested as a man. His father, in his reserved, whimsical way, was rather proud of him and promised not to die before he returned. They corresponded every other week, right on schedule.

"Sir?" It was Reeves, looking at his watch. "It's 2100 hours. You asked me to remind you."

"See you in the morning, Corporal."

"Good night, sir."

He trudged across the field toward the infirmary, his mind ticking off a list of details for tomorrow. Jones was coming in from Washington to take on the Intelligence job, and that would be a relief. Also, he meant to speak to the armorer about fitting on fuselage bomb racks. At the infirmary, Beasley greeted him as if he were a small boy. He stripped and got on the scale, weary of this nightly ritual.

"Not bad, Ops," the doctor said pleasantly. "I'm beginning to be proud of you."

They had some vermouth and talked for a few minutes,

then Osborn headed back to his tent. He slipped his .45 under the pillow and dropped into bed. From the mountain caves high above the valley, he heard rhythmic, frenzied shouts mingled with the baying of wolves.

TWELVE

WALKER LAID DOWN the book of Victorian poetry he was reading and got up from his bed. A pall of ennui and vexation, which had become part of his days ever since he'd been transferred to Special Duty, touched him again. He drifted out onto the balcony of his hotel room. The handsome town of Foggia, until recently an important Luftwaffe forward base, spread around him. To the west a mountain chain snaked its way down to the foot of Italy. To the east and north, where the ground was flat, some of the best airfields in that part of the world were already being used to launch strikes against the fortified German lines not too far way. Walker's gaze moved down into the piazza, now bathed in tawny twilight. The baroque facades of the houses glowed regally. Colors seemed richer and more resonant. British soldiers, part of Monty's Eighth Army, which was moving up this coast, strolled by, talking and smoking. A group of old men sitting at tables drank coffee and chatted amicably. It was clear that everyone welcomed the British, that everyone felt released from the fear and desperation of German soldiers in their midst. Young men still in uniform promenaded with their girls, and a few small children were around. But none of this cheered Walker. He missed the squadron. He missed Appaloosa.

This ain't where I want to be, he said to himself.

He sat down on the bed and withdrew the knife from his boot, studying his face in the glittering blade. A few of the British officers had tried to start conversations with him in the hotel dining room, but he'd always found it hard to talk to educated white people, so he ate in his room. He was hungry now and was relieved to hear the sound of the maid, Emilia, coming upstairs. Then her footsteps came to a halt. He heard her high, prattling voice break out sharply, as if to warn someone off. She moved a couple of steps, only to begin again, her words lashing at some unknown intruder far down the stairs. The door flew open wildly. Emilia, beautiful and buxom, came in, glancing warily over her shoulder.

"Signore Tenente. Signore Tenente," she snapped in alarm and exasperation, pointing to the doorway where a young American sergeant materialized very tentatively.

She reached for Walker's arm, clutching it tightly, a barely audible giggle in her throat as the sergeant stepped across the threshold, looking at them in amazement. He could not seem to take his eyes off Emilia's hand as it rested rather sensually on Walker's tan uniform sleeve.

"Sir, I'm early today," the sergeant said apologetically. "They asked me to come for you right away."

"I won't be able to eat," Walker said to Emilia in English. She nodded attentively and smiled, showing perfect white teeth. Her brown eyes fixed him warmly. She did a little curtsy and then swept up the tray and left the room quickly while Walker strapped on his pistol.

Sergeant Bates brought the covered jeep around to the main entrance of the Hotel Grande Italia.

"It looks like a Model T automobile," an old man said, pointing his cane tremulously at the high rickety top frame fitted tightly with canvas. "That is exactly what it looks like, a Model T automobile. I know because I had one."

Walker climbed in. He took note of a group of Tommies lounging nearby. Yesterday, one of them had remarked that he was probably some kind of colonial mercenary and not a real American. He spat in their direction. Emilia appeared on the steps of the hotel and bustled down to the jeep. She handed Walker some bread and a hunk of salami tied in a kitchen towel, and disappeared around the back. The jeep shot ahead. They rolled through the flat countryside. It was getting cooler early in the evening now, and Walker remembered November was just a few days off. Tonight he could smell the sea breeze coming from the Adriatic. The jeep's headlights hurtled over the barren road. Orange and lemon groves, wheat fields, and small dusty orchards overrun with rocks faded in the dying sun. Walker cut a piece of salami and handed it to Bates.

"Sir, I noticed you were reading a book of poetry," Bates said, as he took a bite of the meat.

For a second, Walker was surprised. "Yeah, man," he replied with a trace of reluctance. "I like a little poetry. It helps me to forget about this war."

Bates smiled faintly and nodded. He said nothing more, and Walker was glad. He didn't want to reveal too much of himself. These Special Duty people were too sharp for their own good. He wondered by and by if he would be killed tonight. Probably not. Probably after all this rushing it would be the same old shit: sitting around that goddamn shack in the middle of nowhere with Borgman, just sitting there on standby until 0200, then riding back into Foggia, half-asleep, on the rear seat to keep from falling out on the road. *Wonder if all the boys are alive and okay,* he thought. *Fremont should be back from Washington by now, if he's comin' back.* At that moment they turned off the road. Minutes later they reached a small airfield. On the runway, the sleek nose of a lone Mustang was merging with the darkish backdrop. The jeep pulled up in front of a low shabby hut lit brightly from within.

The door opened and Major Borgman stepped forward to greet Walker, the gold oak leaves on his collar glistening in the soft light. Bates saluted and vanished discreetly.

"Lieutenant Walker, tonight I've got a job for you," Borgman said as they went inside.

Walker glanced at him quickly. Borgman was taller than he, perhaps a full head taller. He was muscular. As usual, his uniform was incredibly fresh, his shoes dazzlingly polished, his tie stuck between the second and third buttons on a crisp new shirt. A West Point man.

Inside the hut several metal lampshades hung from the low-pitched roof creaking in the wind. Chairs were scattered about. On a blackboard something was written out in big elegant German script. Not long ago this had been a dispersal hut for Luftwaffe pilots flying against the Salerno beachhead. Borgman spread out a map on a small table in front of the blackboard. He and Walker turned a couple of chairs around and studied it.

"Tonight you'll be going to Ferrara," Borgman said carefully. "It's in northern Italy, not far from Venice."

Walker looked at the thoughtful light-brown eyes facing him. He examined the earnest mouth turned down in an expression of concern and suspected for a fleeting moment that Borgman didn't grasp what the Army was asking of him.

"It should be a routine flight, Horace. You'll be doing nothing special, just picking up a man in the uniform of an Italian officer and bringing him back here. The Germans haven't garrisoned Ferrara yet, so you'll be pretty safe."

"Okay," Walker said, letting out a long sigh. "Okay."

"You'll be flying over the Adriatic almost all the way. There should be no flak, and no night fighters that we know of operate in this theater. You'll be well beyond their radar, so you don't have to worry about that."

"Where do I have to turn inland?" Walker asked.

"Right here at the village of Comacchio," Borgman answered, pointing at the map. "It's lodged between the coast and the north shore of a very large lake. You can't miss it in the moonlight. That will bring you into Ferrara on dead reckoning. When you leave the coast, I want you to consult your target map immediately. Navigate carefully, and don't be disturbed by anything, by searchlights, sirens, or any noises that might reach you. The landing zone is here, outside of Ferrara, to the west. When you reach approximately fifteen hundred feet, the man on the ground will signal with a light. Make one pass and check him. Six short flashes. Two long. Six and then two long. Don't forget that. If the pattern varies or the spot is not the one you expect, do not land."

Borgman stared at him tensely, implying that what he said was a direct order subject to stern punishment.

"Always follow this rule, Lieutenant. It may save your life. Sometimes the Germans are waiting, and they try to confuse our pilots with random signals."

"Suppose they're down there anyway, then what?"

"If they have set up an ambush, they won't shoot until you try to take off," was the terse answer. "They want you alive. Therefore, while you are on the ground, you are never safe. You must hustle your contact man into the airplane and get off in no more than thirty to forty-five seconds. If your passenger is frightened, it is up to you to remain calm. Remember, waste no time. We know you have the discipline for this. That's why the general picked you—because you have the discipline."

Silence filled the hut.

Walker's chair scraped against the wooden floor. "Man, give me a fuckin' cigarette," he said peevishly.

Borgman's lighter clinked open. He watched Walker move about the hut nervously, his large eyes flashing anxiously in that round boyish dark face. Over half the men he sent out were killed on their first mission, but he possessed a peculiar and unfathomable trust in Walker. He'd never known any black people before, yet he liked Walker, liked his service record and his strange personality brimming over with crudity and ingenuousness.

Walker came back to the table, hands in pockets, the cigarette dangling arrogantly from his full lips. Borgman fished around in a pile of papers next to him and took out a photograph.

"Is that the dude?" Walker asked, holding it up under the light. "He looks German."

"He's from northern Italy. A lot of people up there have Austrian blood and are fair-skinned."

Walker stared at Borgman very solemnly, as if he weren't sure whether to believe him. His attention returned to the photograph.

"You'd best be quick, or shame on you, brother," he grumbled.

Outside, the sky was still streaked with fiery red bands of sunset. They walked over the grass to the airplane rather slowly, Borgman trailing Walker's diminutive silhouette and carrying his parachute. The plane, a modified P-51 painted dull black, boasted only two machine guns and had no armor plating. A tiny seat was installed behind the pilot. As they came up, the engine kicked over and Bates popped out of the cockpit.

Walker put on his parachute and smoked his last cigarette while Borgman went over final details.

"Don't break radio silence unless you're in trouble, Lieutenant. If your engine isn't running right, return to base. Your contact man is instructed not to stay beyond a certain hour. Another thing, don't get out of the airplane.

Don't ever. And don't shut down the engine for any reason. All you do is open the canopy. The passenger will climb in the back. He'll be carrying a small suitcase. He is not allowed to bring anything else."

Walker got into the cockpit and checked his instruments as Borgman went to work on his straps and looked around surreptitiously to make sure he was carrying a pistol and an escape kit and was wearing clean clothes. A soiled shirt or pants had a bad effect on wounds. He handed Walker a small canvas pouch.

"There's a lot of Italian money inside and a letter describing you as an American flyer lost behind enemy lines. Let's hope you never need it, Horace."

"You can say that shit again," Walker mumbled to himself.

"And here's your coffee," Borgman said with a polite smile as he handed Walker a Thermos bottle. "Don't drink it all. You might have to go to the bathroom."

Walker took the Thermos and stuck it into the spare map case. Gallantly he threw his white silk scarf over his shoulder and waved to the two men on the ground. The canopy closed. He checked all cockpit lights and position lights, then opened his personal escape kit and removed a flashlight. He gripped the shiny metal cylinder thoughtfully and glanced out at Borgman. *He forgot to give me a flashlight! If I didn't have my own, I wouldn't be able to see in all this dark.* "Dummy!" he yelled at Borgman, who could not hear him. "You big dumb ass, quit all that smilin'."

The Mustang began to taxi out. Walker disliked flying a plane when somebody else had started the engine. It was bad luck. He went to full throttle and roared away from the field. The undercarriage retracted smoothly. He climbed over the purple-and-black mountains spotted in their upper reaches by white towns, now yellowish brown in the afterglow of sunset. The plane smelled funny to Walker. The scent of someone else's sweat, someone else's fear, clung to his nostrils. He rode upward in silence, then leveled out at 25,000 feet and shifted to the auxiliary tank. He wanted to use it up as quickly as possible. Like most pilots, he disliked drop-tanks because they slowed him down and tended to develop air locks that could make an engine cut out and send a plane diving out of control.

The Adriatic Sea stretched below him, peaceful, lonely, its gray surface topped by choppy wavelets. To the east somewhere lay Yugoslavia with its dozens of large offshore islands. A numbing cold seeped into the plane, and Walker was glad to be wearing his sheepskin boots. He began to hum to himself, for he could sense a mood of depression coming on. He had come to Europe to fight with his friends and enjoy life for a change, but now he seemed headed nowhere. Things had never really worked out the way he expected.

"Not at all the way I expected," he said aloud. "Life sure fooled me. Never got a shot at squadron leader, then Todd slipped off my hook, if you can picture that. I come up with nothin' so far. Only thing I got are my kills. That's all really. Just them kills. Well, at least they can't take that away from me. But it all could have been so different. If I'd been Rommel, I wouldn't have to worry about any of this shit. That's where it all went wrong, when I wasn't born Rommel."

He reflected on his kills—the FWs, the Messerschmitts, and the Junkers dropping and crumbling from the skies under his blazing guns and devastating cannon shots. He remembered each of them in delicate and exquisite detail. And oddly, they melded in with the soft memories of his childhood and of his hard, lost, bitter years in the Depression. They became something unique to him, something to always hold onto, a constellation of achievement, the beginnings of a mythology. Abruptly though, he recalled where he was and what he was doing, and a fit of resentment seized him.

"They're fuckin' with me again," he said in a feverish irrational voice. "Using me just like a mule in the yard."

An angry cry escaped his lips. He squeezed the gun switch harshly, and the Mustang jolted as spurts of orange flame leapt from both wings.

Suddenly he was more alert. Sound carries a long way over water. He listened for the sound of an engine and, picking none out of the silence, confidently patted the two .45s strapped to his chest.

"I'll blow a few heads if it comes down to that," he whispered.

The danger in this mission, the myriad possibilities for betrayal and incompetence, surfaced uneasily in his mind.

He could not forget the briefing at Tuskegee when they had been given the option of taking L tablets, and he quailed. By that time there were a lot of atrocity stories around. Jewish people were supposed to be disappearing from their hometowns all over Europe. Walker wondered where they had gone. Borgman and people like him, they knew all about it. But they were keeping it quiet. They were sitting behind their desks, smiling like Cheshire cats because they really didn't care. No, they didn't care. After the war, they had the world by the balls anyway. It was them on top and everybody else down in the ditch. Just like old times.

He was very cold now. His toes felt frozen in spite of the heavy boots, his gloved fingers frigid around the stick. Cramps shot up his back, but he couldn't move around because the seat had been placed too far forward. Strangely, his body was damp with sweat.

Out of habit, he searched the sky around the clock. He saw many things along the barely distinguishable Italian coast and sensed the location of others. He noted landmarks, the places where mountains came almost down to the sea, the course of the coast, the changes in direction it took, all this quickly and instinctively. If he ever had to come this way again, he felt confident of knowing the route even if it were cloudy and no moon came out to help him.

He flew on. Time passed more quickly. The town of Rimini, a host of small coastal villages, and then Ravenna drifted under his wings. Only a couple of towns lay between him and Comacchio, the point where he turned in overland again. He studied the target map intently, surprised at how far north he was. ("Damn, I'm halfway to heaven.") Ferrara, his destination, was a mere 150 miles from Lake Como and the sanctuary of Switzerland. He put aside the map and began to descend.

He found the lake easily. It was enormous, glistening down there in the moonlight like a silver coin, and it appeared to be almost a part of the sea. He continued to lose altitude as he followed its northern shore. The target map was very good. A railroad line cropped up right where it should be. He was well inside the target area but felt rather safe. There were no lights, no sign of people.

It was like flying over a country not at war. Ferrara came into view: red tile roofs interspersed among tall cypresses, a cathedral, the cobblestone streets of an ancient town. But something was wrong. His field of vision was narrow. He was low and moving too fast, much too fast. A band of high-tension wires loomed up right ahead, gleaming just beyond his nose. He pulled up hard, listening for a twanging noise as his mouth went dry with terror. The plane was hurtling low, screaming off into the sky. He looked down. A light seemed to be flashing down there, on and off, on and off, plaintively. Ferrara was behind him. Around he came again, disoriented, searching for the landing ground. A dense row of poplars screened out everything. There was no time to maneuver. He burst through them, banking slightly to starboard, trying not to hear the crunching of the wings as the whole airplane trembled fiercely. Momentarily the stick jumped out of his hands. He seized it instantly. He was clear. Only his excessive speed had saved him. He cursed in rage and confusion. The whole town must be awake, even the cats and dogs. He swung west by the compass, scanning the ground once more. Again a light appeared. Short bursts, followed by long flashes. He counted them twice. His man was down there.

In from the east he swooped, gliding in lightly as if nothing had happened, praying he hadn't misread the signal. He was in a huge open space, a meadow of some kind, and had to slow down quickly so there would be room to get out. One hand to the stick, he cranked back the canopy, peering into the darkness. A man came plunging forward out of the gloom. He seemed to take an hour to get to the plane. He was carrying a suitcase and a large canvas bag. Walker squeezed his brakes. The stranger sprinted hard and gained the wing, but just as he was about to climb in, Walker reached over and punched the bag out of his hand.

"Son of a bitch, I only take the suitcase. They told you that," he yelled.

The stranger sat down behind him without uttering a word. Walker turned in curiosity and directed his flashlight right into the man's face. He didn't look too much like the picture. He was thinner. His gray eyes were glazed

with pleasure and a childish sort of mystery. His features
were clean and boyish and sensitive. He possessed thick
tousled ash-blond hair. And he didn't flinch when he saw
the .45 pointed between his eyes.

"Who are you, man? Be quick or be dead."

This was met with an enigmatic smile.

"Pull off the top of that trench coat so I can see your
uniform."

Delicately the stranger drew his black leather trench
coat from his shoulders. His face was flushed with excitement.

Two gold stars over a slanted bar on the shoulder boards
of a black uniform. A single star under two gold stripes,
with the top one in a loop, could be glimpsed on his fore-
arm. "It's him. I can see that now," Walker muttered to
himself.

He picked up the spare oxygen mask and casually threw
it back over his shoulder. Then he saw the headlights come
toward them and stop. Men got out and fired, their pistols
sparking in the moonlight. Gently, the throttle eased inward, and they lunged ahead. Walker squeezed the gun
switch. Soldiers fell or fled from their path, yelling in
German. The Mustang shot all the way out over the Adriatic.

"Put on your mask, boy. We goin' upstairs," Walker
shouted to his passenger.

They leveled off at 15,000 feet and sped southward.
Halfway home, a slim white hand jutted over his shoulder,
and Walker studied it for a minute as if its presence were
a reproach to him.

"Celestino," a somewhat refined voice said. "Tenente
Celestino," the man behind him repeated, introducing
himself.

Walker shook the hand and mumbled something gruffly.

"They won't follow us, my friend," Celestino said in
English. "I can assure you. They have no pursuit planes
to take up this chase. We are safe."

Walker half turned in his straps, amused and already
slightly irritated by this young man.

"Long as you're back there and I'm up here, you don't
assure me of a fuckin' thing," he snapped.

They stayed close to the coast, closer than Walker

thought was really safe. But they had no choice. He was worried. The starboard aileron was badly damaged and hardly responded when he moved the stick. Many of the panels on that wing had been torn loose as he hit the trees, and he feared the wing root might have been weakened. His oil temperature crept up slowly. Flying over the sea in a strange airplane with a hot engine alarmed him much more than coming down near one of these fishing villages. On the ground you could always run until they hunted you down. Over the water you were sitting in your own coffin.

He cut as far back on engine revolutions as he dared. He could tell Celestino was concerned about the strong smell of heated oil in the cockpit, startled by the sight of the huge propellor laboring to turn over, and he felt very much in control of things. After a long while they approached the vicinity of Foggia. Walker broke radio silence to broadcast the code letters which indicated all had gone well. The bright moon swam behind the clouds. Out ahead, somewhere on the dark surface of the earth below, a ghostly flare path of pale blue lights appeared. Walker headed for the center of it in a perfect glide. As he touched down, the path extinguished itself.

He switched off. They got out of the plane without talking, separated by their own weariness. Borgman cruised up in a jeep. His greeting to Celestino, who sat on his suitcase, pulling at a cigarette, was cool and strictly formal. Walker got in back of the jeep. To his surprise, Borgman conversed with Celestino in perfect Italian as they rode in. He noticed a certain tautness and friction between the two men, but he kept out of it. His part was done. He wasn't supposed to know anything more about this. He was just a chauffeur when you came down to it, just somebody hired on to do a little work.

At the hut Borgman came to him.

"Thanks, Horace," he said warmly. "You did a fine job tonight. Congratulations on getting your feet wet. Bates will drive you back to Foggia so you can get some sleep. We'll be in touch."

"Okay, Major," Walker answered, breaking off a snappy salute. "Glad to be of service."

The sergeant emerged, as if he'd been lurking in the

darkness watching things all along. As they sped away, Walker heard violent shouting from inside the hut.

The drive back to town passed very quickly. Walker got out in front of the hotel and surveyed the empty piazza. It had rained during the evening and the stacked chairs where the old men congregated glistened mutely under a street lamp. He was glad to be back in Foggia. What had happened during the last few hours seemed to be a dream. He didn't notice Bates examining him closely.

"Goodnight, Lieutenant," Bates said. "Glad you made it back."

The jeep curved around over the wet paving stones and was gone. Walker strode through the elegant lobby past the plush brocaded armchairs and gilt-edged coffee tables and climbed the sweeping staircase to his room. He was enervated, drained from within by powerful tensions and anxieties he hadn't realized were there. On a bedside stand a kerosene lamp threw its soft full arc over most of the room, leaving the ceiling in pitch darkness.

"Cozy as a cabin," he mumbled, taking off his heavy sheepskin boots.

Someone had put a bottle of Strega and a glass on the floor next to his bed. He poured a drink and sipped at it eagerly, surprised by its sweetness and strange yellow color. The volume of poetry lay where he had left it, face down on the bed. Walker stretched out and began to read a poem by Kipling.

A soft rather formal knock sounded at the door and Emilia came in. As she entered the circle of light, Walker saw she had a tray with fruit, cheese, and a carafe of wine.

"Hello," she said. Her English was somewhat abrupt and strangled.

Again Walker was astonished by her beauty. She was about forty years old and quite tall. Her manner veiled both elegance and brusqueness beneath a strong sensual quietude. Her skin was tan, her black hair streaked with whitish gray. Deep-set, heavily lidded dark eyes studied him. Emilia's mouth curved upward in an expression of private satisfaction, and she smiled, revealing those fine strong teeth. She was one of the best-looking women

Walker had ever seen. Yet he had been avoiding her all along, been a little afraid of her, and now he realized it.

She set the tray down between them and, tucking her long print dress between her legs, swung onto the bed. Her eyes, which often showed haughtiness, seemed to melt with adoration. Walker was drawn to her. *This is a real woman, not no girl*, he thought. Her boldness in coming into his room now, in touching his arm in front of Bates, all this excited him. He had only had a white woman once. One time in Kansas City when he came around to the kitchen door of a big house asking for food, she was back there in the kitchen drinking a little, waiting for the first man that came along. She told him to come back the next night, too. It had to be a trap, had to be set up for her husband to take his revenge. When the hour came he was five hundred miles away from that unlatched kitchen door. Over here in Europe he was supposed to be free. But he did not feel free.

Emilia smiled. She poured them both wine and broke off some of the hard crusty bread and put some cheese on it. He did the same, imitating her gestures.

Walker was touched by her. He spoke to her in English, his tone confidential and tender.

"You don't want me, girl. I'm nobody. I wasn't nobody when I came over here. Nobody at all, really. Just a nigger out back washin' dishes in some hash house. Sometimes they let me make a sandwich. That's all there was to me."

One hand reached forward. A long finger pressed gently against his lips, silencing him. She seemed to understand what he was saying and this surprised Walker. He watched her large rough hands slice the fruit. Her absorbed and calm manner fascinated him. She seemed attuned to him and unafraid of what was harsh and sentimental in his character. Their hands met over the tarnished silver-plated tray, touched briefly, moved away. He took a slice of pear. Their eyes came together hungrily. He smiled as Emilia lowered her eyes demurely. He saw her luscious full breasts straining against the simple flowered dress. She wore no brassiere. Her nipples were large. She glanced at him sidelong now, nostrils flaring just a bit. They were riveted to each other in a moment of silent, powerful recognition. A tiny gasp escaped from her mouth as she fell into his arms. Their mouths sank into each other hotly. She felt good, very good, and was as strong as a potion or a drug. They rolled over, laughing softly.

"So you want to see my Brown Betsy," Walker said before the lamp went out.

She was more tender and carnal than he ever imagined a woman could be. He was overcome by her. She made him so happy he almost cried. They slept together, their heavy brown and tan limbs intertwined. When he awoke at dawn, Emilia was gone, but he knew she would be back.

He arrived at the hut early that evening. Borgman wasn't there. Outside, a very misty rain blew in short, fitful gusts. It got a little colder every day, and Walker dreamed of what it would be like to spend the winter with Emilia, sleeping in his warm room at night. *Took me by surprise. Only woman to do it,* he thought in pleasant disbelief while filling his corncob pipe. He opened the door and stepped into the strange raw weather. The sun came through, spreading a last golden haze over the wet dying grass. Off near the plane a rainbow formed, and he watched it intently. An old man who claimed he'd been born into slavery had once told him rainbows brought good luck to the person who saw them first.

Walker turned. The yellow headlights of a jeep swerved onto the field and came up to him. Borgman, carrying a bulging briefcase under his arm, got out quickly, glancing at his watch. He had about him that air of purposefulness Walker always mistrusted.

"Sorry I'm late, Lieutenant," he said, leading the way into the hut. "Our conference at Divisional HQ ran a bit longer than usual."

Borgman unpacked his briefcase as Walker smoked quietly. His bland face appeared slightly reddened by urgency and by something else, something he didn't talk about.

"I'm sending you very far north tonight, so you'll need an early start," he said at last, revealing a tiny smile that was rather disarming. "For the time being you'll be working with Celestino, dropping him in towns behind German lines, then picking him up in other towns a couple of days later."

Walker puffed on his pipe to indicate he understood.

"This man Celestino is a strange person. Frankly, I

don't care for him," Borgman continued, his voice more serious and reflective. "He's an attractive personality, I'll grant that. And he's a great leader among the partisans operating in the German rear, perhaps the best leader they'll ever get. But he's elusive. Somehow we can never be sure of him."

"You can never be sure of anybody," Walker said. "I know that for a fact."

A heavy brown folder cracked open between them. "Let me give you a little background on the man you'll be traveling with and risking your neck for, Lieutenant. Celestino is a brilliant man, a graduate of the oldest university in Italy. At the age of twenty-six he was a professor of Italian literature, an unheard-of feat. He has a quick brain and a talent for organization that is very impressive. I think he could raise an army in a week if we asked him to."

"Who put all this badness into him?"

"We don't really know," Borgman admitted. "And it is a mite disturbing to the Army. He sold himself to Intelligence the same way he did to the peasants, as some kind of hero. The name Celestino is an alias. It's some kind of a symbolic name, linking him with the heavens or lofty noble ideas. To tell you the truth, I don't understand it myself.

"Our anonymous letter file on Celestino is voluminous. We have information on him from towns all over these hills. But none of it makes any sense. Some denounce him and say he's been implicated with the Germans or the Communists. We also hear he's a Jew. All this uncertainty is confusing, and because it exists, I must caution you, Lieutenant, to give this man a wide berth. In his presence, you are to conduct yourself as an officer in the United States Army should. Be cordial, but maintain a distance. I won't tolerate any other form of behavior."

"Yes, sir," Walker answered quietly. "Whatever you say, do."

Borgman's eyes flared with annoyance.

Barely thirty seconds before takeoff, Celestino arrived in an elegant old dark-blue Lancia sedan. He and Borgman exchanged salutes and spoke very briefly. Then he handed up his suitcase and squeezed into the backseat. They raced down the runway, followed tentatively by the Lancia, which circled back near the field boundary. They climbed out through the brisk cool air, watching the sun sink away in the western sky. Soon the Adriatic appeared under their wings, deep blue and cold. Walker scanned the heavens all around. He wished Celestino would say something, but his passenger remained silent, a leather helmet over his thick blond hair, an oxygen mask robbing his face of expression. Those gray eyes which had so intrigued Walker seemed charged with passion and resignation.

They flew on. Effortlessly, Walker held a perfectly straight course. Just south of the enormous lagoon of Venice, dotted by dozens of tiny islands, they broke inland, losing altitude gradually after passing over Padua. Soon they were near Verona. Walker could make out the ancient battlements on some of the bridges and rooftops. The light signal came up at them, vanished, and returned with more insistence. They came in smoothly on a long stretch of grass. Before jumping off the wing walk, Celestino grasped Walker's right hand in his left, holding it for a moment in a solemn and poignant gesture of friendliness. Voices called to him in Italian. Suddenly he was gone.

When Walker got back to his room that night, Emilia was there to bathe him in a rough wooden tub and then make love to him. They had become quite tender with each other. They seemed to be settling into each other more and more.

Two nights later he picked up Celestino in the town of Pisa, 120 miles southeast of Verona on the Tyrrhenian coast. At home base another argument flared up. Borgman was livid. He screamed at Celestino in Italian, but was ignored. As Celestino went to his car, the driver, a nervous, slim young man in civilian clothes, got out furtively. Walker saw him conceal a machine pistol behind the opened front door.

The flights continued. Every other evening the converted Mustang droned out of Foggia and headed northward over the German lines. Walker grew confident. There was never any trouble. He slipped in and away from Florence and Bologna, La Spezia, and even Rome itself without a single alarm ever being raised. Celestino was the one taking the risks. He was the one strolling off into the darkness never really sure of who was calling to him, who was sitting in the car waiting to pick him up. *He's doing it for glory,*

Walker thought. *He wants to be a statue in the town square or one of them saints begging for mercy. Arrogant. Reminds me of Fremont.*

After the ghostly night flights, after the whispered rumors of sabotaged ammunition trains, mined roads and bridges, murdered collaborators, and ambushed patrols had washed over him, Walker could not wait to get home to Emilia. They were working on her English.

"I have been taught in school as a little girl," she explained shyly. "Also by an uncle who came from New Jersey to visit my mother and was kept here because of the war in Abyssinia."

For a long time she had been afraid to speak much.

"I thought it would make me ordinary, not special to you any more. As a child, my mother said I should always be special," she said, flashing a naughty girlish smile. "My mother protected me. I was her first and only baby. The doctors could not help her have another. The other women in the village made fun of her. My father decided to go to America. He sent money. Then he stopped. We moved into a house in the mountains above any of the towns because my mother wanted to be alone. I grew up strong. I never had malaria. When I was nineteen, I had my first baby. My suitor went away. We stayed with my mother until she got typhus and died. Then I came to work in Foggia. I have been here ever since, Horazio."

Abruptly their romance was no longer secret. They appeared in public, making their way across the piazza in the late afternoons. Walker showed off his best swagger, and a strong light of defiant enjoyment shone in his eyes. Emilia stood beside him, a shade taller, her magnificent features suffused by serenity. People were obviously intrigued by them, especially the old men who played cards over their cheap wine and cigars. ("Look, she treats him like a mother. All soldiers need that. But he won't stay. He will leave her in sadness.")

Emilia was the first woman he had ever known that he did not fight against or try to hurt or blame for his failures. In her presence he was free to be a man and he loved this. He knew that he was sliding into something unknown, an involvement which might warp or maim him, but it didn't matter. The squadron seemed far away, in another theater of war. The thought of going back frankly upset him.

One night he picked up Celestino in Ancona, a coastal town well above Foggia. A bullet had snared his leather coat, badly nipping the fleshy part of his arm. On the way back he passed out in a spasm of silent pain, but Walker managed to revive him with oxygen before Borgman reached the aircraft.

"Come and see me in the morning, Horazio," he whispered as they were getting into the jeep. "My car will pick you up at ten A.M."

When he told Emilia he had an appointment, she asked no questions, but he noticed her watching from an upper window as he stood in front of the hotel waiting for the car. It arrived fifteen minutes late. Walker sank into the plush leather seat and observed the people of Foggia going about their chores and rituals. As always, their acerbic vitality and harshness held his interest. He liked Italy.

The car picked up speed. Soon they were on the outskirts of town in a residential neighborhood of small villas. They turned off down a long private road and stopped alongside a house. Celestino's chauffeur ushered him gravely through the heavy timbered door in front of them. He stepped down into a kitchen where it was cool and dark. Beyond the large unscreened windows four or five armed men sat around playing cards. A rather striking woman of indeterminate age worked busily at a counter cutting meat and vegetables. She eyed him with enormous suspicion. The young man said something to her in Italian, yet she did not seem any less vigilant as she came toward them, stopped, and calmly removed the hunting knife from Walker's boot. The chauffeur avoided her searching gaze. His face went pink with embarrassment. They headed upstairs and came out on a wide balcony overlooking an inner courtyard.

Celestino was sitting at a big table. He stood up. He was wearing his black dress uniform and resembled a naval officer, except that his bearing was a little too theatrical. His blond hair, bleached by the sun, and his wild gray eyes gave him the distressed look of a mediocre character actor. As he smiled and came forward, Walker realized he might never meet anyone as interesting as Celestino again. They shook hands.

"How you feelin'? They fix your arm okay?" Walker asked gently.

"Yes, Horazio," Celestino said, guiding him toward the table. "It was only a surface wound. They cleaned it out and gave me sulfur tablets. Sit down. Have a Campari. You must excuse my formal appearance. I have to meet some of your senior officers for lunch, but we have plenty of time."

Walker glanced around. Along the roofs in the hazy overcast were several men holding carbines. A Browning Automatic Rifle on its swivel tripod covered the courtyard. In a big airy room off the balcony, other men played billiards, yet seemed to take in everything. An enormous Alsatian dog with a nail-studded collar wandered around and growled at Walker once or twice.

"What you see here is my organization, the people I trust," Celestino said expansively. "Everyone else is in the field."

Walker took a sip of the Campari and was appalled by its bitterness. He saw that Celestino was slightly drunk and this relaxed him.

"We don't really know each other at all, and yet we might have to die together, immolated like brothers," Celestino said cordially. "Doesn't that intrigue you, Horazio?"

"It don't make me no never mind," Walker answered, setting down his drink, "cause I don't plan to get burned up."

"Neither do I," Celestino said, "but I should still like to know you. In Italy we know nothing of the black man except the song 'Little Black Face,' which was popular here at the time of the Abyssinian War. Of his mind we know very little. Of his soul, even less."

"Nobody frets themselves about people my color," he said quietly. "They want to know about the heroes, about your kind."

"I am not a hero," Celestino protested. "No, I am merely someone who has undergone a change of heart."

"You mean you fought against us?" Walker asked.

"Yes. Certainly," his companion replied in a confessional tone. "I fought in the desert for an Italian empire because I felt we Italians should be a world power. Fascism made it possible for a lot of us to take pride in ourselves and our country for the first time. People felt they represented the state. I was perhaps the most naive of them all. I suffered all the shortages of food and ammunition, the panic, the murder of my fellow officers, and the desertions every night, before I could see."

"See what?"

"Before I could see the greed and vanity that controlled Mussolini's court. When it all came to me, I wept. But now that Mussolini is gone from the radio and his balcony, everything has changed. I may be wrong or even deranged, yet I believe that I represent the true Italy of the moment. I know I am a transitory figure, but I am throwing my life into seeing the Germans driven from *Italia* this winter."

"What do you get out of this, man?"

"I don't want rewards," Celestino answered, shaking his head reflectively. "I don't want to be president. Frankly, Horazio, I would rather just be remembered."

"You want to be a statue!" Walker said with a big friendly grin. "I knew you wanted to be one."

Celestino knitted his brow in amused consternation.

"It's not a bad idea," he admitted. "Some of our greatest men are now statues in Florence and Rome, but so many others are forgotten. These are the Brigands, the men and women in rural Italy who fought peasant wars against the unjust governments of seventy and eighty years ago. Their graves are often unmarked and unknown. They exist now in the legends of village storytellers and in the memories of their families.

Celestino had been drinking as he talked, and Walker noticed that his eyes were bloodshot and he slurred a few of his words. Still, his face was softer and more boyish than ever. Walker felt rough and hardy in his presence.

"The Brigands did what we are doing," Celestino continued. "They sabotaged, murdered, and held people for ransom. But history was not on their side and they were put down. They lost, as perhaps we will lose. Yet we must fight," he said passionately, "because Italy has not progressed very much beyond their day. Our people are still twisted by superstition and eaten by disease. They exist in the present and dwell in the past.

"Why have your people in America not revolted?" Celestino asked.

"There have been revolts, slave revolts and such. Things you don't hear much about unless you had family there," Walker answered, almost as if he had anticipated this question would be half the cost of getting to know Celestino. "And after the Civil War we began to do a little better. Then they crushed us. Took away everything, man. Since then, we stay to ourselves. We have to survive first. Once in a while we get a little something after a lot of fightin' and hollerin'. That's how we got over here in Europe. All sixteen of us. That's how it goes."

"With so much in the way of riches before your eyes, couldn't you have more, fought more? What did you have to lose?"

Celestino's voice was tight with quiet fervor. Then suddenly he fell silent. "I'm sorry. You live in America. You know the conditions there better than I."

Walker was uneasy. "I'm not supposed to be here," he said to Celestino. "The major told me to steer clear of you. You mystify him. He says he can never be sure of you."

"Forget Borgman," Celestino replied, sounding bored. "He's a virgin. He calls himself the Intelligence Coordinator for this section of Italy, but we Italians find him rather spineless."

They sat there in silence for a time. Celestino drank moodily. At last, he rose and smoothed his hands over his face and hair before checking his watch carefully. The attention of the men on the roof and in the billiard room immediately focused on him. A fleeting expression of disappointment passed over his features as he looked at Walker again.

"Horazio, my friend. I must go to my appointment now. I'll see you at the airplane tonight. And watch out for that Major Borgman. He told me he wasn't sure of you either."

A series of long cold black nights followed. As they sailed over the German lines, over the small towns and cities still in the hands of the Fascist militia and the Wehrmacht divisions, Celestino was more frank.

"You know, Horazio, I'm a little disappointed. I

thought my movement would be a call to arms for all Italians. Instead we are simply partisans like those all over Europe."

Walker turned anxiously in his seat until the straps cut. He didn't want to hear any more.

"The inevitable thing is happening," Celestino confessed. "They are beginning to eat us up. Our people are disappearing from their homes, from the hiding places. We don't have enough guns or ammunition."

"All of a sudden?"

"Yes. Kesselring has planned an offensive for the spring. This winter he wants to camp in one place, undisturbed. He has brought an SS major general, a specialist in intelligence, all the way from the Russian front to see he is not stabbed in the back. This man has become my nemesis. Because of him, Borgman is losing confidence in me. I can see it in his face."

After that evening, things became more desperate. They narrowly escaped an ambush when Celestino was picked up in Spoleto twelve hours ahead of schedule. Several trips were canceled, and two plots against his life uncovered. Celestino retired to his villa and worked on salvaging a hard core of agents who could be hidden over the winter and brought back in the spring with fresh supplies. Walker avoided him until it was time to climb into the cockpit. Most of his time was spent alone or with Emilia. Her affection was more important than ever, for Celestino's plight dismayed him terribly. ("See, nothin' ever works. Just when I thought I had a friend, somebody I could learn somethin' from, it's all changing. Why can't life stand still once in a while and let a man enjoy it?")

"I identified myself too much with that man," he explained to Emila. "I knew he couldn't beat those Germans, but I wanted to believe he could. I wanted it for the boy."

"Perhaps you can still help him," she answered.

"No," he replied. "There's nothing I can do. They'll get him in a corner sooner or later and when they do, I want to be far away."

One evening late the following week, Walker reached the airfield and found Borgman upset and disgusted.

"Let's go for a walk, Lieutenant," he snapped.

They strolled along in the dark, smoking. Walker pretended to relight his pipe so he could glimpse Borgman's face, which appeared taut with silent agitation.

"Lieutenant, I understand you're seeing a white woman in town," Borgman said presently. "Any truth to this?"

"Yes, sir," Walker answered. "There's a whole lot of truth to it."

Borgman turned sharply toward him. Walker could almost feel him seething with disapproval.

"For God's sake, man, haven't you got any sense? The Army doesn't want you people dallying with these women. It's one of the things they dread in this war."

"I don't give a fuck what they dread," Walker came back savagely. "Me and my woman, we're tight," he said, holding up his middle and index fingers pressed together. "Close as two spoons in a drawer. And we gonna stay that way."

Borgman flung down his cigarette and stamped it out.

"Listen, Walker," he began in a floundering voice full of that decency Walker hated. "I know you boys need women too. I'm aware of the problem, believe me. But if this gets out, I'm behind the well-known eight ball. They'll say she's working for the other side or something and ship me to a truck depot in Kansas. You can sink me to the bottom."

"That's tough titty," Walker said roughly. "But I vouch for her personally, if that means anything to you."

Borgman sighed heavily. He looked at Walker again.

"You've done a good job for me, Horace, almost too good," he said enigmatically. "All I'm asking from you now is a little *discretion*. Please don't let this matter get around. I'm going to pretend I haven't heard about it. And I don't want any news of you and this woman to reach me officially. Understand that? If it does, I'll have to take steps."

Walker was boiling inside. He wanted to knock Borgman senseless and stomp on his face until it became an uncomprehending mass of bloody pulp. But he did nothing. He put his hands into his pockets.

"Where's our boy? I didn't see him tonight," he said, quickly changing the subject.

"Son of a bitch isn't here," Borgman answered a bit

helplessly. "He left Foggia this morning for Rome to try and get the SS general who's been kicking his butt."

"Damn," Walker said. "Goddamn."

"I hear he's traveling on forged papers and wearing the uniform of a Fascist militiaman," Borgman continued. "But it's too much of a long shot. He's almost sure to be taken off the train at Campobasso or met by the Gestapo in Rome. The krauts own that town, and besides, they've put a price on his head. That usually signifies the end of a man in Italy. I don't think our friend is going to lead anyone out of these hills to a better life."

"How's he figure on getting next to the general?" Walker asked, casting aside what Borgman had said.

"They don't tell me those things, Lieutenant," Borgman replied bitterly. "I was prepared to help them, but they're pigheaded."

"I believe that boy will succeed," Walker said. "This is the kind of shit you got to handle yourself."

Borgman snorted. They had come to the field boundary.

"Come on," he said brusquely. "Let's jog back. I've got work to do."

Back at the hotel, Emilia had a surprise.

"Tomorrow night we will have dinner at my house," she said sweetly. "There is someone I want you to meet."

"That's fine, pumpkin," Walker said in a puzzled tone. "I'm not gonna be flyin'. Who do you want me to see?"

"My daughter," Emilia answered with a soft prideful smile. "My Vittoria. She's a big girl, you'll be surprised."

For the rest of the evening he felt surreptitious glances examining him. Emilia was clearly very pleased and excited that he'd accepted her invitation without balking. But tonight he found her eagerness and devotion quite annoying. His thoughts shifted and swirled about Celestino. He admired the man enormously. Celestino had begun to make him think. *I'm not gonna go back to being no tramp when this war is over,* he told himself. *Those days are done. It's got to be equal shares for equal men now. I'm ready to come out of the ditch fightin'. Of course, I could be wrong about all this. I might even be losing my mind over here in Europe. A lot of people back home would say so. I got to talk to him more. I got to find out more about what's inside me, what I can be. I ain't no*

*old man. I got some future in front of me. I always
knowed I was a good man, even a better man than Fremont. But I didn't know what made me better. Maybe this
boy can tell me.*

Emilia stirred from her sleep and kissed him lovingly
on the side of the face. He smoothed her hair with long
gentle strokes and then poured some wine from a carafe
on the night table. *I don't see how he can get close to
that general. They know who he is. Somebody's bound to
sell his hide for the reward, just like the major said. But
the boy's hungry. He's crazy and hungry both, that's why
I like him. I got faith in that boy. He'll be there when
I come in to pick him up. I need for him to be there.*

Shortly after seven the next evening they left the hotel
in the old Fiat taxicab always parked outside and headed
into the crowded working-class district of Foggia. They
emerged from the cab in a street of brightly painted but
decaying apartment buildings. Lines of bedsheets and
other washing were suspended from the upper stories. A
few peddlers trundled their wares homeward up the long
sloping streets and people drifted around casually, waving
and calling to friends at their windows. Naked light bulbs
on the corner houses furnished the only illumination, and
through the harsh shadows Walker noticed many pairs of
eyes staring at him and Emilia in immense stark curiosity.

They went into the courtyard of her building and up
two long flights of stairs. Emilia unlocked a large heavy
door and they entered an apartment. It appeared to be
made up of three very big rooms all connected by French
doors. He was ushered through the kitchen and into the
living room, where a wrinkled old woman in black sat on a
sofa, knitting and chatting with a young girl. The old
woman stiffened when she saw him.

"This is my daughter, Vittoria," Emilia said, ignoring
the old woman.

The girl rose graciously. She was beautiful like her
mother and possessed most of the same features, refined
by the purity of youth.

"How do you do, Capitano," she said. "I have heard
so much about you. My mother says you are very brave."

"Why, thank you," Walker answered, surprised at the
courtliness of his tone.

"Tell him Ethiopia is our friend," the old woman whispered to Emilia as she left the room.

Moments later, she reappeared with three glasses of sweet vermouth and smiled faintly but courteously at Walker. Vittoria was excited to hear he was from Texas. She rattled off half a dozen questions before her mother asked her to be quiet. She startled Walker. She was so poised, so sure of her beauty. She had on a nice pink satin dress that was a little out of date and did nothing to hide her gorgeous legs and plump young breasts.

Walker glanced around the room. It was shabby but possessed a few elegant touches: an armoire of beautiful veneered wood, a cane-backed love seat, a slightly worn oriental rug. Not too fancy. Just right. He was very comfortable here, sipping his aperitif and rambling on about his squadron to the two good-looking women who listened keenly to his every word. Yet at the same time he was concerned. He sensed that the flight to Rome tomorrow night might be his last mission. He suspected Emilia had felt this also, and that that was one of the reasons he was there. Delicious smells came from the kitchen. He began to feel like the head of a family, full of fatherly prattle toward Vittoria, who giggled a lot, and rather strongly possessive when his eyes turned toward Emilia. The women were laughing now and teasing him about not being a *capitano*. Everything seemed so secure at this moment, so pleasant, but only in a superficial, diverting way, for Celestino was never far from his thoughts. There were so many questions to be asked and discussions to be initiated. He didn't really know who he was yet. He had a great deal to find out.

As they went in for dinner, Emilia took his arm and explained. "I have hidden her from the soldiers. Don't you think it's a good idea? If anyone knocks, she goes right into the closet with a knife I have given her. They all want to rape her, both the Germans and the Italians."

The meal of rich pasta and thin fine veal was full and hearty and they washed it down with a powerful Barolo brought from the countryside in a wicker-covered bottle. The old woman served them meticulously. Walker noticed a certain majesty in all three of these women. Their courage in the face of this war reminded him of Celestino's strange dauntlessness. He felt wanted.

The dessert was a cheesecake made by Vittoria and strong black coffee. Vittoria was smoother and more genteel than her mother, but still he found her very rustic in an abrupt sort of way. He liked her directness.

"How long have you been with my mama?" she asked as the old woman blushed violently and covered her eyes with a corner of her apron.

"She's a modern girl," Emilia said, her face radiating quiet indulgence, "the only one in Italy. I want to see her become a schoolteacher some day."

In the large bare kitchen, against the blue tile walls, Emilia looked a bit older and more tired than he had ever seen her before. She needed a husband, that was clear; and Vittoria could use the restraint and moderation of a man in the household. Suddenly he felt seduced by the whole evening. He was quiet and thoughtful as he and Emilia drank Strega in the living room. Soon it was time to go. Emilia pleaded with him to stay overnight, but he was afraid. Something told him he might never leave.

"I'm on duty," he protested softly. "I can't leave my post in wartime. They'll go crazy if they can't find me."

"I will go back with you, then. I think you need me."

He said good night to Vittoria, who kissed him girlishly on each cheek. In the darkness near the door, he turned to Emilia, holding a wad of money in one hand.

"Should I leave something for the old lady?"

"Oh, no," Emilia whispered. "She is a distant cousin. She considers what she did a privilege. Offering her money would be like spitting in her face. She respects you because you are an American."

The old woman watched them both from the sink where she had been washing dishes. Her weak eyes focused on Walker. She attempted to smile, but could not.

Walker came out onto the steps of the hotel and gazed at the full moon, large and unshielded by clouds. He did not see Emilia huddled in the darkness of the vestibule with a shawl around her shoulders, watching him in painful concern. It was cold, the coldest night of the year so far. Walker stood there in his leather flying jacket, his cap tilted on the back of his head, and rubbed his hands together. He was tense. He took out a crumpled pack of

Luckies and lit one. He wondered if he would die before
time slowed down enough for him to review his life. There
was a lot to consider. The dinner at Emilia's was one of
the nicest things that had happened to him in a long time.
It was the first evening since his mother died that he had
felt a part of a family. He could feel a craving for the
security of love welling up in him again. He thought of
going AWOL, of marrying Emilia and staying hidden in
some mountain village until the end of the war. But he
wasn't free to do that. It would disgrace the squadron.

The jeep pulled up, squeaking on the cobblestones. He
flicked away the cigarette and got in.

"Earlier today I received a message from Celestino,"
Borgman said as soon as he got to the hut. "He is safely
in Rome. He will make his attempt on the German general
this evening and try to escape during some kind of diversion they have planned. At least I think that's what he
intends to do.

"You will rendezvous in a field north of Rome at 0100
hours precisely. Study this target map for a while, Lieutenant, then try to get some sleep for a couple of hours.
We'll go over everything once again before you take off."

"I don't need no rest. I ain't no baby," Walker said
sharply.

"All right, let's check the essentials again. You are to
wait no more than thirty seconds. If you see anything
suspicious or the Germans arrive, take off immediately.
Don't wait. We will have lived up to our part of the bargain."

"By leaving a man?"

Borgman didn't answer the question.

"One thing, Horace," he said. "Make damn sure it's
Celestino. They could send out an impostor and try to
stall you that way. Be certain before you let him into the
airplane."

Walker lay down on the cot in one corner and leafed
through an old copy of *The Saturday Evening Post*. Borgman flipped him a pack of Philip Morrises. Time hardly
moved. Finally they had some coffee and went over the
route once more. Outside, Bates was having trouble starting the engine. They walked over the hard ground.

"On your final approach be careful of light flak and
machine-gun fire," Borgman said. "Wiggle your ass a

little, going in. You never know, low-level heavy flak
might try to pick you off from a couple of miles away."

They shook hands after Walker was strapped in.

"Good luck. See you later on tonight, Lieutenant."

Walker tossed his white scarf around his neck. He was
ready.

The Mustang rose sluggishly into the night, even on
full power. Walker was anxious. He cursed Bates for not
checking the engine more carefully, but it was too late
now. He was on his way. He climbed very high. The night
was still and icy cold at 25,000 feet. Moonlight dusted the
instrument panel lightly. There was no cloud cover. He
would be able to see the signal from a long way off, and
so could anyone else who might be looking for it. He
hummed softly to himself. Time raced by. The partly
devastated city of Naples lay below him, wan and sickly
beside the ghostly sea. Over the water he steered north
and began to lose altitude. He was right on time for rendezvous. It was almost impossible for long-range radar to
pick him up out here. But he had to get down low. He
couldn't be sure. He found the entrance to the Tiber without difficulty and hung close to the water for a few
minutes before breaking off on a bearing north by northeast. "Aim for the target at all times," Borgman had said.
"Don't be taken in." The landing ground lay ahead, far
from the miles of rooftops comprising Rome. It was twenty
seconds to the hour. He saw the signal, saw it so clearly
it was unreal, and his heart leapt. Twice it was repeated.
The throttle came back toward him. The airplane skidded
badly on the soft uneven ground.

Walker made out an indistinct blob of whiteness bobbing toward him in the quiet cold night. In the long flashlight
beam he saw a blond man in a dazzling white jacket sprint-
ing hard, his features contorted by great exertion. Onward he came for the plane, legs churning with violent
determination. The gold buttons on the uniform jacket
shone dully. A swastika in a wide red band was visible
on one arm. The man started to tear the jacket from his
body. He seemed crazed. Walker believed it was Celestino, but he cocked his .45 anyway. He threw out an arm
to help the man climb onto the wing walk quickly. It
was Celestino. They embraced. Walker could feel him

heaving spasmodically, then suddenly he was in the rear seat.

"We got the general. He's dead," a strained, emotional voice said. "I got into an official reception this evening and put poison in his food. We even talked for a while. He collapsed and died in a bedroom upstairs."

Walker reached back and pounded his friend on the arm, murmuring something inaudible. He was so proud tears almost came to his eyes. Then he realized where they were. At the same time both men sensed how eerily quiet it was. From far off, a siren wailed faintly over the stillness. Another siren erupted, this one closer, followed by several more.

"Horazio, it's a bombing raid," Celestino said, grasping him by the shoulder. "We can get away easily while they hit the city."

Walker gunned the engine. They escaped the clearing and shot off into the night sky. Walker's hand remained on the throttle. He quavered with a terrible uncertainty and reluctance, for he knew immediatey he had made a mistake. He heard no bombers and could not feel their turbulence. The whistling of big bomb loads streaking earthward was absent from the air.

"I fucked up," he said aloud in startled dismay.

On the ground powerful searchlights swung lazily through the sky. They were all over the Mustang in seconds, layer upon layer of them.

"I can't see," Celestino cried. "Get into the darkness."

Walker ignored him. His sharp eyes searched through the brilliant crisscrossing swaths of light for what he knew must be out there. And then he saw them, the night fighters, their long black fuselages gliding through the weird artificial atmosphere like predatory fish in the inaccessible regions of the sea. They were a muddle of Luftwaffe crosses and swastikas, black prop spinners and forward-mounted radar antennae that pronged ahead of their noses evilly. He saw a small armored greenhouse with two men sitting in it and dove on it, firing a long burst from his two machine guns. His fire rushed by the airplane in a narrow converging pattern. He came around for another pass, watching his slow-moving target from the corner of one eye. In an instant he lined up the group of exhaust stubs behind the cowling and aimed ahead of them. A sheet of flame lit up the night and sliced away from him, down and away.

But other planes saw him now. The sky seemed to be full of creeping Dornier night fighters. Cannon fire tore into the Mustang. Walker was disoriented. There was no horizon, no sun to come out of. He broke for the deck, fearful of a collision. They came after him. They had an accurate radar fix and would not let go. He spiraled down toward an immense searchlight, taking hits all over the fuselage. Celestino screamed amid the din and fell silent. They flattened out over the countryside and ran, losing oil and hydraulic fluid quickly. Sweat poured into Walker's eyes. He watched the dull red dials of his instruments. Something knocked them sideways with a hideous bang. Flak roared in from all directions. The airplane creaked and groaned, buffeted half out of control. They streaked through a gap in the mountains lit by moonlight. Men on the ground unleashed a murderous curtain of fire, and finally the Mustang began to burn. Celestino was limp and mute in his harness. Smoke filled the cockpit. They slanted down above the earth, bounced once, and went into a long, hard crash. When the plane stopped, it was burning very fast. Walker freed himself and stumbled onto the wing root. Flames roared up from underneath. He cut Celestino out. They fell to the ground and Walker rolled him over and over away from the plane as it exploded, its frame jerking upwards as bright flaming pieces sizzled through the air.

The two men lay on the cold ground for almost half an hour. Then Walker roused himself. He had cocked both his .45s and put one beside him when he made out the silhouettes of many British pie-plate helmets stalking toward them. He called out frantically, in a voice strange to him, for Celestino appeared to be dead.

The harsh lights in the hospital corridor sliced deep shadows into Borgman's face as he glanced at his watch and swiftly came up to the bench where Walker lay sleeping. Walker had to be shaken several times before he turned over on the bench and tried to fight off the exhaustion which had overcome him.

"They worked on him for three and a half hours," Borg-

man said. "Our medical people observed it. He took five
bullets in all."

"Is he going to make it?" Walker asked irritably.

"His signs are stable. He's got a pretty good chance,
Lieutenant. I'll never know how you gave those night fighters the slip. They had a lot of planes up."

"When can I see him?"

Borgman led him to the entrance to the ward, but did
not follow. He watched Walker smooth out his uniform
and start wearily down the center of the long room lined
with white enamel beds full of wounded British and
American soldiers, the overflow from the packed military
hospitals. Walker saw where they had him right away,
down near the end, cut off from view by two high folding screens. The young man who drove Celestino's car
sat in a small chair nearby. When he approached the
screens, a nurse, who had obviously been listening to his
footsteps, slipped out and scrutinized him coldly. Inside
the enclosed area he found the woman from the villa who
had taken his knife away. She stood on one side of the
bed, hands clasped in front of her, barely taking notice
of his presence. Celestino lay in a narrow bed between
them, his head wrapped in gauze. Those gray eyes which
so intrigued Walker seemed heavy with delirium. Thick
bandages made his body appear almost mummified. One
pale hand, wan and groping, touched Walker's uniform
jacket. Walker held it tightly.

"Thank you for getting me out of Rome, Horazio," the
figure on the bed said to him with some effort.

"Wasn't nothing to it," Walker answered. "Shit, we did
it all the time, didn't we? We were the two musketeers,
my man. You mustn't be thankin' me."

A profound smile whispered across Celestino's lips.

"When you get back to America, Horazio, try to do
as I have done," Celestino said in a faint pleading voice.
"You are needed there."

At this point the woman stared oddly at Walker, then
dropped her gaze again.

"Ain't no point in talkin' about the States," Walker
said patiently. "The Germans are still here in Italy and
we all need you, so please get well."

Celestino merely studied him. His hand fell from Walker's.

"You must go," the nurse said sharply as she appeared between the screens.

In the corridor Borgman was there.

"I'll drive you back to the hotel. You've had a rough night."

They sped through the cold clear morning. Walker was silent and still badly shaken, but Borgman insisted on chatting.

"You boys did a good job. Celestino got the general. I guess you know that."

Walker nodded.

"It's always good to see one of their top men wiped out. Damn good."

At the hotel, Walker collapsed on the bed. He was not aware of Emilia's entering the room, undressing him, and bathing his body in cool water. He sensed neither her anguish nor the tears streaming down her angelic face.

Later that morning he awakened with a start. He lay still, listening to the sounds of people and traffic in the piazza before getting into a class A uniform and leaving the hotel without bothering to eat anything. A taxi sped him to the hospital, where he was alarmed to see two American MPs stationed at the door. They seemed to know who he was and stopped him gently while a third man inside went to get Borgman. He was led to a waiting room where a large family of Italians sat in a corner, the older people suspended in grief, the children restless and talkative. Borgman appeared. He was wearing a fresh uniform. He wasted no words.

"Our friend is dead, Horace," he said flatly. "Celestino is gone. He was killed early this morning, knifed to death in his bed while his bodyguard went to the bathroom. It was all over in less than a minute."

"But why?" Walker asked, his voice shaking in dismay. "Why?"

Borgman examined the turmoil and shock on Walker's face carefully because it made him very nervous.

"The reward," he answered. "It was done for the reward. Whether it's also an act of personal retaliation, we'll never know."

Walker turned away, on the brink of tears.

"Don't let it get you down. It always seems to happen

this way, Lieutenant. These people come along full of life and hope, they help you for a while, then they lose their effectiveness. Celestino probably got a little too big for his britches. He failed to realize Italy was not his until we and the Germans left it to him."

"That's wrong," Walker said sharply. "They're Italians. It's their country."

"It won't be their goddamn country until they're willing to fight for it," Borgman shouted so loudly the Italian family looked at him in fear. "They've got to take the offensive and not wait until the Germans come marching into their towns before they'll fight."

Walker shook his head angrily.

"I know you and Celestino were buddies," Borgman continued. "You weren't supposed to be, but I let it happen. I didn't put an MP in front of your door because you were a damn good pilot for me. Now do yourself a favor and take a friendly piece of advice. Don't jump off the track, soldier. Forget Celestino and whatever weird ideas he put into your head. If you turn fuck-up or radical, your boys won't like it and neither will mine. Forget what happened here. By tonight, you'll be back with your squadron, anyway."

"I don't want to go back," Walker said desperately. "I ain't ready."

"You leave by train at 1600 hours for Matera," Borgman said, looking at him coldly. "Better have someone there to meet you."

"Major, don't dump me," Walker pleaded. "Get me another assignment. I want to stay here."

"I've got nothing coming up," Borgman snapped. "I can't hold out a top combat man if there is no work for him."

"You're trying to separate me from my woman, take away what we have!" Walker cried.

"Don't be ridiculous. This is a world war, not a fucking hayride."

"You know it's true."

Borgman smiled. He touched Walker on the shoulder. A hostile and obstinate pair of eyes studied his hand. He withdrew it.

"Lieutenant, I am only here in Italy to do a job," he explained more calmly, "that's all. Personal difficulties are outside my sphere. All I can tell you is that I want you out of here on that train this afternoon. Bates will drive you to the station. That's it."

"Shit," Walker said.

"Well, good-bye to you, Walker," Borgman said, extending a hand, "and the best of luck to you. I think you've earned a Silver Star for what you've done down here in Foggia."

Their hands touched briefly. Borgman saluted and strode off. It was a very long time before Walker left the room.

Back at the hotel Walker slowly began to pack his canvas suitcase. A harsh, violent sorrow afflicted him, but he did not shed any tears. Through it all, he could not believe Celestino was dead, yet the whole thing seemed so inevitable that he accepted it easily, and this made him angry. He felt as though he were betraying his friend. (*He looked to me to do a whole lot of things I don't believe I'm capable of. I wonder what he saw in me?*) Confusion and unhappiness riled him so fiercely that he flung thc last remaining items in the suitcase and shoved it away from him. Suddenly he hated Borgman and blamed him for everything.

Just then Emilia came softly into the room. Walker got up and went to the window and did not see her eyeing the packed suitcase. She sat down quietly on the edge of the bed and hugged her shoulders very tightly, as if she were cold. Walker knew she was watching him. He had no idea what to say. He waited for her to speak, and finally she did.

"Horazio, will you be coming back to Foggia?"

"Sure, I'll be coming back, pumpkin," he answered in a subdued way. "We ain't but seventy-five miles from here. I'll be in town every weekend and they might even base us here after the front moves north."

Emilia nodded, yet she did not seem convinced. She left the room and came back a few minutes later with his lunch on a tray. The whole town knew about Celestino, she explained. He would get a hero's funeral tomorrow or the next day.

"Wish I could be there. They got no more use for me here, so they're pushing me out," he said.

Emilia stroked him gently on the head. They made love

quietly and subtly, fighting back their depression, searching for a vividness that was not there. Bates came half an hour before the train was scheduled to leave. He was surprised and annoyed when Emilia demanded to be taken to the station. Down in the hotel lobby they passed an American Air Force pilot sitting in a leather armchair. A tough and savagely disapproving look sprang into his face when he saw Walker and Emilia strolling by. Bates saluted the pilot snappily and Walker understood at once that he was the new Special Duty man. A powerful urge to go back and choke him, choke him hard until he slumped dead in the armchair, flared up in Walker. (*Otherwise he'll have Emilia. He'll go after her and get her. I can feel it.*)

The station was packed when they arrived. Italian soldiers in their dull gray uniforms with colorful collar patches circulated everywhere as a handful of stern British officers screamed and shouted at them to form orderly lines along the platform. Walker stood off to one side, holding Emilia by the hand. The train surged in, darkening the station. Walker kissed Emilia for what they both knew would probably be the last time.

"Look for me Friday night," he whispered, " 'long about the usual time."

She began to cry, openly and shamelessly. Walker stepped into a compartment and closed the door, then stuck his head out of the window. Emilia's eyes were riveted to him. She looked incredibly majestic, incredibly hopeful. The train started to move. Panic seized Walker. He grappled with the door but could not get it open. Emilia began to slide from view. In seconds she was gone and Walker felt worn and empty. He turned around and there on a seat was a black leather coat. It was Celestino's coat, the one he always wore. They had almost cleared the station. He searched frantically for sight of the boy, the chauffeur, who must have left the coat. But instead the face of the woman in the courtyard, the woman at Celestino's bedside, appeared mystically from the crowd. He believed she smiled just a little, but he was never sure, for at that instant the train left Foggia.

THIRTEEN

OSBORN CAME DOWN the steps of the Operations van in a sweater and wool helmet liner and greeted Walker in the cold, drizzly night.

"Glad to see you back, Horace," he said amicably as they shook hands. "We haven't been as good without you up there."

Inside, an officer who looked vaguely familiar to Walker served them mugs of steaming hot coffee. Osborn did not introduce him, but Walker soon recognized the man standing by the teletype machine as Orlando Jones, the pilot who had broken formation and run after the first mission. He nodded to him in a not unfriendly way.

"Did everything go well," Osborn asked. "Are you ready to fly?"

"I'm always ready to fly," Walker said calmly.

"Fine. Good," Osborn said, shuffling a few papers. Walker's appearance was disturbing. His eyes were red, as if he'd been crying.

"I'd like you to do me a favor, Horace," Osborn continued. "I know you need some privacy, but I want to put you in a tent with Jennings. I think you can steady him down. He hasn't been the same since Donny Beaumont was killed."

"I'll try it for a few days," Walker said, "but I ain't changin' no diapers for you, Osborn."

"Thanks," Osborn replied as both men got up. "He's in the last tent on the left. By the way, stop past and say hello to the colonel if you have time. I know he'll be glad to see you."

Walker stepped from the oblong of yellow light slanting out of the van and moved off into the blackness. He wore Celestino's leather coat elegantly over his shoulders like a cloak. As he entered the tent area, men began to stir.

"Walker's out here," somebody said, tugging at a tent flap.

A lantern appeared, then two more. Familiar faces drifted in out of the wet night. He recognized Butters and Hollyfield, Colzie, the tail-ass man in Fremont's flight, and Rennie Washington, one of Archie's boys. Silently, he strode on, the long coat almost touching the ground.

"Never thought I'd see his ass again."

"He's togged like a king. Must have taken that coat off a general."

Men called out greetings in the darkness while others made their way into the area, rustling among the tents. Lantern light mingled with that from a big fire to create a soft and bizarre afterglow. Pilots lounged by their tents, watching him pass. Appaloosa appeared and he picked her up without breaking stride. He could feel the expectancy all around him, sense it in the faces of these calm and hardened men who would never again resemble the frightened boys he trained with at Tuskegee.

"Look at this place," he said in a loud playful voice, gesturing toward the figures around the fire. "I leave out of here for a few weeks, and you turn it into a damn niggertown."

This was greeted by harsh laughter. Donaldson came up to him, holding a flask. He took a long swig of cognac, stared at Donaldson, then took an even longer drink draining the flask dry. More laughter surrounded him as he went into his tent.

That night the first snow came, blanketing the hard mass of frozen mud left from the late-November rains. At 0625 the men reluctantly came out of the mess hall and drifted toward the Briefing hut in small groups, talking and smoking. The day promised to be bleak and windy and cold like every other day lately. A heavy mist hung in the mountains. Nothing was visible up there. Trudging along, Walker remembered that Jennings had said landslides were common in this weather. A few days before, a whole family had been swept off a narrow road near Matera.

Walker entered the Briefing hut and sat down on a bench near the front. Jennings sat next to him. Everything seemed as he had left it, the sullenness and tension, the bitter jokes; and at the same time it was noticeably different, perhaps more grim. At any rate he was still slightly confused. Yesterday he had been in Foggia with Emilia. Celestino was alive, hurt bad after the crash, but alive. Today, he was going into combat again. It was unfair. Life was coming at him too quickly. He was exhausted and sore all over, still half-crushed by sadness and a wild hunger for Emilia which had kept him awake most of the night. He was desperate to see her.

Jennings was already beginning to annoy him. The boy talked too much. He brought too damn much bad news: St. Clair's death somewhere in Germany far from his own people, and then Todd taking his life. It was weird about Todd, like some kind of sign from heaven. People still mentioned it, the way the pressure must have built up, the way maybe he wasn't that much weaker than the rest of them. But the world was rife with strangeness and omens and tricks to play on a man. Alfredo Lentieri knew this. That was Celestino's real name, sewn into the lining of his coat. Alfredo Lentieri. It was probably the most common name in Italy.

"Good to see you again," Fremont said as he patted him on the back and moved up front.

A hand touched his shoulder gently from the rear. It was Skinner mumbling a few genteel and encouraging words. Walker turned half around.

"Hey, pretty boy, where were you last night?"

That elusive smile he had always disliked came onto Skinner's face. He put a finger to his lips and sat back.

Against a wall Norvel Donaldson stood off to himself, arms folded across his chest. The briefing had begun, and as usual, every word chilled him. He wanted to get out of flying, resign his commission, and go into the infantry, but he didn't have the nerve to tell Fremont. Lately he'd begun putting a little cognac in his breakfast coffee, so he took the same spot by the wall every day, hoping no one would smell it on him from there.

The briefing went fast. They were flying close air support for an attempted infantry breakthrough. Osborn mentioned something about the Rapido and Garigliano Rivers, the Liri Valley, and the Gustav Line. He detailed everything beautifully. Nature Boy and the armorer finished up. Suddenly it was all over and they were in the truck headed out to the flight line. Hollyfield squinted at a copy of *Stars and Stripes.*

"Hey, we're mentioned in here," he said excitedly. "Seventy-fourth Squadron, Homestead Grays, holding their own in Italy. Who gave us the name Homestead Grays, anyway? I don't remember voting for it."

"Oh, you voted for it just like we all did," Walker said in exasperation. "I put up the name."

"It figures," Hollyfield answered.

"Don't it, though," Walker said in a flash of annoyance. "I always did like that name," he went on. "My father used to play ball with the Grays. He was with the St. Louis Stars and the Pittsburgh Crawfords too."

"What position did he play?" Archibald asked in the effeminate voice he used to denigrate people.

"He played the outfield," Walker said earnestly to Roy Butters, who was sitting beside him, "but he pitched some, too. I got a couple of old clippings on him back home."

"What's he doing now?" Butters asked.

Abruptly a subtle agitation showed in Walker's eyes.

"I don't know," he said. "I haven't seen him since I was a kid. I guess he's around, that's all, just around."

At the dispersal, Fremont surveyed the scene: the pilots climbing into their planes, the whispered conferences with mechanics, the unspoken way men shook off their companions and eased into the controlled isolation of the fighter pilot. He was beginning to wonder if there was any real hope of dislodging the German Army from its mountain redoubts. Perhaps not, but Walker's presence this morning cheered him. It was too bad he had to fly without any rest, yet there was no choice. Every man was needed. Orders from the top were to keep maximum pressure on the Germans, keep them fighting so divisions could not be transferred to Russia where the Wehrmacht's best men lay dying in the snows.

Engines began to start up all over the field. Fremont snuggled into his cockpit. He kept his propellor at very low RPMs until the oil temperature went up. Under the airplane, Friday removed the wheel chocks as the engine got warmer. Fremont checked his gauges and rotated the big fuel tank selector handle. The fuel pressure and flow from each tank was fine. Planes began to taxi as the mechanics clung to the wingtips and dug into the hard ground with their cleated shoes to help them pivot onto the icy runway. Fremont held his brakes and ran up the engine until his spark plugs burned clean. He eased the throttle inward, eyes fastened on the big round tachometer in front of him. He lifted off into the light air, feeling that tiny surge of wonderment which always came to him at the start of a mission. Butters was not with him. He saw the other flights leave the ground without mishap.

"Cobra squadron," he called in. "Check flaps. Turn on your gun- and gun-camera heaters."

It was painfully cold and that kept down the chatter. Breathing was difficult. Almost everyone was on full oxygen. Fremont watched the blinker on his regulator go on and off. On cold days the pressure tended to fall rapidly. He breathed harder. They were knifing across a bleak terrain: mountains, heavy, undulating, and deeply furrowed, crowned by wisps of stagnant stratocumulus; empty stretches of rocky plain; checkered fields resting near the rivers in long, thin family plots; an occasional grouping of houses. The mountains looked bare, lumpy, and vaguely innocuous. But crashing there meant instant death. Through the pale hazy sunlight he saw a couple of huge landslides blocking roads.

He thought about the ground assault today. It seemed inconceivable that the infantrymen up on the line believed they would ever get to Rome. Naples had fallen two whole months ago, at the beginning of October, and Rome was nowhere in sight.

"Closing Sant'Angelo, leader," Butters broke in.

"Cobra squadron, keep a sharp lookout for ground forces," Fremont said tensely into his microphone.

Ahead, the vast Liri Valley was laid out before them. Across its floor, Clark's Fifth Army was to attempt a move into a forward position hard alongside the Gustav Line near a place called Cassino. If they made it, a full-scale breakthrough would then be mounted. The valley was a mess. Rain and light snow had softened it into a quagmire, and tanks couldn't be used because they had no chance of getting within firing range of the line.

"There they are," Walker said, "off to port about nine o'clock low."

It was a disconcerting, almost heartrending, spectacle. Moving across the dismal valley were thousands of men in khaki, American soldiers belonging to the Fifth. Some were dodging for cover from bullets the squadron could not see, but most trudged ahead. They looked huddled, cold, inept. They moved very slowly, as though on the brink of exhaustion. Only a few tanks made an attempt to accompany them, and they were soon burrowed nose-down in the mud. Occasionally a sniper got someone who fell dead in his tracks while others drifted around him. Mines went off in tiny fierce explosions and men tumbled to the ground. As the army creaked forward, mortar and artillery fire began dropping down on it, sparsely at first, then with even more intensity. The fire began to carpet the lead elements, who had stopped as though blinded or transfixed. The whole thing looked sad, futile, and completely primitive.

"Let's get in on those big mortars," Fremont said curtly.

On both sides of them other planes were attacking the Germans. Off to starboard, the P-39s, the Airacobras, released the last of their bombs and then fanned out close to the ground, cutting up anything in their way. On the port side, a squadron of slow, heavy B-24 Liberators began circling back after dropping their loads. One of them erupted into flames which spread over the whole ship, leaving only the big vertical stabilizers visible. It disintegrated with horrifying speed. No parachutes appeared. That was the trouble with the B-24s: they burned very quickly.

The line was very clear. It never changed from its configuration of irregular but overlapping gun positions, some of them on the valley floor. Bodies, mule carcasses, a few of the guns, and a handful of tanks could be made out, but it was hard to spot the bulk of the enemy. The armies down there in their dull gray uniforms seemed to be part of the mountains. A lot of men were hidden in caves and dugouts, behind emplacements, and under camouflage.

There was no milling around. Movements were precise, defensive fire thick and accurate. The whole area facing the line was alive with flame and shell and smoke. Already the long snouts of the .88s sent up bracketing fire.

Fremont picked out a battery of heavy mortars which had all but stopped the Americans within its range.

"The release point will be seven hundred fifty feet. Hit hard, and get the hell out of there. Let's go."

They straightened out, line astern, and formed a bombing circle. Fremont was to be first man down. He gave Butters a hand signal, eased into a half turn, and dove. His engine began to whine murderously. The airspeed indicator rose to the top of its curve and kept moving. Fremont concentrated on the ground below, on the men working at those mortars. Tracers streamed up at him as the .88s pounded away. Fire converged from everywhere, from every hole and crevice. The air was malignant with it. Black smudges from the .88s obscured his vision as he peered through his gunsight and squeezed the release button hard. His bombs went. The ground blast rocked his ship as he pulled into an abrupt climbing turn, angry and disgusted with himself for having just missed the target. Butters and the others had done no better, but Walker and Skinner's boys scored a few scattered hits. He watched Archibald's flight streaking earthward. They appeared to drop below the release point, although he couldn't be sure. He prayed the delay set into the fuses would give them time to escape. Archie and Rennie Washington came away with beautiful direct hits. Busted mortar tubes and dead soldiers lay on the smoking ground. Donaldson was the last man down. Jerkily, he let his bomb go high, way too high, and missed the target off to the right by a couple of hundred yards. The bomb exploded harmlessly on a ridge. Butters looked across at Fremont.

The army continued its attack. A smattering of self-propelled howitzers started crawling up to help the beleagured men and 155 millimeter Long Toms opened fire on any exposed positions. Washington was calling for a damage check. Something had slammed into him underneath.

"Look him over, Four-four," Archibald said.

There was no response.

"Commence damage check," he snapped.

When nothing came through the headset, he glared over and down at Donaldson and clearly, chillingly, saw him remove a leather-covered flask from his mouth and wipe his lips.

"You no good son of a bitch!" Archibald screamed as Donaldson glanced up at him. "You lousy drunken bastard. Get out of my flight. Get out! Return to base immediately."

The others watched as Donaldson detached himself from the finger four and headed home, his solitary craft rocking noticeably.

"Bandits coming!" Walker broke in. "Lots of them."

"I can see their exhausts," Jennings shouted.

"Shut the fuck up," Walker said.

A host of white condensation trails whipped out from behind the planes.

"Here they come. Stay in pairs, everybody."

The squadron flew apart in every direction. But the enemy swooped in and engulfed them. Walker saw it was too late for a getaway. He studied the Focke-Wulfs. They looked like gigantic insects in their winter camouflage of squiggly green lines and circles on a white background. Nobody was in position for a good shot. The radio was filled with confusing chatter ("They're on your ass. I can't see the bastards. Dive. Dive!"). He let one plane overshoot him, then went after his wingman. The German rolled over, but they were tail to nose. Walker's forehead hit the gunsight as he fired long bursts. He felt the heat of burning fuel and metal through his air scoop. The German righted his craft and leapt free seconds before it fell apart.

"His brother's after you, Two-one," a voice in his headset warned.

He banked hard left, wheeling directly into the attacker. He saw surprise and fear on the pale face behind the heavy armored glass. They fired at each other like madmen, but the German was frightened and he missed low. Walker's cannon tore into the powerful Focke-Wulf engine. He skimmed underneath his quarry, whose plane now buckled savagely and smoked. A man in a blue flying suit dropped from the plane as it began to spin out of control. He fell for a long time, then the white cupola

of his chute obscured him. Walker went down to help
Jennings.

Hollyfield came roaring out of the sky, leaving the battle
far behind. A thousand feet below, falling through the
haze, was the Focke-Wulf he wanted. He saw the horizon
slip by, the army on the ground toiling forward, the flak
heavily laced with yellow tracers, but his eyes never left
his man. Any lapse in concentration and he would be
gone. The distance between them closed. The Focke-Wulf
was unsure. He did a nice half-roll, showing his pale blue
belly, and leveled out. They streaked over the ground at
1,200 feet. The sun shifted in and out of the haze, blinding Hollyfield momentarily. Tracers tore at him. He heard
the pinging sound of bullets puncturing his plane and could
see riflemen everywhere standing up and taking aim, but
he pressed on. He wanted this kill desperately, frantically,
for he had only one victim to his credit. A loud bang
exploded in the cockpit. He was hit in the thigh. The
FW began to rise. He was being led into an AA battery
and picked out the guns rising malevolently. Pain shot
down his leg, but he kept his foot jammed against the
rudder bar and banked away at the last possible second.
They were climbing now, hanging nearly motionless in the
sky as their machines pulled them upward. Hollyfield
panicked, fired, and hit nothing. The German was still
close, still clearly in sight. The battlefield spread below
them wider and wider until there were no more charging
men, no more whizzing shells, just a thin pall of smoke.

"Git him, Jasper. Git him."

He saw fewer FWs as they climbed. He was tired and
wondered what the German would do. They reached
20,000 feet. He fired. Nothing. Abruptly the German
flipped over on his back. He was going into a split S. He
was leaving. Hollyfield banked on his bad leg, chattering in
pain. Through the haze he saw his man floating beautifully
in a half-roll, like a butterfly on a summer day. In rage
he fired everything, cannon, machine guns, everything,
and the German was hit. He was hit bad. He was flaming.
It was the end. His plane corkscrewed. Still, the pilot
remained in the cockpit. He spun away, riding on a carpet
of thick black smoke. The snow-covered ground pitched
closer and closer still. A raging fire erupted against the
bleak whiteness down there. Hollyfield turned his regula-

tor to full oxygen and reached for the first aid kit below
his seat.

Donaldson stared out at the blank hazy sky. He was
depressed, vaguely resentful, and quite tired. A pang of
self-pity went through him. Once again his nerve had
given out as it did on almost every mission. But this time
they had found out about it. He had made a goddamn
fool of himself in full view of everyone, just like a tail-ass
turkey should. Then they caught him with the bottle to his
lips, and he knew he was through. He sighed very deeply
and looked at the heavens. He did not know where he
was and he did not care. His compass said he was heading
due east, toward the Tyrrhenian Sea. Below, he could see
the mountains, dark and foreboding. He was up fairly
high, at 22,000 feet, and the German armies were not
visible, although he couldn't be sure about that, for the
mixture of oxygen and brandy made him light-headed.

Quite unexpectedly he spied the Messerschmitt. It was
alone and flying toward him a few thousand feet below,
its dark green camouflage visible against the whitish
ground. He pushed over into a shallow dive. He held the
stick calmly, pulling it back against his stomach. His gunsight was on. He peered into it, roused by a bizarre kind of
exhilaration. The Messerschmitt never saw him. He slipped
down and blew it apart with cannon fire. Every single
shot scored a hit. The plane broke into three flaming
segments and sifted away.

"Beware of the Hun in the sun," Donaldson said with a
wry laugh as he begun to pull up.

But then something on the ground, some movement he
hadn't been aware of, caught his eye. He banked in a
blue landscape of sky and horizon that left him dizzy for
a second. What appeared to be a truck convoy crept along
way down there. He went into a very long glide, hoping
not to be seen until the last moment. They were German
trucks all right, massive vehicles with big fenders and
high-old fashioned radiators. Crossing over them, he
counted seventeen. He came around and zoomed in at
the column, blasting the lead truck with cannon fire until
it exploded and overturned wildly, blocking the road. His
next pass was at the big tractor towing a heavy howitzer
that brought up the rear of the column. The canvas top

began to burn as he poured machine gun fire into it. Men jumped out and tried to get the tractor off the road. Donaldson saw its treads had been smashed by cannon shots. He came in low, strafing and butchering everything in front of him, stitching up the road in long, even rows of .50 caliber bullets. He was so low that smoke from the burning trucks seeped into his cockpit. Three times he came around, cutting down soldiers fleeing in the fields, then tearing up the trucks, which were unable to escape because the column was blocked at both ends. On his final pass, everything was silent. Dead men lay scattered for many yards in all directions. He was stunned. Fear came to him. He had gone too far, been too lucky not to be murdered in return for this carnage. He searched the sky anxiously. *Run, run for home,* something urged him.

He stayed low, flitting and dancing over the snow-white countryside. A sense of awe and childish enthusiasm he hadn't felt since flying school nearly overwhelmed him.

"They can't have me now," he muttered. "Not now."

"Calling Lone Eagle," a strange voice said, easing into the silence all around him. "Lone Eagle, are you in trouble?"

He looked up. High above, a squadron of twin-engined P-38s flew in perfect formation.

"Am okay, Big Birds," he said hoarsely. "Just a little engine trouble. She's cutting out at ten thousand feet."

"We saw what you did back there," the voice said in a conversational tone that nevertheless conveyed real authority. "Beautiful piece of work. We salute you."

"Good to know I had some help around," Donaldson said.

"It was your show. What squadron are you with, Lone Eagle?"

"Seventy-fourth, at Matera."

There was a pause.

"Oh, yes," the voice said more slowly. "One of Fremont's men. Well, you'll be the talk of Headquarters tonight, fly-boy. We'll leave you here. Good luck getting home."

"So long, Big Birds."

They went into a long banking turn, the outside man holding station as if it were no trouble at all. Donaldson watched them go. He knew they, too, were veterans, and he had won their respect. It seemed unbelievable.

The squadron had long since circled the battlefield where Clark's army was pulling back in an orderly but rapid retreat, and headed home. Hollyfield sat rigidly in his cockpit, breathing rather heavily. The morphine he'd injected into his thigh had dazed him, but he was all right. He wondered if they would be blamed for the failure of the attack. And he thought about his kill. The whole thing had happened so fast, his mind still reeled. He was upset to think that he could summon up so much frenzy and desperation to the task of destroying another man. He wasn't like that. He had never been like that, and there was no doubt the fight could have easily gone the other way. Dogfights always unnerved him because they left a man so alone. Now, flying easily in the midst of the squadron, he felt safe. He realized they had just enjoyed a good day, a very good day, and against big odds, too.

They neared Matera. The field was just over the next ridge. Fremont was calling in for landing instructions. No one saw the Focke-Wulf dodging above them. No one heard the whine of its big engine or saw the yellow prop spinner until it was almost on top of them. Gun flashes seemed to fill the air around Hollyfield. The armored glass splintered and cracked. He moaned. The FW, long, lethal, and terribly quick, plunged by his starboard wing-tip. He heard curses. Someone was calling him on the headset. He ached all over, but the smell of smoke and flames pulled him back into alertness. Smoke blocked his vision. He turned up his oxygen to 100 percent.

"Bail out. Get out, Jasper!" someone yelled.

But he couldn't. The canopy was jammed. His hand groped through the smoke for the emergency release handle. He couldn't find it. Flames covered his gloved hand and flicked up from under the seat, playing at his legs. Fire began to blot out everything. It was hot, fantastically hot. At last he found the release handle, but it would not budge. Flames were all around him. He couldn't see the other planes. People shouted wild desperate instructions. He was on fire, his flying suit was on fire. Strange dreadful smells, burning leather and rubber and seared human flesh, filled the cockpit. He headed earthward. He was close to the ground in an open area when he lost control of the plane. The men on the fire truck saw it rocket on its belly and come to a halt far from the field. It was burning brightly.

FOURTEEN

MANY HOURS LATER, Beasley emerged from the infirmary. All the men from C flight and a lot of the others crowded in close to hear what he would say about Hollyfield. He spoke to them calmly. Hollyfield was alive. His condition was critical, but he was expected to live. Bullets had been removed from his thigh, shoulder, and right lung. He had suffered third-degree burns over half his body, including his face. His goggles had saved his eyes. The shock of those burns was devastating. Several transfusions were necessary. He would need further operations.

There was an awesome silence. The men were stupefied. Beasley's assistant, a medical corpsman, stood beside him with tears rolling down his face. The pilots drifted away, angry and disappointed with Beasley without really knowing why.

Fremont walked beside his friend toward the mess hall. New snow was falling. Their feet crunched over the ground.

"Dick, is he really going to live?"

"Probably. The boys on the fire truck did the job they were trained to do, but today they were too goddamn good at it."

"Don't take it too personally. It was one of those things."

"You haven't seen him," Beasley said. "You go back in

208

there and take a look at that boy before you tell me to be cool and calm."

Fremont came to a stop, for the extent of Beasley's despair was becoming plainer.

"It's awful, Jonathan. Just horrible. Burns scare me. That hundred-octane fuel burns hot as a furnace. His hands are all twisted and clawed. His whole face is melted. He's a mummy."

Fremont looked into Beasley's sad eyes, and a surge of terror swept through him.

"What are you doing for him?"

"I have to fight off the risk of infection, that's the big worry now. He's got a massive dose of sulfa in him, and I'm hoping. But if he makes it, I can't deal with all that scar tissue, and there'll be a lot of it. Hollyfield will need a couple of dozen operations. They'll strip his back and chest for skin, but it won't really do much good."

"It's got to help him," Fremont insisted.

"It won't," Beasley replied. "What can he do when he gets back? He'll be the ugliest thing you ever saw. He'll look like . . . he'll look like shit. Walking shit. And he'll be treated that way by everyone who sees him. That boy is ruined, Jonathan. I wish to hell I'd had the guts to kill him when they first brought him in. I wanted to, but I just couldn't. I couldn't do it."

As darkness approached, Fremont drove out to the dispersal. He put on a parachute and trotted to his airplane. Friday watched him in the dwindling light as he released the canopy and cranked it back. He waited until Fremont had finished checking the instruments, then strolled over. "I'm going up to check out my hydraulics, Friday," Fremont said a trifle roughly. "Been having a little flap trouble."

Friday raised an eyebrow to indicate he did not like being confronted with this kind of flimsy story. They both knew it was late, really too late for him to be going up alone. But nothing was said as Friday tightened the shoulder harness and got down.

Fremont checked to see if anyone was standing near his propellor. He was about to close the canopy when Osborn appeared beside him on the wing walk.

"Glad I caught you, sir," he said as the prop wash

pulled at his uniform and blew his cap away. "We've got to make a decision on Donaldson. He's been grounded for two weeks, but a colonel at HQ saw his Messerschmitt kill and the sacking of that truck convoy. They put him in for a Silver Star."

Fremont shook his head in anger.

"I ought to drum him out, Ops," he said. "But if Doc clears him to fly, we'll give him another shot. I want to impress on him that if he's ever caught drinking again, court-martial is automatic."

"Check."

Osborn smiled and waved as Fremont began to taxi. He kneeled thoughtfully on the damp ground as the Mustang roared down the runway and disappeared.

Fremont went into a long climbing turn over the field. The whole place looked pitiful and forlorn, like a frontier town in Montana or Idaho a hundred years ago. Smoke drifted out from the big mountain caves where many of the local people lived. He wondered how they existed.

He headed east, not really sure of where he was going. His thoughts focused on the fighting front. The fighting in western Italy seemed to be shaping up around Cassino and the ancient monastery overlooking it. Without taking Cassino, it would be impossible to gain access to Route 6, the highway leading directly to Rome. It was only sixty miles from Cassino to Rome, but the German Tenth Army had crack divisions around the town and no one could tell when a breakthrough might come. The big attack two weeks ago had cost 1,000 dead and nearly 600 wounded. Amphibious operations in the German rear looked like the best answer.

The lights of Bari, a large provincial town on the Adriatic Sea twinkled below. He crossed out over the water. His clock had stopped and he had no idea how long he'd been flying. He was not aware of the dark water 20,000 feet below. Flying at night was a relief. There was no horizon, no visual points of reference to keep track of. Everything he wanted to know was registered on the big round-faced delicate instruments in front of him. Their soft red light powdered his hands on the stick and his leather jacket. He was totally alone at last, and yet Fremont felt childish in being this isolated. He wondered if he was as stable as he'd been. The trip to Washington and Todd's

suicide had eaten at his nerve more deeply than he wanted
to admit. But there was no way to measure his ability to
lead. Time would let him know about that. Off to starboard now, he saw the navigational lights of another airplane. They passed. It might be a JU-52 coming in from
Yugoslavia or perhaps a British plane. He watched the
lights grow smaller and vanish.

After a while he began to feel guilty. He knew he
should be back in his cottage writing a long sad evasive
letter to the parents of a boy named Fuqua, a replacement
who had been killed by German gunners three long weeks
ago. But he no longer knew what to say in these letters.
The burden of writing them made him both stale and cynical. He still had to contact Hollyfield's parents and that
would be even harder.

He scanned his instruments. He had been climbing for
the last few minutes without knowing it. Gently, he pushed
back a little on the stick and felt the nose fall. The Mustang streamed through the night. The sound of his powerful Rolls-Royce engine driving the huge prop that pulled
him across the vast distances, the feel of the plane snugly
around him, made Fremont realize again how much he
loved to fly.

His mind drifted back to the superb English summer
of 1939, when every day he flew his ancient Gladiator bi-
plane over the bright green undulating fields of Kent. The
pure joy of it, the wind on his face, the smooth respon-
siveness of his plane as it tumbled and rolled through its
maneuvers, the keen thrill of coming in on a grass field
and not skidding as the other cadets watched, all these
fine pure memories forced him to smile in boyish satisfaction. Those might have been his best days back there in
England, yes, they might have been the best after all.

Suddenly he was about to close the coast of Yugoslavia,
a country occupied by the Germans. His airspeed was
300 mph and in no more than two minutes he would be
over the numerous outer islands at 19,500 feet, low enough
to be picked off by a radar-controlled battery. He banked
to starboard and turned for home. A glance at the gauges
told him the wing tanks were almost dry. He had come
too far. Whatever was left in the fuselage tank would have
to bring him home. Tension again seized Fremont.

FIFTEEN

WALKER LAY IN BED, drawing on his corncob pipe. The kerosene lantern on the packing case between them shed more light on him than it did on Jennings, but even from where he was, he could see that Jennings had changed. He had hardened a great deal. Most of the charming naïveté and befuddlement of last summer were gone. He was heavier, rougher looking in his rumpled clothes of corduroy, sheepskin, and army-issue. He seemed to have a continual stubble of beard, even though it had to itch when he wore his oxygen mask. And Jennings smoked more than anyone on the base, possibly three packs of Camels a day. He bought everyone's extras no matter what price they were demanding. But it was his cockiness and perception that really impressed Walker. He felt a sort of compulsion to talk to Jennings now, to make him understand things. That was why he brought up his Special Duty tour this evening.

"That nurse did it, the one who was so snotty to me," he said. "Took me a week to figure it out. She slipped in there and knifed him real good, then kept everybody away until he was about gone. It had to be her. No one else could have got past all those beds without being seen. I'm going to have to go back there and kill that bitch."

Jennings stirred. He propped himself up on one elbow.

"Celestino was quite the man," Walker said. "You

would have liked him, Carl. The son bitch knew truth. He knew like the country preacher knew."

"You believe he passed something on to you?" Jennings said.

"Damn right he did. He said we had to fight and take what was ours and he was right. We haven't done near enough."

"We're trying. We're trying all the time," Jennings replied.

"When this shit is over we got to carry on the fight harder, all the way to Washington. With guns if necessary."

"Horseshit."

"How you gonna sound, tail-ass!" Walker shot back. "You were pissing in your pants the week before last. Now you're a big man and know everything."

"I never said that."

"You didn't have to bother. You got a funny way of makin' yourself known."

"Who's going to lead this revolution across the land?" Jennings asked. "Who's going to get our people, as frightened as they are, to march up to the steps of the White House? Don't tell me it's going to be you."

Walker sat up in his bed.

"You smartass son of a bitch," he blurted out. "I ought to kick your butt."

Then he said no more. His eyes became moist, for he realized he too was afraid, and he was ashamed of his fear. He didn't seem to have it in him, anywhere in him, to rise up and strike at what had caused that fear. Celestino might have helped him cut loose, might have helped him let go with all that rage. But Celestino was dead.

"Sonny Boy," Walker said. "Don't think badly of me."

"I couldn't do that."

Jennings lit a cigarette and passed it over to Walker, whose pipe had gone out.

"What about the woman in Foggia? Do you ever think about her?"

"Sure, I think about her. I love that woman, but things are harder than that, Cricket. Love is hard for me because it's mostly responsibility when you come down to it. It scares the mess out of me. I can't handle it, man. I guess

I'm not from that old-fashioned take-responsibility stock. I wasn't cut out to be nothin' but a rogue."

"Do you think you'll ever get back to Foggia?"

"No. I'd be just another little black face like the nigger in the song. I can't fight that."

Skinner walked through the dispersal area, trying to make his presence as unobtrusive as possible. Most of the planes were chocked and tied down for the night with canvas jackets over their canopies. The ground crewmen worked over the others. A portable generator cast a dazzling whitish light upon the scene. On its perimeter, fires burned in old oil drums to keep the men warm. Through the shimmering heat waves Skinner saw Dummy Jones leaning against the hood of a jeep. He strolled over.

"I got your car here, Lieutenant," Dummy said matter-of-factly. He unscrewed a Thermos bottle and poured Skinner some milky hot coffee.

"What are you asking?" Skinner inquired as he sipped the coffee elegantly.

"I got to have fifteen dollars tonight," Dummy said. "I could lose my stripes for this."

"I can let you have ten," Skinner answered. He disliked all this haggling night after night, but without Dummy he was stuck on the base.

"I got to see twelve dollars," Dummy insisted in a lowered voice.

Skinner opened his wallet and handed over the money.

"Thanks, Lieutenant, you're a fair man. Now we got to gas her up. Can you let me have a couple of dollars toward that? They really watch the gas these days. The man on the pump has to be taken care of, too."

Skinner gave him two dollars, and in an instant Dummy produced a five-gallon gasoline can from under the jeep and filled the tank.

"Sure would like to see you back on the field at 0430, Lieutenant. Crew chief comes out for early inspection then, and if he can't find his jeep, there'll be shit to pay."

Near the gate Skinner pulled to a stop and Archibald strode out of the darkness and climbed in. He held a small white box that Skinner shined a flashlight on. The box was plush with green velvet inside. A beautiful necklace of antique silver glistened at them.

"Thanks, Travis," Skinner said. "She'll like it. We'll settle for this and the jeep when we get to town."

"Whatever you say, pretty face. But let's roll on out of here, baby. Daddy's got a whole lot of business to take care of tonight."

Even in the dark, Skinner could see Archibald looked different tonight. He wore a little lipstick, his cheeks were faintly rouged, and he smelled of an expensive women's perfume. A touch of face powder clung to the silk ascot at the neck of his freshly ironed shirt. His large gold pinky ring gleamed in the moonlight as he tapped it impatiently on his knee. Skinner was both fascinated and appalled. No one in the world would ever believe he was a fighter pilot, but where he was going tonight it probably did not matter. Besides, he liked Archie a lot. He was a funny and agreeable man. He was not ashamed of what he was, not afraid of being an outcast, and for Skinner this courage linked them in an odd way.

They drove rapidly along narrow curving mountain roads above sweeping valleys where human footprints had not yet broken the snow, coming finally down out of the hills to the port of Bari, for centuries a city heavily under Greek influence, now a British Army depot and rest area. The whole trip had taken forty-five minutes. As they crested the last hill, the smell of the Adriatic came to them in the cold penetrating air. Archibald directed Skinner to a small paved square with a marble fountain in the center that was coated in ice. They agreed to meet back there at 0330 and exchanged money for the necklace and the cost of the jeep.

"We won't have much leeway, Archie," Skinner explained. "I can give you five minutes' waiting time and then you're on your own."

Archibald nodded and checked his watch. Once again Skinner was struck by his ugliness. He was a tall, superbly proportioned man, but it all seemed ruined by his hideous face, by the broad flat lips and small sharp animal eyes.

Just then a car entered the square, an old upright black sedan. It crept into a dark corner and stopped.

"Sweetheart. Over here," a well-bred English voice called to Archibald, who smiled at Skinner and flounced away, tossing a coy mischievous look over his shoulder as he neared the car.

Skinner let them leave first and then began driving through the streets of Bari. If anyone stopped him, he was searching for a friend. That was his cover story. Within minutes he was in the wealthier section of town, in an enclave of villas and small palaces in the Byzantine style. He pulled the jeep off to the side. Cautiously he approached a large stone house where tall elegant cypresses stood grouped at each corner like minarets. He noticed several big imposing automobiles, including a few Chryslers, U.S. Army staff cars.

He loped around to a back door and entered with a key, stepping into a sort of drawing room. It was dark, but soft light slithered under the heavy polished doors at the far end of the room, leading to the grand salon. He could make out a gentle melding of voices, low cultured laughter, glassware clinking, and a string ensemble playing something baroque. Gina's father had been Minister of Finance in the Mussolini government; now that fallen government had fled to Bari and was virtually powerless, and it disturbed him that they were still having a good time while the war droned on. He wondered if Alexander or Eisenhower was in that next room. *"Buona sera,"* a devilish little voice said.

It was Gina's maid Anna, her white cap and apron standing out in the gloom.

"This way, please," she said coquettishly as she led him up the back stairs, the way they always went. When they reached the big gold-and-white sitting room in Gina's suite, she was not there. Her cigarette burned in a marble ashtray on a coffee table next to the love seat. Skinner put the box with the necklace in it beside him as he sat down. Then Anna handed him a drink ("British whiskey, the way you like it"), and he waited.

After a while the door opened halfway. He heard Gina's rich, luxurious, insouciant laugh in the adjoining room. A blond afghan hound trotted in. Gina came around the door and leaned on it lightly so the man on the other side, an RAF officer in blue, could not follow her. Skinner glimpsed a corner of his face. He had sandy hair, a flushed countenance, a thick aviator's mustache.

"Gina," he said as the glass in his hand shook violently.

"Please. You're not being fair to me. I must talk to you. It's important and God knows when I'll see you again."

"You'll try to see me next Thursday as you always do, and it won't work. Good night, Group Captain."

Before he could say another word, the door was slammed shut and locked.

Gina came across the exquisite parquet floor in her long sashaying aristocratic stride. She was both beautiful and elegant and she knew it. Her full wavy shoulder-length hair was a tawny color that set off her eyes, which were blue and sparkled like sapphires. A slight bulging in the hips and a thinnish mouth were the only things that kept her from looking too wild, too exotic.

She sat down beside Skinner, wearing a Chanel suit, several bracelets of Florentine gold, and a lush perfume. He kissed her hungrily until she wriggled free of his embrace and laughed.

"I'm not going to let you stay away for a whole week ever again," she said, looking at him. "Where have you been, Percy?"

"They've had us up on the line," he said, picking up his drink. "They're recreating World War One up there."

"I like the necklace," she said, holding it up to her throat so that he could see it. "It's superb. But I don't have much time to give you tonight, Percy. There is a big reception downstairs for senior Allied officers, and I'm expected to entertain. Could we make it Saturday. Rather late?"

He leaned over and kissed her on the mouth.

"Of course," he said, although he was irritated and let-down.

She held his handsome head away from her, running one finger over his dark skin.

"You look marvelous tonight," she whispered. "You belong down there in the salon, talking to my father and the others. That should have been your destiny."

"I know," he said.

He kissed her again, softly and with immense tenderness. He adored Gina. She was strong, fiery, intelligent, and imbued with that unshakable confidence which always accompanies money. She reminded him of Helene, far away and long ago in Germany before the war. He felt her tremble in his grasp and pressed on subtly. Her hand was inside his shirt. He stroked the inside of her soft silken thighs. Their legs scissored together as they slid onto the lush oriental rug. Gina moaned and whispered in his ear while Anna peeked through the slightly opened door, her small fat hands fluttering uncontrollably in passion.

"Gina," someone outside the door shouted. "Gina, let me in."

"Go away," she said, rolling over on her back. "I am busy."

"Gina, open this goddamn door!"

She let out a long sigh of angry disappointment.

"Percy, I have to," she said in a pleading, resigned tone of voice. "If I don't let him in, he'll go to my father and make enough noise to ruin the whole evening."

"Who is he?" Skinner asked, for the voice sounded southern and raw.

"His name is Maynard Evans. He's an American from Georgia, a major or something."

Evans began to pound on the door. "I'm not going to let up," he called.

"Saturday at eleven," Gina said, pressing Skinner's hand. "I am sorry about this, Percy."

They kissed. The back door was open and Anna stood beside it, holding a candle. As they started down the stairs, Gina unlocked the front door. Maynard surged into the room, one hand in his pocket, a lock of heavy black hair dangling over his forehead.

"I damn near busted my hand out there, Gina," he said. "Hey, you look funny. Who the hell was in here with you anyway?"

Gina picked up a table lighter and lit a cigarette.

"A friend of mine paid a call," she said. "He's a very handsome lieutenant from your army."

"Well, where the hell is he?" Maynard said, searching the large room in some confusion. "What kind of a man runs and hides when a brother officer enters a lady's sitting room?"

Gina smirked. "You wouldn't like him, anyway. He's not part of your code."

"Well, what is he, a Jap?" Maynard asked.

"No, my dear Major," Gina said ironically. "He is a Moor."

"You mean a nigger?" he said. "In here? Gina, you sure are crazy. But you shouldn't joke me like that, girl. Where I come from, niggers are only funny when we tell them to be."

"Say what you like, my broad-minded friend," Gina replied as she rose from the love seat. "But I've always been honest with you. Don't forget that."

Maynard glanced at her.

"Damn, Gina," he said in a conciliatory way, "you're just talkin' a whole lot of stuff and nonsense. Come on, let's go downstairs and have some champagne and enjoy this thing. I still don't feel I know your father."

Moments later the back door flew open and Skinner stalked into the room with Anna in his wake. She seized him by the hand, pleading with him to leave the house.

"Tenente, please. Go outside. Go *away*," she repeated over and over again in an imploring voice as he strode through the richly furnished apartment and yanked open the sliding doors giving on to the corridor. Here he seemed to freeze, and Anna crept up behind him, still holding the candle in one hand. She hooked his arm and he turned on her, his controlled face forced into a harsh visage of rage. She let go and touched him reassuringly, almost as if she dealt with these symptoms all the time. He strode off, heading down the long carpeted hall to the marble balcony surrounding the grand salon. At a discreet distance Anna followed him. What he saw below in the huge chandeliered room filled him with wonder and envy. Medieval tapestries covered the walls. Dozens of high-ranking officers stood about talking with older men in well-cut dark suits while maids in black and white circulated among them, serving glasses of champagne from silver trays. There were a few women around, wives and daughters of the Italian cabinet ministers. The richness of the scene, the profusion of stars and uniforms and medals glinting in the soft light as a string octet played sprightly baroque music, all of this overwhelmed and stunned Skinner. He recognized some of the men down there in their custom-made evening dress uniforms. And he felt compelled to descend the sweeping main staircase, to speak to them, to reveal to them that he too was present. In that instant Anna reappeared and pushed him back rudely. She removed her apron and touched his brow with it, wiping away the beads of sweat. He was breathing very deeply. He was ready to leave now.

SIXTEEN

A HOT FIRE SIZZLED in the potbellied stove near the stage in the Briefing hut. Osborn stepped forward, holding a brown manila folder under one arm. He looked down at the men, who were crowded into the first two rows, except for Donaldson against the wall.

"Good morning, gentlemen," he said a bit more formally than usual.

The men understood that in his way Osborn was delivering a New Year's greeting, for it was the second day of 1944. Osborn inspected the pilots carefully. They appeared clear-eyed, healthy, and well-rested after a nine-day layoff because of bad weather. He remembered the big Christmas celebration with roast boar and potatoes, a party for the children in the cave dwellings, and presents of food from the villagers who wanted to thank Beasley for giving them free medical care. Osborn had not seen the men as relaxed since Tuskegee.

"Ops, we hear a lot about an invasion of northern Europe in the next few months," Jennings said. "We'd like to know what you hear about this."

Osborn checked his watch and decided to take a few moments out to discuss the question. Fremont nodded in agreement.

"Gentlemen, let's look at the map," Osborn said, picking up his pointer. "Germany still holds most of Europe, a chunk of Russia, and two-thirds of Italy. We have North Africa, southern Italy, and the British Isles. We're winning in the Atlantic. The convoys are getting through, but in spite of everything the Reich is still very much alive."

"We know all that," Walker said. "Tell us something we don't know."

"Rumor has it, and remember this is just scuttlebutt, but they say assignments for the power thrust into the heart of Germany are now being given out to the top generals."

"When do we get in on the big stuff?" Walker asked.

"You're in on the big stuff now," Osborn said. "This fight around Cassino will be a turning point, like Stalingrad and Tunis last year. There are soldiers on the line from all over the world—Poland, New Zealand, France, everywhere. And mountain troops have arrived from India and Morocco. This is the first real international military effort, and I don't want any of you forgetting it. They'll be writing about this for a long time, so keep your mouths shut and don't let anybody down. Understand?"

He finished and gave way to Jones, who showed them some enlarged photographs of the hilly area they would be attacking.

"We are now operating along a front that shifts considerably from day to day," Jones said. "The infantry has probed and found a lot of soft spots. Along the sector you'll be working today, troops have gotten into the mountains. These men are fighting in clouds, sometimes, and in sleet and blizzards. There are no roads up there, just horse and mule tracks."

"What can we do here, Jonesy?" Rennie Washington asked. "We're having trouble picking out targets under our noses half the time."

"You're going to try," Jones said evenly. Pantelleria was far behind him. He worked hard and knew his job well.

"Without command of these hills we'll never get through, and to get through we must destroy enemy mortars faster than he can replace them. The mortar teams are going to be everything in this fight. Our big guns can't hit a lot of the German positions because they are blocked by ridges and we can't risk moving up and showing ourselves in the open. The mortars have taken over. They're deadly on those narrow ledges and reverse slopes. I've pinpointed some of the more prominent positions on this recon map.

But look everywhere for the flashes. They'll be dug in
like fleas on a dog's ass."

At the dispersal the pilots clustered around Fremont.
Most of the mechanics stood close by.

"Now I'm sure all of you noticed Ops was a little upset
this morning," Fremont said, his breath coming in thick
vapor. "And he has damn good cause to be. It seems the
Germans resent the fact we've made a name for ourselves.
Their intelligence boys have put together a profile on us.
They say we're deviants and mutants from an inferior
race. That's what the reports say," Fremont shouted over
the grumbling and cursing. "Berlin has ordered the Luftwaffe to destroy us. So let's look alive up there today. We
may be jumped, anything may happen. Okay. That's it.
Start engines at 0655."

They took off and swung west. The sky was gray and
dull, the ceiling low. The flight to the battleground seemed
to take only minutes. It was all too familiar by now: the
battered hollow town of Cassino, the railroad station where
men died for possession of a doorway, Hangman's Hill,
Phantom Ridge to the northwest, the Monte Villa barracks
straight ahead, and Route 6 parallel to the railroad tracks
running north to Rome.

"We are supporting hills four hundred forty-four and
four hundred forty-five," Fremont reminded them as the
squadron passed over the magnificent walled Abbey of
Monte Cassino, designated hill 516, the highest elevation
for several miles.

On the upper ridges of 444, a fire fight was in progress.
A British brigade flanked by American units had run into
a line of machine guns. They were torn to shreds, slaught-
ered as they ran and dived for cover. The Germans refused
to stop firing even as the planes closed in. Their helmets
never moved. No one looked up. They just kept shooting.
Antiaircraft fire crackled through the air. Fremont pulled
his men up for the attack on 445. On the Allied side, the
hill was alive with various national flags and colors.

"We'll split into two sections. You boys up top don't
make a move before we come off that hill. We don't want
to get jumped down there."

"Right, leader," Skinner called in.

Fremont went down first. He was amazed at how many

men clung to the surface of that blasted ground. Some of them waved and pointed to the targets. It was a good run. They got good angles on the German dugouts and killed nearly every man in them. Skinner's and Archibald's flights zoomed in, yellow and red tracers streaming all around them. They left a line of heavy bluish smoke and smashed gun positions. The Allied soldiers charged upward.

"One more strike apiece and we'll get the hell out of here," Fremont barked.

They started down, line abreast. It was noisy. There was more fire than Fremont had anticipated. He concentrated on the flickering guns among the big boulders. Suddenly he heard a cry in the headset.

"I'm burning!" a man said. "Right wing."

A plane veered off from them, dropping below Walker and heading for a ridge near the top. The Mustang skittered along near a flat space and crashed on its belly. There were no flames. Not far away, not a hundred yards below, Fremont noticed a French tricolor. The French had seen the plane resting on its side and moved up. Then mortars zeroed in on them. Some of the French crawled forward, but the fire was too heavy for quick movement. Fremont racked his men around and bore in. Strong fire beat them off. A squad of German soldiers made its way down the slopes toward the plane. On the other side the French ran and dodged, trying to get closer. The top guard swooped upon the persistent laboring figures in long gray coats, hitting them hard, yet they kept coming. Everyone was tense, anxious. The pilot was out of his plane now, facing the Germans, pistol in hand. Fremont scanned the heavens for enemy planes while the last two flights pulled up. It was hopeless. The pilot was firing, but it was hopeless. The Germans were on him as they scrambled over the dead bodies of their comrades. The French fired in desperation but hit only the plane.

"They got him," Archibald said as the pilot raised his hands. "They got Greenlee."

"Give us one more run," Walker said. "Just one more."

"No," Fremont answered. "We don't want to lose another man."

They banked steeply to port. The French were still pinned down. Greenlee was surrounded by German helmets and overcoats. He walked stolidly, hands on top of his head, and glanced up one last time before they pushed him into a dugout.

"Leader," Butters said, "have spotted four tanks in the vicinity of the town. They're sneaking in from the north."

They dropped down to 1,500 feet. Now he saw them, too. The tanks were big and very wide.

"They're Tigers," Butters said.

Fremont pushed his stick forward and began to dive. He was too close to the ground, but he kept on. A yell escaped from his lips. His eyes were misty with tears because he knew what awaited Greenlee. He knew Greenlee would die like an animal in one of the special German hospitals, and the thought of it plunged him into a silent numbing frenzy. He watched the ground rise up and did nothing. The tanks were directly in front of his prop. His forehead slammed against the gunsight. He cut loose with all his machine guns and cannon, seeing only the tanks, only their hideous monolithic advance. His teeth were jammed together. Perspiration ran down the sides of his face and under his goggles. He came right in on the lead tank, firing at the huge gun in the revolving turret. His cannon shots tore at the treads, and the vehicle stopped clumsily. The next man in echelon fired at him, scoring hits on the fuselage as he passed not a hundred feet above. Turning, he streaked in behind them low, aiming at their radiators. He got the last two. They were smoking.

He circled back, head-on, as the crews tried to get out and run. Looking in the mirror, he saw bodies sprawled over the burning tanks and in the mud. The lead tank attempted to move on its broken treads, then gave up and poured fire into the village at random. But the second tank was getting away. It wheeled powerfully, smashing through a grove of decimated trees, and made for safety. Fremont overshot it and cursed, slamming one fist hard against his knee. The tank was fast, faster than he thought, and the driver knew how to maneuver in the open field. He zigzagged. Through fences and over a couple of ditches he rolled, his long aerial whipping in the wind. The big turret gun whirled malevolently, belching fire as it sent shells roaring in his general direction. Finally, he flattened out and came in at about 200 feet. Ground fire picked him up and the plane pinged with solid hits, but his cannon shots tore through the thin armor protection on the motor, and the tank began to burn. Fremont wished he had napalm so he could roast the men inside. As he passed overhead, the hatch flopped open and the crew scampered out. Butters cut them down from behind. Fremont breathed hard. He had trouble remembering where he was.

He mopped his brow and took a gulp of oxygen. He felt lightheaded and sad and unsure.

"Call them together, Roy," he said in a whisper. "We're going home."

"Sir, I think you did the Army a real service today," Butters said, smiling. "I noticed swarms of panzer grenadiers waiting in trenches to follow the next wave of tanks. When they saw what happened, no one came out. They never made a move. You beat back a whole attack, Colonel. I hope you save the gun-camera film on this one for your grandchildren."

Fremont stared at Butters with his mouth slightly open. He had not heard one word. Osborn came over and put a Coke into his hand but the bottle felt cold and repugnant to his touch. He took a sip as Osborn ran down a list on his clipboard.

"Walker had two kills. Skinner, one. Archibald, one," Osborn said. "Preliminary damage report, moderate."

"What about Greenlee?" Fremont asked.

Butters strolled back to his airplane.

"Sir," Osborn said quietly, "Greenlee is probably gone. We can make all the proper inquiries, but we both know it won't do much good. I think at this stage, sir, that we cannot allow the capture of any one man to become an issue of emotion. If we do, it can undercut us. That is my feeling."

Fremont gazed off into the distance.

"Okay, Ops," he said. "I accept that, but do what you can."

"Yes, sir, I will."

They stood watching the planes make their final approaches into the brisk crosswind, lower gear, flare out, and touch down. The ground crewmen were everywhere, waving planes in, helping pilots out of their harnesses, and checking damage. In spite of the noise and turmoil, there was a lot of conversation, a lot of joking. Some of

the men said it was the best time of the day, those first
few relaxed minutes out of the cockpit before the truck
left for debriefing. Archibald's flight came in now, but over
and above it a roar built up in the air. People turned and
searched the heavens.

"Planes! Planes!" one of the mechanics standing near
the runway cried.

They stood mute and unbelieving as the tiny specks in
the gray distance closed the field. The planes were white
and light blue underneath. It was hard picking them out
of the dismal sky. No one moved from where he stood.
Fremont recognized the slanting nose, the long sectioned-
glass canopy, the enormous protruding bullet-shaped cowlings of the Messerschmitt 410 bomber-destroyer. He made
out twelve in two groups flying six abreast.

"Get down. Get the hell down!" he shouted.

The Messerschmitts dropped low, huge cannons sticking
out of the bombbays. Shells whistled overhead and explosions erupted all over the field, releasing huge shock waves.
A tide of burning gasoline unfurled on the main runway.
Men screamed in the searing, choking heat. Machine guns
ripped into the turmoil. Planes trapped on the taxiways
were hit and started to burn. The Messerschmitts seemed
to drone by very slowly, giving an impression of incredible
power and invincibility. Fremont saw their black wing
crosses and the gesturing pilots behind the armored glass.
Another salvo was fired, then another. The hangar and
mess hall were blown apart. Fires raged in the tent area.
The second wave swept in, loosing incendiary rockets in
a fierce whitish glare. Several Mustangs jumped high in
the air and disappeared in a roar of flames.

Then everything was quiet except for the crackle of fires
and the confused choking of men in the smoke. The attack was over. It was nearly impossible to see. Helpless
moaning came from every direction. Bodies were everywhere. A lone Mustang raced by in pursuit and shot down
the last Messerschmitt as it went into a climbing turn.
Fremont kicked something. He stared down. He had stumbled over Beasley, unconscious and bleeding beside his
burning ambulance.

SEVENTEEN

THE SUN had just about set as Fremont emerged from his tent. His eyes scanned the partially rebuilt field, the new infirmary and mess hall, the half-finished main hangar, the neat rows of bright green tents. He found it hard to believe six weeks had passed since the surprise attack. Five men had lost their lives that day, including two mechanics and the crew chief, but the squadron went on. He stepped inside out of the chilly air, rubbed his hands together and poured himself some scotch before sitting down at the metal folding table which served him as a desk. He felt tired in a deep-seated, cumulative way. Harsh wrinkles drifted away from the corners of his eyes, and he discovered a few more gray hairs in his head almost every week. He was also mentally tired. He questioned things in a more intellectual way, as if he were a civilian, and it often surprised him to think of himself as a professional soldier.

He sipped his scotch and thought about the men who were killed in the air attack. He hardly knew them, hardly ever had had a chance to get to know them as men, as people. The only man he had a clear recollection of was John Laidlaw, the crew chief. During that first confused day at Tuskegee, Laidlaw had come to him with a story. He was a tall, thin dark man, very intense and emaciated-looking in his coveralls.

"I'm from Kansas City, Mister Fremont, sir. In the nineteen twenties I was a crackerjack automobile mechanic. Some people claimed I was the best mechanic in the Middle West. I worked on Pierce Arrows and Packards and brought a whole lot of business into the garage. But I had to work out back where no one saw me. I had to let the white boys, the owner's sons, take all the credit for my work, just to earn a decent buck. Sometimes people would see me and ask who I was. And the boys would say, 'Oh, him, he's just the nigger. We let him change tires.' When the Depression hit, they put me out on the street with nothin'. I hit the freights, went to California eventually to get a job sweepin' up in an airplane factory. When I showed I was good with my hands, they put me on the line. I'm an airplane mechanic, believe it or not. That's why I come."

Fremont still could not remember what he had done that day after they got Greenlee. He studied the gun-camera film over and over in disbelief. Osborn said some of the colonels over at HQ were worried that he might become a general after a few more days like that, but he was certain the episode would amount to nothing. He asked HQ for antiaircraft protection and received no answer, even though HQ knew the Germans were after them. This was not the way they treated future generals. Spare parts and replacement machinery for the hangar had yet to arrive. They were putting up only a dozen planes, yet nobody at HQ seemed to care. No one came around to inspect the bomb damage or offer a word of encouragement. It was hard to accept.

A loud rustling sound came from the tent flap and Beasley entered, slumped heavily on the crutches he used to keep the weight off his broken leg. He said nothing, but went directly to the small stove in one corner and began putting wood on the dying fire. Fremont watched him. Beasley had aged too. His bushy hair and beard were now more gray than black, and he'd put on a lot of weight since he was hurt. His leg seemed to be coming around slowly and that disturbed Fremont. Beasley needed medical care himself, but he refused to take the time off. After the air attack, he had lain on the ground in terrible pain and calmly given instructions to Osborn, who set his leg and put a splint on it. He had worked that evening until the last man was treated or sent in a truck to the hospital in Foggia.

"Hasn't anyone told you that influenza is rampant around here, General," Beasley said as he came over to the table holding a lantern. "We've had a lot of pneumonia, too. I lost one of the new boys last week. Better keep this tent warm, Jonathan; this is an unhealthy place we've stopped at."

Fremont smiled and poured his friend a drink. Beasley scrutinized him.

"We're getting to be a big hit stateside," he said. "The boys tell me we've had two magazine stories this month alone."

Fremont nodded and pulled at his drink.

"Heard from Marva lately?" Beasley asked, his voice cleaving to a delicate line between discretion and meddling.

Fremont looked at him. His face remained poised and neutral.

"She sends Christmas cards, birthday cards, that kind of thing," he said. "The boys write. They tell me what they're doing. Thank God for that."

"You know, Jonathan," Beasley said. "I always thought you should have married a more ordinary girl, a quick vivacious type. Marva is a lady, a fine lady, but she really helped to lock you into the role of military man. She was so correct and intellectual. She made it easy for you. That was never really you, Jonathan. I could see that much."

"You never did want me to be a soldier, did you Dick?" Fremont asked with the hint of a smile. "Come on, Battle Surgeon, get it off your chest."

Beasley chuckled.

"You would have made a good doctor, you really would have. I always hoped you'd go to medical school with me."

"Oh, I don't know, Dick," Fremont said. "Could be you're right. Everything was so distorted back then. We had to be supermen just to hold our heads up. We were so afraid of failure, so afraid of being niggers."

Beasley nodded, staring into the middle distance.

"It was too goddamn tough," he admitted, "but what we're doing here in Italy is a lot harder. I can't get accustomed to war, Jonathan. I've tried, but the whole thing haunts me. I still live with the Hollyfields and Greenlees."

Fremont gazed up at the terrain maps taped to the walls.

"The only man who seems to be at peace with himself is Walker," Beasley continued. "He really racks up those kills. If he comes back here without one, he's in a rage. They tell me he's going to be the top fighter pilot in the Med."

"He's different," Fremont said.

A fine misty rain swirled around Skinner and Archibald as their jeep sped along the slippery winding road to Bari. Skinner thought of asking Archie to slow down, but he, too, was in a hurry.

Lately he'd taken to studying Italian and brushing up on his Spanish. His goal was to escape, to desert, to flee with Gina and find a small village somewhere in Europe and stay there until the war was over. His defection would be a blow to Fremont and he was sorry. He admired Fremont and had tried to serve him courageously, really tried, but now he wanted something else.

He sneaked a glance at Archibald. Archie was becoming more frenetic as time went by. He was worried about survival. ("According to the statistics I should be in Arlington now.") He wore a bit more makeup now, drank a little more, drove faster, and had taken to talking and singing in falsetto. Skinner was somewhat alarmed. He wished he could do something. Archie had invited him to parties a couple of times, but he had declined, and this surprised him. He was not quite as liberal as he liked to think. Archie knew it and was amused. ("You want to know what we do, don't you Percy? Of course. Everyone does.")

"How's your little girl friend—what's her name— Gloria?" Archie asked.

"Gina. Her name is Gina," Skinner replied.

"Gina," Archie said, savoring the name. "Brisk and sophisticated. Charm and guile. Am I right, Percy?"

Skinner smiled and shot Archie a look of amused forebearance.

"Thanks," Archie answered, "because you'll be needing my advice. Your ass is going in the stockade, handsome. You're fucking out of your class and that's a good way to get that little pecker you've been hiding snipped right off."

"That's never worried me," Skinner said. "I can handle anything that comes up."

"Then go ahead!" Archie said. "Go right ahead, don't listen to me. No, don't listen to what Archie says because he's just a crazy nigger faggot. I know that's what you think, so go ahead. Bang away. But look out for what's behind you, Percy. It could be somebody with a hot poker in his hand."

Through his gunsight Walker could see the sprawling Benedictine monastery atop hill 516. It was still an awesome and beautiful building despite the heavy rain of bombs and shells on its majestic walls. ("The Benedictine monastery at Monte Cassino," Osborn had read to them one day from a file card. "Stormed by Lombards in 581 and Saracens in 883. An outstanding center of the arts and church historical scholarship in the early Middle Ages. Reconstructed in the eleventh century. Damaged by earthquakes in 1349 and extensively rebuilt in the sixteenth and seventeenth centuries. We've laid off it for a long time. Now, say goodbye to it.") Those high walls pierced by arched doorways leading nowhere fascinated Walker. They rose up out of the hill so defiantly they appeared to be part of its structure. His eyes roved over the place, picking out the smashed cupola of the main chapel, the crumbling red tile roofs, paved courtyards, statuary, and wide staircases leading from level to level, building to building. It all looked so eerie in the late-afternoon sunlight. His gaze wandered downward. On the side of the hill, right in the middle of the German dugouts and caves clustered down there, he spotted the bright blazing wreckage of the Messershmitt he'd just shot down.

He banked to starboard, slicing over the broad earth, looking for another kill. As usual, shelling was going on everywhere. Men were dying below, although at 20,000 feet it was difficult to believe. He saw the squadron spread out around him as they disposed of an inept surprise attack from above. Then his Mustang was hit, hit hard. It rocked and wobbled almost out of control. Strange noises came from the engine as the dials before him jumped under the ferocious impact of 20 millimeter cannon shells. He did nothing. He didn't believe what was happening, and he did nothing until smoke poured in from behind the ripped armor plating over his shoulder. The heavy cannon shots stopped reverberating in his ears. He was headed downward. He could see field pieces and tanks glinting in the sun.

"Get the hell out!" Fremont ordered him. "Jump."

He was trailing flames and smoke. In a minute it would be over.

"Blow the canopy!"

His head went down. The canopy flew away. He flung himself onto the starboard wing and lunged forward before rolling off. The slipstream grabbed him and he whirled away like a scrap of paper. He fell wildly in the cold, cutting air, gasping for breath. The packet on his back burst open, yards of limp silvery parachute cloth trailed behind him; and then a loud pop and he was jerked upright. He descended slowly. It was quiet. There was no sign of the war. He must have glided a long way after they hit him, that must have been it. He came down near a road and cut the noisy billowing chute away from him, watching it blow across a field and collapse.

"Never saw the son of a bitch," he said shaking his head. "He must have spotted all them swastikas on the side. Some people are jealous of everything. Now how the fuck am I gonna get home?"

He checked the magazines in both .45s and headed for the road, charging up the embankment in three long, powerful steps. No vehicles appeared, and after a while he sat down on a large rock, disgusted and annoyed with everything. His head ached and he found dried blood around his nostrils. He was still dazed, still shocked to find himself on the ground and on foot. About half an hour later, an antiquated vegetable truck chugged around the bend and rumbled toward him. He leapt in the middle of the road pointing both pistols at the driver, who stopped some distance from him, cowering in the cab.

"Where you goin' man?" he said with a big smile, one foot planted on the running board. "Why aren't you fightin' today?"

The driver, a hawkish-looking man in corduroy cap and jacket, surveyed him fearfully.

"Napoli," he said. "Napoli. Napoli," he repeated, thrusting a finger forward.

Walker smiled again and shook his head.

"Matera," he said, pointing his pistol ahead. He wiggled his hands to indicate the twisting roads.

The driver nodded obsequiously and Walker climbed
into the cab, which smelled of axle grease and livestock
and cheap gasoline. They rolled through the mountains for
a long time. But he was happy to be alive, happy to have
gone through the experience of being shot down. Nothing
to it, just get out of the motherfuckin' plane and find a
soft spot to land. Suddenly, though, he was irritated. The
truck was not moving fast enough. He made the driver
stop and took over the wheel. They rambled through the
undulating sunlit landscape, forcing people off the road,
scattering a flock of goats. Walker grabbed and tussled
with the wheel like a little boy.

"Hell, don't you worry none," he said to the man in the
corduroy cap. "You'll get some money and chow out of
this, and I'll be home in time to hear Front Page Farrell."

It was early evening. The last pale rays of the late winter
sun had just dissolved in the sky when Skinner approached
the villa. He came by a new route, slipping through hedges
and climbing fences, for this was no time to be stopped
and questioned. At the back door he looked around before
fishing out his key. The door sprang open. Anna stepped
out and handed him a note, then she pushed him away
from the house before he could read it.

"Go away, Mister Percy," she said in great agitation.
"Go back to your home. Quickly go."

One by one all the lights in the house went on. He
stumbled back into the shrubbery. Men began to run in
his direction, shouting in Italian. The two Great Danes of
the house came tearing out of a side door. He began to
run, dodging and scrambling to get away. The male servants in their striped jackets and the dogs thrashed about
him clumsily but could not locate him. There was someone else among them, shouting instructions. It was Maynard Evans. Skinner saw him running with a pistol in his
hand, cutting back and forth, beating at the dense thickets
with a stick. He circled out of the area, opening ground
between them rapidly. For an instant they spotted each
other, and he could see Evans' eyes grow large in surprise
and hate. A shot was fired.

"Get that nigger," Evans screamed. "Get him down."

More shots came, but they were wild and faraway. The
house stood elegantly in the distance. The servants were

tired. They rounded up the dogs. He could hear Evans arguing with them, his strident voice growing dimmer as the party headed back. He lay down, gasping for breath, and read Gina's note. She wanted to see him about 3:00 A.M. at a stone farmhouse south of Bari near the village of Triggiano.

He got to the farmhouse early and parked the jeep in back. Gina's Alfa Romeo, its headlights off, crept along the road shortly after the hour. Gina got out. She was wearing a fur coat over her nightclothes. Anna had come too. She smiled and giggled, then settled down on the running board to watch for cars.

Gina was very insistent and tender as they embraced. Skinner was thrilled by her, thrilled by the dark starry night and the audacity of what he was doing. He loved adventure. Gina took his head in her long delicate hands and kissed him.

"My father and Maynard have vowed to kill you," she said in a hush. "I'm very afraid for you, Percy. I don't know about running away."

They sat down and talked, sharing his last cigarette. Evans was after her to marry him. His plan was to send her immediately to Atlanta where she would stay with his family until the end of the war.

"Then he will redeem me like a lost parcel."

But she had rejected his proposal half a dozen times. Gina was adamant. She would never marry Evans.

She said nothing for a time. She sat holding his hand and looking out over the rough barren rocky fields.

"We'll try it for six months, Percy," she said. "And if things go badly, promise you'll let me come back."

"I promise you that much, Gina."

He would make all the arrangements because she was bound to the house and closely watched. She had lots of money, Swiss francs and English pounds, and that was their stake. They agreed again. Soon Italy would be behind them.

When Skinner arrived at the piazza, it was very late. Archie sat on the rim of the silent fountain and glared at him.

"Where the fuck have you been?" he said, pushing into

the driver's seat. "You tryin' to get my ass busted to private?"

Archie zoomed out of Bari and raced along the foggy roads. He was incensed. Fremont might be out on the flight line to meet them. But Skinner didn't seem to mind. He began to talk about his frustration with the war, about failing to be a top fighter pilot, about growing stale and slowly older, and all the rest of it about Gina just came out.

"Percy! Mercy! Why do this to your pretty self?" Archie said when he'd finished. "The war ain't gonna go on forever. Why not wait and do it the right way? They can shoot you on sight as a deserter, and they won't think twice about doing it to a nigger. But Archie suspects you know something about that."

A bitter, obstinate smile came to Skinner's lips. Archibald felt sorry for him. Percy was doomed.

The darkened field stretched beyond the mess hall windows as Fremont sat alone drinking a mug of coffee. It was late. A heavy rain drummed on the metal roof, drowning out the music on the radio out back where the cooks sat around enjoying some whiskey and a last cigarette before leaving. Around Cassino a far-flung and savage battle was entering its last days. New Zealanders, Maoris, Gurkhas, and a few Americans were fighting hand to hand out there in the dark. In the mud which had turned the Liri Valley into a replica of Passchendaele and the Somme, they were starving, starving and crawling forward in the mud to slash at the entrails and inflict a mortal wound on the great German armies of the Gustav Line.

The front door banged open and Osborn came in out of the rain, wearing a glistening rubber poncho and wool helmet liner. He made his way to the table circumspectly and removed a folder of reports from under the poncho.

"Thought you might want to glance at these, sir. Today's work. I'm impressed, myself."

"Sit down, Ops," Fremont said. "Have some java."

Osborn sat down and produced a cigar.

"Actually, sir, I'm here because we got a strange request on the teletype today. A Major Evans stationed in Bari has asked for a copy of our squadron roster. No reason given."

"Do you know the major?"

"No, sir. I checked around with some of my gremlins on the radio network and they say Evans is just a liaison officer to the British. Sounds a bit out of line to me, sir."

Osborn puffed at his cigar. Just the slightest trace of consternation fled over Fremont's face.

"Hold off on that request, Ops," he said. "Ask around. Find out who is getting off this field regularly and where he goes. Keep me posted."

"Yes, sir."

At the dispersal, most of the mechanics stood around eating sandwiches and drinking hot pea soup. The new spare parts shipment had come in and it meant a lot of work. Sergeant Harris, the crew chief, came striding over. He was agitated and very upset about something.

"Jones, I want to see you," he said, taking Dummy firmly by the elbow.

They walked a few steps away from the group. Harris put his hands on his hips. His close-cropped graying hair and steel-rimmed military spectacles gave him an air of immense authority.

"Let's talk a few facts, Jones," he said. "My jeep is beat to hell. The tires are going. The sparks and batteries are shot. The engine needs an overhaul because some son of a bitch has been running it like a goddamn taxicab. Now, I never leave this fucking base, so I want to know who does. And I want to know now."

"Chief," Dummy said, "I couldn't tell you. I see that jeep out here at night sometimes, but other times it's gone."

"Listen, wise ass, the man on the gas pump tells me you run your own rental service. Now, who the fuck uses my jeep?"

"Don't know," Dummy said, shaking his head.

"I ought to cut those goddamn stripes off your arm right now. Come on," Harris said, seizing Dummy by the shoulder and leading him toward the jeep. "We'll take this matter before the colonel."

Walker strolled casually from around the side of his airplane, hands in his pockets.

"You there, Chief," he said loudly. "Turn that man loose. That's my man there. Unhand him this instant."

"Stay out of this, Walker," Harris shouted back. "This is an enlisted man's matter."

Walker strode over as the mechanics stopped work and watched. He didn't like Harris. The man wore his eyeglasses up on his forehead when he drank a glass of beer in the base club. The jeep started up. Walker put his foot on the front bumper.

"Who the fuck you talkin' to, Tech Sergeant," he said. "Talk to me like that and I'll blow your fucking head off."

"You irresponsible son of a bitch," Harris said. "Why do you have to mix in everything? This man is going before the colonel. He's a small-time crook and I'll prove it."

"You ain't provin' nothin'!" Walker yelled. "You take this man in front of Fremont and we'll have to talk about something else, too. You know what I mean. I know all about that little young girl you were humping at Tuskegee. She sort of disappeared, didn't she? Where she go to have the baby, Harris?"

Harris released his tight grip on Dummy's elbow. Fremont had warned them time and again about getting women in trouble at Tuskegee. He cringed as the men stared at him. He would be failing in his duty, failing to handle all the details under his charge, if he let Jones get away with this. But if they went into the colonel's quarters, he would be destroyed, would no longer be a crew chief. He shut off the engine and sat stonily behind the wheel of the jeep. Jones left his side.

"Thanks, brother," Dummy said to Walker with a silly smile. "I was just about plucked chicken."

"They don't call you Dummy for nothin'," Walker said. "I only saved your ass because you fix my plane good. Now you can tell me. Who burned out his jeep?"

"I don't know nothin' about that jeep," Dummy answered.

"Nigger, don't hand me that shit!" Walker bellowed, turning on him. "Who is it? I want to know, dammit."

Dummy looked around. His eyes took on a veiled expression.

"It's Skinner. But don't tell nobody."

"Skinner," was the disgusted reply. "Shit, I thought there was something to it."

EIGHTEEN

INSIDE THE WALLS of the tent, which had begun to glow with dawn, Skinner sat on the edge of his cot, dressed for battle in his leather jacket, boots, and flying helmet. In one hand he held his grandfather's old Colt revolver. He examined it thoughtfully. A strange sort of quiet reigned. The tents were empty. Most of the pilots were at breakfast. It was a good time to think.

Skinner was determined to leave the squadron, although his reasons became vaguer all the time. He had never done anything like this before. He'd been beaten and disappointed before, but he'd never quit, never run away. He felt weak and foolish. The men in his flight admired him. To them he was the ultimate in coolness and sophistication. And he enjoyed that role, he reveled in it, giving advice here, shoring up confidence in a man who needed it, and making everyone feel needed. But like nearly everything his life had touched, it was not enough. Even if it were, he would not be satisfied for long. Restlessness seemed to be part of his nature.

Fear accounted for it, not any particular source of terror, but a general apprehension about life dating back to his boyhood. His family and most people he knew back in Muskogee had been so afraid of not being proper, of not being educated, accepted, and normal. He had absorbed all of this; he had won the football games and the scholarships. And it all had damaged him terribly because he was still afraid and on the run from that fear.

Living with Gina might change everything, though; this was his hope. Gina was kind, perceptive, and intelligent. He was sure that living with her in a quiet setting would grant him the kind of peace, the respite from life's rigors, that he needed. Gina was not from his background and this was good. He could explain everything to her, let her see him objectively, let her calm him.

He got up from the cot and stomped around the tent. Abruptly he realized the whole thing was absurd. He could not escape. He had no civilian clothes except for one suit, barely $400 in cash, and no papers at all but an expired passport. It would be foolhardy and dangerous to go back to Spain. Republicans were still being hunted like weasels. He would be denounced on the street the very first day. No, Spain was out. They would have to go to Lisbon to be safe. But first they had to reach Sicily and get the day boat for Tunis; after that they could move by train to Oran, then on to Casablanca for the weekly plane. They might well end up in the Canary Islands.

"Desertion is stupid, it's cowardly, and it's suicide, Percy," Archie had said last night, speaking more passionately than Skinner had ever seen him before. "Take off that uniform and you're a dead man."

Archie was right, but he was going to desert anyway. The lure of a new life, the possibility of fresh adventure was too powerful to resist. He holstered the pistol and stepped outside. A light morning fog had rolled down out of the hills, but the sun was breaking through steadily. Blades of bright green grass sprouted here and there. He recognized the sweet delicate scent of spring in the air as he jogged toward the Briefing hut.

Late-afternoon shadows spread over the field as Walker came in for a hard, bouncing touchdown. The squadron had just completed the second of two dive-bombing assaults against the Germans who were dug into the slopes of hill 516, and he'd lost a pilot from his flight. La Grange, the man who took Donny Beaumont's place, was dead. On the bombing run he went way down, maybe too low, maybe not. When he released his bomb, it exploded right under the plane, blowing it to pieces. He hadn't said anything about the bomb jamming, so it had to be the

time delay set into the fuses. The delay was short. Somebody's ass was going to be stomped.

Walker's Mustang taxied in very slowly. He gazed
through the armored glass. The activity on the field, the
dust, the noise, seemed foreign and distant to him. He
couldn't be sure, but he seemed to be blacking out for
seconds at a time. He reached the dispersal and climbed
from the plane with great effort. The engine was still running. The propellor was windmilling as he started to wan-
der away.

"Man, switch off!" someone shouted. "That baby could
run wild and cut us all to hamburger."

He got back into the cockpit. Memory glided his hands
over the instrument panel. Ignition switch off. Fuel shutoff lever off, also the radio and electrical switches. He
dropped to the ground again. Dummy came over holding
an icy bottle of Coca Cola from the bucket and handed it
to him, then he went to work chocking the wheels.

La Grange had vanished in seconds. He was snuffed out.
No oxygen at all, just fire and something tearing him out
of his seat, tearing at his arms and legs, sucking out his
eyes and stomach so fast he probably never felt it. The
rest was roasted into vapor by that heat, lost in that high
swirling black cloud the Germans pointed at in awe. Harris
had to take part of the blame. He was supposed to check
those goddamn fuses. He ought to be shot dead for what
happened, the incompetent nigger bastard.

Walker sat down on the damp ground, drawing up his
knees and drinking the Coke. The bottle slipped from his
hand. He watched the foamy brown liquid spill over the
earth and disappear. The boys were piling into the truck,
heading for debriefing. He believed people were calling
to him but couldn't be sure. It was hard to breathe. His
stomach was tight and burning, his head ached all over.
He lurched to his feet.

"Shit, I'm all right," he said to no one in particular.
"Ain't nothin' botherin' me. I was shot down and got home
before the supper bell, so how can anything get to me
now."

*It happened so quickly. I was alone, all alone, and then,
pop-pop-pop, that man I didn't see, that man they tell you*

about, he showed up. He shot my ass off, shot me right up the tail like it was my first day up there. He was as quick as a motherjumper and I ain't seen him to this day. Nobody saw him. He was too quick.

"I rule the skies," he said aloud. "They don't know which way I'll break, which direction I'll come from. I have no pattern, man."

A couple of the mechanics stared over at him. He picked up a stone, hefting it in his hand.

Emilia. My pumpkin. Nicest woman I ever met and she's gone out of my life. Where am I going to find another woman to love what I am?

Lazily he flung the stone into the distance.

Those nice evenin's in my room were somethin' to remember. Maybe somethin' to cry over when I get old.

He threw another stone, this time with more urgency. He was thinking about the dinner now, the night in Emilia's apartment where the old lady lived. His third stone hit the Mustang, smacking against the fuselage with a loud bang. He fired another rock, hitting the airplane again. He was bending over and piling up rocks in his hand.

I should have been born Rommel. Look what happened. I'm an ace and nobody knows. These niggers around here take me for granted, even after I've gone out of my way to save half of them. They know all the other aces, the white aces, Bong, Gabreski, and them. I hear 'em talkin' about it. But nobody knows me 'cause they don't want to. Ain't nobody ever seen my picture. I can't win. I'm trapped in this goddamn flying machine. Trapped in this motherfucker until they kill me in it and I fall out of the sky.

He threw stones at the plane furiously, rifling them at the fuselage and canopy so fast and hard it sounded like several people throwing. The noise reverberated all over and still the stones kept clanging into the Mustang, falling on the wings, hitting the damp earth with startling frequency. His eyes bulged. He continued his assault, stoning his airplane with methodical, crazy fury. He was yelling and screaming when they grabbed him. Spittle showed at the corners of his mouth and his eyes looked tiny and blank. He struggled fiercely, bellowing incomprehensible words, but they held him. Dummy appeared before him, his face sad and shocked.

"Sorry, old buddy," he said.

The punch caught him flush on the side of the jaw and Walker went limp.

In the Briefing hut everyone sat huddled shoulder to shoulder in the first couple of rows. It was a cold morning and the fire in the stove was out.

"Men, Colonel Fremont wants to speak to you a minute," Osborn said.

"Gentlemen, good morning," Fremont said as he came to the edge of the stage, arms behind his back. "I have important news. During the night I received a message from Supreme Headquarters, Allied Expeditionary Force, London. We have been recalled to England to take part in the invasion of northwest Europe, the big French and German campaigns everyone has been waiting for."

There was no reaction from the pilots. They sat leaning forward, their faces serious and intense.

"Personally, I have mixed feelings about this. I'd like to stay here in Italy and see this Cassino fight through to the end. But it doesn't look as if we're going to get a shot at it. The invasion forces are probably shoving off sooner than we think. Now, there is an important option I want you to consider. We can go home. We can return to Tuskegee if we want because our tour is over. I know many of you are weary and would like to see your families again. I understand that. What I want to ask is that you adjourn to the mess hall and decide among yourselves whether to go on to England or pack it in right now and catch the boat home. It is your decision entirely. Report back to me in one hour. That is all."

The men left, not talking, just pulling up their fur collars and trooping off. Osborn remained where he was, sitting on the stage with his map pointer in his lap. He produced a pack of cigarettes and shook one out. He did not look at Fremont, who was busy starting a small fire in the stove.

Fremont warmed his hands in front of the half-opened grate. He was upset and angry about the recall order. The message had come from a source he did not really want to hear of again: Captain, now Lieutenant Colonel Paul M. Love, attached to Ike's staff in London. Love was a goddamn lieutenant colonel already. He was young, too damn young, devoid of any combat experience and yet he'd been able to move up without difficulty. Soon Love would be wearing that first star on his collar, forming his own staff, sending young first lieutenants and captains around to see how the black men were doing.

Daylight streamed through the big windows of the mess hall. The pilots sat around smoking, drinking coffee, and watching each other. Butters was the only man standing. He held a note pad and pencil in one hand.

"Pedro?" he said to Johnson.

"Okay, Roy. I'd like to come in over Berlin. Sure. Sign me on."

Donaldson nodded in agreement, so did Rennie Washington.

"Where's Jennings?" Butters asked.

"He went to the infirmary to get Walker's vote. He says he's in for the duration."

"All right," Butters said with a trace of satisfaction. "What about you, Archie?"

"Don't ask me a whole lot of silly questions, Roy. You know I want to see Paris."

"Oh. I forgot for a minute. Percy?"

"I like it," Skinner answered, showing a smile that was just a trifle false. "I'll buy a ticket."

Archibald shot him a long inquiring glance. At that moment Jennings came in. He had spoken to Walker in the infirmary, where he was still under mild sedation. His condition was diagnosed as severe battle fatigue and exhaustion.

He wanted to come over and join in the vote, but Doc said no. He says, yes, it's all right for us to go ahead."

"Fine," Butters said. "I'm counting myself in and that makes us unanimous."

In the middle of the next afternoon, an aging brigadier general arrived from Twelfth Air Force HQ in Foggia to present the squadron with its combat medals in a formal ceremony.

"So you're the Homestead Grays," he said as he stepped from his staff car. "I've heard a lot about you. You boys get more publicity than the whole goddamn Army combined, and I can't see the fairness in that. But let's not quibble. Let's get this thing over with."

Everyone had put on his class A uniform for the occasion, and at 1430 hours the flyers and the entire permanent base company paraded out of the tent area and down to the flight line where they formed ranks. It was a gorgeous April afternoon. Fresh breezes had blown away all trace of clouds. A pleasant warmth suffused the air. In the distance, peasants were working in the fields, bending and stooping in ragged unison as they had for hundreds of years.

The general made a short pompous speech ("You brave boys are helping valiantly to save Europe from the dawn of another dark age"), and then went down the line handing out little black boxes. Fremont was first ("For your important work, Lieutenant Colonel, in fostering brotherhood"). He received a Bronze Star. Butters was outraged. He touched Fremont gently on the shoulder. He had gotten a Distinguished Flying Cross; so had Archie, Walker, Donaldson, and Greenlee in absentia. Pedro Johnson and Walker got Silver Stars; Jennings and Skinner, Bronze Stars; Hollyfield, a Purple Heart. The others got Air Medals with clusters and ETO ribbons with battle stars. Good Conduct Medals and American Defense Medals went to the enlisted men. It was all over rather quickly. The general departed as soon as possible.

In the distance Skinner could hear the chow bell ringing, but he continued to pace back and forth in his tent. The familiar urge to get out there with the men running for the mess hall pulsated in him. He sat down on his footlocker, trying not to hear the bell, waiting for its clamor to die away on the evening air. *I need a fresh start,* he told himself. *I'm tired of running for bells, running for briefings, being there to kick over my engine on time.* He fingered the Bronze Star hanging by a gaudy ribbon over the breast pocket of his Class A uniform. A Bronze Star was all he deserved, and that was part of the reason he was getting out. The scuttlebutt now was that the squadron would leave Italy the next afternoon and fly to England. He wished them well. By then he hoped to be approaching the shores of North Africa, rested for the trip to Oran, where forged papers were available.

All was quiet. Everyone was in the mess hall. He pulled his packed suitcase from behind the nightstand. It contained a few shirts, ties, a pair of brown shoes, and the black double-breasted suit he'd worn in Spain and across the Pyrenees to France after the war. He was ready to go. He took his grandfather's Colt and stuck it inside his tunic, then dropped his Army automatic on the cot. He wished Jennings or Archie or Butters were around to say good-bye to, but they weren't. Darkness had set in when he left the tent. He walked off into the wilderness toward Matera and did not look back.

About a quarter of an hour later Archibald arrived at the tent. Everything appeared in order except for the .45 lying on the far edge of the cot. Percy loved pistols; it wasn't like him to be careless with one. Archie sat down on the cot. He flipped open Skinner's footlocker. All of his Army gear, his helmet, leather jacket, and the rest of it, was there neatly folded in place. Archie lay down on the cot, brooding over the situation. Soon he was asleep.

Briskly Skinner covered the three kilometers to Matera. But near the town he decided to get out of uniform. He would have to change back later because he needed the uniform to get out of Italy; but he wanted to put on his suit so Gina could see him as a civilian for the first time. He inserted the Colt in his belt and headed for the town hall. A taxi driver there agreed to take him to Bari for ten dollars.

The taxi dropped Skinner on the outskirts of Bari. He approached Gina's house on a long roundabout course. Gina had promised to be ready. Her parents were dining with friends and she was to join them later. There would be twenty minutes when the house would be empty except for the servants, and they had to leave during that period. Their plan was to drive as fast as possible to Reggio and catch the ferry for Messina. On Sicily, people wouldn't ask questions. By dawn they would be in Marsala; early evening tomorrow would find them in Algiers.

At the house everything was silent. One of the Great

Danes appeared and Skinner stroked his head. He listened at the door and then inserted his key. When he entered the rear drawing room, Anna was bringing down the last suitcase. She kissed him lightly on the cheek and he went upstairs. Gina was there. He startled her for a second, for she had just slipped a pistol into her handbag and closed it as he came in. They embraced and she took his arm.

"Are you ready for our great journey?" she asked, fixing him with adoring eyes.

"I've never been more ready for anything," he replied, kissing her gently behind the ear as they went downstairs.

Gina sat on a sofa watching him and Anna getting ready to take the bags out to the car. She did not hear the massive doors leading to the grand salon sliding open on their rollers until it was too late.

"All right!" Maynard Evans shouted.

He advanced into the room holding a .45 in his hand. Anna dropped her bags and screamed in a piercing, terrified frenzy. Time seemed to rush to a halt.

"Put that suitcase down, Cap," Evans snarled. "You ain't goin' nowhere. You've run your race, nigger."

Slowly Skinner let the bags touch the floor. Evans came forward. He was still behind Gina, who remained seated on the sofa. She was opening her handbag carefully.

"Who are you, boy?" Evans demanded.

"Lieutenant Percy Skinner, United States Army Air Force."

Evans smiled. "You're through, Skinner."

He had his back to Gina now. Her hand was coiling around the pistol when a sudden spate of shouting came from the salon. Gina's father burst into the room, followed by three male servants in striped jackets. They looked a little bewildered, but one of them held a shotgun. Gina stared at Percy, her eyes quivering in dismay. She lowered her head and snapped the handbag closed.

Gina's father was beside himself with fury. He was a short, stocky, spruce man, wearing glasses, a black suit, and a wing-collar shirt. In one tremulous hand he clutched a Beretta .25 automatic, a lady's pistol. He advanced on Skinner, shouting and screaming in Italian, the corners of his mouth turned down in hatred. He burst into heavily accented English.

"You monster. You disgusting animal! Why do you come to Italy and steal what is not yours? Why? Why don't you stay in Africa with your kind, the black faces, the cannibals. You are a savage like them; go back there and eat people," he said, working his jaw.

Aiming for his groin, he kicked the black man in front of him high up on the leg. Then he smashed the pistol to the side of his head. Evans laughed gleefully as Skinner staggered for a moment. Gina cried out. Her father spit into Skinner's face. Evans moved in with the servants.

"All right, Vittorio," he said. "That's enough. Stop it now."

The old man glared at him, his dark eyes hot, vague, and uncomprehending. Skinner's wrists were bound in front of him with rope. Both Anna and Gina sobbed on the sofa.

"You call yourself an officer, but you're wearing civilian clothes," Evans said, fingering the label of Skinner's suit. "I think you're trying to bullshit me, friend. I say you're a goddamn deserter. You're out of uniform and on the run. They're going to shoot you, nigger. That's what the Army does to cowards."

Skinner bowed his head.

"What have you got in your belt there?" Evans said, opening his jacket and taking out the revolver. Slowly he read the blurred inscription.

" 'Amos Skinner. Oklahoma Territory. 1884.' Grandfather, huh?"

"Yes."

"He must have been a hell of a fella," Evans said. "But look at you, Percy. Hell of an officer you turned out to be. You're reckless and wanton. You disgraced the country before these people. I wonder what old Amos would say about that."

There was more movement in the room now. Gina and Anna were led away still sobbing. They looked back at Percy, tear-stained and shocked, then disappeared up the stairs. Gina's father stood resting one hand on the arm of the sofa, his small intense eyes fastened on Skinner.

"I'm taking you to Twelfth Air Force Headquarters in

Foggia," Evans announced. "They'll dispose of your case there. It's getting a little late. We'd better get a move on."

Skinner was led through the deserted grand salon and out the front to Evans' car. The servant holding the shotgun accompanied them. As he was put into the car, a lady's handkerchief floated down and fell at his feet. Upstairs two figures watched from an unlighted window.

Slowly they drove out of Bari. To Skinner, the lush padded interior of the Chrysler felt strangely comfortable, but the rope binding his wrists cut off circulation and his hands ached. His mind was surging and swirling with confusion over what had happened. When they cleared the city, Evans seemed to relax. He glanced over at Skinner now and then.

"What will happen to Gina now?" Skinner asked. He expected to be hit in the mouth, but Evans just looked his way sharply.

"You got a hell of a nerve taking an interest in a white woman," he said in a cold voice. "From the look of you it ain't the first time it's happened either. But I'll tell you, because it doesn't make any difference now. We both missed out, soldier. Gina is going to another part of Italy tonight with her daddy. She won't tell me where, not that I'm surprised. I was never really polished enough for her, but you were, weren't you, Percy?"

Skinner made no reply. He watched the headlights slant over the cramped two-lane road. A car passed them. It had come off one of the numerous roads leading in from the coastal towns. Skinner saw its red taillights grow small and vanish.

"Percy, where you from?"

"Oklahoma. Muskogee."

"Oh, I heard of Muskogee. Everybody has. You didn't happen to play any football at the colored high school there, did you?" Evans asked.

Skinner nodded and smiled a bit to himself.

"Yeah," he said, "we had some real fine teams."

"State champions?"

"My last two years, yes."

"Your daddy must have been a doctor," Evans said. Skinner turned toward him for the first time.

"Mine was, too, although you'd never know it to hear me talk. Where'd you go, Harvard or Yale?"

"Howard University."

"Oh yeah, up there in Washington where all the rich black folks go. I've heard about that place. Damn," he said suddenly, "I hate to meet you under these circumstances, Percy.

"What went on between you and Gina? What did she see in you?"

Skinner stared at Evans in mild surprise. He saw a nice-looking American boy, probably captain of the tennis team at Georgia Tech, a major in the Army, and it all infuriated him. He pressed his lips together.

"So you're not going to tell me. It's something you want to keep to yourself, carry to your grave. Well, a man in your position has that right, I suppose."

They were more than halfway to Foggia now, climbing into the mountains again.

"You're an ace pilot, aren't you, Percy? One of those jockeys who gets a new man every day."

"I've got one kill," Skinner answered.

Evans obviously didn't believe him.

"So have I," he snapped. "So have I."

Time passed. Foggia was fifteen kilometers away. More traffic appeared on the road. It began to rain. Evans glared into his rear-view mirror. Something funny was happening. A pair of jeep headlights was behind them and had been there for a long time. Evans speeded up, but the jeep stayed with them, about thirty yards behind. He began to push the Chrysler along the slippery road. The noise of the windshield wipers cutting away the heavy rain made him more nervous. Skinner didn't look at him.

Evans was afraid now. He sensed acute danger, but he couldn't go any faster, and the jeep was gaining. It hit the rear bumper and he nearly leapt out of his seat. They were slammed into again, then again. The jeep was coming alongside; still he couldn't see the driver, see who or what he was. Panic ripped through him. He was being forced into the oncoming lane. He fought wildly with the wheel, seeking to bolt away, but the car skidded. Then the tires seemed to stop moving under them, and in seconds they were off the road and plunging downward. They hit ground and bounced over sideways, careening to a loud violent stop. Flames licked at the Chrysler from underneath. Skinner swam in and out of consciousness. He heard something heavy sifting down toward them. He was jerked out of the side window. Rain wet his face. He smelled smoke and fire and cried out because his hands were tied. Then he wasn't there anymore.

PART THREE

NINETEEN

TAKEOFF WAS AN HOUR AWAY. Fremont was tense. He stood in front of the Briefing hut, watching Harris and Osborn stroll toward the Operations van. The transfer operation was going smoothly, but that did not allow him to relax. He had nothing to do for an hour and this idleness increased his anxiety. Over in the tent area he could see men loading their footlockers and duffel bags onto the truck so they could be shipped out on the transport tomorrow. Children from Matera and the cave dwellings were around saying good-bye to their friends. On the flight line, engines screamed as the mechanics ran them up one last time.

Fremont was still disappointed about leaving Italy. Several of the men had told him that they too wanted to be in on the fall of Cassino. He checked his watch and kicked at the dust softly. Hardly any time had elapsed at all. He turned and was greeted by the bizarre figure of Horace Walker striding purposefully in his direction. Walker was wearing pajamas, a bathrobe, white woolen socks, and slippers, all of this partly concealed by a magnificent black leather coat with a Silver Star pinned on the lapel. Fremont could see he was very disturbed.

"General! General, I got to speak with you," Walker cried in an agitated voice, as if he expected Fremont to walk away.

"What are you doing out here, Horace," Fremont said,

putting a hand on his shoulder. "Who cleared you to leave the infirmary dressed like that?"

"Colonel, sir, I got to make this flight. I just got to go with the boys."

"You're scheduled to leave on the transport, Horace," Fremont said. "You're still under medical care. Leave this alone."

"But I can't stay here," Walker pleaded. "I got to come into England with my outfit. I'm the top ace down here. How's it gonna look for me to arrive in a cargo plane wearin' pajamas? It ain't right, Colonel."

Fremont examined Walker's face for signs of stress, but the man appeared remarkably calm. Still, Walker was the only human being he had ever heard of who'd stoned an airplane.

"See Doc for clearance; if he says okay, you can fly. But don't pull anything fancy today, Horace. Stay in line. Understood?"

"I read you, General," Walker said with a friendly wink. "Thank you, sir. I was awful sorry to hear about that Bronze Star they put on you, Colonel. It wasn't fair to a man of your character."

"These things happen," Fremont replied softly. "After all, I'm not an ace like you."

"You're an ace," Walker said. "You're the best. All the boys think so. Me too."

All engines started on time. Fremont led them down the runway and up steeply into a full-power climb in perfect formation. The field, the town, and the mountains melted away below them, becoming tiny and insignificant. For twenty minutes they nosed higher into the heavens. At 40,000 feet the order came to level off. It was calm, limpid, cold, and silent, like flying in space without the unending darkness. They could see to infinity. The rough heavy boot configuration of Italy was clearly visible between the Tyrrhenian and Adriatic Seas.

The Gustav Line, so formidable and treacherous at low altitude, was hard to pick out. Only large barren areas and an occasional puff of smoke or gun flash gave away its location. Beyond it the mountains and towns were peaceful. The planes droned on, their pilots secure behind heavy armored glass, breathing in pure oxygen. Up the west coast they moved. The vast Po Valley of northern Italy opened up before them. They made out Milan, Torino, and Genoa. Near the horizon lay the great silvery fingers of Lake Como and Lake Maggiore, storybook places they had only heard about.

"I can see the snow, the Alps. That must be Switzerland over there," Jennings said.

Fremont changed course. They bore west, away from the snow-frosted crags rearing up to the north, and crossed over the lower Maritime Alps stretching into southern France. They were over Provence now, following the lovely Rhone River, which ran down sylvan valleys to the Mediterranean. Almond, orange, and citrus groves marched along the rich green plateaus. Tiny villages roofed with red tiles clustered among the beautiful angular fields. Skinner breathed deeply. He was glad to be out of Italy. He had not yet begun to comprehend all that had happened in the last twenty-four hours. Archie pulling him from the burning car, its wheels still spinning furiously. Afterward Archie went crazy and tried to shoot Evans. At least one shot was fired into the air. He remembered showing Archie the lump in Evans' broken neck, the limp way his head hung down on one shoulder. It was an accident, his screaming voice had ranted, an accident. Early in the morning he woke up in his tent and Archie made him change clothes. His back hurt terribly, and one wrist was alive with shooting pains, but he was out of Italy. He was safe.

The idyllic countryside unrolled beneath their planes. Saint-Etienne, Lyon, Dijon, and all of Vichy France were well behind them. They began to see airplanes as they veered northwest in the direction of Paris. German fighter squadrons roamed the château country of the Loire, casting their predatory shadows over the ancient moats and towers. Bands of RAF Spitfires and Typhoons and Mosquitoes bobbed up all over. And then the B-17 bomber formations made their appearance, whole trains of them, not twenty-five or thirty ships, but hundreds strung out in enormous fleets blanketing the sky. They set up tremendous turbulence as they lumbered on, contrails flying, toward their targets inside Germany.

"Damn," Walker cried excitedly into his headset. "This is interesting. I didn't know all this went on in France."

"Leader, something strange off to starboard about three o'clock," Butters said. "Two specks, possibly aircraft, closing us at incredible speed, sir."

"I've got them," Fremont answered.

They were German planes, he could see that at once. Huge bullet-shaped appendages bulged from under each wing, but they weren't bombs. They served some other purpose. The planes rocketed in on them and were gone almost simultaneously in a fierce unearthly roar.

"They got no propellors, you see that!" Walker shouted.

The thin blue sky seemed to swallow them up, but they wheeled and streaked back.

"Jet aircraft approaching," Fremont warned his men. "Hold station. Repeat. Hold station."

The jets crackled by overhead, sleek, beautiful, incredibly swift. Fremont watched them in fascination as they turned immense distances away and returned almost immediately, climbing, darting, circling with more ease and power than he'd ever seen in any aircraft. No fire was exchanged. The intruders merely toyed with them. Then they zoomed out in front one more time, leading the squadron toward the English Channel, where they waggled their wings in farewell and simply banked out of sight to the northeast.

No one spoke as they crossed the Channel, losing altitude over the numerous barges and line-astern formations of the British Home Fleet. They skirted London and dropped down on a grass field outside of Oxford.

After helping the RAF ground crews tie down their airplanes, the men rode in to their new quarters, a long drafty Quonset hut where they settled down and waited for the evening meal. Fremont was assigned to a tent some distance away. He had been alone for only a few minutes when an orderly came by and politely called to him.

"Colonel Fremont, sir, a signal has just arrived for you."

The message was from Love. Love asked him to come to dinner in London that evening at 1750 hours. They would eat at the Connaught Hotel. He barely had time to shower, change into a class A, and find someone to take him to the station. He found an empty compartment in the train and sat back in the heavy cushions, watching the English countryside drift by, lighted by the mellow waning sunlight. It was all so familiar and refreshing, the farms, pastures, grazing horses, and stolid figures walking in the fields. But near London a lot of military traffic materialized on the roads. He noticed more and more big airfields, Quonset huts, and guarded checkpoints. A low-flying squadron of B-17s glided in over the train, which soon pulled into the massive shed of Victoria Station. He fought his way to the cabstand through surging throngs of soldiers and sailors, many of them American, and shared a cab with four people going his way.

The main dining room of the Connaught was filled with high-ranking British officers in their neat, trim uniforms, clipped mustaches, shined boots, and regimental badges. He could feel their cold inquiring stares flickering at him in a surreptitious, well-bred manner. A waiter led him to a far table where Lieutenant Colonel Love rose to meet him, smiling pleasantly.

"Damn good to see you, Colonel Fremont," he said, shaking hands. He seemed a little heavier than he was when they last met in Washington. But he was obviously more sure of himself.

"We're glad to be up here, Colonel," Fremont said. "Italy was rough."

There was another man at the table with Love. He was tall and possessed the snobbish aspect of a polo player or race car driver—all of this despite the immaculate uniform whose epaulets showed the crossed baton and sword below a star, the mark of a major general.

"General Clive Scott-Woolf," Love said casually. "Colonel Fremont of the Homestead Grays."

The general frowned slightly.

"You were at Sandhurst, weren't you, Colonel?" Scott-Woolf asked.

"Yes, I was an exchange officer before the war."

"Very good," Scott-Woolf said as they sat down.

A waiter in white brought them boiled beef, potatoes, cabbage, and an inferior claret. Love kept glancing at Fremont.

"General Barker is here in London, too," he said with a faint air of amusement. "Just thought you'd want to know."

They talked mostly about what Love was doing, about his job on Ike's staff. Love assured them that the invasion, when it came, would be a complete success. The Italian campaign had helped to insure a good landing in France by drawing some of Hitler's best divisions into the meat grinder around Cassino. Now these divisions were decimated.

"Hitler would have been much smarter to hold a line in the foothills of the Alps and bring those crack divisions back to France."

"How are your plans going to liberalize the Army?" Fremont asked Love. "May I pay a social call to you at your office, or wouldn't that be advisable?"

"Not advisable," the younger man replied. "But we're making progress, Colonel. I sense it. I really do. Of course, your squadron is showing the way because everyone knows you. They hate you, but they know what you've done. It's hard to measure this kind of thing during the course of a war, but I must tell you there have been some unfortunate incidents, rapes, riots, things that have been kept out of the papers. I'm working as hard as I can to lay this problem before the top people. But their minds are elsewhere. It is slow work."

Fremont nodded as if he understood and sympathized, but he was angry.

"As soon as the invasion is established and on its way, your squadron will be based in France," Love said. "Your duties will be bomber escort. Right now we're using Thunderbolts for escort work, but their range with belly tanks only takes them to the Ruhr and we're striking deeper into Germany every day. Your ships can go all the way to Poland or Rumania if necessary. We need you if we're going to win."

"Colonel Fremont," Scott-Woolf cut in smoothly, "may I ask your reaction to the race riot in Detroit, Michigan, a few months ago."

Fremont turned to the general, his face carefully composed. He knew little about the riot beyond what Osborn and a few of the others had told him. He was mildly shocked that black people would turn over streetcars and battle white people at the factories, but he understood.

"The reason I ask is because I think it's an important event," the general continued, sipping his Benedictine and brandy. "Things are going to change after this war a lot faster than our good-hearted young friend here believes."

"But you're talking about the colonies, Clive," Love said.

"Yes, the colonies," Scott-Woolf came back suavely, his aristocratic voice striking a note of regret. "We know we can't hold India or most of Africa much longer. No one can hold these lands for many more years. They've put us on notice that they want their freedom. And I expect the black population in America will be swept up in this tide of liberation."

"Maybe," Love said.

"No 'maybe' about it, sir," the general replied more sharply. "We have a committee in the House of Commons studying this whole development. Friends of mine. According to our prognosis we are even going to have trouble with the British soldier when he gets back. He wants his social security, his health services and old-age allotment. Churchill says this isn't true. He's thrown the report in the wastebasket several times. But the signs are there, Colonel, I assure you."

"Clive, you're a Socialist at heart," Love said. "If Montgomery ever finds out you've been drinking tea with intellectuals, he'll assign you as his driver."

Scott-Woolf ignored him.

"Colonel Fremont, you must come round to the House and sit in on one of our study groups. Wednesdays, usually. Here's the address. We'd like to see you, sir. We really would."

The weeks passed slowly at Oxford, although all around him Fremont sensed the invasion was ready to go. Too many soldiers clogged the cities and towns, too many trucks were parked in long lines along the country roads, for everything not to be set. Osborn predicted the invasion would push off on the sixth of June, a night with just enough moonlight to help the armada setting sail for France. The pilots didn't really seem to care. Most of them had found girl friends in London and weren't around much. Jennings spent a lot of time at Oxford listening to madrigals and talking to the physics research staff. Many of his friends were dons. Skinner brooded. He lay on his bunk for hours at a time staring at the ceiling. Fremont did not approach him. Along with everyone else, he'd read the long account in the British newspapers about the

torture and execution of a former finance minister in
Mussolini's government. The man, his wife, and daughter
had been waylaid by the partisans of Verona. All three
were beheaded as a warning to other political fugitives.
Their bullet-torn bodies hung upside down from a tree
on the main road into town. They had been living in
Bari, but the fact was of no significance to Fremont.

"Jonathan, we've got to go down to London and see
Hollyfield," Beasley kept reminding him. "They're working
on him down there at the Allied Military Hospital and
I want to see what kind of a job they've done. Come along
with me and Osborn. He'll be glad to see you."

Fremont had dreaded this moment ever since he'd
known they were coming to England, but strangely he still
held on to Hollyfield's Purple Heart instead of sending it
home to his parents. He would present it to him in a very
formal little exchange and leave. Fear of what waited for
him in those bleak hospital wards made him nervous and
irritable.

They arrived promptly at the start of visiting hours. A
pretty nurse led them to the ward set aside for burn cases.
It was permeated with an overpowering antiseptic smell.
Mummified expressionless faces watched them.

"They are here to see Jasper," one of the patients said
in a loud, cheerful voice.

Immediately people began popping out of their beds.

"Anybody got any cigarettes or magazines? You chaps
don't realize how starved we are in this place for news.
They won't let us out. I wonder why?"

Osborn and Beasley stopped to chat with the faceless
young men, some of whom wore silk scarves and RAF
sweaters and carried pipes. They seemed happy enough
and were full of eager self-deprecating prattle and bitter
jokes. At the end of the ward, Hollyfield emerged from a
bathroom. He saw his old friends and rushed forward,
tears welling from his eyes and running down his dark,
scarred, undefined face. Fremont embraced him.

Cassino had fallen. A contingent of Polish troops took
the monastery, its buildings destroyed and art treasures
ruined. Hundreds of Polish and German corpses lay en-
tangled in the rubble. An incredible battle of attrition was

over. One week later a colonel in the Free French Forces
came from London to see Fremont, bearing a com-
mendation signed by General de Gaulle. They spoke in
French. The colonel said France was eternally grateful
for the magnificent support afforded its troops at the
Cassino front. He expressed concern over the fate of the
pilot captured by the Germans and promised inquiries
would be made. Fremont thanked him for everything in
the name of the squadron. Their eyes met. Subtle shadings
of weariness and respect, admiration and surprise passed
between them. They saluted, not looking at each other.
Quietly, the colonel left.

The invasion hit Normandy on the sixth of June. Osborn
collected $200 in the squadron betting pool as more than
5,000 ships moved in on the northern French coast. Fremont expected them to be sent up the next day, but no
orders came. A week dragged by. The five initial beachheads were consolidated, and troops began to move inland, fighting their way through the tough hedgerow country. Other squadrons flew over several times a day, heading for the front. In the middle of the month, Fremont
tried to reach Love at Southwick House, Ike's headquarters in London, but Love was never there, and he wondered if he'd been foolish in ignoring all those dinner invitations. He decided to wait, to study the situation and
wait calmly.

He knew the Luftwaffe was in trouble. Many of their
fields in France had been raided and destroyed, leaving
no place near the front line to move in their reserve fighters. Provisional airfields were set up, but conditions were
chaotic and primitive. Camouflage didn't exist and these
emergency fields were discovered every day and bombed.
Weeks drifted by slowly. The men began to look at Fremont questioningly, for coming to England began to smell
like a double cross. July was moving along. It began to
rain incessantly and all planes in England sat on the ground,
waterlogged by the heavy squalls blowing in off the Channel. The important harbor at Cherbourg was captured by
Bradley's First Army and much of the hedgerow country
had been breached. A climactic battle shaped up around
Falaise, where a huge German force was almost encircled.
Fifty thousand men were bagged, but most of the Germans
escaped eastward toward Paris. The rain ended, to be re-

placed by midsummer heat. Instructions, orders, and priorities streamed back into England. The squadron was activated. A former German airfield in France would be their base. Fremont briefed them. They sprinted to the planes.

TWENTY

SKINNER STEPPED FROM HIS TENT into the early morning warmth, a towel wrapped tightly around his waist. Dawn had just come up softly and sweetly in the high late-August sky. Birds twittered loudly in the woods below the ground where they camped, as Skinner made his way between rows of tents and headed for the lake. He could hear water splashing and calm voices floating toward him on the luminous air. Under his bare feet the grass was rich, thick, and cold with dew. A lone deer bolted into the woods, which were still ghostly dark in the last shreds of night. Behind him on a rise stood the château, white, aristocratic, and very elegant with towers, turrets, and many chimneys. This was an out-of-the-way place the brass had picked for them: 140 miles south of Omaha Beach, 100 miles southwest of Paris, nestled in the lush, rolling, beautifully wooded Loire Valley dotted with châteaus. The squadron would be here until the war was over, and he was glad. He had expunged most of Italy from his mind. He remembered Gina as she was so many nights when they had time to talk and love, but there was enough adventure in the war to satiate him now, Skinner was sure of that much.

He continued toward the lake. It seemed impossible that France was actually at war and huge army groups surged across her landscape, bound for rendezvous in the Saar and Ruhr. In crossing the Channel and coming upon Normandy, there had not been too much evidence of carnage and destruction. A few overturned assault boats bobbed in the water; ruined tanks and trucks and bloated farm animals littered some roads; a plane or two was down, but Normandy hadn't visibly been ripped apart. Later they were told about the German bodies in the hedgerows, in the haystacks, farmyards, and copses, where they lay heaped and rotting until the French were forced to bury them. A mist covered the lake, hiding the men from each other as they bathed. Fremont emerged onto the bank and put on a towel.

"Morning, Percy," he said.

"Morning, sir, how's the water?"

"Couldn't be better. By the way, Percy, remind the others, briefing at 0800."

"Yes, sir."

Fremont strode away. He mounted the rise leading to the château in long powerful strides. He loved France. Its history and culture drifting back to the wildest beginnings of Europe fascinated him. Southern Italy, too, had an intriguing past, but France was somehow different, somehow much sharper in his mind. He stopped to gaze at the château as its windows glistened in the rising sun. It was one of the smaller châteaus of the Loire, a mere twenty-seven rooms. He'd been in only half of them so far, traveling the austere hallways by himself, inspecting the luxurious apartments, ballrooms, and the art gallery. He wanted to live here forever like a medieval king or duke. Yet he was curious about the owners, who had fled to Switzerland until the war was over, curious about what had brought them to such an isolated existence.

He entered his apartment and dressed in leisurely fashion, then opened the windows, which faced the formal gardens leading to the main entrance. He could hear the men struggling up from the lake toward their tents. Twice already he'd told them it was all right to move into the château, but no one had joined him except Beasley and Osborn with his two clerks. The men seemed to be in awe of the place.

"I ain't movin' up to the big house, Colonel," Walker explained. "I been in the fields all my life and I'm stayin' in the fields."

Later, in the fall and winter, they would change their minds. But Fremont wished they'd come and look around out of curiosity. Abruptly he wondered where Love was and what he was doing. He must be very concerned these days, for after the tremendous push out of Normandy, the campaign was starting to lose impetus. Fremont grimaced and brushed his hair into place one last time. He regretted not seeing Scott-Woolf again. He really should have gone to the House of Commons Study Group, but England had put him into a subdued and irritable state of mind. Perhaps it was Hollyfield, or maybe it was something else, thoughts of home or something.

A knock came at the door, echoing into the large room. "Breakfast is on the table, sir," Reeves said.

Fremont checked his watch. The good thing about bomber escort was that you didn't have to be up too early.

Osborn had converted the first-floor ballroom into his Briefing Room. The pilots moved across a huge expanse of parquet flooring, past gilded mirrors and windowed doors through which the sun streamed in thick brilliant shafts. They took their places on benches which had been brought in from outlying buildings beyond the deer park. A dozen or more small gilt chairs were pushed into one corner. Everyone was in a good mood after their breakfast of ham, omelettes, brioches, and coffee prepared by the cook who worked for the owner of the château.

"Gentlemen, good morning," Osborn said as he peered at the contents of a folder.

"We have some escort work for you this morning. You'll be riding shotgun for a B-17 formation going to Munich, where they'll bomb the railroad yards. The rendezvous point is twenty-five thousand feet over Orléans at 0940, weather in England permitting, but we'll get back to that in a minute. First, I think we should have a little talk about what has happened to the Luftwaffe since the invasion. There seem to be a lot of misconceptions around."

He put the folder down on one of the delicate little chairs and went to the map.

"When we hit Normandy, Galland, chief of their fighters, tried to transfer about six hundred of his reserve planes to France. His boys let him down. According to Intelligence there was a lot of equivocation and changing of destinations in flight because emergency airfields were put out of action. Also parts of each unit had to remain in Germany. Their aircraft were unserviceable. The result was that units had to merge. They began to lose their identity. They had big trouble with crashes, accidents, et cetera, and the crews found themselves overworked and couldn't salvage much."

"What happened to the fighters already in France?" Archibald asked. "Coming up from Italy we saw them buzzing around like bees looking for honey."

"Most of the operational fighters in France were based north or northwest of Paris," Osborn explained. "The beachhead was within their range, but only from the flank, and this made it easy for the RAF to patrol the area and stop them during the approach. The Luftwaffe had planes; they were just sealed out of the invasion area, that's all. When they got through it at all, it was only in the east. Americans never saw any German planes; therefore, a lot of people don't think they exist anymore."

"We haven't seen any since we've been here and that's been a whole week. Where have they gone, Ops?" Jennings inquired.

"Mostly back to Germany," Osborn said. "And you've got to give them all the credit in the world for that, Jennings. The turmoil was probably fantastic. They had women and civilians filling in on their intelligence and communication units. These people slowed them down, cost them planes, something like three hundred a week. In 1940 similar conditions swallowed up the French Air Force in practically no time at all. But don't be fooled. Nobody reorganizes like Germans. I look for a revival of fighter strength by the end of the month, if not sooner. And I'm talking about a strong revival. Keep a sharp lookout up there today."

The men stared at Osborn a trifle glumly. He ignored them and motioned to Jones, who stepped forward and began discussing the heavy flak concentrations on the way to the target.

They left the château in a group, smoking and chatting as they strolled across the grass toward the woods and the field beyond. Among the trees and shrubs their orange Mae Wests stood out brilliantly against the lively green. A couple of deer watched them from a safe distance. Walker eyed them hungrily.

"Cricket," he said to Jennings, "we've got to have venison at least once while we're here."

They came onto the wide, thick grassy meadow which served as their airfield. The runway area was outlined with big whitewashed stones. The Mustangs were dispersed around a few leafy trees, their starter batteries connected. While the ground crews made final checks, each flight leader pulled his men together because this was their first mission inside Germany.

"Don't forget," Fremont told Butters and the others, "the Reich is still out to get us. Be alert for any surprises up there, but don't leave the bombers. This is imperative."

"Let's stick together and make this a success," Walker said to his flight, looking each man in the eye. "Remember, none of you dudes has permits to be on Reich property. We need each other."

"Stick with me like I was flypaper," Skinner said. "Don't freelance. Don't fuck up. We don't know how these bomber guys will react to us. It could be another Pantelleria. Enough said."

Archibald thought he smelled a slight trace of alcohol on Donaldson as D flight huddled.

"Norvel, embarrass me today and I'll shoot your ass out of the fucking sky myself, DFC or no DFC."

They took off without incident, rising into the limpid sky at close formation. The sun poured through their canopies, dazzling and pure. But it became very cold quickly. They could feel ice forming in the oxygen lines, and their exhaust contrails streamed out elegantly behind them. At 27,000 feet they turned and found themselves virtually over Orléans. Dark specks resembling beetles appeared on the horizon, layer upon layer of them, yet they weren't spread out too far. It was a relatively small formation, about five squadrons, thirty four-engine heavy bombers. As they came closer, Fremont thought about those Luftwaffe jet planes tearing over France unmolested. In England the brass acted as if they didn't exist.

"Our boys have seen them too, sir," one of the RAF fitters had told him in confidence, "but it's all very hush-hush. No one has seen more than two at a time. We think they're based up near the North Sea. Messerschmitt probably. That fellow has given us a lot to think about, hasn't he, sir?"

The bombers passed over Orléans thirty seconds late. Fremont broke radio silence.

"Soho formation, this is Mercury squadron reporting in."

"Roger, Mercury. Man are we glad to see you. You'll be taking us to the target and back here. Escorts are spread kinda thin today. Say, where are you fellas, anyway? Come on down and join the party."

They dipped down to the formation and leveled off.

"We'll break into two units," Fremont said crisply. "C and D flight, take the starboard side. The rest of you, stick with me to port. Stay close to the bomber boys. Report anything suspicious immediately, but do not leave the formation on your own, no matter what."

They took up station. Below, the sunny landscape of France slipped by, the meadows, rivers, fields, medieval villages, forests, and then Chambord, a 440-room hunting lodge near Auxerre. Dijon could be made out far to the south, hiding behind patches of smoke trapped down in the warmer layers of air. Jennings scanned the translucent sky. He wondered why the formation was so small. This was probably a diversionary attack for something bigger. But if that were true, they might pull a lot of planes out of position and he'd heard about what happened then. He hoped after all these years the Luftwaffe was not that easily fooled. His gaze wandered down to *Brooklyn Bridge, Dough-re-me,* and *Kiss my Tookass,* the last three planes in the low squadron to port. They held station perfectly in a rigid V formation leaving 50 feet of clearance space from nose to tail and wingtip to wingtip. The 17s were spread out all over, stacked in squadrons of six, with the last three planes 150 feet below the leaders.

Jennings watched the planes below him carefully. They were huge powerful superdreadnoughts of the sky, more than twice as long as the Mustangs, clumsy, difficult to maneuver, and fitted out with just enough advanced technical aids to give them a sporting chance if they stayed together. The crews knew they flew in death traps which might kill a man in any of half a dozen ways. Jennings could see the navigator of *Brooklyn Bridge* lying flat in the plexiglass nose of his ship. During combat he and the bombardier handled three .50 caliber machine guns between them, one to each side, and another facing forward.

But at this moment the navigator seemed unconcerned with fighting and death. He rose to one knee and studied a chart, his helmeted head bent over it intently. He nodded to the bombardier seated just aft of the dome in a small compartment housing his control panel. Their ground speed and heading were probably all right, with perhaps a trace of drift in the steady crosswind. The bombardier now crawled into the dome, his leather flying suit glistening in the bright sun. Jennings banked slightly and waved. Both men glanced up and waved back.

They moved on in total silence. The top turret gunner right behind the pilot's cabin swung his two guns around in their electric-powered plexiglass dome and shrugged his shoulders. Putting one hand to his forehead he scanned the heavens, then pounded his gloved hands together. Jennings couldn't see the radio operator, but his machine gun protruded starkly from a small glass-covered opening that resembled the sunroof of a car. Below it the operator sat strapped in a chair surrounded by dials and switches. Toward the rear, the waist gunners stood in their windows, leaning on their gun magazines, waiting. Their fur jacket collars and leather caps with earphones clamped over them were all that could be made out. Behind them in the back compartment the tail gunner knelt on special pads, his two machine guns commanding the rear approaches. Jennings remembered he had forgotten a man, the man locked in the ball turret underneath. That was frequently the case. The small sturdy man sealed in his own whirling, chattering maelstrom often died without anyone knowing or else found himself trapped beneath a jammed lid as his empty airplane spun to its destruction.

Up ahead, Walker waggled his wings. A waist gunner poked his head out and stared down at a thin silvery strand of blue, the river directly below. The Mustangs in front of Jennings bobbed in and out of place, buffeting him a little.

"Germany," a taut voice said in the headset. "Germany below."

Jennings breathed quickly and his palms began to sweat as he groped in the map pocket. Holding the stick between his knees he spread open the map of France and Germany. Orléans was on a direct line to Munich. The river they had just crossed was the Rhine. They had skirted Freiburg, the only big town in the area, and were now flying above

the Schwarzwald, the Black Forest, home of elves and
trolls, Hansel and Gretel. Forty-two minutes had elapsed
since rendezvous. Approximately ninety-eight miles lay between them and the railroad yards at Munich. German
radar had them, but no fighters came, not yet anyway.

"Maybe we'll be lucky," Jennings said to himself, folding up the map.

Ahead, black puffs of smoke began to appear amid the
lead squadron. Huge black smudges obscured some of the
planes, but they flew on as if nothing were happening. The
air was rough and violent with shock waves. Jennings expected them to be jumped at any moment. He glared at
the sun anxiously. One of the Fortresses in the low squadron to starboard was hit. Three of its engines erupted
into flames as it spun helplessly out of the formation and
dived to oblivion. Another plane was hit, but it held station, belching thick black smoke. Gradually the smoke
thinned out and disappeared. They were losing altitude
now. Some light flak batteries sent up bracketing fire.

"Nine minutes. Nine minutes to target," Fremont said.

Through the light patchy clouds, Munich was visible in
the distance. It looked like a very large German village
with its precise rows of houses, intermittent church spires,
and air of pastoral tranquility. The main railroad station,
a huge shed sprouting tracks in all directions, lay straight
ahead. Jennings glanced into the plexiglass nose of *Brooklyn Bridge*. The bombardier had moved from view, for
the planes were on their bombing run now, and he was
in total command of the airplane until the run was over.
All his instructions had to be obeyed without comment or
delay. Bombardiers interested Jennings. The job required
a careful, scientific approach. And not only did the bombardier have to know his instruments, he also had to
possess a range of crucial skills including loading bombs,
fusing them, clearing jammed machine guns, and making
minor repairs on the ship.

Out front lay the railroad yards, long tenuous strips of
track blossoming out like an immense tulip. Hundreds of
boxcars were strung out on various tracks in a languid
design. There were sheds, switch towers, and a big roundhouse. None of the heavy smoke screens the Germans
often used were in operation, but the flak started up and
in seconds it was dense and accurate. Practically all the

bombers showed hits. Black smoke thickened the air. Jennings heard the big guns pounding, pounding. No evasive action was possible now or the target might be missed. Jennings knew the bombardier would be working hard. His mind would be racing through the bombing problem and its variables: altitude, true airspeed, wind drift, actual time of bomb fall. The imaginary circle in the air through which the bombs had to be dropped in order to smash that yard, this is what the bombardier was searching for. He was actually piloting the ship through the autopilot mechanism on his control panel. He was flicking switches, talking to the pilot, asking him for a level, for a holding altitude. The bomb-bay doors folded open. They were right over the yards, right on that thicket of crisscrossing tracks. *Brooklyn Bridge* let go a stick of bombs. From the other planes, bombs squizzled down in their fat-bellied, malevolent, obscene dive to the earth. Jennings could see nothing down there except gigantic plumes of grayish-white smoke covering the faint orange color of the explosions. Still, it was amazing that from that height bombs fell only on the yard. Buildings 200 feet away stood unscathed. The smoke was still very thick as they came off the target. They began a turn over the city, turning for home.

Everything was so peaceful down there, so untouched and tranquil, Jennings could not believe Munich hadn't been evacuated. He couldn't hear the air raid sirens, but he was sure they were wailing. Flak still popped up at them, sending off currents of buffeting air. The bombers made for the rally point where they would re-form. Anyone late at the point might have to go home alone.

"Messerschmitt 410s coming from the north," Skinner said calmly. "About four o'clock."

"Roger," Fremont answered. "I have them in sight."

They were moving very fast in a loose formation which disintegrated as more and more of the bomber-destroyers sifted out from behind the leaders and pulled into a solid line, making for the bombers head-on. They had to be cut off.

"Move out," Fremont snapped. "Stay with your wingmen. Don't scatter."

Jennings looked back and over at the marshalling yard. The smoke had begun to clear. He could see no trains, no roundhouse or sheds, just dozens of craters. The ground appeared terribly devastated, wasted and forlorn as a child's sandbox does an hour after a heavy rain. He gasped sharply, fighting for breath and words.

"Messerschmitt 410s coming behind us. Behind us!" he shouted.

"Too late, pardner," someone said grimly.

The forward wave of 410s fired its rockets at the oncoming bombers. Brilliant searing flashes of light blinded everyone. The lead ships were hit. Glass from their greenhouses splintered into the cold sunny air. Another salvo was fired as the Mustangs pounced. The bomber formation had broken up. Several planes were burning. More rockets came as the bomber-destroyers plowed ahead into the Fortresses, firing at will, scattering the planes, ignoring the Mustangs nipping at them for soft spots. Jennings found himself caught in a scene of utter turmoil. Barbette machine guns mounted on the fuselages of the 410s raked his airplane. The Fortresses lit up at all their gun positions, fighting for life. But they were all over the goddamn sky, slugging it out in the open where they had no chance. A second gaggle of 410s closed in from the rear, slicing up the air with 20 millimeter cannon. They handled themselves arrogantly, refusing to be drawn into dogfights. The Fortresses took them on valiantly, but it was no good, they had drifted too far apart. Orders were shouted through the headset. Jennings was lost. He was on the edge of panic. Then Walker got one of the bomber-destroyers, riding his tail with flaming guns until he burned and nosed over.

"Don't turn into these fuckers. Hit them from above and behind."

Fremont notched a kill, his prey erupting into a ball of flame. A Fortress went down. Miraculously, it was the first one. Jennings counted five parachutes. A second Fortress was in trouble. Both inboard engines blazed fiercely. One of the outboards was feathered. It went down, battling to stay out of a spin. Moments later, it was on the street surrounded by rubble. A fire engine came up. Jennings zoomed after another 410. It fired underneath a Fortress, blasting out the ball turret, but several Fortresses had bunched up and crossed their fire effectively; more joined them as the 410s, depleted of rockets and shells, started to break off and return to base. The noise died down. Jennings was frightened. Everyone must be getting short on ammo and they had a long way to go.

Slowly the bombers began to form up, crisscrossing aimlessly until they had arrived at an approximation of their original formation. Two planes were missing, but about half a dozen seemed on the verge of disintegration. Many of them had gaping holes in their fuselages and tail planes. A lot of the greenhouses had been shot out, killing the bombardiers and navigators. Here and there in the top turrets, men lay collapsed against their guns. Some of the waist gunners, wounded or dying, had disappeared from view. Hardly any of the planes flew on four engines. The straight-on assault had started many engine fires, and sprinkled throughout the formation were feathered props, a few dangling from burnt-out cowlings, streaking the wings an ugly black.

They limped away from Munich over the picturesque countryside. Near the Schwarzwald, Focke-Wulfs appeared, dozens of them buzzing in from all directions so quickly the squadron was soon overwhelmed. Big radial engines, yellow, red, and orange prop spinners, harsh cannon fire, filled up Jennings' windscreen. But the FWs weren't interested in dueling. They wanted the bombers and tore into them. The gunners fought back as if crazed, as if they knew they'd never get out of their ships alive. FWs fell burning and blazing, yet others took their places. Walker drove away two by turning directly alongside a bomber. He blew another apart. One of the bombers was on fire. The crew jumped almost immediately and they were lucky, because at that instant the entire tail section dropped away and the forward half spun down into the forest below. The FWs regrouped in the sun and plunged back. Jennings turned into them and fired. He scored. Smoke, gray and ominous, poured out of the engine, obscuring the rest of the plane. Then an explosion sounded in his ears. He was stunned, hesitant; another terrible bang went off. His cockpit was hit by cannon fire that just missed him. The glass was cracked and split badly. He dove, waggling his tail in stark headlong terror.

"Git up here," Walker said. "He's not on you. Git back fast."

The attack was just about over. They had crossed into France and the FWs seemed leery of being surprised by

Thunderbolts and Lightnings. They headed back toward Germany. But the flak took over, rocking the battered ships without respite. The course was changed three times. On a camouflaged airfield below them, Fremont saw a squadron of planes with black crosses on their wings take off. They climbed swiftly, menacingly. He recognized the big twin engines, the long canopy and fuselage of the Messerschmitt 110 fighter. But the 110 was a very old plane. All the 110s could do was lurk around hoping someone would drop down. Soon they went away.

At Orléans Spitfires closed in from the north and picked up the formation.

"We're fine now, Mercury," the leader told Fremont.

"They worked you over pretty good. Sorry we couldn't do more."

"Shit, this is nothin', man. We see this every time up. These crates are built to take it, but it's rough on the crews," he added. "Be seeing you, little friends."

"So long, Soho."

They dodged home, skimming the peaceful countryside, their magazines nearly empty, their nerves frayed and blunted. Escort work was going to be a real bitch.

TWENTY-ONE

FREMONT WROTE the last paragraph of a letter to his sons
in Los Angeles and folded the paper. He wondered if they
had any conception of who he was and what he was trying
to accomplish so far from home. He suspected that Marva
had diminished his memory in some way, though perhaps
not consciously. Sometimes he hated Marva and couldn't
remember why he'd married her. But it was a funny thing
about her, the women he knew over here in Europe, the
wife of the shopkeeper in Matera and the lady writer he
was seeing in Paris, both wanted to know about her. At
first he was puzzled and resentful, then he saw they were
measuring and comparing, for they had never known a
black woman. He was starting to use Marva as bait to
trap women, and this made him dislike her even more.

Paris had fallen a few days before. But Eisenhower's
armies did not stop to celebrate. They continued to explode
across France in pursuit of the Germans. The Canadians
and the British under Montgomery sped northward into
Belgium, striving to encircle the Ruhr before winter. Bradley's First Army swept up from Paris, headed for the Ardennes. Patton, driving his tank columns day and night,
sliced eastward toward the Saar. Supply trucks moved on
the nearby roads in an almost constant shuttle, but the word
coming back was that gasoline, ammo, and food were
very low. Trucks broke down from overuse. The Germans

began to stiffen. The war would not be concluded in September as some of the generals had predicted.

Still, the drive across France had electrified the squadron. Slowly the men seemed to accept their surroundings.
They were moving into the château to get out of the chilly
late-August nights. The elegant swagger of earlier days
returned again to their dress. The delicious cuisine aroused
their curiosity, and it wasn't rare to see men asking the
cook about the food and wine. They appeared intrigued
by the indulgent and baronial style of life around them
and took a certain whimsical pleasure in examining the statuary, paintings, furniture, and tapestries. They had spread
out all over the house. Most everyone lived in his own
room, and in the afternoon it became a custom to sit on
benches in the formal gardens while reading or writing
letters to home.

Fremont was glad to see all this. Leisure and privacy
gave the men just enough time to gather themselves together for the tough missions over Germany. They had
maintained their fighting edge well and no one had been
lost yet.

Walker sat on his bed in the enormous room he shared
with Jennings. He lit a cigarette and then got up to close
the glass doors leading onto a terrace which overlooked
the formal gardens. Jennings' stuff, his bed, dresser, desk,
and footlocker were all at the other end of the room. He
was downstairs with the others, drinking and sitting around
the fire and talking about the weekend trip to Paris they'd
just returned from. Walker was glad not to be there. He'd
liked Paris all right; it was older than he expected, quainter,
and incredibly beautiful in the early-morning mists. But it
made him think about Emilia and that was bad, very bad.
He thought about her the whole time he was there, even
after he picked up a pretty French girl. He was never
going back to Paris again.

What in God's name is to become of me, he thought.
*I'm a DFC and a Silver Star, but time is runnin' out. I'll
be goin' home soon and then what? I ain't gonna pull no
more cotton, I know that. I ain't gonna nigger around,*

so what is there for me? I should have stayed away from Celestino, just like the major said. I didn't have to know he saw somethin' in me. I don't want to be a leader, a goddamn troublemaker. I want to be happy like I was. I'm worried for you, Horace. Scared. You never were much of a fighter. You believed in the good things and cried when they didn't come true. But you stayed in the place set aside for you. Now you thinkin' of changing everything; you're looking to get cut open or hanged in a swamp somewhere. You can't change nothin' in this world. Nothin'. Nothin'. Nothin'. Jennings. That fuckface kid! I should have kicked his ass the first time he tried to show me I wasn't shit. I'll beat him to a pulp yet. I'm the man to do it. Then I'm going to be the man to show people a whole lot of things. I'll get them off their haunches and show them a motherfuckin' thing or two. I'll be a liberator. I am a liberator. I am . . . George Washington. I am Simón Bolívar. I am . . . I am . . . Attila the Hun! I'm a better man than Fremont and now I know why. I can speak to the people, walk in those fields, make my way in them towns. I don't need someone in a tweed suit taggin' along to make it official. People will listen to me when I say, "Don't let this man stomp on us no more. Don't take any more shit." They'll see I'm a nigger just like them and they'll listen. What I am, that will be my power. I'll start with the veterans, the survivors in their rags 'cause they'll be a bunch of angry and hungry niggers. There ain't gonna be no jobs for them and no handouts either. I'll get with the veterans. We'll move from place to place talkin' to people, making them fight for what is right. We'll force this white man to see what he's done. We'll get out of the ditch for good.

A door at the far end of the room opened noiselessly and Jennings came in from the brightly lighted corridor.

"Why is it so dark in here? Why the hell don't you come down and have some wine, Horace?" he said, walking over quietly. "You look pensive."

"You're fuckin' right I do. Sit down, Carl. I want to talk to you and I don't want any lip."

It was twilight. The squadron swept in from the east, losing altitude as they circled down into a landing pattern.

Rising out of the dark green earth, the château glistened snowy white and pristine as a newly baked wedding cake. The countryside was serene and restful to their weary eyes. A group of hunters trudging across the fields looked up at them, and then Walker saw something quite incredible. Below them, and not too far off to port, flew a pair of old JU-52 transports. He could make out the bright red swastikas on their big horizontal stabilizers. He studied them for a moment in shock, for this reminded him of Sicily, where he'd picked a transport out of the half darkness, followed it into a valley, and gotten a kill. But that transport was headed somewhere behind German lines. There was nowhere these birds could be going, yet they ambled along as if they hadn't a care in the world. He called in.

"I've got them, Two-one," Fremont answered. "'They're climbing, probably waiting for us to land so they can pounce on the final approach. We'll attack by flights. Four-one, keep your men high until I join you."

"Roger."

"Hit hard. We haven't got much ammo."

They dove violently to port, and Walker could feel the anger and outrage of the tired men in the cockpits around him. Fremont was already firing. Walker switched on his gunsight. The old trimotor Junkers were pitifully slow. Their corrugated bodies showed rust, peeling paint and heavy oil stains around the engines. Their two machine guns sent out thin streams of defensive fire. One of them was already flaming along the starboard wing. Walker cut loose with his cannon. The Junkers began to fold up when Archie shouted in the headset.

"It's a trap! Get up here. FWs everywhere."

Immediately they wheeled from the transports and climbed to meet the attack. There seemed to be dozens of Luftwaffe crosses skimming through the air. Dogfights and turning duels broke out all over the sky. And enemy planes began to fall. Their powerful cannons hardly scored any hits at all. It was almost too easy.

"Who the fuck are these people?" someone asked.

It began to grow dark, although only a few minutes had elapsed. Mustangs dropped out of the fight as their gas and ammo reserves were used up. Soon, only four or five planes remained in the air, but they continued to battle on their last drops of fuel because never had kills come so easily. Burning and shattered planes were strewn over the fields. Finally the Germans broke off. The Mustangs descended, one right after the other. No one had to crash-land.

TWENTY-TWO

FREMONT POKED AT THE FIRE burning lazily in the sitting room of his apartment. He went over to the window and watched the rain coming down, shrouding the formal gardens and the delicate spruce trees beyond in a soft mist. It had been raining since early morning and no missions were being flown. Most of the men were in their rooms playing cards or reading. Fremont sat down in a comfortable armchair and lit a cigarette. At that moment, Reeves appeared at the door.

"Lieutenant Osborn would like to see you in the Operations Room, sir," he said.

Fremont followed Reeves down the hallway and into Osborn's domain, a large formal chamber whose rich languorous curves, heavy gilt, and polished mahogany were set off against the drabness of portable generators, battered teletype machines, radio equipment, cables, and wiring strung from the chandeliers. Jones was busy on the phone. A second clerk studied aerial maps. Cigar smoke hung thickly in the air.

"Sir, I just pulled this off the teletype," Osborn said, getting up to hand Fremont a message.

It was brief. It said Ross Greenlee, the pilot captured at the Cassino front, was reporting for duty and had left Cherbourg by car at 0900 hours.

Fremont pulled at his cigarette and looked at Osborn. He noticed something like hesitancy and hope and cunning restraint in the familiar face opposite him.

"With the roads clogged as they are he should be here in about an hour and a half," Osborn said. "The problem will be what to tell his replacement."

"Any idea how he got away from the Germans?"

"No, sir," Osborn answered. "I've got nothing else on it."

"Send him in to me as soon as he arrives."

"Shall I tell the men?"

"No," Fremont said. "Don't alert them until we know what this is all about."

Fremont returned to his room. He had never expected to see Greenlee again and now there was some chance, some bizarre possibility he was returning at this moment, speeding at this moment over the 180 miles of rain-slicked roads leading down from Cherbourg. One thing was certain, the Germans hadn't released him. They'd taken too many casualties on that hill just to get him alive. He was valuable to them as a laboratory animal, as a war criminal, perhaps as a plaything. Fremont looked at his watch. An hour and five minutes were left, on Osborn's estimate. He went to the window and stared into the mist. A pot of coffee was brought in from the kitchen. Fremont remained at the window, cup in hand. At last, an old black Citroën appeared. A few of the men had seen it and drifted outdoors. The car rolled right up to the front of the château and Greenlee got out. He looked thin but lively. Fremont could tell the men were stunned as they approached him. Jennings embraced him while the others crowded around him in the rain. He was being carried on their shoulders now. Fremont could hear clapping. He felt overwhelmed and dazed by emotions he hadn't known were there. He didn't want anyone to see him like this, so he stayed at the window until the Citroën had circled back toward the main road and vanished.

In the Operations Room Greenlee sat behind a folding table, smoking a cigar and telling his story. Fremont motioned for him to continue and sat down.

"After they picked me up I was kept in a dugout until nightfall," Greenlee said, his young face and grayish eyes still alive with wonder. "They treated me with respect and I ate some of their food, dried sausages or something. They lived in real filth, man. Everything was smelly and rotten, even their clothes. I thought Germans had it all figured out, but these were desperate people. They knew they were gonna die. They couldn't even go out to take a shit. Stuff like that does funny things to your mind. It made them tough. It made them want to die on those goddamn guns."

"Did the SS get you, Bluey?" Archibald asked.

"Yeah, Archie, soon as they heard about me they came banging on the door. See, I was taken to Rome that same night after I came down. I was technically a Luftwaffe prisoner. They were surprisingly okay, man. They promised to get me to a POW camp for American flyers. I was scheduled to leave the next afternoon for Germany when the SS showed. They acted crazy. I've never seen people so wild and arrogant. I was immediately whisked into a hospital. My head was shaved and measured. The doctor said he could tell how intelligent I was that way. They measured every inch of me."

"What kind of questions did they ask you?" Beasley inquired.

"Well, they wanted to know why I was so light-skinned and if one of my parents was white. They couldn't account for my eyes. Everybody examined them until they got red and started hurting. They asked why I wanted to fly and if I was a suicide pilot. If he didn't like my answers, the doctor slapped me in the mouth. But it wasn't too bad until they started measuring my penis every day. Then I got scared. Finally they said I was being shipped to Milan, where the planes left for Berlin. A doctor explained to me I'd be hospitalized indefinitely. When I heard that, I knew it was escape time. But I got lucky. On the way north the truck convoy was stopped by partisans in the mountains. I jumped out of the truck in the dark with an Englishman and he was shot by mistake. The partisans took me and some other dudes along. We moved all the time to caves and villages where they fed us. We did all this moving for nearly three months. I was down to skin and bones. Finally, they smuggled me and a couple of other boys into Lugano, Switzerland. The Swiss were so mad they wouldn't talk to us. We were expelled to England the same goddamn day. I've been there for six weeks."

"You see Jasper?"

"Yeah, I saw him in the hospital. They're doing something for him. He's coming along. He says hello to everybody."

From where he stood near the door, Beasley studied Greenlee. The boy talked more slowly than he had before. He was obviously very tired. His eyes seemed watery and veiled by signs of prolonged shock. He should not have been sent back to the front.

"Lieutenant Greenlee, I'd like to see you in the infirmary," Beasley said. "We can get back to this another day."

Dawn began to crack through the dark purple sky beyond the ornate windows of the Briefing Room as Orlando Jones came forward. He was much heavier than he had been in his flying days. Somehow he had mastered the ability to sound both official and humble at the same time.

"Gentlemen, we called you in a little early because it's time for a review. Too many people in this theater are getting the idea the war is about over. Let me tell you straight out that it is not. We've had a good summer on the ground. But now it's time to forget the horseshit. The Germans are regrouping along the Siegfried Line fronting on France, Luxembourg, Belgium, and part of Holland. In the meantime, our ground commanders are bitching among themselves like girls at a sweet-sixteen party. Patton's got his dander up. He talks about the Saar but thinks Berlin. Bradley's pissed off because people have forgotten him. From what I get, there is no way we're ready for a full-scale assault on Germany."

"Jonesy, what about the Luftwaffe?" Greenlee asked, taking a sip of coffee from the mug in his hand.

"German fighter strength has gone up and it's still climbing. Even with the bombing, we can't seem to slow them down for more than a week or ten days at a time. Check these figures. In July 1943 they turned out twelve hundred fighters a month. Now it's a little over two thousand. The number of assembly stations and repair workshops has proliferated."

"But how?" Walker said, his voice rising with annoyance and frustration. "We're bombing the shit out of these people. They got to be hurtin'."

"They've gone where we can't hurt them anymore, Horace. Underground. Here are some of the facts. Last January the Reich made a survey of all quarries, caves, and other suitable underground sites for factories. Junkers 188s are being manufactured in sections of the Berlin subway. Messerschmitts and FWs are coming out of mine tunnels that have been widened and shored up. Planes are assembled and hidden in railway tunnels. The list gets longer every day."

"The other day when those FWs surprised us coming in, I noticed they were different," Jennings said. "They seemed more streamlined and a hell of a lot faster. We had our hands full for a few minutes."

"Part of the German effort is the mass production of improved or new planes," Jones explained, producing some pictures from the small table behind him.

"The planes that hit you out here were FW 152Cs, the new long-nose Focke-Wulfs. They go four hundred forty to four hundred eighty miles per hour, turn with the best of them, and come at you with four cannon. Show them some respect. This is the new Me 109, the K⁻ model, a lighter equivalent of your Mustang. In capable hands it can test you. Here's the jet, the Messerschmitt 262.

"I love this plane. It's a sensational plane. Twin jet engines, thrust unknown. Heavy armor plating. Four 30 millimeter cannon. Twenty-four 55 millimeter rockets. Speed in excess of five hundred ninety miles per hour, really unprecedented speed, gentlemen. They say it's a tricky number to fly, but I'd love to try it just once. More and more are being seen every week. Right now they're used for tactical reconnaissance over the front because nothing can touch them. But I want to stress this aircraft is essentially a strategic weapon. The day they appear in large numbers, our bombers are obsolete. So are you, probably. We could all find ourselves back in Normandy."

Walker leapt to his feet.

"You go too far speaking about Normandy, man. They got some good planes, I grant you that. But what about the men? I see some pretty bad fellows in this room. And the other day when they came here looking for us, I noticed young boys flyin' those long-ass Focke-Wulfs. Where have all the men gone to?"

"Good question," Jones replied. "A lot of pilots lately have come back and said their opponents were young and inexperienced kids. That may be true now, but it won't hold up."

"Why?"

"Well, let's look at the composition of the Luftwaffe pilot corps. Unlike us and the RAF, there doesn't seem to be any middle category, not many average guys. After the Battle of Britain and the push into Russia, they rushed up a lot of men who weren't ready, mostly due to shortened or improper training. A great many of these people got knocked off and were replaced by even younger men. But the cream of the Luftwaffe, the top twenty percent or so, is still pretty much intact."

"After all the shit that's happened?" Walker said.

"Yes," Jones snapped. "Some of these boys learned their trade in the Spanish civil war. Almost all of them date from 1940 onwards. That means England, North Africa, the works. Up until recently they were rotated between the Western and Russian fronts so we could never be sure how many survived. Now that the fatherland is in jeopardy, they are in our backyard and will be tougher than ever. They have priority as to planes, spare parts, and fuel."

"Jesus Christ," someone said too loudly, "just when I thought I was going to get out of this goddamn thing alive."

Walker sat down, hands in his pockets.

"One final word. From now on keep an eye out for small airfields. The Luftwaffe has dispersed its fighters to hundreds of fields all over the goddamn map. This situation cannot be allowed to continue. It threatens the integrity of the bomber fleets."

Below, Butters could see the huge synthetic-oil plant situated on the outskirts of Magdeburg. Berlin, enveloped in a light cloak of smog, sat majestically in the distance. ("We've got to take out these oil plants," Jones told them. "Whatever the Germans dream up next, it will probably run on oil.") The lead Fortress of the ten-squadron formation was within moments of releasing its bombs. Butters was tense. For seconds at a time he heard nothing whatsoever. Then the demonic noise around him, engines, guns, voices on the headset, returned with a violent roar. The flak was so thick it created a dark gray fog which obscured the guns themselves. Many of the bombers were badly battered and some didn't make it at all, for they had run into ferocious spoiling attacks along the way. The smoke generators around the plant went full blast, but Butters could still make out most of the target. He saw complex lines of horizontal pipes, vertical stanchions, dozens of round, domelike fuel tanks sheathed by concrete blast walls, sheds, railroad tracks, and guns, everywhere, even in the outlying fields. The bombers cut loose with their loads, which squizzled down and vanished in the smoke screen. The ground blast was tremendous; Butters felt it in the soles of his feet. Immediately a hideous thick black smoke boiled upward. It was filled with strange smells, alcohol, menthol, and something acrid. It grew quite dark. A bomber lit up the dimness as it burned out of control and fell away. They wheeled off the target.

In the sky not far ahead, Butters noticed what looked like hundreds of fighters swarming in. He alerted Fremont. At Magdeburg they were farther from home than they had ever been, a long 435 miles. All of central and western Germany lay behind them.

A stunning explosion erupted right in the middle of the formation. Planes were blown around in the turbulence like scraps of paper. Covered completely by flames, one of the Fortresses broke in half. Another explosion. The wings of one plane dropped off and careened into another, setting it on fire. Both planes spun helplessly toward the earth. Butters saw parachutes. Another plane was going.

"Spread!" someone cried in terror. "Spread out. They're bombing us from above."

All eyes turned upward and there, making off, their bomb-bay doors just closing, was a pack of Messerschmitt 410s.

Voices sliced thin by panic and shock babbled over the radio. The top turret gunners, radio operators, and tail gunners opened up with everything; but it was too late: the bomber-destroyers were far out of range.

"Here come the fighters," Archibald warned his flight. "Go for the good shot."

A line of FWs zoomed in straight at the bombers, holding steady, waiting until they were a mere fifty yards away before opening up with their cannons. These murderous attacks at zero deflection always astonished Butters. He didn't understand where these Germans got the courage, the uncontrolled audacity, to fly level at another plane.

Before the squadron could move, the first wave had scored its hits and run. A second wave was on the way, and behind that, a third and fourth wave. It was relentless. As dogfights broke out, the later waves pressed their attack unmolested. The bombers fought back bravely but some began to go down. Fighters wheeled and jockeyed all over the sky. There were three Focke-Wulfs for every one Mustang. Butters was attacked from below by two fighters who tore at his underbelly like sharks. He climbed to get away, nearly colliding with a bomber, and then blasted an FW crossing his gunsight. These were newer FWs. They had cannons mounted in gondolas under their wings and hit extremely hard. Men yelled desperate instructions into the headset. Gradually, though, one voice predominated. It was Walker. He blotted out Fremont. He seemed to be everywhere and see everything. His guns blazed sparingly, but two, three, now four FWs fell away from them, barely smoking yet mortally hit.

"Get an angle on him, get a good angle. Shoot him! Shoot him! Good. Good."

"I got him off your ass. He's below you. Go with him. Hit him as he rolls."

"Good fucking shot! Never seen you take a man from the side."

"Don't turn with that fucker! Break low. I got him. He's mine."

Finally, the attack was broken off. They were very low on ammo now. The bombers closed up. Behind them was nothing but smoke. Below, Germany looked sleepy and at peace.

They changed course to avoid the flak corridor between Braunschweig and Hannover. It was an exceptionally clear day, sunny and cloudless, the best kind of flying weather. But the men in the Fortresses could not enjoy it. Hardly one of the Fortresses flew on all four engines; most were badly holed and had lost fuel and glycol. Wounded men lay in the passageways stupefied by morphine. The bombers flew on toward their home base. Those twelve .50 caliber machine guns had saved them, for it took twenty to twenty-five solid hits to bring a Fortress down, and it was hard, very hard, to score those hits without getting chewed up in overlapping fire.

Skinner watched the tough vigilant face of the starboard waist gunner on the plane level with him as the man shaded his eyes and checked the sky. He stared down, scanning the green-and-brown fields, then suddenly his attention was riveted on something. Skinner banked slightly, searching for what the gunner had seen. Flashes of light so sharp and brilliant they stood out even in the strong sun met his eyes. He pressed the microphone button.

"Rockets coming at five o'clock low."

"I've got them," Fremont answered calmly as he watched the projectiles climbing on them at a speed almost beyond belief.

"They aren't rockets," he said a moment later. "They're planes."

"These fucking Germans are crazy!" Walker cried.

They were tiny airplanes, stubby in the tail and wing but quite heavy and thick through the fuselage. Their camouflage was a dirty dark-green mottling over baby blue. The sun bounced off their small blue-tinted canopies. They looked like six overfed pigeons as they drew closer and closer before spreading out.

"Hold position. Let them make the first move."

"I've lost them."

"They're under the bombers."

Donaldson in the rear saw them cut loose with their rockets, a salvo so intense and powerful the miniature planes shook nearly out of control. Tubes of blinding light leapt from under each wing and directly up at the bombers. Two planes erupted into balls of strange bright rolling fire. Others were hit and wobbled badly. The rocket craft zoomed out and away, circling far from gun range as they peppered the formation with heavy cannon. They dove, falling like rocks, and could no longer be seen.

"Two of them crashed and burned on landing," Washington reported, but no one answered. The whole attack had taken less than three minutes from start to finish.

A quarter of an hour passed. The German border lay ahead. Fremont noticed the bombers had slowed down. He urged them to try and make the Channel, but they seemed to cower at the prospect of crossing the Netherlands, a country dotted by dozens of fighter interceptor stations. As soon as they crossed into Holland, Me 109s appeared and finished off another Fortress before they were driven down into the undercast. A moment of hopelessness had been reached. There was hardly any ammo left. The lead ship, *Dixie Pixie*, began to drift back.

"Five minutes to the Channel," Fremont told the pilot.

"Not sure we can make it, leader. Copilot dead. Radio out. I don't know who's back there."

"I see one of your waist gunners."

No response came. The big bomber slanted downwards, shuddered violently, and then righted itself.

"Can you cover them, four flight?"

"We've got a burst or two left, that's all the ammo."

"Go as far as you can."

"Roger."

"We can't hold altitude," the bomber pilot said to Archibald, his voice quavering in desperation.

"You've got to," Archibald snapped.

He scanned the flat greenish earth for fighters taking off.

"I don't know about reachin' that Channel," the other voice came back slowly. "We're throwin' everything over, but we're sinking, little friends."

Archibald monitored his instruments. *Dixie Pixie* was losing 400 feet every thirty seconds. Donaldson shook his head sadly. Flak batteries opened up. The ground was closer. The sea was visible now; it stretched tantalizingly beyond their noses. A direct hit staggered the Fortress. Archibald thought he could see the big motor launches in the water circling in wide expectant patterns, but it was a mirage. He knew it was a mirage.

"We've had it now," the pilot said.

Moaning and screaming could be heard in the background. Fire was spurting out from both inboard engines.

"So long, little friends. Thanks for tryin'. We got that refinery, that's the main thing."

The radio went dead as the Fortress slid down in a long arc. They were too low to bail out. He was going to try and land, try to put it down before it exploded in his face. The Mustangs wandered along in its wake. The plane hovered close to the ground throwing an enormous shadow. It came to rest right at the water's edge and broke in half. Archibald came in low, dipping one wing to the three men standing there in the wet sand. Then he climbed away toward the southeast, toward France.

One afternoon two weeks later a battle spreading out over twenty miles of sky erupted near the château. Two hundred Fortresses coming from south Germany were waylaid by Messerschmitts and FWs near their rendezvous point at Orléans. Everyone went down to the lake for a better view. Hundreds of contrails streaked and sliced through the heavens. The men stood there shading their eyes and watching transfixed as planes wheeled and killed each other off without mercy. An armada of Spitfires arrived from England and plunged into the holocaust. Fighters dropped from the air like harmless toys. Almost directly overhead a Messerschmitt was hit and began to flame.

"Tried to turn inside and his engine cut out," Osborn said, watching the damaged plane through binoculars.

The Messerschmitt began curving downward. Fire broke out along the fuselage and a thick plume of black smoke smudged the bright blue sky. Osborn followed the doomed craft. The tiny awkward figure of a man could be seen hanging in space near the port wing.

"Parachute!" he cried in excitement.

The group of flyers standing by the calm, still water strained their eyes to make out the first billowing of silk, but Walker had seen the pilot before anyone and he took off. Across the spacious lawns he sprinted. The parachute was fully open and easy to track. In front of him lay the deer park. He darted through the trees quickly, coming out at the field. The ground crewmen had been watching. Friday came up in a jeep and drove him past the planes, where the crews pointed eagerly to the dropping parachute, and out to the field boundary. Here Walker plunged into dense woods again. The chute had disappeared at treetop level somewhere not too far ahead and to the right. He bore straight ahead, searching right. He was wild with excitement and anticipation.

I got to have me a German, he thought. *Got to see one, smell one, cut his throat myself for all the boys that died, for Celestino. I want all them ribbons they wear, all that fancy shit and them boots. It's them boots that make 'em special. They wouldn't be able to strut around like that*

*without them boots. I'm gonna have a pair today or my
name ain't Horace Walker. Goggles too. Goggles like Rommel had on his hat in Africa.* He found what he was looking for just off his right shoulder in a small sunlit clearing. The German pilot was there. He'd already gotten out of his parachute harness and was unzipping a gray flying suit under which he wore a full Luftwaffe uniform. Using both hands, Walker swept back the branches and entered the clearing. The German glanced over at him and stepped away from the suit on the ground. He showed only a momentary quizzical kind of surprise at seeing a black man, for his face and entire body seemed taut with fear and a strange, disarming resignation. Walker snarled something inaudible and went into a crouch. He had no gun. His only weapon was the bone-handled hunting knife he carried in his boot. The German circled timorously away from him. Walker eyed the man hotly. He looked resplendent in his dark, bluish-gray Luftwaffe uniform with its orange collar badges. His black boots glistened with a high, beautiful shine as Walker stared at them. At his neck, instead of a tie, hung a large black cross edged in silver and held in place by a black, white, and red ribbon, the legendary Knight's Cross with swords and oak leaves. Only one thing was wrong: the arrogant spacious blue eyes and flaxen hair whipping in the wind were missing. The German had brown hair and ordinary brown eyes. This infuriated Walker. He sprang forward. The German drew a pistol from his holster. He stared wanly at the crazed stubby quick little black man not six feet away. The safety went off. Hadn't he heard it? Didn't he understand that in an instant his brain could be shattered, his life obliterated. They faced each other as Walker inched up on him. Then Walker smiled, waving his knife. The German was flabbergasted. He smiled back at Walker and tossed the pistol away in irritation. Out came his dagger and Walker nodded with pleasure. They snarled at each other. The fight began. Both men were nicked immediately on the arm. They dueled back and forth, lunging, thrusting, and diving, switching hands, spitting. Men sifted through the trees, forming a circle around them. This gave Walker incentive and he charged his opponent, yelling, slashing at him until he was down clutching at a shoulder in pain. Walker stood over him in the stance of victory, knife held high

waiting for the signal. A nervous laugh went through the men. Finally they showed thumbs up. Walker fired his knife at the ground in mock disgust.

"Shit," he cried. "I wanted his scalp. Why'd you have to go and stop me."

He helped the dazed and frightened German to his feet and carefully untied the Knight's Cross from his neck. Someone else took his wristwatch. Donaldson got his dagger. A blanket was placed over his shoulders. Slowly they filtered through the clearing and back to the château.

At exactly 1900 hours the chandelier in the main dining room went on. Moments later Fremont came in, followed by the German pilot and the rest of the squadron. The men sat down quietly. They noticed that the best linen, silver, and glassware had been laid out. A certain stillness and reserve hung in the air.

The German seemed at once grave and genteel as he sat there between Fremont and Osborn. He had slept, bathed, and shaved, and appeared to be over the initial shock of being shot down. He was a thin man of medium height with very lively eyes and an ironic mouth, tight at the corners. He again wore his Knight's Cross and the elaborate chronograph watch, which Fremont had returned to him. Everything in his bearing was strictly military and precise. His name was Werner Hartmann. He spoke good English. Osborn had already explained to him that he would be driven to Paris in the morning and interrogated at length by Intelligence officers. The prospect did not seem to disturb him.

The meal was substantial and motley. It began with scrambled eggs and lark pâté, then moved on to *gigot de mouton* with chestnut puree, asparagus, potatoes, and some exceptionally fine Bordeaux. The whole thing was put together by the regular kitchen crew because the French chef had refused to cook for a German and gone off angrily to her cottage. When the meal was almost ready, the kitchen boys changed into dress uniform so they could take turns serving.

Everyone started eating. Nothing was said for a while. Fremont was the first to break the strange hush.

"How's the food?" he asked their guest.

"It's really very fine, Colonel," Hartmann answered. He seemed to smile a bit at all this formality.

"Tell us something about yourself," Fremont prodded him.

"I am Kommodore Werner Hartmann. I come originally from Frankfurt am Main, and my *Geschwader*, my group, is number eighty-three."

"Based where?" Osborn said.

"Near Stuttgart, sir."

"What's a *Kommodore*, man?" Walker asked. "I always thought that was a Navy title."

"In the Luftwaffe," Hartmann explained, "it is a courtesy title given to certain group leaders who have attained the rank of *Oberst*, or in your army, colonel."

Walker nodded respectfully. He understood from this and the Knight's Cross that Hartmann was an unusual man, a killer and a leader.

"How do you feel about eating with black people?" Archibald inquired in that sweet, deprecating way he had. "In America, you know, this whole thing would be impossible. It just wouldn't be done."

"I find that unfortunate," Hartmann said with a surprising seriousness. "In the last five years I have found myself in many different lands. I respect a man for what he is. That is all I'm going to say about it."

"Have you heard of us?" Greenlee said.

"Of course," Hartmann replied. "Everyone in the Luftwaffe knows who you are. It's not as if you were here on a secret mission."

"Why they come here and fuck with us, Werner?" Walker said.

"Orders, my friend. Orders from Berlin, the kind of orders that cannot be countermanded. You must understand that those in high authority have a very narrow concept of the world. Anything that violates that conception is a threat to their existence. Therefore it must be destroyed."

"What about their destruction?" Donaldson said. "We're sitting on the German border right now. What do you think will happen, Kommodore?"

Hartmann's glass was refilled. He savored the fine rich vintage and set his glass down carefully.

"Gentlemen," he said, showing a charming and sophisticated smile. "I believe Germany will win the war. This is

an objective prediction. Frankly, I'm not so sure I want
to see it happen, but I think Germany possesses sufficient
means to win."

"You mean them jets?" Walker asked.

"Yes, the whole family of jet-powered aircraft. They are
a beginning. They can put an end to the bombing. And
after that, in the underground factories, a new generation
of heavy rockets guided from Germany by new, unheard-
of apparatus. Believe me when I say London may not be
standing by the end of this year."

More wine was poured. Bottle after bottle of Bordeaux
had been consumed as the discussion went on. Now two
huge plates of pastry were brought in and set on the table.
The pilots pushed their chairs closer to Hartmann.

"Kommodore, how long have you been fighting and in
which campaigns?" Jennings inquired.

The lines around Hartmann's eyes deepened with satisfaction as he grinned, revealing long straight teeth.

"Let me see," he began, taking a sip of cognac from
the large snifter in his left hand. "I was posted to Spain,
but we never left because the war ended right away. I
was in Poland, though, piloting the Stuka at that time, and
also in France, supporting the Wehrmacht. The Stuka terrified the civilians fleeing south on the roads out of Paris.
It made a terrible sound when we pushed it over into a
dive, but it really wasn't that good an airplane. You don't
see them anymore. In early 1940 my *Gruppe* got the Me
109E. We fought against the British in those planes and
they served us very well. After Britain there was nothing
to do, so they shipped us to Africa, to Libya. I was in
the Twenty-seventh Desert Fighter Wing, do you know
it?"

Jennings nodded. He had heard about the 27th; they
were the best Germany had in North Africa.

"In Libya I flew with Marseille, Hans Joachim Marseille,
the African pilot. He was the top pilot in this war, believe
me. Hans was the summit of perfection, and I'm not just
talking about his one hundred fifty-eight victories.

"The way in which those victories were achieved was
so remarkable it is hard to describe. Hans was a great shot,
an uncanny shot. He could bring down several aircraft
with very little ammunition. No one could shoot with him.
He used every ounce of concentration in his body. In his

last four weeks of action he shot down fifty-seven aircraft, gentlemen. When he finally died at Tobruk, gloom spread over the front for days. It was as if Von Richthofen himself had died."

"Did you go back to Germany after the Allies landed in Africa?" Rennie Washington asked.

"Yes. We backed up in Tunisia and it was time to get out. I miss Africa even today."

"We know what you mean," Greenlee put in.

"Germany was very idyllic for a few weeks in the autumn of 1943, though. The daylight bombing had not yet begun. It was an ominously peaceful time, and we Germans knew it couldn't last. I was sent to Russia at the beginning of that winter."

"What are those Russians like to fight against?" Walker asked. "They don't seem like the type to go in for much flyin'."

Hartmann smiled.

"Tactics were very different in Russia," he said. "The Russian pilots liked to fly in large irregular groups. This is the way they went about everything in fact. In the beginning we had experience and it was really like swatting flies. Later on, the quality of their personnel improved. But the Russians never had the daring or the individual flair of the Western Allies. In a way they bored us."

"Then it was very difficult for you?" Skinner said.

Hartmann shot him a questioning glance.

"The most difficult thing I have ever endured in my life. You have no idea what it was like, what it did to the mind. Every day we flew over the steppes. They were utterly flat and covered with snow. They went on and on. Men became hypnotized. But you had to find the landing grounds and there was often little fuel. Russian artillery could appear anywhere in mass. The Russians killed German pilots automatically."

"Do you fear the Russians?" Beasley asked.

"Yes, Herr Doktor, we fear them. They have courage and stamina. I saw this many times in Russia. Their armies swarm about. They don't look as if they're doing anything and suddenly you are surrounded and suffocated to death. The Wehrmacht has lost a lot of its arrogance in Russia. But you know, I firmly believe that without the equipment you sent them, the war there would have been over in early 1943."

A silence descended on the room. More cognac was poured, but the men seemed tired and spent. A full moon hung languidly beyond the glass doors.

"Gentlemen, it is late," Fremont said. "I think we should end our evening here and thank Kommodore Hartmann for being our guest." Glasses were raised to the German, who bowed his head graciously. The men got up and filed out. They all exchanged a few words with Hartmann before leaving. Finally everyone was gone but Walker, who sat with his head in his hands staring into the night. Hartmann reached over and put something on the table in front of him. It was his Knight's Cross with oak leaves and crossed swords.

Hartmann spoke in his peculiar English. "I have already presented my dagger to your colonel and my service pistol to Herr Osborn. The Cross is for you. I know you'll understand what it means."

Walker picked up the decoration and glanced at Hartmann's bone-white shirt front. His thick fingers closed slowly over the medal.

"Thank you," he said. "Thanks for the Cross, Werner. I guess you know I always wanted one of these."

Hartmann looked at him quizzically for a second.

"Good-bye, my friend," he said, shaking hands.

"So long, Kommodore," Walker replied, getting up to leave.

A long, wailing, sickly scream erupted into the peace and quiet of the château a few hours before dawn. The Operations Room clerk stepped out in the hallway and looked around. A few of the men woke up, startled by this bewildering cry of anguish. In his bed, Skinner was jerked upright. His mouth was still open wide even though the scream had escaped and died away on the ornate ceiling. Butters snapped on the lamp between them and stared over, hs eyes filled with alarm.

"Another nightmare?" he said in a voice rapidly losing the hoarseness of sleep.

Skinner nodded, almost as if the dream were still clinging to him.

"Yeah. I'll be all right, Roy. Go back to sleep."

Butters did not move. He studied the handsome face opposite him that was now haggard with tension.

"What's causing all this, Perc? It's been happening too much lately."

"Roy . . . Roy, I'm afraid. I keep thinking my life is used up. When the war is over, I'll have no place to go. What am I going to do, Roy?" he asked.

"I don't know, Perc," he said. "Try and get some sleep. You never know what they'll throw at us in the morning."

Skinner leaned back against the headboard, breathing harshly and still shaking. He said he would switch out the light in a minute, but he was terrified of the dark and the vivid cruel dreams it brought into his mind. Butters turned away from the light and pulled a blanket over his head. He didn't want to report a buddy to the doc, but he might have to if this continued. An unsteady man endangered everyone in the air.

Skinner threw his head back and exhaled. This last dream never seemed to fade. He had gone through it three nights in a row and he was exhausted. In it, Gina was executed. She was beheaded in some kind of shed or hut. Her head fell from the edge of a chopping block into the hay where the heads of both her parents rested, bloodied, gray-haired, and oddly alive. Gina's torso writhed. Her beautiful clothes were torn and dirty. He was in the hut, too, stunned by her last words to him: "Percy, you belong down there in the salon talking to my father and the others. That should have been your destiny." Then unseen hands seized him. He was dragged forward screaming and crying to the bloody, slippery chopping block. His wife, his pretty, innocent, naive little wife, held the axe high over her head. He screamed for mercy. Helene, his German sweetheart, his teammates at Berlin, his mother, and even his father and the neighbors back home in Muskogee stood watching and laughing wildly. A group of black boys shot dice in a corner and drank from a brown paper bag. They looked over disdainfully as the blade fell.

Skinner's mouth went dry and he wiped at it with the back of his hand. He thought about Hartmann, the German pilot. Like Hartmann, he'd come to rest. He was out of adventures. Gina was his last suicidal fling. When the war ended, he'd have to return to D.C. or Muskogee and become just another nigger. He slammed his fist down on the bed.

"No!" he cried out sharply. "Not me. Not me, please."

It terrified him, everything terrified him. He thought again of suicide.

TWENTY-THREE

Norvel Donaldson sat in his cockpit and surveyed the bank of instruments before him. They had forty-five seconds to go, and already Donaldson was weary. They'd flown a lot of miles lately and time was moving fast. In a few days November would be on them and soon after that, Christmas. A whole year had nearly vanished from his life and Donaldson was depressed. In spite of all the briefings and explanations he couldn't understand why the war wasn't over yet, why the Allied armies had stalled in and around the Siegfried Line and were on the defensive in many sectors. He wanted to go home.

Beyond his canopy the French landscape looked wan and forlorn in the faded pastel shadings of early winter. Most of the trees had lost their leaves and appeared as stark and elegant as driftwood. France was a country Donaldson liked. The people in Vendôme, Orléans, and Cléry were polite and restrained. The food was excellent. The wine and cognac were even better, so good that he was embarrassed at the cheap coarse bottles he'd been drinking all his life. Twice he'd stolen into the wine cellar and made off with half a case of cognac and calvados. He drank at night now and only rarely in the mornings, but he was still drinking far too much and this frightened him. He was getting slower every day. A dreadful cumulative tiredness had taken possession of his body and mind.

"Switch on."

The engine turned over immediately. He watched the gauges come up, listened to the familiar whine in the cockpit. They taxied out for takeoff. Today there would be no bomber escort, no long enervating hours of tension and pressure. Today was going to be like the old days in Sicily, free-lancing and roaming, jumping people, cutting throats. Osborn had told them to go after trains especially, to follow them into the stations if necessary. As long as the trains ran, Germany would continue to function.

After touchdown the men left their planes more quickly than usual and climbed into the back of the truck, cursing and grumbling. The mission had yielded no kills and no real action except the busting of one lousy locomotive.

La Grange banged on the cab and the truck engine strained to turn over but could not.

"What the fuck is wrong?" Archibald shouted to Dummy Jones, who was taking his turn as driver. "Why isn't this pile of shit moving?"

"You got ears, ain't you?" Dummy yelled, sticking his head out of the window.

It began to rain. The men sat in the open truck as Dummy nursed it to life. It chugged away from the field along the soft muddy road leading through the deer park. Walker sat slumped in his place. He was wearing Hartmann's Knight's Cross pinned to one of his shoulder holsters because Fremont had forbidden him to tie it around his neck. He stared at Donaldson in mild disgust.

"What the fuck was that all about up there, Norvel?" he asked. "How can you follow a man down when he's flying on a jet booster? What the hell goes through your mind, dumb ass?"

"Archie said it was my plane," Donaldson snapped. "Besides, what would you have done, since you know so goddamn much?"

"Shit, I wouldn't have dove after somebody moving that fast. I've seen planes crumble doing that shit. How many times have I got to tell you, the first decision you make is whether to attack. And to attack, you got to be close enough to move in for a good pass. You weren't, that's how you lost that son of a bitch."

"How close do I have to be?" Donaldson shouted. "He was right under my nose."

"You thought he was," Walker retorted. "The secret is to get in tight, less than a hundred yards. Then you got a good chance for a kill."

"I don't want to take those kind of chances," Donaldson ranted. "It's too easy to collide."

"You got to take chances," Walker said. "Otherwise you can't live up there."

As Donaldson sank into an embittered silence, Washington said, "Horace, suppose you miss at that distance, then what?"

"Then nothin'. Break away quick. Use the split S and dive like they do. Clear the area so they can't turn on you and slice you up."

"That's when I'm always nervous," Butters said.

Walker shrugged. "We're all nervous, Roy."

"A lot of the time I try to do it your way, Horace," Skinner said. The water was dripping off his cap and he clutched at the sodden parachute on his lap. "But it doesn't work out. Something's missing."

"You fall into old habits, Perc, that's what it is. The way things are goin' now with all this new shit the Germans got, we got to forget about dogfightin' like we did in the beginning. That kind of duelin' is over, man. You can't experiment. You got to have the advantage at all times. Don't fall into no pattern. Let's face it, maybe we ain't got the best planes anymore."

"Do we have to know all this?" Jennings broke in. "We've done enough killing and maiming, do we have to talk about it all the goddamn time."

Walker looked down the aisle at him.

"What else is there to talk about?" he said. "Look where we are, stupid."

"I just don't like where it's all leading," Jennings shouted. "You make everything sound as if we can conquer the world from this little piece of France. We can't handle everything the way we do Messerschmitts and Focke-Wulfs."

"Fuck you, buddy," Walker shot back. "I'm through savin' your schoolboy ass. You're full of shit. I know what's eatin' you. You're out of date. You want to think the same way you've always gone around thinking. You want to go back to school and wear a suit and tie and teach science like a privileged character. But that's not what you are, fuck face," Walker yelled. "There ain't gonna be no fancy job for you, you mealy-mouth son of a bitch. No laboratory will have you around like they did over in England. No girls gonna run around in them long white coats doing your biddin'. You'll be dogmeat like the rest of us! But right now you don't believe me. You're still thinkin' ahead even when I'm talkin' to you. Tell you one thing, a few crumbs from the table ain't gonna make you a man. Get the fuck out of my sight."

Some of the men broke into raucous embarrassed laughter.

"That's enough out of you, Walker," Fremont said coldly. "Shut up. I won't have you talking to another officer that way."

In a sly gesture, Walker touched the bill of his cap. Rennie Washington, Archibald, and a couple of the others patted him on the shoulder.

The cold disc of Beasley's stethoscope touched Fremont on the chest. Beasley listened carefully to his heart for a long time. Fremont stared at the dark paneled walls and stained-glass windows of the old chapel being used as an infirmary. His thoughts took the brooding anguished configuration of these last few days, and he found himself hypnotized by the fearful message contained in the letters and legal papers still scattered upon his desk. He was divorced. The State of California had decreed that he and Marva Fremont were incompatible. The shock during that first day was unbelievable. He told Beasley right away, just to hear the news come out of his own mouth. Sedatives eased his passage through the night, but in the morning he felt hollow and weak.

"Turn around, Jonathan," Beasley said. He placed the stethoscope alongside his spine.

Marva wanted another life, she explained in her letter. She felt he was too heavily committed to the military. ("I don't know that you'll ever return home again, Jonathan. After this war there'll be another one somewhere, and you'll want to go. Your honor will be at stake if you don't, and I can't live with that honor anymore. It's consuming me.") The military had always appalled her. She thought it was inhuman, cold. ("Who knows what you'll be like if and when you get back. I'm sure by now most of those boys you took overseas are gone. That terrifies me. It will change you for the worse. The boys and I want to remember you as you were.") Not much was different at home, she said. Black people were still poor and despised. The war had enriched a whole new class of people, but Negroes still clung to the lowest jobs. Discrimination was getting very bad in California as more white people came in from the South. ("You'll find it hard to adjust, perhaps too hard, Jonathan. I'm not sure we'd be able to adjust to you again either.") The thought of going back to Army posts and small apartments on the wrong side of the tracks made her cry herself to sleep at night. ("I only want to remember the good years, the years full of hope. I love you for giving me those years and I always will. Good-bye and God bless. Marva.")

"Open your mouth there, young man. Ah, fine teeth. Okay, let's get your blood pressure."

When he was finished, Beasley opened his file and began making notes in a small precise hand.

"Am I all right, Dick?"

"Yes, you're all right. Completely normal, straight across the board."

"Too normal," Fremont said.

"No one can be too normal," Beasley said a trifle sharply. "I want you to take these," he said, producing a small bottle of pills. "Two every night before retiring. And don't forget."

"I don't need drugs to keep me going," Fremont protested.

"Listen, Jonathan," Beasley said, "you've just been kicked in the head. That kind of thing hurts even after the pain is gone. You'll take these pills as I've instructed you or you don't get flight clearance, understand?"

The two men faced each other. Fremont's hand closed around the brown bottle and Beasley smiled.

"It's always safe to be sensible," he said without a trace of rancor. "You'll want to see your sons again, and they'll want to see you. How about a drink to celebrate your good health?"

Fremont felt a relaxed smile broadening on his weary face.

"Okay, Dick, whatever you say."

TWENTY-FOUR

OSBORN REMOVED HIS HEADPHONES and put them down on the table heavily. For a long moment he stared off into space. Then he turned to Reeves.

"Sergeant, go find Colonel Fremont at once," he said.

Reeves came back with Fremont a few minutes later. Fremont had been outside in a snowball fight between pilots and ground crewmen. There was snow on his uniform where Walker had hit him. Reeves put on the headphones and began jotting down information.

"Sir," Osborn said, "something incredible has happened. At dawn this morning at least eighteen German divisions crossed our lines along the Ardennes forest in Belgium. They splintered the three divisions facing them along a seventy-five-mile front and have moved on strongly. We don't know where they came from or where they're going."

The teletype message started clacking again. Jones pulled off a sheet.

"Colonel, Intelligence at General Bradley's HQ at Versailles has identified twenty divisions. A hell of a lot of panzers. A group of SS divisions has moved in from the north. The Ardennes is a huge area, sir, a great deal of heavy forest that is not really good for tanks. But they're driving through and, from what we gather, doing it well. The reports from the front are a jumble. Units are cut off and wandering, but the Germans don't seem to have much interest in them. Also Germans wearing GI uniforms and speaking English have appeared and are spreading confusion all over the goddamn place."

"Then it's big," Fremont said. "That's the tip-off."

"Yes, sir."

"Could it be Antwerp?"

"It's wild, but that really has to be their strategic objective, Colonel. All of our supplies, American and British, arrive here by ship. If Antwerp fell . . ." He shrugged.

The pilots began to drift in, in threes and fours.

"What do you hear on the radio, Sergeant?" Fremont said to Reeves.

"Frankly, sir, depression. And a little despair. A lot of people near the top can't seem to believe it's happening, from what I can pick up."

"Lieutenant, we're going up," Fremont said. "Maybe we'll see something worthwhile or get a chance at a tactical strike. In this weather those armored divisions can cross half of Belgium before anyone finds them. Alert the crews."

Osborn motioned to Reeves, who picked up the phone.

"I want every one of you down at the field in five minutes," Fremont said to the men standing around near the door. "Find your wingmen on the double."

"Jonesy, tell Nature Boy to get his charts. He'll ride in the truck and brief us on the way."

Half an hour later they climbed into the heavy, frigid air. It took that long to warm up their planes and clear the runway of snow. They approached the Ardennes from the south, flying at 8,000 feet, fighting their way through thick bands of stratocumulus. Near Verdun, Fremont had them drop down. The forest was dead out in front. A gray mist hung everywhere. Far in the distance a squadron of twin-engine Lightnings prowled about, trying to sniff out the German armies. The Ardennes was a strange place: foggy, dense with endless stands of fir trees, deeply snowbound, virtually roadless, vaguely evil. It provided the right setting. Fremont brought them down to treetop level. Visibility through the mist was still meager, but they could see troops in white uniforms sifting among the trees and tanks, big tanks, grinding through the snow with fir boughs giving them camouflage. They quickly disappeared in the mists. Fremont was afraid someone might crash into the trees and he had them climb a bit, which made it even more difficult to see. Finally he decided it was hopeless. He radioed the men to head for home.

At that moment Walker was separated from the squadron. The other Mustangs simply banked away into the dense clouds and were gone. He cursed.

"Trying to get rid of me, huh? Well, it won't work. Bordeaux squadron, this is Two-one. Bordeaux squadron, Two-one calling in. Where the fuck are you?"

There was no answer. He slammed the radio control box at his side with a violent blow.

"Goddamn you. Talk. Talk, you son of a bitch."

He examined his compass. It whirled erratically before his eyes.

"Can't trust you either," he mumbled. "I'll be lucky not to come out over Germany and get the shit knocked out of me by those damn guns on the Siegfried Line. Isn't this some shit? All this cold weather killed my radio. It's all Fremont to blame. He had to come out and stop the German Army, as if what they did was any of his fucking business."

The extreme cold sneaked into the cockpit. The heaters could not keep it out. Walker debated whether to try and use his compass. He'd marked true north on it with a red pencil, so it was possible to tell how much he was off. He had to make a decision soon. He was lost and he knew it. The low rolling cloud banks made the forest below very spooky. He could make out the German division as they emerged in remote clearings or when columns came together at little crossroads. They never stopped. They moved on as if guided by a powerful will, tramping, tramping, incessantly through the heavy snow. Walker dropped down and buzzed a few men trudging along between stands of trees. He waggled his wings. In the mist, they thought he was a German and waved back, but their assurance and their ability to keep moving forward frightened him.

"Wonder where the fuck they're goin'? England, I guess."

The cold was really bothering him now. It was time to make an effort at getting home. Suddenly he burst out of the cloud cover and there, not two miles away, was a pack of Me 262s. He had never seen that many together before. They were beautiful machines. The trim elegant body rushed forward into a very long ballistic nose. The engines were big, but their tapered cowlings extended from beneath each wing in a sweeping simple design that harmonized with the shape of the fuselage.

"I want one of those things to take home," he said. "With one of those I could get above everything, up where nobody would dare fuck with me no more."

Then the Messerschmitts saw him. He watched them come, his eyes gleaming. Just as they roared into cannon range, he ducked into a cloud bank and glided down to the deck. If they found him now, he was a dead man. It would be easy to cut him off. But first they had to find him. He could hear their strange and dreadful jet engines filling up the air with immense volume all around him. Flame spurted from the back of those engines, coloring the clouds a dull orange. One passed a mere fifty feet above. He saw it fuzzily, yet it wasn't until the plane disappeared that Walker realized he was unusually attentive.

"I seen somethin'," he said. "Yes, sir, I seen it. There's somethin' I can do they can't, and that's how I'll get 'em."

He listened. The jets still searched for him, but they were in the distance, crossing and crisscrossing in streams of muffled sound filled with high-pitched whines.

"They're gaining altitude. They think I have climbed out. Fooled 'em. F-o-o-led 'em! Well, so long, suckers."

He turned and headed due west out of the Ardennes. Ten minutes later he came upon a company of American infantrymen in the square of a tiny village. They waved. He felt sorry for them ("If you knew like I know, you'd cut that shit out"), so innocent and cheerful down there. They had no idea how much armor was surging through that forest at them. It was a damn shame. At Amiens he changed course southward, knowing that Paris had to be somewhere out there on the horizon. He flew directly over the heart of the city without looking down. Seven minutes later he made his final approach over the château.

Two weeks later they crossed into Germany on bomber escort. The bad weather began to break up. A turn northward was made at Heidelberg and soon Frankfurt was visible.

Most of the city was gone. Night area bombing and precision day raids had devoured block upon block. The city appeared to be composed entirely of crumbling houses standing in vast empty lots of dirty, pulverized brick, barren rooms, and devastated furniture. Very few buildings had roofs. All the bridges were down, the trees withered. The streets led nowhere but to more of the same bleak landscape. Here and there a church spire stood, blackened by fires of unimaginable intensity.

"God punished them people," Walker said.

They continued flying north, flying parallel to the Rhine. The bomber crews rarely looked down. They watched the sky, waiting for the moment of attack. The bombers picked up a little speed. Cologne drifted toward them over the horizon. If Frankfurt was terminally ill, then Cologne had been violated and mummified, for it consisted almost entirely of ruined walls standing in a limitless acreage of ground, lumpy and malignant with bomb craters. No streets or even paths existed. The earth looked wasted and sandy. The flyers could feel the cold wind down there, smell the stench of bodies, cringe at the bestial loneliness which came over human beings when no walls sheltered them and no food passed into their mouths. They felt civilization was dying in Germany and perhaps also among the people who had done this. It was an act of savagery beyond their comprehension.

Their eyes did not linger over Cologne. This whole mission was very strange: the postponements, the raped cities, and the absence of German fighters troubled them.

Fremont checked the sky for any sign of gathering fighters. He ordered the men to spread out a little more than usual. They would need maneuvering room when the attack finally came. Dusseldorf lay off his port wing. The target wasn't far. Through the open radio he heard the bomber leader talking to his copilot. Then their conversation sounded a bit strange to him. Something made him rotate the volume knob at once and listen in.

"Hell of a day," a young incredulous voice brimming with annoyance said. "First we get that collision in the goddamn fog and now this. Will you look at that son of a bitch? Shit, we're right in the middle of fighter country and he looks like he's out for a Sunday stroll. Those bastards were supposed to go straight through to Berlin and they're limping back home already. They'll bring half the goddamn Luftwaffe with them."

Fremont edged out ahead of the lead squadron and looked to starboard. There was a lone Flying Fortress coming toward them from the northwest on all four engines. His bomber-group letter stood out in white on the high, rounded horizontal stabilizer. Fremont was astonished. Fortresses never flew alone over enemy territory.

"Hi, big birds, glad to see you," the pilot radioed in.

"Where you headed, pardner?" the leader asked.

"Ipswich, I hope," a pleasant voice answered.

"What the hell are you doing out here alone?"

"Engine trouble. Number one and three conked out over Hannover. Just got 'em goin' again."

"Shall we let him in, Randy?" the copilot was asked.

"Oh I don't know, Bob," he answered. "He's probably a fuck up."

There was friendly laughter on both sides.

"You better pack in with us, pal. There are a couple of hundred airfields between here and the Channel. You've got as much chance of making Ipswich as a snowball in hell."

"Thanks, fellas, it's appreciated. By the way, where you goin', anyway?"

"Oh, a little garden spot outside of Essen. Bet you never heard of it."

The lone bomber circled around and began taking up a rearward position.

"You shouldn't have told him anything, Bob," the copilot said. "He didn't use the call sign."

"He doesn't know the call sign, genius."

"You still shouldn't have revealed our destination."

"Aw, fuck it. Check with the bombardier and see what's cooking."

Fremont switched channels.

"Four-one."

"Yes, leader," Archibald replied.

"Have your boys keep an eye on that stray. He doesn't look mangy enough to me."

"Can do."

Donaldson watched the newcomer. Nothing about the ship was unusual, but the crew wasn't particularly friendly. When he dipped his wing to say hello, the waist and top turret gunners nodded rather stiffly.

"Prejudiced bastards. Fuck 'em."

"Three minutes to target. Three minutes."

Essen was directly in front of them. The city appeared

partly smashed, but smokestacks still sent up a shroud of
black mist which spread for miles. Donaldson's radio
crackled and hissed. And through the heavy static he heard
something funny. He listened, pressing the phones to his
ears. Somewhere in the ether a transmitter was sending
out German words. A man was talking. Distinctly he heard
the word "Essen." Essen. The Fortress beside him had
peeled off. It was angling away on another course. He
didn't know what to do. He knew who was in that plane,
but what if he was wrong? Tension pounded in his head.

"One minute to target. One minute and counting."

Donaldson yelled. He flung himself on the Fortress like
a madman, all of his guns and cannons blazing. They
plummeted through the sunny sky.

"Norvel's gone crazy!" someone shouted. "Stop him.
Stop him."

His shots tore at the wing nearest him. He was on top
of the big plane. It filled up his gunsight as he fired in
blind determination and watched the bomber erupt into
bright flame.

"Somebody get him."

"They're Germans. They're Germans!" His voice burst
from him, frenzied, jubilant, and confused.

The stricken bomber rolled away, sheeting a solid wall
of burning fuel hundreds of feet long. Parachutes appeared.
The men dangling in them wore grayish-blue flying suits.
Luftwaffe suits. The ball turret gunners ripped them to
pieces. Bombs began to stream down on a cluster of old
sheds and a barn near the edge of a wide field. Donaldson
could make out the configuration of something like a runway painted brownish green. The bombs hit with beautiful
accuracy. Enormous explosions shattered the buildings.
More and more went off, welling up from deep underground. As they turned for home, the assembly station
was still blowing itself apart.

The pilots sat around in chairs and on the floor near
the fireplace in the drawing room that served as their club.
Most were drinking or smoking. Beasley was sunk in an
armchair, reading a newspaper.

"Colonel, that was pretty daring stuff the other day,
going after that jet fighter base. Are we going to keep
playing it both ways?" Johnson asked hopefully.

"Sure, Pedro, we've got to. We can no longer remain a defensive force on escort missions. We've got to go to the attack and suppress these people."

"Hey, Osborn," Walker said. "What's happening in the woods, man?"

"You mean the Ardennes," Osborn said.

"Yeah, you know, over there in the woods."

"The Ardennes offensive is now called the Battle of the Bulge, Horace," Osborn said. "They named it that because the line is bulging out like a balloon."

"Or something else I could name."

"What's that?" Archibald cut in.

"Nothin' you ever had, Buster Brown."

Archibald pretended to pout and the men laughed.

"In a way the Germans are winning," Osborn said. "They've made some interesting progress. They managed to wear down a hell of a stiff defense at Saint-Vith, but I suspect it took them a lot longer than they wanted it to. Anyway, the Bulge is getting bigger every day. Bastogne is still surrounded. The big boys have something to conjure with here."

"Duane, what do you see in the old crystal ball?" Beasley asked.

"Patton's trying to fight his way through and relieve Bastogne," Osborn replied, shrugging his shoulders. "We'll see what that brings."

"I read the other day where the British have a new way to get the two hundred sixty-two," Donaldson said.

"Where'd you pick up readin'?" Walker muttered.

"The British don't try to catch them by scrambling," Donaldson said, "because they cross the lines at six hundred miles an hour. Instead they head for the base where they came from and wait. They ambush them when they come into the landing pattern with their flaps down."

"I heard about that," Jennings said. "It worked for about a week, but then the Germans put in one hundred sixty low-level guns along a corridor near the strip."

"Of course they did," Walker said. "They can outsmart Norvel any day and twice on Sundays. I'm the only one around who knows how to handle them jets."

"I saw that the other day when I was giving you the last rites," Donaldson said.

"Never you mind," Walker answered.

"I saw you flying in circles with your head in your ass," Archibald shouted. "And I'll thank you not to do it again."

Walker laughed and filled his corncob pipe. Somebody handed him a snifter of cognac and he put it down beside him on the floor.

"Radio says a lot of brothers have gone into the field," Butters said. "They're all service personnel, cooks, stevedores, truck drivers, and such. I bet most of 'em are country boys."

"Wish 'em luck," Pedro Johnson said.

"God bless 'em."

"They'll need it."

"I don't know why they'd want to do it," someone put in. "The Army had no use for them. It consigned them to the nigger jobs, and now they're bustin' ass to help bail Eisenhower out of this mess."

"I'd still like to see them do well," Walker said, taking a sip from his glass.

"Why would you want to side with them?" Archibald asked. "They aren't soldiers. They'll just go out and get themselves killed."

"Are we the only soldiers?" Walker inquired.

"Hell, no, Horace," Archibald answered. "But you know what I meant."

"Yeah, I know what you meant," Walker replied. "And I don't like it one goddamn bit."

"Why?"

"Because I see a lot of us in what they're doin'. Those boys want to do something for the country, too. They want that identification, that recognition in history for doing their part. I feel for them. I wouldn't mind walkin' around in that Ardennes forest shootin' a few Germans myself."

"What do you think, Cricket?" he asked, turning to Jennings. "You ain't said nothin' much tonight."

The others looked at Jennings.

"I think what they're doing is in the right spirit," Jennings replied. "I hope they make a name for themselves."

"You talkin' sense for once," Walker said.

"But," continued Jennings, "I don't see where it's all leading. I think you are all placing too much significance in this. Where the hell does it fit in the larger scheme, what becomes of any of us when this is over?"

"Forget the larger scheme, Carl," Walker said without rancor. "We never know too much about that, anyway. We're put on this earth to fight and dream, especially our people. I wouldn't lie. You people here are my family. You all I got. I ain't gonna tell you somethin' that's not right."

On Christmas Day, as a spearhead of the panzer armies in the Ardennes came within five miles of the Meuse River, the squadron dined on roast suckling pig in the upstairs room of an elegant Paris restaurant. Most everyone knew this would be the last Christmas they'd share together, but no one mentioned it. The after-dinner talk flowed for an hour and a half before the group broke up on the street below. Fremont went to see his friend, the lady writer who thought she was in love with him. Skinner left quickly to spend the night at the apartment of his girl friend in the exclusive Paris suburb of Saint-Cloud, where Field Marshal von Rundstedt had lived for the past four years. Archibald went in the opposite direction. He too was in a hurry. He'd taken up with a famous sculptor and was already a couple of hours late for a party the whole art world of Paris was to attend. Beasley departed soon afterward, bound for the high-class whorehouse where he had become a well-known figure. The others had dates or were following up good leads.

Two days later they were back in the war, this time over Chaumont, a small town south of Bastogne, where the 101st was still surrounded. In the dawn mists of the following morning, advance parties from Patton's 4th Armored linked up with elements of the 101st, the Battered Bastards of Bastogne. The town was liberated, never to be recaptured. Patton was preparing to drive northward in an attempt to cut off escape routes back to Germany. Allied counterattacks had begun in two places along the lines. The Bulge was starting to collapse.

That night around the fire, Fremont talked about the battle.

"The way I look at it, Carl, the key to the battle lay in the north. The Germans had four Panzer divisions up there, elite forces, SS troops. The Fifth Army under General Hodges absorbed the punch and slowed them down. The Germans took Saint-Vith way behind schedule. And to do it they needed concentrated power, which kept them from moving around or even sliding down to Bastogne to help. Hodges deserves a hell of a lot of credit. Too bad he'll never get it."

Walker grumbled to himself. He lashed out at Fremont.

"Colonel, what you said is a lot of bull. I believe in my heart Patton won it for us, and now you're trying to take away the credit and give it to some other general."

"What I gave you was a professional appraisal," Fremont said. "The realities," he added.

"Damn the realities, Colonel! You're the only professional military man around here. What the hell do the rest of us need realities for?"

Fremont took a sip of his whiskey.

"What would you prefer?" he asked politely. "How would you go about finding the truth?"

"I ain't got no use for the so-called truth. Give me the legend," Walker answered with great force. "Give me the legend every time. That's what moves people. What we need over here is folks who can write their own legends on the run. Most of us need it, anyway."

TWENTY-FIVE

OSBORN SAT ALONE in the Briefing Room as the pale winter sun began to come up. A few weak bars of light strayed inside. He looked at his watch. In another five minutes the empty benches in front of him would be filled. It was the second day of 1945. He could hardly believe another year was already upon them. Where had all the years gone, he wondered, where the hell had they gone? He was finding gray hairs in his head now, and last week his father had died. He had suffered a cerebral hemorrhage as he sat in his favorite armchair reading the *Philadelphia Bulletin* and listening to the radio. The paper boy came in the next afternoon and found him still sitting there, stiff with rigor mortis. An aunt from Pittsburgh had notified him. She said many of his former students had come to the funeral, and she wished he could have been there too.

He was proud of the squadron as the new year opened up. The boys were in pretty good shape for an outfit that had stayed on the line this long. They'd gotten through the whole summer and autumn without a casualty. Morale was high and Greenlee's return from Italy made everyone feel fate was on their side. Fremont was doing a fine job, he thought. His subtle style wasn't appreciated, but he was a top squadron leader. Everybody benefited from this.

It was too bad about Fremont's divorce. He had to be badly shaken by the news that his former wife had married a prominent Los Angeles surgeon within the week. Osborn wondered how in hell it got out. Fremont was scrupulous when it came to his personal affairs; yet it appeared he had deliberately let the men know of his predicament. Perhaps it was a way of letting them know he, too, was human and vulnerable. He wished he knew Fremont better and that his father could have met the man. They would have admired each other.

The pilots began to arrive. First La Grange, then Jennings, Skinner, Archibald and his crew, Fremont and Butters. He picked up his pointer and came toward them. He felt he ought to be optimistic and bouncy, but he was not. He recalled Hartmann's assertion that Germany would win the war. Fierce armored battles were going on in the Ardennes this morning. Allied troops still bivouacked in France and the Low Countries. Who could tell what the year held? Maybe the Germans had a long-range rocket underground somewhere and were waiting to unleash it in the direction of New York.

"Gentlemen, good morning," he heard his voice say briskly. "This morning at approximately 0620 strong formations of FWs and Messerschmitts flattened twenty-seven Allied airfields stretching from Brussels to Eindhoven."

"Oh shit," a despairing voice cried.

"They moved in groups of three hundred to four hundred planes. They hit the British up there like dynamite. Almost nothing got off the ground. In the first few minutes hundreds of aircraft, including Fortresses, were totally destroyed. We'll be called upon to cover in that area until things are normal again. I'll get back to that shortly, but first Jonesy has some info for you on new enemy aircraft types."

Jones stepped up. The men studied him. Word of new planes fascinated them. Jones began by telling them about the exotic new single-seat jet bomber, the Arado 234. He showed them a somewhat blurred photograph and warned that the plane was fast, how fast, no one really knew.

"She's known to carry at least four thousand pounds of bombs and two heavy cannon. Watch out for this number: they may throw it at you in place of the bomber-destroyers."

The second plane was the Heinkel 162, the Volksjäger,

or People's Fighter. It was easy to build and fly. Factories
all over Germany were putting them together. One of the
pilots started to ask a question and stuttered.

All of January was bitter cold. The pace was enervating.
For ten days they flew fighter sweeps over Belgium and
Holland, with its monotonous flat surface, windmills, canals,
and indistinguishable towns. Gradually the RAF Tempests
and Typhoons returned to service. The panzers had retreated from the Bulge, leaving 80,000 American casualties.
Osborn said the Allies would now begin to move on a
broad front to the Rhine, cross it, and strike into the
heartland of Germany. The Mustangs roamed in central
Germany every day, strafing troop trains, busting loco-
motives, wrecking supply convoys, shooting up airfields.
The flak was murderous no matter where they went.
Their nerves began to quaver and shred. On the last day
of the month La Grange was killed by a 262. He'd spotted
it whistling along at treetop level and closed fast. He
knocked out one engine, but it turned on him as he drove
in for another shot and blew his Mustang all over the
countryside. At the start of the next mission Greenlee got
back into a regular slot for good.

"There are now two distinct types of Me 262," Osborn
said, reading from an Intelligence report. "The Me 262A-2a,
the Sturmvogel, or Stormbird. This version carries two 550-
pound bombs plus the regular cannon. Sometimes they
load it up with cameras for low-level recon. The other is
the 262A-1a, the Schwalbe. The Swallow. One of these got
La Grange. You all know what they can do."

"They're everywhere," Washington complained. "What's
being done to stop them?"

"The fields they operate from are watched continually.
It's hard for them to move because they need a runway
eleven hundred yards long. Their flak protection is what
allows them to get off the ground and accelerate. We're
doing all we can, Rennie."

"Any specs?" Walker wanted to know.

"Not many. They seem to have a special parachute
harness and portable oxygen bottle for bailing out at high
speeds and great altitude. The tail plane is adjustable during flight to change the aircraft's trim at supersonic speed.

They've got multiple ailerons, radar, rockets, and some new kind of sight we can't figure out. Gentlemen, do the best you can."

The fighter sweeps continued into February. Three large army groups were now inside western Germany. Daily the bomber fleets appeared, tier upon tier of them. The condition of German cities was appalling. People had gone underground and into the forests. Kills mounted among the squadron as they met more and more younger pilots. If the older pilots were flying anything but jets, their number had been obliterated by youth and inexperience. ("I don't mind killing another man. That's a fair bargain," Walker said, "but child murder is somethin' else. I don't much care for it.") On the night of February 13, Dresden was attacked by 1,000 RAF bombers. The devastation was total. The next morning Dresden existed only on the map. Then the word was passed to all squadrons: hit every possible target in Germany, everything that stands, moves, or breathes. Fighters ripped over the countryside, tearing up hamlets and farms, machine-gunning men in the fields, people on the roads. In the middle of the month the enormous Russian armies, which had fought back all the way from Stalingrad and Baku and Moscow, surged into eastern Germany along the Polish border.

"The Red Army under Marshal Zhukov has arrived at the Oder-Neisse Line, thirty-five miles from Berlin, and established bridgeheads across the water," Fremont announced.

"Does that mean we can go home now?"

"Not yet, Norvel."

Fremont thought back over the tough day they had just finished. He was alone in the sitting room of his apartment drinking champagne. He pulled the cold bottle from a silver ice bucket and slowly poured some more. Down the hall everyone was in the drawing room. The floor-model radio in there was blaring, but he heard the small table set next to him very distinctly. The news this evening was good. General Hodges' First Army had crossed the Rhine at Remagen. Shouting erupted from the drawing room. Fremont walked over and closed his door, then snapped off the radio. He smiled thinly. At last the war was ending. He'd waited years for this, and now that it

had finally come, he was embittered. His life was going
absolutely nowhere. He was divorced, separated by an
ocean and a continent from his sons. Marva had remar-
ried a little too quickly to suit him. The newspaper
description of the ceremonies sent by his sister was already
brown around the edges.

He sat down and drank the champagne. Ordinarily he
liked to savor the ironies in any given situation, but tonight
he was sad. He'd created this goddamn squadron, scratched
and begged for it, only to find himself overshadowed by
Walker. It wasn't really Horace's fault. He didn't want to
be a hypocrite and go around hating and loathing a man
who meant so much to this enterprise. But envy and resentment tore at him because Walker had exposed all of
his weaknesses as a commander. Walker was a remarkable
man without trying to be; this was what hurt so much.
He'd done the big important job of keeping the men in
touch with their feelings and thoughts. He was the older
brother in all of them.

Fremont refilled his glass. *This is what I get for being
a goddamn Army man,* he thought, *the shit end of the
stick.* He sat down wearily. The champagne made him
light-headed, and all the sources of his bitterness intensi-
fied. He remembered all the humiliation heaped on him in
Washington, the snide presumptuous generals sitting behind
their long table, the hostile audience, the coldness in his
presence. Yet he took all like the fool he'd always been.
He proved his nobility. He was stupid enough to shake
hands with the secretary of war over Todd's dead body
and promise not to tell what had happened. For this they
promised him a squadron. What a joke! He'd written the
secretary three long polite letters asking why the second
squadron remained in the Alabama woods. He got no
replies, nothing, not even an acknowledgment. On long
flights he sometimes felt he was going to snap in that tiny
cockpit. After the war he might resign his commission and
tell the whole story surrounding Todd's death. That would
scare the shit out of those bastards.

Someone knocked loudly on the door. He took the
champagne bottle off the floor and placed it back in the
ice bucket. Fremont buttoned his collar and pulled his
tie up, then put on a jacket. He went to the door and
opened it. Skinner followed him in.

"It's a beautiful apartment you have here, sir," he said.

"Thanks, Percy," Fremont said in a brisk, commanding way. "Have some champagne with me."

They sat down in heavy gilt chairs, facing each other. Fremont leaned back. Skinner noticed he looked a bit frayed and careworn.

"Because you're one of the original boys, I'm going to get right down to cases, Percy," Fremont said with toughness. "Roy's been to see me."

Skinner flinched.

"He meant well. It was either me or Doc Beasley. He says you cry out in your sleep, you're up half the night. What is it, combat fatigue?"

"I wish it was, sir. To be truthful I don't know what's eating me. Maybe it's that the German government still hates us and wants to destroy us. I'm tired of being hated every place I go, Colonel. It's too much."

Fremont nodded. He looked at Skinner. If he hadn't climbed into the military straitjacket, he might have become the same kind of young man.

"I know I've got no right to ask, but I have to. What's your personal life like?"

"Until recently I was just like any of the other guys. I had somebody in Paris, and we saw each other a couple of times a week. She had a little money and we lived it up. Then her fiancé returned. He was a collaborator, they say, a real tough guy. He went into hiding when the Allies arrived. He threatened to kill me, even took a shot at me once, but I got the gun away from him. I'm seeing an older woman now. She seems to understand."

"What about your folks, do you hear from them?"

"Yes, they write. My father wants to see me back in Muskogee as the local M.D. I've got a daughter who'll be nine years old in June. She lives with her mother in Washington and sends me a note once in a while. I'd like to see her again."

Fremont took another sip of champagne. Skinner seemed so confused and easy to hurt. It was no wonder he'd never reached his potential as a pilot.

"Well, Percy, you lead an interesting life," Fremont said. "What are you going to do with all this nervous energy when the war is over, go to medical school and get that shingle?"

"I doubt that, sir," Skinner replied. "Frankly, I'd like to drive race cars for a living."

Fremont chuckled.

"Suppose it doesn't work out?"

"Then I'll try my hand at prospecting for gold and diamonds in Africa."

"I see. Have you mentioned this to Horace?"

"Horace doesn't think in these terms, sir," Skinner said. "He's a rebel. I admire a lot of the things he says, but I don't expect to see many of them happen in my lifetime. I need room and time to live like a human being, Colonel. I can't use myself up fighting everyone who wants to spit on me. I'm just not that much of a pioneer."

Skinner seemed to be more relaxed, but Fremont refused to let himself believe this talk had subdued the demons chasing the man. He was almost sorry he'd made Skinner a Flight Leader. Both men drained their glasses and stood up.

"Lieutenant, I'm glad you came in to see me," Fremont said as they strolled toward the door. "I want you to try and hold out until the end of the war. If you can't make it, we may have to ground you for the duration, and that's not a good way to go out, Skinner. See Doc for sleeping pills if you need them. Don't let yourself crack up. It might take you years to come back. Good night."

"Good night, sir. Thanks for the champagne."

The squadron took off at 0900 precisely and climbed northeastward into the cloudless sky to Arras. They arrived on time and found an armada of planes coming at them, layer upon layer, wave on wave, spread out in every direction almost to infinity. Nearly 1,000 B-17s were part of today's raid on Leipzig. It had taken them more than an hour to form up. Thirty full squadrons escorted them. At 25,000 feet the noise of massed engines was overwhelming. The squadron fell into their assigned place and moved on over Belgium, glancing down now and then at the Fortresses, which seemed stacked right down to treetop level. Soon they became vaguely depressed. This whole operation was too big, too anonymous. They felt no one really needed them.

It took twelve minutes for the formation to cross the German border. Almost immediately the escorts spread out. Some of the squadrons took off on their own, strafing and menacing targets as far as fifty miles away. Here and there the men noticed gaggles of Messerschmitts and long-nose FWs trying to reach the bombers, but it was impossible. They were screened out, kept far in the distance, where they burned up their precious fuel in meaningless dogfights.

They swept over the Rhine near Koblenz. More planes appeared everywhere. Most of them had no connection with the raid. Jennings looked around in amazement. ("Yesterday," Osborn had told them before T.O., "there were four thousand planes in the sky over western and central Germany. We don't know what the Soviets had up.") He began to distinguish the different craft. Below and off his port wing he made out a group of Spitfires. They possessed an old-fashioned loveliness, a brash daredevil air softened by their big rounded wings, which reminded him of a butterfly. Four and a half years ago they had saved a nation, but sadly their time was gone.

"Looks like Route Sixty-six on Labor Day," Walker said to no one in particular.

To starboard, Jennings saw a pack of Tempests and Typhoons chasing a train. It was hard to tell the two planes apart except that the Tempest had a bubble canopy. But it was the Typhoon that fascinated Jennings. Here was a strong, unruly, thoroughbred machine boasting the sporty lines of an elegant touring car. The Typhoon was the only fighter plane that looked truly expensive. Its small neat angular canopy seemed to be handmade. Pilots feared the aircraft. It was difficult to handle and would not pull out of a dive easily, but it was very fast, especially in the lower altitudes, and packed murderous firepower.

The flak began to thicken and rock the bombers gently. Escorts continued to come and go on their mysterious little errands. Donaldson watched the other Mustang squadrons operate. About ten miles away in the transparent sky he spied a desperate battle taking place. German fighters swarmed over a small formation of B-17s, like angry hornets. The scene was a gorgeous, compelling tableau of flak smudges, exploding planes, squiggles of tracer bullets, parachutes, and wild contrails. Soon, though, it was behind them. But the radio crackled with violence and death, with reports of jammed guns, engine fires, stalls, spins, empty magazines. The bombers continued across Germany as if nothing much were happening.

Fremont pulled his squadron farther away from the bombers. He scanned the peaceful landscape below. A group of Gloster Meteors, the RAF turbojet fighters, roared by. They were dramatic-looking in their white paint, but the Meteor was not a fast plane and its presence sparked activity on the ground. Messerschmitt Komets, the little rocket planes, came tearing up to challenge them. Climbing in their mottled green camouflage, they resembled embryonic tadpoles. They ripped into the Meteors, cutting them off and butchering them with rockets. When their fuel was used up, they glided for a while and got one more before slanting down to the earth, where Fremont saw them land with the aid of drag chutes. No sooner had they touched down than a pack of Typhoons pounced and blew them to pieces.

"Six minutes. Six minutes to target."

Ground-to-air rockets appeared. At first Fremont wasn't sure what they were. He saw their explosive takeoff and thought he might get his first glimpse of the Natter, the new manned projectile. According to Osborn, the Natter carried twenty-four smaller rockets to be fired when closing in on a Fortress. Then the pilot pressed a button, the craft broke in two and he was ejected in a parachute. But these were not Natters coming up. They seemed too graceful and thin riding on their tails of white smoke in the harsh sunlight. Their accuracy was fiendish. Two bombers in one of the low squadrons flying an evasive course went down within moments of each other.

"Leader," Fremont heard Jennings say, "what is that, due north?"

Fremont glanced over and cringed for a second. The entire horizon seemed to be on fire. An enormous red conflagration roared up as if the earth itself were ablaze. Fremont stared at it in horror.

"That's the city of Dessau," he said.

A gaggle of 262s appeared and a prearranged defensive plan went into action. Fighters made for them from every angle and altitude. They found themselves completely surrounded, and yet they cut through the grid of planes and escaped, knocking down three of the Fortresses with their blazing silvery rockets before anyone could act. In seconds they had vanished. Bomber-destroyers attacked the low squadrons. They looked absurd in comparison to the jets, but planes fell and crumbled in their wake. They fired one last terrific salvo of rockets and dived under the cover of low-level flak. None of this saved Leipzig. The bombs tumbled earthward right on time, and when they did, the whole city disappeared in a tidal wave of explosions.

Nearly three hours later, the Mustangs glided out of their final approach and landed, one right after the other. They taxied to their dispersal areas. Voices, tired laughter, and the sound of engines being cleared and switched off drifted across the field. Fremont talked with Jones and Osborn about the ground-to-air missiles they'd seen.

"It's almost hopeless trying to pinpoint these things," Osborn said as he looked at a map on his clipboard. "Most of these rockets are fired from trailers. They're never in the same place twice."

Fremont glanced around. Most of the pilots were drinking Cokes and smoking. It was time to unwind before going back to the château for debriefing. Suddenly Fremont noticed that one of the Mustangs was still on the runway. It sat there turned at a slight angle, flaps hanging down, propellor utterly still. Fremont was furious. He'd told the men to always get the hell off that runway fast in case of a surprise attack. Now somebody was fucking up.

"Who is that man?" he snapped.

"Looks like Norvel, sir," Jones said.

Fremont strode toward the plane. This was the last goddamn straw: drinking on a mission, lack of air discipline, insubordination in the Briefing Room, and now stupidity and negligence. Donaldson had it coming. This time he was getting the shaft. Osborn, Jones, and Beasley were at his heels as he approached the plane. And then a chill came over Fremont. He was mesmerized by the bulging yellow spinner, by the huge four-blade prop painted black with bright yellow tips, by the way that sunlight struck the plane and made it appear forlorn and abandoned. A strange urgency prompted him to run. In seconds he was on the wing walk yanking back the canopy. Donaldson sat slumped in his harness. Fremont lifted his head. His coloring was faded and pasty. His lips were turning a dark blue. Fremont clamped the oxygen mask over his nose and turned on the regulator. Beasley climbed onto the wing. His fingers searched for a pulse. One meaty hand reached inside Donaldson's flying suit. His bag was handed up and he prepared a syringe and jabbed it into Donaldson's arm.

"His heart has stopped, Jonathan," he said in a quiet, emotional voice.

Five minutes went by. Donaldson remained motionless. Beasley sighed.

"Norvel's gone," he said. "He's dead. He must have died on landing. Look, he turned off the engine with his last strength to keep the plane from running wild."

Fremont let the oxygen mask fall from his hand. Beasley got down and closed his bag. Now everyone was gathered around the plane. There was not one sound. Fremont bowed his head in momentary bewilderment. His body was shaking terribly. Walker was beside him. He seemed shocked and distraught.

"Horace," Fremont said, "get him out of there."

Walker cut the straps and lifted Donaldson in his arms. He got off the wing gingerly and stood there holding Donaldson and staring off into the bleak late-winter landscape. The men removed their caps. Some of them were in tears.

"He gave more than he had in himself," Walker said so softly that only those closest to him could hear. "He stayed with us until he just didn't have another breath left in his body. He was a good pilot, and a better man. I joked about Norvel, but I loved this man. God bless his soul."

"God bless his soul," the men said in unison.

The way was cleared for Walker. He carried Norvel across the field, through the deer park, and all the way back to the château, with the others following, their steps slow and humble.

Dummy Jones wheeled his jeep to a stop near the big oil-drum night-fire on the field and got out holding a bottle of brandy. He went over to the fire and opened the bottle with deliberate and theatrical slowness, not unaware of the hungry eyes watching him. He took a long swig and passed the bottle on. It changed hands rapidly.

Through the leaping flames he saw the faces of his friends and enemies, the other crewmen. They looked both angelic and shrewd, intelligent and mean. He caught a grimace here, a satisfied scowl over there. The brandy bottle came flying through the air and slapped against his palms. He pulled the cork, drinking the hot smooth liquid freely, then tossed the bottle to his left, wiping his mouth with one sleeve.

"Spring's comin'," Friday said. "I guess that'll be about the end of this war."

"How you figure that?" someone said.

"Army's got 'em good and tight by the balls. It don't matter how many rockets or jet planes they shoot off now. Germany's overrun with death."

"It won't be a minute too soon," Harris said. "These planes are beat to hell. I don't know how to keep 'em together for another week, and there ain't no goddamn parts comin' through."

"Why in hell won't you tell the colonel?" a man they called Stubby said across the fire. "Why take the responsibility on your shoulders, Chief?"

"Haven't got the heart to go to him," Harris replied. "He's one tired son of a buck, and after what happened to Norvel, he don't want to hear my troubles."

Dummy looked up toward the château. Most of the lights were burning. The building stood resplendent and regal against the black starry sky.

"They livin' high on the hog up there," he said. "I hope they ain't forgot how bad things are back home."

"Some of 'em never knew," a bitter voice commented.

"I don't like that big ole house," a man named Upshaw said irritably. "Damn house that big with no furnace. It don't make sense no kinda way. No wonder the owners ain't here. I wouldn't be either."

"Wasn't that a damn shame about Norvel?"

"That hurt me," Coco, Donaldson's mechanic, said. "Just tore me up to see him go that way. I don't think anybody ever understood Norvel. He liked a drink now and then, but he was a good boy and had a DFC to prove it."

"I wouldn't be surprised to see a few more die right out here in the cockpit," Upshaw said. "That Lieutenant Skinner is on thin ice, if you ask me. Don't know how many times I seen him shakin' so bad he can't get out of the harness. He just sets there until he stops shakin' so the others won't see him."

"I guess I shouldn't say this, but Archie, he's been flyin' on his nerves the last six months. Well, he's high-strung anyway, you know how those kinda fellas are. But his hands are shot to shit. Can't hardly hold his hands steady to shoot no more, but he keeps goin'. No complaints. They say he's peculiar, but I say he's much of a man."

"He's that, all right. But how about that Walker. Did you hear him talk at the service for Norvel? Why that man could preach anytime he wanted to."

"He's just the legal limit."

"Ain't he, though?"

"He's gone back a little bit," Dummy said quietly. "He ain't really been the same since he took to throwin' stones at his plane. He says he's not as quick. He has to get closer for a good shot."

"I fear for these boys," Coco said. "None of 'em ain't gonna have no lungs when this war is over. That oxygen burns out your lungs. Half of 'em throw up blood every day. Think they'll see a doctor? Hell no."

"Doc Beasley ought to put his foot down."

"Colonel wouldn't let him. He'd never go against these boys. Besides, he knows Doc don't like war, and it makes him mad."

"I know what Doc does like. He likes them women in Paris. Why, he gave me the address of this house in Paris where there was so much white titty I thought I was inside a lemon meringue pie."

"Is it true that the colonel got a Dear Johnny letter from home?" Cap, Rennie Washington's mechanic, asked.

"What in hell would make you ask a question like that?" Friday inquired with savagely controlled anger. "What goes through your head to ask that?"

He got no reply.

"Answer me, you chickenshit son of a bitch!"

"Well nothin'," Cap said. "I thought I heard it around last week, that's all."

"You didn't, you goddamn ingrate. Colonel gave us jobs, made us skilled men, and brought us over here to Europe. I'm not gonna hear any words against him."

"I take it back, Friday," Cap said.

"You damn well better," Stubby put in.

"I want some more of that cognac brandy," Coco said. "Feel a little chest cold coming on."

"Bottle's empty," Harris said, holding it upside down, "and it's too late to get another one. Put some of that coffee in you and get back to work. They're leavin' early in the morning, Lieutenant Osborn said."

The month of March crept by very slowly. Nearly every day the squadron rocketed past Orléans and off into the skies over Germany. More American columns moved up the roads and trudged across the vacant fields. The number of German corpses in uniform mounted. Dead men seemed to be everywhere: in village squares, on railroad tracks, scattered at the base of flak towers. Yet the air war gained in ferocity. The Luftwaffe refused to capitulate. One day sixty-nine bombers were shot down approaching Berlin. It was the worst day of the entire war for the Eighth Air Force. Two days later fifty-four were lost. Airfields lay abandoned all over the country. Many German planes were simply left out in the open, well camouflaged. Others were hauled into the forests after every mission and covered with boughs. ("They've gone back into those dark forests where they came from," Walker said.) During the day they were towed out again. Frequently their wings were damaged and they had to be junked; but it was all very eerie, this lingering fanatical desperation, this fierce ardor to be obliterated from the face of the earth.

As spring came on, the men began to pray Germany would stop fighting. Oberkommando der Wehrmacht remained silent. Hitler urged his forces on. Resistance continued into April. The Ruhr was encircled by Bradley and Montgomery, yet something was missing. The British cast their eyes toward Berlin.

"Whoever takes Berlin gets credit for winning the war, no matter how hard the others busted their butts or how much ass they kicked," Walker said.

"Haven't you read the papers, dumb ass?" Archibald broke in. "It was all decided at Yalta or someplace. Germany's been cut up like a fryin' chicken, Horace. The Russians get Berlin."

"Fuck that. I don't want to hear that shit. *I* want Berlin."

"The Russians are on the Oder-Neisse Line with a couple of million men," Butters said.

"Who's with 'em that's bad, Roy?" Walker asked. "Nobody. It's Zhukov and a whole lot of peasants. Let me see a show of hands. How many of you dudes are for moving on Berlin?"

Everyone raised his hand.

"That's what I thought. How about you, Colonel Fremont, sir?"

Fremont swirled the deep amber cognac in his snifter. He glanced at Walker roguishly.

"I'm with you, Horace. It would be the right touch of glory. But the politicians are going to take it away from us, wait and see."

Walker's face went glum. He turned to Fremont, shaking his head.

"Can't believe it, sir, just can't accept it. I know in my bones some crazy son bitch is gonna bust through and get it for us. I just got a feelin'."

TWENTY-SIX

FREMONT AWOKE WITH A START. He snapped on the light and examined his watch. It was barely 0400. He tried to go back to sleep for another couple of hours, but couldn't. He just lay there in the cool darkness, brooding. He got up, put on a robe, and started a fire, then wandered outdoors barefoot. He walked for a few minutes and found himself down by the lake. He undressed and slipped into the cold water, swimming lazily to the far shore and back. He returned to the château. He was sad and restless. He knew all sorts of ambiguous feelings had taken hold of him, but it was very hard at this moment to say exactly what they were. All he could focus on now was the news Osborn had brought to his apartment last night.

As soon as Osborn came in, it was apparent he was tense, but he stated his business quickly.

"Sir, I've just received a call from HQ. Russian and American forces met this afternoon near Torgau on the Elbe River."

"What have they got for us tomorrow?" he said.

"Tomorrow," Osborn replied, "we've got a long-range sweep over the Hannover-Berlin corridor. We are to overfly the capital before heading home."

They looked at each other for a long moment.

"Then this is it?"

"Yes, sir. This will be our last mission."

"Thank you, Ops," Fremont said, breaking off a rather formal salute. "I'll inform the men."

"See you in the morning, sir."

He strode to the drawing room and made his announcement. The pilots listened to him in utter calm and, when he had finished, returned to their drinking and card games without comment.

Now Fremont sat before the fire in his bedroom and dressed. He felt cold. Gone were the days when he did a series of exercises each morning. His body couldn't stand that kind of tension anymore. He sat down and wrote a long letter to Mark and Tony in Los Angeles. If anything happened today, he wanted them to have this last word from him. Dawn was coming up rapidly beyond the glass doors. He could see the statuary, the unclipped hedges, and the low stone benches sitting in the desolate splendor of the formal garden. He checked the magazine on his .45 and stuffed it in a shoulder holster, put on his leather jacket, and tied a brand-new white silk scarf carefully at his neck.

Jennings sat on his bed at the far end of the cavernous room he shared with Walker. He had just finished dressing when Reeves knocked at the door.

"Briefing at 0720," Reeves said.

"Sergeant, you've been hanging around Osborn and Jonesy too long," Jennings said pleasantly.

"Could be, sir," Reeves answered.

Jennings slipped into a chair, resting his hands in his lap. He couldn't believe this would be their final mission, because he hadn't expected to be alive when it came. Two years of combat had gone by and here he was, a survivor. That would be his accomplishment in this war, he thought, not medals or kills but survival with a little honor. His mind drifted back to that first mission out of Medjez-el-Bab, and he saw Donny Beaumont sitting there on the bed, smoking a cigarette in his ivory holder. All of that seemed an eternity ago, the Mediterranean sultriness, the heat of Sicily, and finally the big invasion; it was hard to believe poor Donny hadn't died in another war.

Down at the other end of the room he watched Walker getting ready for the day's work. He seemed inordinately busy. Curiosity prompted Jennings to get up and stroll over. Walker was inserting his big hunting knife into one boot. As he saw Jennings, he straightened up. He was armed with two .45s in shoulder holsters and extra ammo clips. On his nightstand he placed a small bulky leather case that resembled a shaving kit.

"What have you got there, Horace?" Jennings asked.

"Uh, nothin'. My survival stuff."

"What kind of stuff? We weren't issued anything like that."

"Never you mind, boy," Walker said, going to a bureau drawer and taking out a pristine white silk scarf.

"Horace, what are you going to do when you get home? I thought I had my future figured out, but I've been thinking lately and now I'm not so sure about anything."

"You not bein' sure about something ain't news," Walker said. He plopped down on his footlocker, crossed his legs, and lit a cigarette.

"I been thinkin' about home, though," he said. "I can't wait to see Texas again even if I don't know what I'll do when I get there. You see, I never did have many friends. I think I'm gonna go out and try to find my pappy." He nodded his head and looked Jennings straight in the eye. "I'd like to see that old coot again. I figured out I'm more like him than I thought. I'll have to look in every gin mill between Atlanta and Corpus Christi to find him, but he's bound to be in one of 'em. He ain't playin' ball no more, I know that. He's too old now even for the Homestead Grays and them other nigger teams."

"Do you think you'll preach?" Jennings asked. "Travel through those small towns telling people now is the time to stand up for their rights?"

"What?" Walker said. "What the hell are you talkin' about. I'm talkin' about my pappy. Shut up with that other racket. Get out of my face! Give a man time to think!"

Appaloosa tiptoed into the room and Walker scooped her up.

"It's too damn cold in here for you, ain't it?" he said to the cat as Jennings went back to his end of the room. "I'm takin' you back down to the kitchen now. You stay by that stove until I tell you to come out. Good weather'll be here in a couple of days."

When Osborn stepped to the edge of the briefing stage, the pilots got up from their benches and clustered around him. For a moment his eyes roved over them. Skinner wore a dazzling white flying suit. An old revolver was jammed into his belt. Walker had on his World War One sheepskin aviator's boots. The Knight's Cross tied at his throat stood out against his dark skin in savage beauty. Archibald wore a red wool cap knitted by his mother. The others were dressed in jodhpurs, cavalry boots hand-made in Paris, suspenders, helmet liners, and corduroy vests. No one would have taken them for officers in the United States Air Force. They looked more like the cast of a high-school play.

"Gentlemen, good morning to you all. Our mission today is to patrol the Hannover-Berlin corridor and suppress fighter strength in that area."

"Why in hell do we have to go to Berlin when the other squadrons in France have already been grounded?" Walker asked in a cutting tone.

Now Osborn saw how nervous they really were, how much fear and tension they concealed beneath their swagger. The idea of doing battle one last time had tightened them up.

"You're needed," Osborn said bluntly. "You're the best, and when you get that reputation, they use you and use you until you're not the best anymore."

"This sector his turned into a real son of a bitch," he went on. The new German aircraft types, the ultramodern stuff, is operating between the Oder-Neisse and the Elbe. They're causing significant casualties among the troops and destroying material. Everybody up there is scared shitless. The brass in Wiesbaden wants this plundering stopped."

"It all sounds very funny to me," Archibald said. "Every airfield in Germany is supposed to be bombed to pieces, from what I hear."

"Most of them have been smashed, Archie," Osborn said, "but the Luftwaffe has changed its mode of operation. They are no longer flying from fixed bases. Fanning out from the Berlin area is a series of secondary fields, gen-erally with one good permanent runway. The fighter wings that still exist move between these fields, never staying in one place more than a couple of days. These bases were not bombed originally because they were almost never used and lay far away from more important targets. Now they've turned into a regular rat's nest."

"What about flak?" Washington asked.

"Flak's going to be a problem. Each field is protected by a flak battalion and these boys are good. They've got the latest gyroscopic sights and some big guns too, so be damn careful. Relays of experienced spotters watch the sky in all directions for a radius of six miles. Okay, Jonesy's got some intelligence for you."

"What's happening in Berlin?" Jennings asked.

"The Russians are there, Carl. The Third Shock Army of the Belorussian Front, Zhukov's men, are in the suburbs of Berlin and closing the inner city."

"Where's Hitler at?" Walker demanded.

"He's holding out in an underground bunker, we think."

"How long will the war last? Give it to us straight, Jonesy," Greenlee said.

Jones sighed and made a grim face.

"How long will the war last?" he said raising his eyebrows. "A week. Two weeks. Maybe more, depending on the situation up north."

"That long. Jesus, then we might have to go out again."

"Oh man, shut up," Walker said. "Where's this up north you're talkin' about, Jonesy?"

Jones brought the map stand over to them and took pointer in hand.

"This thick outcropping of land north of Hamburg is what I'm referring to," he said. "Up here is Kiel. If the Germans want to hold out on the Kiel Canal line, in the Danish Islands and in Norway they can keep the war going until the middle of the summer. This development poses an interesting situation. German airfields in Denmark are jammed with planes. Every bight and estuary and many of the beaches are holding fleets of Blohm und Voss and Dornier flying boats. The center of this retreat is Norway. Convoys leave from Kiel every day. Flying boats have been spotted crossing the Skagerrak in large numbers. What the Russians find in Berlin and whether anybody with authority is still around to give orders will determine what this activity in the north means."

"Can we go up there today?" someone asked.

"No. Do not go north. There are hundreds of anti-aircraft guns up there. Stay in the corridor. The British are doing all they can in flying strikes against the convoys leaving from Kiel."

There was a pause.

"Any more questions? All right, one last warning. If by chance you have to put down, don't land at abandoned German airfields. They've all been heavily mined."

Nature Boy stepped up wringing his hands. He cleared his throat and smiled.

"The best thing about today is the strong tail wind going out," he said. "Otherwise, you're not in luck. You'll run into heavy showers in central Germany, eight-tenths strato-cumulus in some area, four-tenths altocumulus straight up to twenty thousand feet."

"Thanks, man. Thanks a lot."

Nature Boy moved away. Fremont appeared in front of them. He was businesslike.

"Synchronize watches at 0745. Start engines at 0800. Take off is at 0805. Watch radio discipline. They may be listening in."

"Good luck," Osborn said.

"Wish I was going with you," Jones called after them.

"No, you don't," someone shouted back.

After everyone had piled out of the truck Fremont called them together for a final word.

"We'll have to do a lot of improvising today, so I want you to stay the hell off that headset unless it's damn important. Keep a sharp lookout and let me know about anything strange as soon as you can identify it. Okay, you flight leaders, you've got exactly thirty seconds to huddle."

"The main thing," Skinner told his men, "is to relax. Be natural. If you start to overcompensate, you're in trouble. Do things the usual way, or be prepared not to come back."

"I've lost a lot of men from this flight, but I'm still here, so stick with me, understand?" Archibald said. "We'll fly as a three-plane unit. We've got a better chance that way, without Norvel to cover for us."

"Touch my hand, everybody," Walker said, removing one glove.

"You heard me. Touch my hand, go ahead."

The men glanced at each other and then rested a hand upon Walker's until his was obscured.

"That's better," he said, placing his free hand on top of the pile. "That's the way comrades should act. Now, I'm not going to pretend like the others that this is just another day. It ain't. It's our final day together up there against them. We've become men, warriors, and somethin' else besides. You all know what I'm talkin' about even if I can't explain it. Let's do good today so we can all come back and enjoy what life gives us and laugh and tell lies about this whole thing thirty years from now, amen."

"Amen."

Jennings lingered a few seconds after the others had left.

"I'm sorry I got mad at you back in the room, Carl. You know how I can be at times. I just wanted to tell you I'd like for you to come down to Texas this summer and meet my daddy. Maybe we can travel around and raise some hell in those country churches and get the people talkin' about their deliverance."

They stared at each other for a long moment as Walker put his glove back on. Jennings nodded. Suddenly he grabbed Walker by the shoulders. They embraced.

All over the field, pilots in their patched and battered Mustangs checked out their gunsights and radios, oxygen masks, surface controls, and rearview mirrors. They talked in clipped voices with the mechanics strapping them in. Beasley leaned against his ambulance, watching the crews scamper to the starter batteries and check their watches. Sunlight rippled over the fresh green grass. Jones, Reeves, and Osborn stood together near a jeep as the engines started up in a tremendous roar and planes began to taxi. Ground crewmen clung to the wingtips, helping them to pivot smoothly on the wet grass. They waved as the planes lifted off, looking thick and vulnerable with their big drop-tanks slung underneath.

Walker was still on the ground. His engine had quit as he moved away from the dispersal and he was wild with rage as Dummy came running up and climbed the wing.

"You worthless son of a bitch," he screamed. "You fixed me up with a dead plane."

"How'd I know she was gonna quit?" Dummy said.

"Fix it! Start this plane or I'll blow your fuckin' head off," Walker cried in a frenzy.

Harris and Friday sprinted over, followed by the other mechanics. Dummy pulled the starter battery across the ground and plugged it in.

"I could hear you bellowing on the other side of the field," Harris said with obvious relish. "Why don't you shut the hell up and let this man work. We'll have you out of here in no time."

"You're fuckin' A right you'll have me out of here or I'm gonna kick some ass," Walker shouted back.

"Leave it the fuck alone!" Dummy yelled at someone under the wing. "I can start this son of a bitch by myself."

"What's wrong, Two-one?" Fremont asked over the radio.

"It's these chumps down here. They fucked up my ship; now they're tryin' to blame me."

"Get it straightened out. We'll give you five minutes."

"Don't leave me holdin' the baby," Walker said.

"Work it out fast, Horace."

"Roger."

"Crack the throttle," Dummy cried from under the plane.

He materialized in front of the propellor. Jumping up, he grabbed one of the big blades and began pulling it through with all his strength. Harris and Friday retreated in fear. Walker hit the starter and ignition switches. The blades began to turn laboriously. Dummy seemed to have trouble geting off. His legs dangled. Finally he stumbled to the ground and pitched forward, his head missing the roaring propellor by inches. He crawled under the plane, struggling in the prop wash, and came up behind the wing. Walker saw him in the rearview mirror and slammed the canopy shut. Dummy banged on the side of the plane. The battery was disconnected. He flashed the thumbs up sign. Walker returned it and smiled. The Mustang taxied out, but Walker was fighting a sudden siege of panic. As the engine turned over, he realized he didn't want it to. Its power sounded ominous and fateful to him. He wanted to shut down, to quit now while he was still alive, but it was too late for that. The Mustang gathered tremendous speed. Everything he passed turned to a blur. He gave the ship plenty of right rudder to keep it straight. His head pounded with fear and indecision. Then the aircraft felt lighter, freer. The Rolls-Royce engine in front of him pulled the plane upward. He felt like a kid on top of the Ferris wheel at an amusement park. Then fear touched him again. The château, the lake, the deer park grew quite small. He banked to port and stared down at the frail green landing ground. His eyes checked the sky in a quick sweep. He exhaled deeply and rode into the heavens, closing the minute swarm of planes circling above him.

They zoomed across the French landscape at low level, bobbing gently in the turbulence. Horses galloped in large pastures among fields of brown and yellow and a luscious velvet green. Poplars bloomed along the roadsides. Fine blue smoke drifted up from the chimneys of stone farmhouses which had stood there for generations. All was quiet in the villages and large towns. Then they crossed into Germany for the last time. At first, things appeared no different, but as they approached the Rhine, changes came over the land. Railroad tracks were obliterated for miles on end. Every junction of rail and road travel was squashed. Trains sat empty and abandoned in the middle of nowhere. Flak towers dotted the field, forlorn and unmanned. They dipped down again, their stark shadows racing over the earth. People were nonexistent. Bomb craters pockmarked everything, some of them stretched a hundred yards across. It grew very cloudy. The gloom was unnerving. They huddled together, plunging through zero visibility and relentless rain.

Near Bonn they broke out into the sun again. Fremont took them down. The earth below had a blasted sandy texture. It looked like the surface of the moon. Panther tanks, the indestructible Panthers, lay scattered all over this wasted landscape, their eight huge drive wheels and 75 millimeter guns smashed and useless. They looked like the carcasses of prehistoric animals.

Walker frowned as he gazed around. Apprehension and worry nagged him. He feared an encounter with the jets, and yet he knew it must come. He thought perhaps he didn't know how to fight them after all. He was both giddy and heartsick. Concentration eluded him today, of all days. Strange noises emerged from his headset. He heard German voices far away, violent storms of static softening into passages from a symphony by Beethoven followed by weird ghostly reverberating sounds electronic in nature. He wondered if he was losing his mind, for the sounds came and went with unpredictable frequency. Below, he could see an army moving, thousands of helmeted men picking their way along, supported by tanks, trucks, and guns embossed with the American white star. The squadron was fired on by nervous GIs. More clouds obscured the sun now. They plunged into another storm.

On the other side, farm country lay beneath their wings. The burning crops, leveled buildings, and dead livestock moved by very quickly because they flew almost at roof-top level in the rolling, shifting sunlight. Airfields shattered and churned up by the bombers lay in all directions. On an autobahn, a clean stretch of white ribbon miles away to port, there was some activity. Planes took off and tore away with the speed of rockets. The squadron circled in to see what was happening. The planes were new to them, long in the fuselage, indescribably sleek, and painted dull black. Their shoulder wings appeared tapered to the thin-ness needed for supersonic flight. The compact nose was rounded into a small dome of tinted glass. Four jet engines powered their escape. They launched themselves one right after the other and streaked into the northern sky, headed for Denmark, the Skaggerak, and Norway.

"Beautiful planes," someone said.

"Yeah. Beautiful."

"Approaching Hannover," Fremont said.

They could make out the city. It was wreathed in smoke from fires burning out of control. A pack of Heinkel 162s, the People's Fighters, roared overhead, driven by single jet engines clumsily mounted atop the fuselage aft of the pilot's cabin. In moments they, too, had executed a turn northward and disappeared.

"Messerschmitt 420 destroyers closing from behind, leader," Washington called.

"All planes go to full power."

They moved out just in time. The bomber-destroyers cut loose a salvo of rockets which seemed to gain on them before trailing off at the end of their range. The destroyers slanted away and made for their base.

Another storm overtook them outside of Hannover, heaving them all over the sky, dropping them a thousand feet at a time. Somehow they managed to stay together and break out into the good weather again.

"Airfield at three o'clock low beyond the road. FWs on runway."

"Attack at once," Fremont cut in. "Follow me down. Each man pick out a target. Open fire at seven hundred yards."

He pushed into his dive. Auxiliary fuel tanks from the other planes fluttered around him. The terrible sickening pressure of plunging at the earth rippled over his stomach. The airspeed indicator climbed. Flak batteries started firing. A heavy curtain of boiling smoke and bright gun flashes obscured the field and 37 millimeter guns picked them up. Their familiar black smudges mingled with the white puffs from 20 millimeter low-level stuff. Fremont heard his engine whining out every bit of its immense strength. He swept under the 37s. Butters and Johnson were on his wings. Tracers laced through the air, scoring hits. Sweat poured off his body. He could see ground crewmen running wildly.

"Flatten out," he cried. "Get in low. Low!"

A loud bang sounded at the side of Jennings' Mustang. He was hit hard for the second time. He heard other planes being hit and could almost smell the desperation and near panic. They closed the field boundary barely 100 feet off the ground. It was eerie to travel at this speed and yet see buildings and people clearly. Jennings felt as if he were flying through a tunnel. Planes were trying to take off. They had yellow-and-orange bands painted around the rear fuselage. He was firing now. Long-nose Focke-Wulfs jumped in the air and exploded. Anyone in the open was butchered. A huge cloud of burning gasoline rolled toward him through the smoke. He pulled up and came out unharmed. He and Walker and Bluey blasted a large wooden hangar to pieces. Someone came running at them with a machine gun. Double tracks of .50 bullets drove him to the runway. They were climbing. The flak was incredible. Everyone was hit, everyone, but no one exploded. They spread out over the sky. Smoke from the airfield drifted up thousands of feet. Jennings was trembling in his harness.

"Form up on me," Fremont told them.

They continued on in the direction of Berlin. The men were very quiet. The flak had gotten to them, had shaken them to the depths. They couldn't take any more. That was all, they just couldn't go down again into another flak curtain. Berlin loomed before them. No one could tell it had once been a cosmopolitan metropolis. Large sections of the city were completely burned out by fire storms. Millions of bricks from disintegrated buildings had cascaded into the streets. Trolleys stood mired in rubble. Over-turned trucks used by the last fanatical defenders burned. Vaguely familiar tanks crept along in the center of the city. Then a swarm of Russian fighters appeared from nowhere. They were Yak-9s, Jennings said.

"Our escort is here," Archibald said.

"Funny looking, aren't they? I see a little Spit, a touch of Me 109, and more Mustang than I want to see. God-damn copycats."

The Yaks pulled in tighter, their nondescript forms painted an ugly brown color ("Shit brown," Walker growled) with big red stars on the tails, and enormous, crudely lettered squadron numerals stretched over the rear fuselage. One of the Yaks was flying wingtip to wingtip with Walker.

"Get away from me with that fucking humpmobile, you communist motherfucker," he screamed. "Get off me, I said."

He was waving his arms, but the Russian pilot eyed him with a blank stare.

"Get on back to Minsk!"

The Russian continued to hold station, although his face showed traces of alarm now, for Walker was pounding the side of his canopy in rage. Then he turned on the Russian. His thumb hit the gun switch. Bright flashes of cannon fire streaking over his canopy lit up the Russian's terrified expression as he babbled into his radio. Instantly the entire flock of Yaks departed.

"Horace, you might have caused an international inci-dent there," Fremont said with a hearty laugh.

"Shit, I don't care none."

"Leader, I see the Russian flag flying from the Reichs-tag," Jennings cried.

"There's another one going up over there. Jesus, they've got them up all over the place."

"Don't look now, anybody," Archibald said, "but we've got company."

"I knew this would happen."

"Swallows, leader," Butters broke in.

"Stay in flights," Fremont warned.

"No! Don't stay in flights," Walker yelled. "Go to pairs. It's your only chance."

The Messerschmitts were among them in seconds. They were brand-new. Their freshly painted swirling green net pattern, the rarely seen wave mirror pattern, gleamed in the thin rays of sun breaking through. The jets turned once majestically and came in again.

"They have to slow down and maneuver to get their sights on you," Walker barked into the headset. "I saw them doing it over the woods in Belgium. When they slow down, you speed up. Keep changing speeds until you get position."

Fremont counted nine jets. In seconds, planes were blazing away at each other. Everyone was in trouble. Cries for help filled the headsets. Two of the jets picked him out. They had altitude. He felt helpless and naked as the first one zeroed in on him. He flipped his Mustang over violently, rolling to get out of the way. His starboard wing resounded with a series of solid hits. It was holed. As the jet roared over his canopy, its tremendous slipstream threw him out of control for a moment. He grabbed at the stick in terror as his plane spun and in that instant the second Swallow came down and missed him. He climbed at full throttle, almost colliding with another Mustang. His pursuers whipped around and came for him again. It was unbelievable the way they climbed. He was forced to fire too quickly and missed both of them. Panic seized him. He slammed the stick forward, hoping to outrun them in a dive. No good. He leveled off on shuddering wings and gasped for breath. The Swallows were back, looping above him now, getting ready to blow him apart. He cut back on his speed. He saw cannon fire converging well ahead of him. Then he went to full throttle. They missed him again. He whirled around in a tight climbing turn. Beads of perspiration stood out all over his face. He would be underneath them for a split second. He fired a long burst into the beautiful flat pale blue underbelly of the lead ship. An explosion rained debris down on him. The Messerschmitt was flaming. He saw the pilot eject free, tumble a few times, and fall until his parachute popped open. Cannon fire raked his fuselage as he shot past the second Swallow. He had altitude. The German seemed stunned and uncertain. Fremont fired everything he had, but the Swallow took his best shots and dove for safety.

Another jet was on Skinner. He could see its evil triangular body and big engines very clearly in the mirror. It toyed with him, flying alongside in a dive, cutting off his turns, peppering him as he climbed. He felt ready to die. He couldn't remember what Walker had told them to do and he was afraid, paralyzed and afraid. His only chance was to try and disappear in the clouds. He broke away from his zigzag course, plunging into the undercast. It was like falling down a manhole filled with steam. For a second, he broke into a patch of sunlight. The Messerschmitt was there. Tracers sped toward his tail. The Mustang rocked under the impact of 30 millimeter shells. He was in the clouds again, falling like a stone. His altimeter said 3,000 feet, 2,000. He had to pull out soon. He found himself in the open again. The jet was lining up, getting set for its final barrage, when a hail of fire ripped at it from the side. It wobbled crazily. The pilot never had time to eject. His craft exploded in a ball of white-hot flame. Skinner saw a large piece of jet engine swirling away like a scrap of refuse. He searched around. Not a plane was to be seen. Then Walker's gruff voice crackled in his headset.

"Get on back upstairs, Pretty Boy."

"Where the hell are you?" Skinner asked.

"Get the fuck back up there or I'll tear your ass apart too."

Archibald closed on one of the jets. It had slowed down to turn and line up Greenlee for a perfect kill. He had nearly 500 feet of altitude to dive in. The outline of the Messerschmitt ballooned in his gunsight. He was almost on top of it now. His thumb slammed against the gun switch. His cannon fire streamed through the elegant glass canopy. The reverberation jarred him in his harness. He kept firing until he saw plumes of black smoke and flashes of fire. The whole cockpit was a cauldron of flames. He couldn't stop watching it, couldn't break off. A series of tremendous explosions erupted all around him. Quick frightened voices yelled in the headset. A daze came over him. His canopy was shattered. Blood cascaded down his right arm. Don't dive, something told him. His left hand drew back on the stick, hugging it to him. He climbed slowly, dreamily, waching the earth tilt away.

"Go to one hundred percent oxygen." He pressed the

mask against his nose and breathed deeply. Darkness dropped over his eyes and brain. When he awoke, Archibald was flying level. Brilliant sunlight bounced off the huge cloudbanks below. He was quite alone.

Washington saw black wing-crosses edged in white plummeting out of the sky above. It was too late to try and climb past the jet closing him. In confusion he yanked the throttle back toward him, almost shutting down the engine. The German missed him with two long bursts. His timing was way off. Washington smiled in satisfaction as the bullet-shaped plane hurtled by him and streaked into the clouds. For a moment he sighed, overcome with relief. The chills rushed down his back. He felt isolated and stricken. It was terribly quiet. His Mustang began to tremble as if it were about to fall apart. He had no power. He was stalling. In seconds the plane would tumble out of control. He slammed the throttle home and pushed the stick away from him, leaning hard on it. The Mustang hung in space neither climbing nor flying. It eased into a dive, engine roaring to life. The tachometer rose slowly. Washington shuddered. Fear released its grip on him. He never looked into his rearview mirror or heard Greenlee screaming at him. The jet angling in had all the time it needed. Greenlee saw sparks flying from the fuselage behind Washington. Then the Mustang flamed. Its engine whined and it tore apart into a million fiery fragments.

Jennings could hear his heart pounding wildly. He was by himself for the moment, flying an evasive course. Below, the battered and wrecked city of Berlin spread out through a gap in the clouds. He was drawn into a corner of the battle. Two Mustangs had cut off a jet as it climbed for safety. The Messerschmitt wheeled into a violent skid. Jennings blasted away at him, but the stream of bullets and shells skimmed around the plane as the German broke into a twisting pattern. Someone hit him from above. Jennings poured cannon fire into his starboard engine cowling. Thick black smoke roared out behind the beautiful craft as it made for Jennings and tried to ram him. All of the Mustangs nearby blazed away, their guns flickering with a lurid, deathly light. Slowly the Messerschmitt began to come apart as Jennings bore in, still firing. It burst like an overripe tomato, spewing itself in all directions. Jennings streaked through the debris. He was clear, but smoke poured into his cockpit mingled with a terrible odor. Something was lodged in the air scoop. Jennings pushed into a dive. A bundle of smoky debris popped out of the scoop. He examined the seared blond hair with astonishment. The bundle, which he now saw was the head and armless upper torso of a man, fell rapidly and was gone in seconds.

Walker had just gotten another Messerschmitt, blasting it off Johnson's tail as he fled into the undercast. So far, so good. No one suspected he was lurking around the cloud base in the shadows waiting. He smiled to himself, his eyes colored a hideous yellow by the illuminated gunsight. He flew into the clouds and made a 180-degree circle, then held position while he listened to the transmissions from above. The jets were still giving them hell. The boys were tired, very tired, he could hear it in their voices. Someone was in a dive, calling for help.

"I got another customer," he said with a weary smile.

He turned 180 degrees to starboard and proceeded along his entry route. Emerging, he saw nothing. Then a Mustang flashed by, half-falling, half-diving, and trailing a thin veil of smoke. He led the Messerschmitt perfectly and knocked it on its back. He was on top of it, tearing away with his cannon. The craft flamed orange. The pilot ejected free and floated down into the hands of the Russians.

"Poor bastard," Walker mumbled. "They'll probably shoot him dead before he hits the ground."

He banked around to watch the spectacle, and his plane was hit. It jerked and skidded through the air. He knew he was hit bad. He grabbed the stick, choking on the cordite and acrid smoke filling the cockpit. His canopy was shattered, but the shells had come in at a narrow range, and many had bounced off the armor plating behind his head or he would have been killed. All of his instruments on the starboard side were shot out and some of the others fluttered and died before his eyes. He felt glass underfoot and saw fragments of black-and-white dials hanging from bits of dangling wire. Above him and far to port, the only surviving jet raced back to its home base. Walker watched it sadly.

The sky was empty. An odd poignancy was in the air.

The men gathered themselves together in the solitude of their cockpits. A sense of exhilaration rose in them as they realized they'd just defeated the best planes that Germany or anyone else had to offer. They got on the headset, adding up the kills and near kills.

"I feel like goin' up north and getting a few of those big seaplanes."

"Hell no, man, we're beat up as it is."

"Horace, you had four jets, didn't you?"

"Damn real. But we lucked out, Pedro. They didn't have the rockets today. If they'd had them, we'd all be gone."

Someone was sobbing. His radio was open and his anguish could be heard quite distinctly as it rose from a low muffled series of choking sounds to something that resembled weeping. The sound was embarrassing and eerie, but everyone listened just the same, perhaps because it was what they all felt.

"All right," Fremont snapped at last, "whoever you are, let go of the microphone button."

The sobbing broke off. Fremont thought it was Skinner, but he couldn't be sure and it didn't matter. The squadron was spread out over miles of sky. It was vulnerable to another attack. Greenlee and Butters had already put out engine fires. Radios had failed and men signaled each other by hand. The time had come to run for home.

"Archie, what kind of shape are you in?"

"I've got morphine in my shoulder. I can make it, leader."

"Okay. Everybody pack it in fast. Let's get the hell out of here."

"'Leader. Two-one's not keeping up," Butters advised him.

"What's the matter there, Horace? You're lagging."

"Can't be helped, Colonel. I'm hurtin'. I got no instruments."

Fremont twisted in his harness and stared at Walker's plane. It was full of gaping holes. The canopy was half blown away, and a long white stream of glycol spun out from the engine cowling. If any of that glycol got into the cockpit, Walker would be unconscious in minutes.

"You're losing all your antifreeze. There's no way you

can make France in that kind of shape. You'll have to put down on the other side of the Elbe behind our lines."

"Whatever you say, General."

"Bluey. Jennings. Give him top cover."

"Right, leader."

They crept along over the sunny landscape. The morning showers had cleared the air and visibility was good. Walker's engine began to run hot. He fought to keep altitude, but it was impossible. After a long silence he spoke up.

"I've run my race," he said without emotion.

"Try and make the Elbe, Horace," Fremont replied. "It's not too far now."

"I can't make that river, General," Walker said in a voice suddenly hoarse. "I got to get out of here. This thing is hotter than a pistol."

Fremont was quiet. He didn't know what to say, what to do.

"Don't hesitate," he finally responded. "Bail out now and walk due west to our lines. We'll pinpoint your landing."

Walker had no time to reply. Dry hot smoke from the engine seeped in on him. He smelled glycol. But he didn't move. He could feel himself tensing, straining, holding back, even though he knew it could be fatal. Then his hands whipped at the seat belt and shoulder harness until he was free. One hand yanked the emergency release lever and the splintered canopy flew back. The noise of wind rushing past hurt his ears. Off came his oxygen hose. Debris, bits of glass and torn metal, swirled around him. He closed his eyes against the blinding wind.

"I'll be home before you will," he shouted into the headset.

He crawled along the wing. Air currents, suction, and turbulence tore at his body. He raised up on one knee and waved at Jennings and Greenlee. Then he was gone, hands folded over his face. Down he fell, down, down, toward the patchwork fields below. Jennings counted to ten twice. The chute was open, it was open and looked like a ball of cotton blowing in the wind. Jennings rapped on his canopy in excitement, and Greenlee rapped back. Fremont and Butters were down there with him. Instructions were being radioed to First Army HQ at Magdeburg and to Osborn in France. Walker was on the ground and out of his chute. He was waving his arms wildly and jumping up and down. He was okay.

TWENTY-SEVEN

SEVERAL PLANES WENT IN ahead of Fremont. Archie was first. He had a tough time, wobbling and yawing until he touched down hard, bouncing wildly for a second before settling into an erratic taxi turn. Butters and Jennings landed next. Then it was Greenlee's turn. Blue flames tipped with orange streamed from beneath his cowling. His landing gear was stuck. He dipped down very fast, swerving all over the runway as the fire truck chased him. The plane was sprayed as soon as it stopped. Mechanics pounced on it and had Greenlee free in an instant. Fremont dropped out of the go-around and let his flaps down all the way.

At the far end of the field, Archibald sat shivering in his cockpit. The morphine was wearing off. A deep sharp cutting pain sliced across his chest and down into his stomach. His arm and shoulder felt destroyed. There was blood all over the instrument panel. He fought to keep from blacking out, fought to keep hearing the noises around him, engines running, people shouting. But through it all he was immensely sad. All he could think of was Horace. He remembered him saying, "Archie, I want to get a ranch with my back pay and live on it with my pappy. That would be something nice. This will be my first property, you know. Of course, you can come down anytime you feel like, just remember to behave yourself." The canopy slid open. A knife lashed away at his harness. He could hear Beasley talking. He was lifted up by many hands, lifted high above everything, it seemed, and then he was unconscious.

Jennings sat clutching the stick in shock. He scanned the field for sight of Walker's plane, but it wasn't there. Horace wasn't with them. It was incredible the way he had dropped out, so brief and cruel. He had waved from the wing, Jennings could still see him doing that. He knelt there near the wingtip and waved as if to say good-bye forever. But it didn't mean anything. How could it? In a day or two he would stride in juantily, cursing and yelling as always. He'd come back to them many times before. The last one would be easy.

Skinner turned up his oxygen regulator and gulped into the mask. He slumped back, staring blankly at the field. He couldn't believe the war was over for them, finally over. It took everything out of him, but he'd made it. His mechanic slid back the canopy and began unstrapping him. When he asked about Walker, Skinner merely shrugged.

Fremont cleared his engine and switched his ignition off, fuel shutoff lever off, battery disconnect off, for the last time. He could feel somebody underneath, chocking the wheels. Friday got him out in a hurry. He didn't mention Walker, but it was clear that word had spread quickly over the field. It was very warm. Flies buzzed and circled everywhere. Most of the pilots were out of their cockpits. They sat in the shade of their wings, drinking Cokes. A jeep pulled up with Reeves driving and Osborn lodged in the back. As Fremont climbed in, he saw Harris and one of the pilots talking to Dummy Jones. Jones listened to them, holding his head in an attitude of weird intensity. He covered his eyes. He seemed ravaged by despair and agony. Then he rushed headlong toward the jeep, waving his arms frantically.

"Colonel," he shouted. "Colonel! What happened? What'd they do to him? My boy ain't comin' back? Is he dead? Tell me, nobody will tell me."

Jones extended one hand in supplication. Tears rolled down his face. Rarely had Fremont seen anyone so distraught. He placed a hand on Dummy's shoulder.

"It's all right. He went down near our lines. It'll be all right."

Jones turned away, pulling down the long bill of his

cap. Friday put an arm around him and led him toward the crewmen's shack.

"What have you got, Ops?" Fremont said as the jeep started to roll.

He was overcome by weariness. Spots appeared before his eyes. He shook his head.

"I've notified General Simpson's HQ at Magdeburg to be on the lookout for Walker. They know where he went down, but all they can do is keep a lookout. They can't cross the Elbe."

"What are his chances?" Fremont asked.

"Depends on who picks him up. The SS and Gestapo will be rough. The Landwehr are a bunch of toothless old men who will probably give him shelter. His best bet is the Kriminalpolizei, the civilian cops. They would see to it he's repatriated. And the Russians are at his back, and our boys are in front of him. He has every chance in the world, Colonel."

They rode on toward the château in silence.

"By the way, sir, Hitler is dead. He committed suicide today, presumably in his bunker."

"Positive identification?"

"No, sir. Not yet."

Fremont nodded. He was skeptical. Hitler was probably in Norway right now. There was still traffic out of Berlin in the late morning.

"Don't let up on this," Fremont said as the jeep came to a stop. "If at all possible, try and get word through to the Russians. Call me as soon as you have anything."

Dinner that evening was subdued. Rennie Washington was gone and Walker's chair was empty, too, and nothing else seemed to matter. Men dropped by the Operations Room every hour or so. Each time Osborn had to tell them the same thing.

"Nothing yet."

Walker peered into the darkness through the slats of the barn he had been hiding in since late afternoon. He looked at his watch. It was after 2100 hours and he was uncertain whether to stay all night where he was or set out on foot. He thought back over what had happened earlier, searching for a way out of his quandary. Bailing out was a shock. Fear had made his body rigid and slow. He thought he'd never get away from the plane. He felt himself disintegrating several times over before falling clear. He came down in a potato field and was dragged by his chute. Finally he snapped open the harness. There was no time to rest or think. He sprinted to a nearby farmhouse. The farmer and his wife confronted him with terror in their eyes. They indicated that he must follow them into the barn immediately. A while later he was fed a sausage, bread, and a small potato by the wife. The farmer conveyed to him by a series of motions and gestures that he was to remain out of sight. Then the door was closed. The long day waned without the sound of tanks or trucks or airplanes. He felt abandoned.

An hour later he heard a car coming. The big barn door was pulled back and an ancient Mercedes-Benz drove right in and lurched to a stop. Walker surveyed it with both guns drawn. Slowly the driver got out. He proved to be a harmless-looking old man dressed in a suit and vest. A smile of fascination and amusement flitted across his face as he strode up to Walker.

"So," he said with a polite smile, "you are the black American. Welcome to Germany, Herr . . ."

"Walker. Horace Walker, man, United States Army Air Force."

The elderly man nodded.

"I am Doctor Lipfert. I come from the village. This is my pleasure," he said, extending a hand.

"Same here."

"I suppose now you want to get back to your army," the doctor said ironically.

"Just get me to the Elbe River, man, that's all I want."

"The Elbe," the doctor chortled. "That's a long way from here. Let me explain a few things, my friend. Since this morning the Führer is no more. He abdicated all his wonderful promises to the German people by shooting himself. But what can you expect of an Austrian? You have had the misfortune of coming down in an area controlled by neither the Russians nor Americans. Nazi order still prevails here."

"Why can't we just get in that jalopy and drive to the river, Doc? I'll take care of the Nazis with these," Walker said, holding up his brace of pistols.

The doctor frowned.

"Dangerous," he said. "Foolish. Take my advice; remain here until the Allies come and order is established. The war cannot last out the week."

"I can't lay around for a week. I got things to do."

"That I very much doubt," the doctor replied, "but I will try to help. I will hand you over to friends in Brandenburg. In exchange I want you to do one thing for me."

"What, Doc?"

"Please take off that Knight's Cross. There are still Germans around who will shoot you at the sight of it."

They waited another hour and then set out. The doctor drove his old Mercedes carefully, but Walker could tell he knew the way very well by the manner in which he anticipated every curve and rise. At about 0100 hours they came into Brandenburg. Lipfert relaxed and began humming something from Beethoven. They pulled around to the back of a neat gray stucco house. A man in his late forties wearing a bathrobe and nightcap came outside holding a flashlight. He spoke to Lipfert in abrupt sentences and turned to Walker.

"We are pleased to have you with us," he said in English that sounded a little sinister. "Step this way, Lieutenant."

Walker followed the man up a flight of back stairs to an attic.

"We talk in the morning," he said with a friendly smile.

He went out and locked the door behind him. Walker took off his jacket and settled into a big rocking chair near a window overlooking the street. He placed a cocked .45 in his lap. Below he saw a pair of SS troopers stroll by on the cobblestones. A feeble street lamp exaggerated their shadows. He noted the time. An hour later, two more soldiers passed, but he couldn't tell whether they were the same men. He wished to God he hadn't let his survival kit go down with the plane. There was no telling when he might need the grenades, hatchet, compass, K rations, and extra ammo he carried in it. But he could do nothing about that now. He pulled his fur jacket collar up around his neck and dropped off to sleep.

Early in the morning he heard a key in the lock. He raised his pistol. The man who had taken him in last night appeared in the door. He was balding and long wisps of blond hair were tucked behind his ears. He wore baggy trousers and a striped shirt without a collar.

"Come down to breakfast, Herr Walker," he said.

They moved down to the kitchen in silence. The room was flooded with bright, pure sunlight. Walker was motioned to a chair.

"My name is Josef," the man said. "I cannot reveal my last name for obvious reasons. This is my *Frau,*" he said, smiling at a plump, handsome woman in a print dress and white apron. She nodded to Walker.

"This is my oldest boy, Hans."

A muscular young man well over six feet tall hobbled into the room. He had enormous forearms and thick blond hair. He shook Walker's hand and sat down.

"Hans works in the fields all day. He lost a leg on the Eastern Front."

Hans shrugged as if to indicate none of this mattered to him so long as he could eat three big meals a day.

"And this is Gunther."

A slim blond boy about eleven years old, who had just bounded down the stairs, halted in the doorway. His eyes fixed on Walker. They betrayed instant coldness and enmity. Gunther came forward slowly and deliberately. His brown eyes were still on Walker as he pulled his chair back and plopped down.

Big steaming bowls of porridge were served, followed by sausages, black bread, and some weak tea.

"I'm sorry we don't have coffee," Josef said.

"Y'all eat good," Walker said. "I didn't know there was any food left in Germany."

"We manage. I go into the fields three days a week with Hans, and we have a little garden also. At one time I was the town pharmacist, but my shop has been closed for a year now. There are no drugs."

"Is that how you know the doctor, from your store?"

"Yes. For many years Doctor Lipfert was a Brandenburger. We are old friends."

Josef now spoke with his wife in rapid, confidential tones. His face turned to Walker's.

"Can you tell us, Herr Walker, when the Americans will arrive? We have been hoping to see them for two weeks."

"They're comin', man," Walker said. "Any day. Just hold on."

Josef translated and the others smiled.

"Will you put in a good word for us? It is all we ask."

"I'll speak to the general myself," Walker replied.

He felt mean and shoddy, but the urge to laugh almost overcame him. His eyes rested on Gunther's brown uniform. He saw each button was embossed with a swastika and the boy wore a shiny Nazi medal over his breast pocket.

"What kind of getup you call that," he asked. "You in the Boy Scouts?"

"I am in the Hitler Youth and proud of it," the boy responded.

"Hitler's dead, Sonny, ain't you heard?"

"It is ridiculous," the boy replied promptly. "The Führer lives. I know this for a fact."

They eyed each other with great mistrust.

"Why do you carry two guns. Are you an outlaw?" Gunther challenged him.

Walker did not answer.

"Who are you? Who sent you to Germany?"

"Gunther!"

They finished breakfast in silence. Hans excused himself and left for work. Josef and his wife went out back to their garden. Gunther remained at the table playing with his fork. His eyes never left Walker.

"Give me one of your pistols," he said, "and I won't tell anybody you are here."

"I'm gonna slap you upside your head," Walker responded, pointing an angry finger.

"What? What are you talking about? Please try to make some sense."

Walker reached over and swatted the boy to the floor in one swift movement. Gunther began to cry, more in surprise than anything else. His red face materialized at the edge of the table. He got to his feet and shook a fist right in Walker's face.

"You will be sorry. You will regret that you ever put your hand on a German."

Then he ran into the living room. Walker watched him go.

"I never did like Boy Scouts," he muttered, taking out a pack of cigarettes and lighting one.

Early that evening Josef tapped on the attic door.

"Herr Leutnant," he called. "Herr Leutnant."

Walker stood beside the door with both .45s ready and told him to come in.

Josef sat down on a dusty window ledge. He spoke too quickly and Walker had a hard time understanding him.

"Leutnant, Hans and I have been talking and we think it would be better if I drove you to the Elbe River tonight so you can cross your lines. You see, Gunther has been upset. He's just a boy and I'm afraid he might say something."

Two hours later, a truck filled with hay pulled around to the back of the house. Josef's wife waved Walker downstairs. She gave him some sausages and bread in a small package and patted him on the back. Hans got out of the cab and lifted up the hay with a pitchfork so he could get under it. They shook hands. Josef cautioned him to be very quiet. He said the drive would take between two and three hours. The truck started up and rumbled out of Brandenburg. Walker parted the hay and stared at the countryside. Germany looked remarkably like parts of Ohio and Indiana he had seen from freight cars. There seemed to be a lot of soldiers around. He noticed them bivouacked in the fields and occasionally heard an officer barking orders. A few antiaircraft searchlights had been turned on. They stabbed brilliantly into the night, but there was nothing out there for them to find. The silhouettes of 20 millimeter flak guns dotted the landscape. Crews clustered around them, talking in low hushed tones which carried a long way on the warm night air. The truck headlights picked up a man urinating by the side of the road. Shortly afterward, they were stopped. Josef spoke to the soldier who climbed onto the running board. A flashlight was shined on his papers. The truck started up again. The old man at the next checkpoint waved them through when Josef slowed down and called out a few friendly words. Half an hour passed. A soldier in full battle dress emerged from a blockhouse and signaled them to stop. Papers were exchanged once more, questions asked in a taut probing voice which had lost its edge of authority.

It was all play acting. Nobody cared what was in the goddamn truck. Nobody cared about anything. They just wanted to keep on eating, keep on having a little fun, keep fucking and having children, that was all. Josef and the soldier were laughing. The soldier had his helmet off and was drinking from a bottle Josef had handed him. Walker felt a terrible urge come upon him. He was going to sneeze. He tried to hold it back. He pinched his nose and closed his mouth, but the sneeze grew gigantic within him and exploded loudly in the night, followed by two or three lesser sneezes. The soldier found this incredibly funny. He was beside himself with merriment. Josef was chuckling. They had another drink. Finally the truck rattled away. When the blockhouse was well behind them, Walker popped out of the hay. He banged on the back of the cab and Josef stopped.

"I'm riding up front," he announced.

"But it is dangerous," Josef protested.

"Don't worry about it, nobody ain't gonna be expecting me. That's for goddamn sure."

Once again the old truck moved ahead.

"Where's that bottle you're hidin', Joe? I saw what went on back there."

He took a long drink. The hot liquid seemed to burn a path down his throat.

"Damn, that's good shit," Walker said, wiping his mouth on his sleeve. He turned the bottle around and tried to read the label but it was in German.

"How long to the river?"

"Twenty kilometers."

They drove for a while in silence. Walker stared out into the clear, starry night. He had a full moon to cross by and that was good.

"Man, I'm homesick," he said turning to Josef. "I can't wait to get back home."

"You mean back behind the Allied lines?"

"Yeah, I'd like to see my buddies again. But I'm talkin' about gettin' back way over yonder where I come from."

"You have relatives?"

"Just Pap, and he don't even know where I am. Didn't have time to tell him I was going overseas."

"Well, at least you are going back to a country which

is your own. Here we may have to live under the Russian boot."

"They gotta go home sometime, Joe."

"I suppose so. In a way I really don't care. I'm just glad the war is at an end. At first it was an adventure. We were winning and everyone was proud. I personally didn't like the Nazis. I didn't like the way they treated our educated men, the professors and artists who disagreed. But I enjoyed what Germany was doing. I admit that."

"Can I do anything for y'all when I get to the other side of the river?"

"Yes. Please tell the Americans about us. Tell them we wish to be placed on the list of those who are to be trusted."

Walker sighed. He didn't have the heart to tell this man that the Americans weren't coming and his destiny belonged to the Russians.

"I'll do what I can," he said, "but your story would go a whole lot further if you'd speak to these people yourself. Why don't you come across the river with me? Send for the wife and kids later."

Josef gripped the wheel tightly.

"I cannot do it. I am needed. I must go back to Brandenburg," he explained.

"Joe, make it a short trip," Walker replied.

Soon they arrived opposite the broken and crumbling city of Magdeburg. They headed south now, traveling parallel to the river and watching it glisten in the moonlight.

"This is the Elbe, Herr Leutnant."

"So this is the fuckin' Elbe I been hearing so much about."

Josef continued on until they were about three miles below the city, then he pulled off the road and parked under some trees.

"I will be back shortly," he said.

"Where you goin'?"

"Don't worry. I will rejoin you in a few minutes."

Walker listened with trepidation to Josef's fading footsteps. *Suppose he don't come back,* he thought. *Suppose he brings the Gestapo or the SS or one of them. He didn't want to make the crossin' and now he's gone off somewhere. I don't like this.*

He got out of the truck and wandered down to the damp and soggy riverbank. The Elbe rushed by. It was much wider than he had anticipated and the current looked strong. Immediately he gave up the idea of swimming across unless he had no other choice. He lay down in the tall weeds near the road within sight of the truck and checked both .45s. It would be easy to nail Josef. He waited. The minutes crept along. Something in his pants pocket cut against his leg. He pulled out Hartmann's Knight's Cross and examined it in the moonlight. *We don't have anything like this,* he thought. *This is a real medal, a token of honor. I never did have anything of honor before and now I do.* He sat up, opened his collar, and tied the Cross around his neck, flattening it against his naked chest. Then he stretched to wait a while longer.

Three quarters of an hour came and went before Josef strode back to the truck. He seemed alarmed to find the cab empty. Walker scrutinized him as he searched the area in apparent despair. There was no one with him, that much was clear. Walker strolled out of the weeds.

"You back already? I went down into the bushes to take a leak."

"I have found a boat for you. It's nearby. I think we should hurry. I must get back home before the morning."

"Okay, you first."

Josef led him down the bank and into the marshes. They fought their way through reeds over their heads and at last came out at a tiny dock of rotting wood. Josef helped Walker into the rowboat there.

"Sure you ain't comin', Joe?"

This was answered by a reluctant nod.

"All right, but don't call me back when I get halfway across."

"I will be tempted," Josef said, "but I cannot. Goodbye, my friend, and good luck to you in America. Please don't forget to mention us to the authorities. The name is Braun. We are depending on you."

"I'll take care of it. So long, Joe," Walker said, shaking his hand. "So long, buddy."

Josef waved to him from the dock and he waved back. He was alone on the dark water, struggling to keep the boat in a straight line. The oarlocks moaned and creaked with every stroke.

Dammit, I'm rowin' backwards. I never did learn how to handle a boat, Walker thought.

The far shore melted away. A bat or two sailed past his ears. *Well, I guess I've about seen the war. I enjoyed it, I really did. Came in with nothin', got three meals a day, and went home a top pilot. How's that for nigger luck. I'll miss Emilia, though, and Celestino and Josef and all them people out here where I thought I'd never be. Pap won't believe all the people I met. He'll take a stick to me for lyin'.*

He could make out the trees on the near shore now. He began to plunge his oars deeply into the strong current. The boat swept forward in a powerful sustained glide. He hummed part of an old church song he'd learned as a child. A rifle shot crackled in the night. One oar slipped from his hand. His chest felt hot and weakened. Shots whizzed all around him. His chest seemed to explode. Pain and numbness coursed through his body. A knee was blown away. He screamed in agony, lurching to his feet.

"Don't shoot," he yelled. "It's me. Don't shoot. It's me. Me."

He was in the bottom of the boat fighting to get up, but he couldn't. A bloody foam came to his mouth.

"Dear Jesus God, it's me," he mumbled.

And then Walker was gone.

TWENTY-EIGHT

OSBORN CLOSED THE FOLDER on his desk and ran one hand through his hair. He reached into his breast pocket for a cigar but decided this was not the time for one. He picked up the folder and left the Operations Room for Fremont's apartment. The corridor was filled with equipment crated up for the trip back home. Down at the field the Mustangs were lashed into place and hidden by tarpaulin covers, for they would never fly again. The schedule today called for a departure to London in two hours. Any minute the C-47 transport would land. The war was over. The document of unconditional surrender had been signed that morning at Soviet Headquarters in Berlin. ("The mission of this Allied force was fulfilled," Eisenhower cabled Marshall in Washington.) Osborn felt lost and empty. There would be no more operations, no more waiting for the teletype bell to ring, no more voices straining and cracking in the maelstrom of combat. It was all over except this one last detail.

Fremont had just about finished packing his belongings. He took his leather-bound editions of *Caesar's Gallic Commentaries*, *Napoleon's Diaries*, and *Thucydides* and pushed them to the bottom of his suitcase. He placed the tinted photograph of Marva and the boys on top of everything and let the lid drop. He was ready to go. But he double-checked his desk drawers and found there was something lodged in the back of one. He removed the long black wooden sheath containing the dagger Kommodore Hartmann had presented to him. The razor-sharp steel was of a fine bluish gray, a beautiful mournful color unlike any he had ever seen. At the base of the long black handle he could distinguish the blurred silver outline of a Nazi eagle with a swastika at its neck. Hartmann had worn this dagger for a long time, perhaps since he had first become a pilot. It was a shame he'd felt the compunction to part with all that it meant to him.

Fremont sank into a chair. Yesterday, for the first time in his life, he had done something unsoldierly and insubordinate. One of the brass in London had arranged for them to be driven to Freiburg, a town in the Schwarzwald, and there accept the surrender of a Luftwaffe *Staffel* and its Messerschmitt 262s. The men were overjoyed. They chatted and joked all the way down. At the tiny field the German pilots lined up on the runway before their planes. A young lieutenant said the MPs would arrive shortly to take them into custody. The Germans were neither abject nor hostile. Fremont walked down the line, nodded to each man, shaking hands with a few. ("We have met," he was told, "near Essen. I got one of your bombers.") When it was over he felt like a complete fool. The thought of these men in a military compound infuriated him. He strolled up beside the Oberstleutnant and spoke to him in French.

"Tell your men they are dismissed. I am dismissing them. They are free to go."

The Oberstleutnant listened carefully to make sure what he heard was real. He stepped back and saluted Fremont.

"You are a true gentleman," he said. "We appreciate this gesture of dignity."

Fremont twirled the dagger on his desk top. He understood now that he should get out of the Army, yet it seemed cowardly even to entertain such a thought. He slipped the dagger into his briefcase and lit a cigarette. Footsteps approached the door. He heard a loud, ragged knock.

Osborn came in wearing a pitiful look on his face. As usual, he stated his business at the outset.

"Sir, Lieutenant Walker is dead. I just got the news."

Fremont sighed and rested his head in one hand. He wanted to cry.

"He was shot while crossing the Elbe at night," Osborn

continued in a heavy voice. "The man responsible was a buck private from Nashville, Tennessee, named Orville Perkins. Perkins was on guard duty near the riverbank. Through binoculars he spotted a man wearing a Knight's Cross and fired six shots. Most of them hit Walker."

Fremont got up and walked over to the window.

"Here's the official report, Colonel," Osborn said, placing a folder on Fremont's desk. "Perkins isn't being disciplined. Ninth Army washed its hands of the whole matter."

Fremont whirled.

"Well, I haven't," he yelled at the top of his voice. "I damn well haven't."

His eyes bulged from his head. Both men stood there, staring at each other, staring into the same burning core of violence and shame. They knew nothing would ever be done.

"Walker's body is on the way here now by plane. We should get the official photographs in a few days."

"I don't care about the goddamn photographs, Duane," Fremont said in the same raging tone of voice. "But we are not leaving here until he arrives. We'll take Horace back home with us or we won't go home."

"Yes, sir. I understand."

Jennings lay on his bed, brooding. He wore his class A uniform for the hop over to London. An overseas cap with his lieutenant's bars glistening on it sat rakishly on the side of his head. His polished shoes were propped against the packed suitcase near the foot of the bed. He shook a cigarette from the pack of Luckies next to him and struck a match.

Three times in the last half hour people had knocked at his door. First it was Bluey, sounding stricken and apologetic; then Skinner showed up; and finally the colonel was out there tapping softly and asking him to be reasonable. Fuck them all. He knew what they wanted. He knew exactly how they would sound when they gave him the news, and he didn't want to hear that shit. He was sure Horace wanted him to act this way.

Time went by. The floor was littered with cigarette butts. Jennings examined his watch, but the hours and minutes meant nothing to him. Someone scraped against the door at the far end of the room. Jennings saw the doorknob turn. Reeves came in and looked around. He began to go through Walker's things. Jennings leapt from his bed.

"What are you doing there, Sergeant?" he shouted. "Get the hell away from there. Those are Lieutenant Walker's things."

"The colonel sent me," Reeves said.

"I don't give a good goddamn if Eisenhower sent you! Put those things down, Reeves."

"Lieutenant, I don't like this. It's awful. They had to practically force me to come in here. But this is an Army matter now. I've got no choice, sir."

Jennings averted his eyes.

"What are you taking?" he snapped. "I want a complete accounting. You'll have to give me a receipt for it, Reeves."

"Regulations say I've got to have his clothes, blankets, musette bag, gas mask, and hats. I don't want anything personal, just his Army property."

"You be quick about this."

"Yes, sir, Lieutenant."

Within five minutes Reeves was gone. Jennings took his list of items, balled it up, and flung it away in rage and frustration. He opened Walker's footlocker and took out the black leather trench coat with the small bullet hole in the right sleeve. Horace always said he would tell him the story of that bullet hole, but he never did, and now it was too late. He walked over to the big gilded mirror they shared and put on the coat. It fit him well. That's probably why Horace said he should wear it when the time came, because he looked right in it. He felt powerful and solemn standing there. He picked up his bags, opened the door and went downstairs.

The whole squadron sat around a large circular table in the dining room of their hotel in London. Two emaciated-looking waiters in white aprons and black jackets served them lunch. Wine was poured. Everyone was in a sad but expansive mood, for they still had time to relax before going to Victoria Station and catching the train for Scotland where a plane was to take them home. A group of tommies with their helmets on and a few American soldiers dating English girls stood near a piano at the far end

of the room. Their off-key voices rose and fell in a medley
of songs from the early war years. A hotel porter appeared
at Fremont's side.

"Your tickets," he said in a polite cockney voice. "The
Flying Scot, sir. A fine train."

Fremont handed him a pound note and he bowed
graciously. His raincoat was soaked. It might be hard to
find cabs if the rain didn't let up, but that was all right
with Fremont. He was really in no mood to go anywhere.
A mellow sort of reverie fogged his mind. He was almost
unaware of the others at the table. His thoughts meandered
back over the past couple of days. They had left France
on one of the most beautiful mornings he could remember.
The transport rose heavily off their narrow grass runway.
Crowded at the windows, they could see the château, as
rich and imposing as a new monument, then the lush deer
park, the cold blue lake, the cook's cottage, a sprinkling of
tiny villages, and, for the last time, their landing ground.
They counted the Mustangs sitting there, chocked and
covered with tarpaulin, waiting to be trucked to Cherbourg
and shipped home, where they would be cut up into scrap.
The green velvety landscape sped beneath them. They
said good-bye to France forever as the wind-driven Channel
slipped under their wings. Forty-five minutes later the
transport touched down at an RAF station in Surrey. The
coffin containing Walker's body was taken off first.

Fremont picked up his wine glass and drained it. He
wondered what in hell the future held for him. Turmoil
and anger boiled over in him and he'd been doing wild
things. Last night he'd called HQ for a staff car. He was
told there were none available. He rushed out into the
streets, muttering and cursing. In front of the Connaught
Hotel he found staff cars parked three deep. He absconded
with one bearing the two-star plate of a major general and
nearly ran down a sergeant who tried to stop him. Rain
began to fall as he raced along the Thames. London fell
behind him. He sped over the narrow wet roads through
Chatham, Milton Regis, Canterbury, and down to Dover,
where he made his way to the cliff edge. He could hear the
sea heaving up tremendous waves. He walked into the darkness. He was through as an Army man, he told himself. He
had done everything they asked, fought like a champion,
acted the gentleman, and caused them no trouble. In return

he got nothing, no second squadron, and no promotions for his men. They were back where they started. When they mustered out, that was the end of the black man as a fighter pilot. He had come all this way for nothing. And he had Brigadier General Love on his back again. It was Love who had arranged their transportation and hotel. It was he who had taken it upon himself to set up a special flight home so they could be spared the embarrassment of berthing in the hold of a segregated ship. Love had called him a dozen times since he'd arrived in London. The calls kept coming, even after he changed his room. Then, mercifully, a note was left for him. He was ruining his career, Love said, alienating the people he would need later. He'd heard it all before and it made him heartsick. Night passed as he sat on the running board smoking cigarettes and nipping from a flask. He wished Horace was alive. This was the kind of thing he needed to talk to Horace about.

He missed Horace Walker. Horace was a man who had the guts to be what he was at all times. He'd never allowed himself to really appreciate that quality, and now Horace's death haunted Fremont. It was so unjust that he should lie in a box at Victoria Station with an American flag draped over it, so wrong and unjust. And now, ironically, he was the custodian of Walker's personal belongings, including his pilot's wings and second DFC. But there was no place to send them. Walker had no home. His only address was a post office box in Corpus Christi, Texas. Later, after Horace was buried in Arlington with full honors, he would have to go down to Texas and trace the Walker family, even if it took another year of his life. It was the very least he could do.

"Congratulations on your DFC, sir," Osborn said, pouring more wine into his glass.

"Yes, congratulations, Jonathan," Beasley put in. "It's been too long in coming."

"Thank you," Fremont said.

Glasses were raised to him in tribute. He lifted his in acknowledgment. Everyone took a sip. They seemed more relaxed now that this ritual was over.

"Wish my boy could be here," Dummy Jones said. He was seated next to Friday, directly across the table from

Fremont. All the ground crewmen had been asked to come, but they were the only two who had showed up.

"He was some hell of a pilot," Butters responded in the mournful silence that followed Dummy's remark. "I sure as hell wouldn't want to face another mission without him in the group."

"You can say that shit again."

"They say he's one of the top three in Europe," Dummy continued. "But he's got to be number one. There couldn't have been another man as good."

Friday patted Dummy on the sleeve. Dummy bit his lip and said no more.

"Well, Mr. Osborn, what are you going to do with yourself now?" Fremont asked.

Osborn smiled.

"It'll be the Army for me, sir. My father is gone now, so the Army's my home."

"A good choice, Ops," Fremont said. Osborn might just make it and get that first star. He was right for the job. He grasped everything quickly and he had the easy unpretentious style needed to get along with people like Love. Also, he was an Army man. Osborn would make it all right, and he'd pull a lot of people along in his wake.

"What about you, sir?" Osborn asked him.

"I'm undecided. I'm not sure, Duane, that I'm cut out for the military, or much else, for that matter. I've got a lot of thinking to do."

"I wish you'd stay, sir. I know Horace would want you to. The tougher it got, the meaner he was. He thought of you in the same terms."

Osborn was beginning to sound like a fighter and Fremont liked that.

"Jasper, how do you feel?" Fremont asked Hollyfield, who had said almost nothing.

"Pretty well, sir. I'm glad you signed me out of the hospital and put me on your flight. I appreciate it, although I don't feel I belong here. I've been away so long."

"If you don't belong here, then where the hell should you be?" Archibald inquired in his sharp, mocking voice.

"How's the rehabilitation coming, Jasper?"

"I've got three more operations, skin grafts. I feel more confident, sir. I really do."

"You ain't havin' no more operations," Archibald went

on. "You look too good already. I don't want you lookin'
prettier than me."

"Roy, what are your plans?"

"I'm thinking about a police job in New York, Colonel.
If I don't get on the force, I'll try for a liquor store license
with my back pay."

"Pedro?"

Johnson smiled. He had received a DFC at last and he
was very happy.

"I'm going to be teaching high school, sir. I've got a
girl back home. It looks like marriage."

"I'll miss you, Pedro."

"Same here, sir."

Fremont turned back to Dummy, whose face was veiled.

"Dummy, what's your real name?"

"Ain't free to tell you, Colonel," Dummy said with a
small bashful smile. "It's out of the Bible, that's all I'll say."

"You gonna re-up?"

"Got to re-up. Can't get three meals a day no place
else. Besides, all I know is airplanes. I'm crazy 'bout 'em."

"Friday?"

"I'll be at Tuskegee, sir. I want to work with the young
pilots."

"Reeves?"

"Army all the way, sir."

"Archie, what in hell are you going to do away from this
bunch?"

"Drift, Colonel. Lay up under the trees and enjoy
nature. Spend my back pay slow and easy. I won't miss
these clowns at all."

Fremont chuckled.

"Jonesy?"

"I'm going to stay in, sir. I like this life."

"Mr. Skinner, may we have your attention?" Fremont
said.

Skinner looked up. He was wearing the black double-
breasted suit which had been folded at the bottom of his
footlocker since the day he'd arrived at Tuskegee.

"I'm not going back, Colonel," he said. "I'm not going
back to the nigger trains, the nigger buses. It would kill
me. I don't understand how any of you can go back. In
six months we'll be forgotten. In a year people will claim

we never existed. Don't look at me like that. You know it's true."

"Oh, Percy," Archibald cried.

"Where are you headed, Lieutenant?" Fremont asked.

"Sweden, sir, or Denmark. I plan to study architecture, build a house for myself way out in the woods. In time I'll marry and settle down, but for now I've got to have solitude."

Fremont nodded.

"I respect that," he said.

"Richard, have you got anything lined up?"

Beasley let out a big, hearty laugh.

"Not a thing, Jonathan," he said, finishing off his brandy and gesturing to the waiter for another. "I'll go back to making my rounds on the public wards, but if you get into another war, expect me."

"Okay, Battle Surgeon."

"Carl, I imagine you'll be going back to school."

Jennings pulled Walker's black leather coat around him. He felt some sort of statement was expected of him.

"No more school for me, sir, not for a long time, anyway. Horace opened my eyes to a lot of things. I'm going to try and help people. I'm going to walk through the South and see the life I've never seen before. Our people need deliverance, sir. I'm going to try and bring it about, because Horace would want me to."

"You watch where you go on those back roads," Archibald warned. "The South can be mean, boy."

"I understand that, Archie."

"Bluey, I'm sorry I got to you last. It's not an oversight."

"It's okay, sir, because I've really got nothing to say. I expect to go back to Tennessee and sit on the front porch all summer."

"What then?"

"Maybe medical school, sir. My parents want it and I kind of like the idea, too."

Fremont surveyed the familiar faces around the table. They had been with him through some of the toughest days of his life. He couldn't believe it was finally all over.

"Let's have a minute of silence for the boys who aren't with us," he said.

The singing around the piano, which had begun to thin out, now died completely. The men lowered their heads. A few mumbled to themselves. Dummy Jones dabbed at his reddened eyes with a handkerchief. The minute passed, crowded to the bursting point by a tumult of unspoken fears, unspoken sorrows.

Fremont looked at his watch. The instant he dreaded was upon them.

"Gentlemen, it is time to go," he announced. "In ten years we'll get together at Tuskegee and do this again."

They left a pile of bills in the center of the table for the waiters and filed out, slinging their musette bags over their shoulders. The rain had stopped. A warming sunlight spread through the busy London streets, drying the sidewalks. Osborn hailed a couple of cabs.

"Jonathan, ask the men to hold on for a minute," Beasley said. "I want one last picture."

They lined up by flights on the hotel steps. Dummy, Friday, Osborn, Jonesy, and Reeves sat cross-legged in front. Beasley snapped away.

"One more. Just one more."

"Hurry it up, Dick."

"Okay, that's it."

THE INTERNATIONAL BESTSELLER!

KG 200

J. D. GILMAN
AND
JOHN CLIVE

A Luftwaffe squadron that spoke perfect English.
If they'd succeeded, we'd all be speaking perfect German.

"This novel of aerial assassination, inspired
by actual historical events, booms right along to
an explosive finale."
Publishers Weekly

"Masterful ... the implications are spine-chilling."
The Denver Post

Selected by 2 Book Clubs

Avon  39115/$2.25

KG 9-78

THE BIG BESTSELLERS
ARE AVON BOOKS

☐	The Thorn Birds Colleen McCullough	35741	$2.50
☐	The Homestead Grays James Wylie	38604	$1.95
☐	Sweet Nothings Laura Cunningham	38562	$1.95
☐	The Bermuda Triangle Charles Berlitz	38315	$2.25
☐	Lancelot Walker Percy	36582	$2.25
☐	Oliver's Story Erich Segal	36343	$1.95
☐	Snowblind Robert Sabbag	36947	$1.95
☐	A Capitol Crime Lawrence Meyer	37150	$1.95
☐	Fletch's Fortune Gregory Mcdonald	37978	$1.95
☐	Voyage Sterling Hayden	37200	$2.50
☐	Lady Oracle Margaret Atwood	35444	$1.95
☐	Humboldt's Gift Saul Bellow	38810	$2.25
☐	Mindbridge Joe Haldeman	33605	$1.95
☐	A Fringe of Leaves Patrick White	36160	$1.95
☐	To Jerusalem and Back Saul Bellow	33472	$1.95
☐	A Sea Change Lois Gould	33704	$1.95
☐	The Surface of Earth Reynolds Price	29306	$1.95
☐	The Monkey Wrench Gang Edward Abbey	30114	$1.95
☐	Beyond the Bedroom Wall Larry Woiwode	29454	$1.95
☐	Jonathan Livingston Seagull Richard Bach	34777	$1.75
☐	Working Studs Terkel	34660	$2.50
☐	Shardik Richard Adams	27359	$1.95
☐	Anya Susan Fromberg Schaeffer	25262	$1.95
☐	Watership Down Richard Adams	19810	$2.25

Available at better bookstores everywhere, or order direct from the publisher.

AVON BOOKS, Mail Order Dept., 250 West 55th St., New York, N.Y. 10019

Please send me the books checked above. I enclose $_____(please include 25¢ per copy for postage and handling). Please use check or money order—sorry, no cash or C.O.D.'s. Allow 4-6 weeks for delivery.

Mr/Mrs/Miss_____

Address_____

City_____ State/Zip_____

BB 9-78

A Wide-Canvas American Epic!

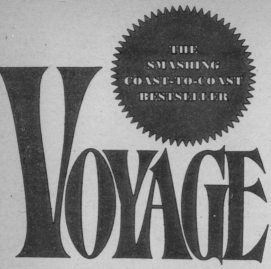

THE
SMASHING
COAST-TO-COAST
BESTSELLER

VOYAGE

A NOVEL OF 1896
STERLING HAYDEN

"A ROUSING EPIC . . . BIG, MUSCULAR,
PROFANE, CYNICAL, ROMANTIC."
Chicago Daily News

"A FAST-MOVING, HEART-POUNDING SAGA
. . . PURE PLEASURE TO READ."
San Francisco Examiner

**MAIN SELECTION OF THE
BOOK-OF-THE-MONTH CLUB**

 Avon 37200 $2.50